Praise for

'Gripping and tantalisingly sexy'
Holdfast Magazine

'A beautifully written, flowing Urban fantasy with a terrific
story and some really great characters'
Liz Loves Books

'Instantly absorbing . . . will certainly leave a lasting impression'
SciFi Now

'I loved this book. The characters, the atmosphere, the humour, the
romance, it all worked. *Marked* is a wonderful debut for Tingey'
A Fantastical Librarian

'A compelling debut . . . a brisk paranormal tale with outstanding
world building, a large cast of well-drawn characters, and an intricate
plot filled with intrigue and adventure. Reads like a PG-13
version of the Sookie Stackhouse series'
Booklist

'Any Neil Gaiman fan should feel right at home with the style of this book,
as it's smartly and compellingly written with some confident prose'
The Fictional Hangout

'Great fun and a delight to read'
Upcoming4.me

'The kind of story that sucks readers in very quickly and you end up
completely losing track of time while you're reading . . .
A fantastic start to this new series'
Feeling Fictional

'I was enthralled. A strong and interesting debut'
Draumr Kopa Blog

'A thrill ride to the very end. The intrigue and action began immediately,
drawing the reader in and keeping their eyes glued to the pages . . .
I cannot wait to see where it goes from here'
Fangirls Read It First

Also by Sue Tingey

The Soulseer Chronicles
Marked

THE SOULSEER CHRONICLES BOOK II

SUE TINGEY

CURSED

Jo Fletcher
BOOKS

First published in Great Britain in 2016 by

Jo Fletcher Books
an imprint of
Quercus Editions Ltd
Carmelite House
50 Victoria Embankment
London EC4Y 0DZ

An Hachette UK company

PB ISBN 978 1 78429 078 8
EBOOK ISBN 978 1 78429 077 1

10 9 8 7 6 5 4 3 2

Typeset by Jouve (UK), Milton Keynes

Printed and bound in Great Britain by Clays Ltd, St Ives plc

To Lucy
A true friend

One

As I watched, ten small specks of black grew to dots and then to figures on horseback as they charged through the valley towards us, leaving a trail of dust in their wake. I had been back only three days and they had already found us.

'Jinx!' I called, my eyes not leaving the advancing riders. They were close enough now that I could see sunlight glinting off the armour that marked them out as Lord Baltheza's royal guard. I supposed I should be grateful for the small mercy that they weren't the chief executioner's men.

In a moment Jinx was beside me, 'What's wrong?'

I gestured towards the valley. 'We have visitors.'

He stared down at the fast approaching horsemen through narrowed eyes. 'Come on,' he said, taking my hand and leading me inside the isolated herdsman's hut serving as our home for the night.

Jamie was sitting on a low stool – one of very few usable pieces of furniture. He didn't look up from the thin blade he was sharpening, but continued the rhythmic turning of the steel as he rubbed one edge against the stone and then the other. The three rabbits Pyrites had caught for our supper lay at his feet, ready for skinning and cleaning. My drakon was sprawled on the floor beside them, his eyes fixed on Jamie, mesmerised by the motion of the blade.

'Ten riders heading this way,' Jinx said without any preamble.

Jamie still didn't look up. 'Amaliel?'

'Baltheza's guard.'

I let out a shuddery breath. What were we going to do? We couldn't keep running forever.

'Fight or flee?' Jamie asked.

'If they were here for a fight brother, they'd have approached by night so we wouldn't see them coming.'

Jamie lifted the knife to examine its edge. 'That should do it.' He looked up at last and flashed me a smile that would normally make my toes curl and my stomach give a little flip, but today my heart felt like it was weighed down with fear.

'Lucky,' he said, getting to his feet. 'Jinx and I will go and see what they want. You stay in here.'

I tried to smile but failed miserably. 'Isn't it obvious—?'

'Not necessarily. As Jinx says, if they wanted trouble they'd have come after dark and there'd be more of them.'

'Pyrites, stay with your mistress and guard her with your life,' Jinx told my drakon. Pyrites puffed out his chest, sat to attention and began to grow to the size of a great dane – not that he really needed to; he had firepower and, where my safety was concerned, he wasn't afraid to use it.

Jamie hugged me close. 'Stay in here,' he repeated.

Jinx handed Jamie one of the swords resting by the doorway and strapped another around his own waist, then stepped over to me, rested his hands on my shoulders and gave me an encouraging smile. 'Don't look so worried,' he said and gave me a kiss full on the lips that went on for so long I began to feel dizzy.

'Jinx,' Jamie said with an exasperated sigh.

Jinx pulled away from me and winked. 'Keep that thought,' he said and followed Jamie out of the hut.

'Be careful,' I said from just inside the door, and Jinx waved once before calling out to Bob, his big, black powerhouse of a flying horse.

Despite my nerves, seeing Jinx and Jamie standing out in the sunshine together made me catch my breath. Two men couldn't be more different, yet in some ways so much the same. Jamie – all blond hair, blue eyes and tanned skin – could have been human if not for his huge, snow-white wings. Jinx, on the other hand, couldn't have been more daemon, with glossy, maroon skin, horns, an arrow-tipped tail and long maroon hair so dark it was almost black, hanging in a braid to just below his waist. They were both beautiful in their own way and I cared for each of them a lot more than was entirely good for me.

Jinx called out again and within moments I could hear the beating of wings and a dark shadow passed overhead. Bob glided down to land in front of the hut with a grace that belied his bulk and fierce demeanour, and in one fluid movement, Jinx had grasped his shaggy black mane and pulled himself up onto the creature. Bob snorted and stamped his hooves, his red eyes glowing with infernal fire. Unperturbed, Jinx gave him a slap on the rump; the beast surged forward and, with two powerful flaps of his leathery wings, was airborne. Jamie gave me one last smile, unfurled his own wings and then he too was flying into the sky.

I shut the door and sank down on to the stool. Three days: it had taken them only three days to find us and it made me wonder whether the Underlands was really the place I should be making my home. How could I ever be safe here?

Pyrites somehow knew where my mind was going as he put a claw on my knee and made a small mewing noise.

'I know. If I went back I would have to leave you and Jinx, and I couldn't bear to do that,' I told him, scratching the underside of his chin. And it was true: I couldn't take even a small drakon into my world, and I certainly couldn't take a daemon who, on earth, would leave a trail of death and destruction in his wake. And without them – well, without them I was lost.

The last time I'd returned to my world I had lasted only five days alone. I'd missed them hugely and I'd known it was no safer on Earth than in the Underlands – even less so without my daemon guard – so, by the end of the five days I was a nervous wreck with every unexplained sound causing me to reach for a strategically placed carving knife or hammer. Of course, there was also the matter of Lord Baltheza: if he had sanctioned a visit by one of the court assassins I would have been history in no time without my friends.

I started thinking about all I'd learned over the past few days. I'd tried to find out as much about my new home as I could – as if the knowledge would somehow protect me – and I'd begun by asking questions. Every time we'd stopped in our travels, or settled down for the night, I'd put every question I'd thought of to Jamie and Jinx. One of my first was: were there other countries in the Underlands? But apparently there weren't; instead, the Underlands were divided into states overseen locally by their individual lords, but ultimately ruled over by Baltheza.

Another question I'd asked had been: how come Amaliel has so much power? This was something neither Jamie nor Jinx could answer. Everyone, except for perhaps Baltheza, hated him, and yet he appeared to wield almost as much authority within court as Lord Baltheza himself.

If he was one of the approaching riders I just knew we were destined for trouble, which set me to worrying about my two men yet again.

They were gone a long time; at least it seemed that way. I kept getting up and walking to the door to peer out, but from the cabin I couldn't see the valley below and that was where they would be. I was tempted to go outside to take a look, but I knew from experience that if Jinx and Jamie had told me to do something it was usually for good reason, even if it didn't always sit easily with me.

Actually, this was something I had planned to talk to them about. I hated that sometimes they treated me like the 'little woman'. Jinx might not know any better, but Jamie bloody well should having spent a lot of time in my world, and if anything he was the worst of the two. Of course, now they were gone risking their lives for me, and I was alone and worrying about them, my getting bolshy about this seemed pretty pathetic.

When I thought I couldn't stand the wait any longer, Pyrites' head jerked up and his ears pricked forward. He gave a low rumble in his chest and jumped to his feet, growing a few more sizes until he was as big as a small pony. He moved so he was between me and the door and stood glaring at it, snorting puffs of steam which gradually changed from white to grey to black.

'What is it, boy?'

He gave another low grumble. I grabbed the knife Jamie had been sharpening from where it lay and backed towards the bedroom. The handle to the front door began to turn and Pyrites roared . . .

'It's only us, you stupid sod,' I heard Jinx say as the door swung open. Pyrites stood his ground until Jinx appeared in the doorway followed by Jamie. 'I swear, one day he's going to roast us.'

'Why do you think I always let you go first?' Jamie said with a grin.

'And there I was thinking you were being deferential to your elder and better.'

Pyrites gave a puff of smoke, shrank until he was not much bigger than a Yorkshire Terrier and scampered out of their way as Jamie closed the door behind them.

'Well?' I asked.

Jinx gave a bob of his head in Jamie's direction giving him the job of telling me the bad news, as I knew it must be from the change in their expressions.

'Just tell me,' I said.

'An attempt has been made on the life of Lord Baltheza.'

'Is he dead?' I asked, though I didn't really care. Baltheza was, in my opinion, a sadistic monster – if he was dead, he deserved it.

'He lost two of his guard and another was injured, but Baltheza was unhurt,' Jamie told me.

More's the pity, I thought. Until something else struck me: 'Does he think Kayla and I were somehow involved?' As he had only recently ordered me to be executed for plotting to kill him, this was a real concern. It was also why I was on the run: in this world justice was served out fast and with little chance to defend oneself.

'No,' Jamie said, 'not *you*.'

My two daemons were studiously avoiding eye contact with me, which sent my anxiety levels soaring. 'What about Kayla?'

'She and her entourage have disappeared.'

'I thought that was the point: she's in hiding.'

'Well, it didn't take him long to find us; he has spies everywhere,' Jamie said. 'Anyway staying in a mini palace on the coast is hardly hiding out. She might as well have sent Baltheza a postcard.'

'And now Kayla's gone,' Jinx said, 'leaving not a trace of her or her guard. It doesn't look good.' I scowled at him. Upon seeing my expression he gave me an apologetic smile. 'I'm only telling you how it is. That they have truly disappeared makes Baltheza suspicious.'

'I suppose Lord Daltas has convinced him she's as guilty as sin,' I said. He was the daemon who had got me into this mess in the first place. He thought he could use me as a lever to get Kayla to marry him, which would have brought him one step closer to the throne. His plan had misfired, and now I doubted Kayla would marry him if he was the last daemon in the Underlands.

'Daltas is currently *persona non grata* at court. Though this could change at any time,' Jamie said.

'Why would Baltheza think I had nothing to do with it, but Kayla had? He was pretty sure I did before.'

'Why would you send armed assassins to kill a man when one of your consorts is a Death Daemon?' Jamie said.

Put like that I suppose he had a point. 'So, what of the riders?' I asked.

'Here.' Jamie pulled a small scroll of parchment from his pocket and handed it to me. 'They were coming to tell you all charges against you have been dropped and to escort you back to court.'

'Like that's going to happen,' I said as I opened up the document and scanned the contents. Sure enough, it confirmed I was no longer a wanted woman, but although it should have made me feel safe and secure, I couldn't help but think it was some kind of trick.

'I think perhaps you should go,' Jinx said.

Jamie swung around to face him. 'Are you mad?'

Jinx leaned back against the doorframe. 'Do you believe Kayla had anything to do with the assassination attempt?'

Jamie's brow furrowed for a moment then he shook his head.

'Nor do I, and yet she has disappeared. *Poof!* she and her guard have completely vanished. Does that not strike you as strange?'

It was true; Kayla and Baltheza may not have a typical, cosy, father-daughter relationship, but she'd chosen Vaybian over Daltas when Daltas would have seen her on the throne. By all accounts, Daltas would have had no qualms about killing Baltheza to seize power – Kayla had told me that herself and it hadn't sat well with her, so it made no sense for her to want to kill her father. I said as much to Jamie and Jinx.

'Unfortunately, it makes sense to Baltheza,' Jinx said.

'Only because she's disappeared,' Jamie said.

'Where do you think she's gone?' I asked. 'Do you think she's all right?' And then, slowly, something started to make sense to me: if Kayla hadn't tried to kill Baltheza, was it possible someone was trying to make it *look* like she had? I glanced at Jinx, whose expression was grim. My mouth went dry. 'Is it possible Kayla has been taken by someone against her will?'

'By whom?' Jamie asked.

'Now there's the question,' Jinx said. 'We should go to the villa where she was staying and take a look around; maybe we can persuade Baltheza that Kayla is in as much danger as he is.' Then he smiled his dangerous smile, the one that meant violence was not very far from his mind.

Two

Jinx and Jamie went back down the mountain to tell the riders we would be returning to court in due course, and to request that they pass our felicitations – whatever that meant – to Lord Baltheza. I still had my doubts about returning to the palace. Although Baltheza had claimed I was his daughter, he certainly didn't trust me and I wouldn't be at all surprised if he only wanted me at court so he could keep an eye on me. Either that, or he wanted to use me to draw Kayla out into the open. Of course, it may also have been the case that the pardon wasn't worth the parchment it's written on, and his intention was to arrest me immediately upon arrival. Though, if that were a possibility, I imagined Jamie and Jinx would be more worried.

We set off early the next morning. There wasn't much to pack; we'd been travelling light as we'd gone from one hiding place to another in an effort to keep one step ahead of Baltheza and his men. That we had failed miserably wasn't lost on me; I'd just have to hope my supposed father and I wouldn't have any further falling outs, though I wasn't going to hold my breath on that one.

I hadn't slept a wink, but neither of my two daemons had any trouble. Even Pyrites, who was usually most sensitive to my moods, had begun snoring as soon as he'd curled up on the pillow above our heads. Consequently, by the time we set off I was tired, I was worried and I was fractious. Jamie and Jinx both knew it and didn't even bother to try talking to me.

Kayla and her guard had been staying at a villa not far from the mountain where Pyrites and I had holed up last time I was on the run. I recognised some of the landscape flashing by beneath us as we flew over small villages and fields of rust, copper and bronze crops. Soon, though, we left the rural areas behind and the vegetation changed to tall forests of scarlet and burgundy pines. As we sped closer to the mountains, the lush maroon, purple and red foliage faded away to be replaced by grey rock. Unlike the last time I'd been here, we carried on up over their snowy peaks where the air turned frigid and I was glad of the cloak Jamie had insisted I tie around my shoulders.

As soon as I saw the villa in the distance I knew Jamie was right; this was not some bolthole or hiding place. It *was* a mini palace. Kayla was obviously not as afraid of her psychotic father as I was.

The villa was quite beautiful; a vision of midnight blue marble and gold. Had I been Kayla, I would have been happy to live out my days in such tranquil surroundings. So why did Baltheza think she would leave such an idyllic place to live in a fortress and be saddled with a position that would very likely get her killed? She had forsaken court for over twenty-five years to be with me, she had left Vaybian to be with me – these were not the actions of a woman hell-bent on becoming queen. And if nothing else, knowing this made me fear for her safety even more.

'I think we were right,' I said, as we walked through the marble hallways and past a huge swimming pool filled with water the colour of amethysts.

'Right?' Jamie said, turning to look at me.

'I don't think Kayla left here by choice.' In my heart I knew she hadn't, but if Baltheza hadn't taken her, then who had? I felt totally miserable. Kayla and I may have had our quarrels recently, but I still loved her as my sister; we had spent so long together.

Jinx nodded in agreement, but his mind was elsewhere. He stopped and turned full circle. 'This place has recently seen violence,' he said.

My heart skipped a beat. If anything had happened to Kayla . . .

'There's no blood,' Jamie said. 'If she had been taken there would be blood. Her guard would have defended her to their last breaths.'

'Blood can be washed away,' Jinx said.

'Jinx,' Jamie warned and looked my way, his brow creased with worry.

'There's no point hiding this,' Jinx said, 'the air reeks of hostility.' He turned to Jamie. 'Can't you smell it; feel it?'

Jamie gave an almost imperceptible nod. 'Come on,' he said, 'let's search the place.' So that's what we did, even Pyrites trotted around sniffing and snuffling like a little bloodhound.

'Here,' Jinx called. 'What do you make of this?'

Jamie hurried to his side and I followed as Jinx pointed at a spot about waist high on one of the marble columns. We both leaned in close to take a look.

'It's been chipped,' I said.

'Hit by a sword,' Jamie agreed.

'Judging by its colour, it's quite recent,' Jinx said, running his finger along the blemish.

Pyrites made a mewing sound and when we looked his way he started to paddle from foot to foot in agitation.

'What is it lad?' Jinx asked.

Pyrites pawed the floor then sat back on his haunches waiting for us to come and see. We all crossed to where he sat and as soon as we joined him he jumped back up onto his feet and once again began to paw the marble slabs.

Jinx crouched down beside him with Jamie opposite. 'I can't see anything,' I said, peering over their shoulders.

Jinx squinted at the floor. 'We can't see it, but Pyrites can smell it. Is it blood boy?' Pyrites made the mewing sound again.

'Let's check the bedrooms,' Jinx said to Jamie and me. 'They would have come at night.' Both men got to their feet and together we went looking for the bedrooms.

The master bedroom was another expanse of dark blue marble; the bed took up most of the far wall and was big enough to sleep a small army of bodyguards, which it quite literally did. At last count Kayla had seven, though this could have changed.

The bed had been freshly made with clean, silken gold sheets and pillowcases. Jinx picked up one of the pillows, sniffed it and threw it down, repeating this action with all of the others.

'What are you doing?' I asked.

He picked up a fifth pillow and lifted it to his nose, his nostrils flared and he ripped off the case. 'Look,' he said.

I moved a little closer and gave it a tentative glance, scared at what I might see, but there was nothing. 'I . . . I can't see anything.'

'Smell it,' he said holding it out to me.

I moved closer and he shoved it under my nose, so I did as he said and took a tentative sniff. 'It doesn't smell of anything much.'

'Exactly,' Jinx said.

Jamie gave him a puzzled look and took the pillow from him and he too sniffed the fabric. 'It's new,' Jamie said. 'As in: never been slept on.'

I frowned at him, took the pillow back and turned it over in my hands, then sniffed at it again. It was true – used pillows normally smelled musky, or at least a little like the person who had slept on it.

'I wonder if they went as far as changing the mattress?' Jinx said as he started stripping off the sheets. He gave a grunt. 'Give me a hand turning this.'

Jamie stepped forward and grabbed the other side of the mattress. Being so large it was difficult to manage, and they struggled to lift it as it bent and flexed in the middle, so Pyrites joined in by stuffing his snout under its foot and pushing upwards until it flipped over.

'Oh hell,' I said.

Whoever had taken Kayla hadn't been thorough enough; there was a dark green stain right in the middle of the mattress. Pyrites padded over to take a sniff and gave a little whine.

'Blood?' I asked.

'Blood,' Jinx said.

'Maybe it isn't theirs. Maybe the bed was already stained. Maybe . . .' I came to a halt as both my men and Pyrites were looking at me as though I was the village idiot.

'They must have come at night. Kayla's guard were overcome and she, and most probably her men, were taken.'

'Would they have bothered taking Kayla's bodyguards as well?' I asked.

Jinx blew air out through pursed lips and lifted his fist to his chin in thought. 'Only in as much as they wouldn't want to leave any signs of violence: if the guards were overcome, either they or their bodies would have been taken. Kayla can't be both villain and victim.'

'Do you think she's . . .?' I hesitated, not wanting to say the word.

Jinx shook his head. 'They may well have killed her guard, but I doubt they'd have killed Kayla. What good is a dead scapegoat?'

'I hate to point it out, but if she's dead, she wouldn't be able to argue her innocence,' Jamie said, giving me an apologetic grimace. My fists clenched at my side so hard I could feel my nails biting into my palms – I wanted to believe Jinx, but Jamie had a point.

'Like Baltheza would listen,' Jinx said. 'You know how he is when he gets all of a lather. And this last attempt on his life was too close for comfort; he won't be happy until he has someone's head on a spike. If two of his guard hadn't died trying to save him he'd probably have had them executed for incompetence anyway.'

'I knew he was insane,' I said, 'but it's like he's getting worse.' I hoped it didn't run in the family, though I still couldn't really believe he was my father and didn't think I ever would. As for my mother – well, that she was meant to be Kayla's aunt didn't sit very well with me either. I couldn't be totally daemon, I just couldn't.

'They do say power corrupts, and he's been ruler of the Underlands for a considerable amount of time,' Jamie said, interrupting my maudlin thoughts. 'The power and the temptation to use it for personal gratification have gradually turned him and his court into a hotbed of decadence and depravity. Once on that slippery slope, insanity looms large.'

'I think he's paid that price in full,' Jinx said, 'he's as mad as a rat in a cage surrounded by a pack of cats.'

'So, what do we do about Kayla?' I asked.

'We carry on searching the place and hope we find something that might give us a clue as to who has taken her – and where.'

We searched the villa from top to bottom, then the gardens. Pyrites scampered ahead of us, sniffing and snuffling as he went. When he reached an area of lawn he started to grumble again. As I drew nearer, I could see watery streaks of jade decorating the russet blades and the red earth below. It looked as though the attackers had tried to wash the blood into the grass.

'Do you think it's Kayla's?' I asked.

Jinx frowned at me. 'She's a royal.'

'So?'

'Kayla's a blue blood. Green is the colour of a lesser daemon.'

'When you were wounded your blood was red,' I said to Jamie.

'Jinx and I are Higher Daemon, our blood is red, just like yours.'

'Oh,' I said. 'But that would mean that if Baltheza is telling the truth my blood should be blue?'

'I suppose it could be purple. I've never seen the blood of a daemon-human cross,' Jinx said.

'Purple?' Jamie said.

'Red plus blue equals purple.'

'I don't think it works quite like that, Jinx.'

'Baltheza told me my mother was Kayla's aunt,' I said.

'Hmm.' Jinx and Jamie both pulled faces of disbelief. 'I'm not so sure about that,' Jinx said.

'Me neither,' Jamie agreed. 'We've been giving it some thought and it doesn't really make sense that you're totally daemon – for one thing you can shed tears – but then, a lot of the things Baltheza says and does are a mystery, so who knows?'

'I guess we can give it more thought later, but we have enough to worry about for the moment,' Jinx said, 'like finding Kayla.'

They were right: Kayla had to come first. If it was the other way round, I was sure she'd give everything to find me. I followed the three of them across the grass, Pyrites surging ahead, his snout moving from left to right as he scented the ground and the air. Then we entered a grove of trees and he put on a sudden spurt of speed and disappeared into the undergrowth. I heard a pathetic little whimper and he began to howl, a terrible heart-wrenching sound. Both Jinx and Jamie pulled their swords.

'Look after Lucinda,' Jinx said and strode through the grove to find the drakon.

I went to run after him and Jamie grabbed me by the arm. 'We wait here.'

'Jamie, Pyrites sounds like he's been hurt.'

'He's upset 'tis all.'

'He sounds more than upset.'

'We wait here until Jinx tells us otherwise.'

'But Pyrites—'

'Pyrites will be fine.' I pulled my arm free and hugged myself. 'Honestly, he will be fine,' Jamie promised. I really hoped he was right.

The seconds stretched into minutes, and had there been walls to climb I would have been climbing them. Then Jinx called, 'It's all safe,' and Jamie took my hand and we moved through the trees.

I didn't need Jinx to tell me that acts of violence had occurred within the grove. Trees were gouged and green bloody handprints stained the bark, marking the passage of a fierce battle, and despite the heat of the day I felt cold and sick with apprehension.

The trees gave way to gardens and there was nothing they could have done to hide the evidence of an almighty fight here. Flowers were trampled and bushes and saplings crushed and snapped. More blood stained the flagstone pathway that led out through a gate, and on the other side we found a cliff which dropped away sharply from us.

Jinx was standing at the edge, overlooking the sea, with his hand resting on the drakon's head. Pyrites was puffing black smoke and his wings were pulled back tight against his body.

Jinx turned his head to glance our way. 'I wouldn't come any closer,' he said, his voice bleak.

'Wait here,' Jamie said to me and walked over to join Jinx, who gestured downwards with his head. 'Oh shit,' he said, when he'd looked down.

Jinx uttered a curse, turned his back on the cliff's edge and went to walk away, then hesitated mid-step. 'Did you hear something?' he asked Jamie.

Jamie leaned forward to peer over the edge. 'I thought so.'

Jinx strode back to join him and they both looked down. I moved a few steps towards them, my own ears pricked and listening hard. I wanted to know what was down there, but I'm not good with heights and I couldn't quite bring myself to get any closer to the edge.

'There,' Jinx said.

Jamie frowned in concentration as he listened, then all of a sudden launched himself off the side of the cliff. It was so unexpected I gasped and started towards the edge before remembering Jamie had wings and could fly.

'What is it, Jinx?'

'Stay where you are,' he said.

'Jinx?'

'They threw their bodies over the cliff,' he said. 'I suppose they hoped they would eventually be washed away by the tide.'

'Bodies? Whose bodies?' I asked, rushing to stand beside him, my fear for Kayla outweighing my fear of falling.

Jinx grabbed hold of me and pulled me away from the edge. 'Kayla's bodyguards.'

'Kayla?' I asked struggling to break free of him.

'No,' he said, 'Kayla isn't down there.'

I looked up at his face and he gave me a gentle smile.

'You're sure?'

He pulled me to him and kissed the top of my head. 'Quite sure.'

The sound of beating wings had us both looking back towards the cliff edge as Jamie appeared from below.

'What in the name of Beelzebub?' Jinx said, and let go of me to hurry to Jamie's side as he dropped down to land. Cradled in his arms was a daemon. A daemon I knew only too well: Vaybian, Kayla's lover.

'Is he alive?' I asked as Jamie gently laid him down on the grass.

'Just,' Jamie said.

Vaybian's usually deep jade skin had paled to the tone of over-cooked peas and was smeared with darker green liquid. A nasty gash scarred his brow and an open wound encrusted with drying blood sliced across the top of his thigh. A similar cut ran across his chest down from his left shoulder to the bottom right side of his rib cage, though to my inexpert eye the thigh wound looked the worst.

His eyelids flickered, and for a moment I thought he was about to wake, but then his head slumped to one side. I looked up at Jamie in alarm.

'It's all right,' he said. 'He's unconscious, that's all.'

Jamie carried him back to the villa where we laid him down on one of the couches in the living area while Jamie and Jinx did their best to clean and dress his wounds.

'They must have thrown him over the cliff thinking him dead,' Jamie said.

'Considering all the trouble whoever did this has gone to, you'd have thought they'd make sure he was,' Jinx said. 'A fall off a cliff won't kill one of our kind and none of these injuries are fatal.'

'The others all had their throats cut,' Jamie said and he and Jinx exchanged a glance.

'Yet Kayla's lover did not,' Jinx muttered.

'It's mighty strange that he's the only one to survive. If it were I who'd orchestrated this intrigue, he'd have been the first one dead.'

They were right – it was damn weird. I glanced at the unconscious daemon willing him to wake up. We needed to know what had happened.

'Unless of course, they knew we'd come and they knew we'd undertake more than the cursory search of Baltheza's soldiers,' Jamie murmured almost as if to himself.

They both turned to look at me. 'I think Lucinda needs her full complement of guard,' Jinx said.

'Aye,' Jamie agreed, 'and sooner rather than later.'

'We can't travel while Vaybian's like this,' I told them.

'I'll send a message to Kerfuffle and Shenanigans,' Jinx said.

'You can do that?' I asked, surprised.

'We may not have mobile phones and the internet in the Underlands, but it doesn't mean we live totally in the dark ages,' Jamie said, smiling for the first time in quite a while.

'Actually,' Jinx said with a grimace, 'we do. I was going to send a raven.'

'A raven?'

'I have a very good relationship with the harbingers of death.'

'It figures,' I said with a sigh.

It was so easy to forget that such a sexy and funny man was a Death Daemon; *the* Death Daemon, and I didn't really like to be reminded of it, though I guess it was better to have him on my side than not.

That I was apparently 'marked' by him, as well as by Jamie, put me in a very unusual situation. I allegedly belonged to them both and any daemon causing me harm would be on the receiving end of their very rough justice. Jamie's mark alone was enough to make a daemon think twice, but being marked by Jinx was something else altogether. I had seen members of the court edge away from him as he passed. Whenever we visited the Drakon's Rest the conversation stuttered into silence and tables cleared to allow us to sit.

'I'll go and send the message,' Jinx said.

I watched him walk out into the courtyard and put his head back to gaze up into the sky. Within moments, several black birds appeared above him and dropped down to land on the flagstones at his feet. They sat there, heads cocked to one side as though listening to him, until he held out his right hand and one flew up to alight upon his outstretched fingers.

'Will he tie a message to its leg?' I asked Jamie, my eyes not leaving our friend and his little companions.

'There's no need. Kerfuffle and Shenanigans will know who's sent the message and why.'

'But how will they know where to find us?'

'The raven will tell them.'

That made me look at him. 'The raven can speak?'

Jamie laughed out loud. 'Of course not. It's a bird, albeit an intelligent one.'

'Then how will it tell them?'

'By leading them to us. They will literally follow the ravens.'

When I looked back out into the courtyard Jinx was stroking the bird's feathers with his fingertips and I could see his lips moving as though he was speaking to it. When he took his fingers away, the bird gave a little bob of the head and fluttered up into the sky followed by his other feathered friends who had been waiting patiently at Jinx's feet. Jinx watched them fly away, his hand shading his eyes against the glare of the two suns, and then turned to come back inside.

When he saw me watching him his lips lifted into a smile and his tail curled around his leg to give a little wave. Jamie gave a derisive snort.

'What?' I said, giving him a sideways look.

'He knows you're totally fascinated by his tail.'

'I'm not,' I said frowning at him. He raised his eyebrows into a 'yeah – right' expression. 'I'm not,' I asserted again.

'You're not what?' Jinx asked as he strolled through the archway into the room, but from his grin I suspect he knew full well.

I ignored him and went to take a look at Vaybian. His colour had improved and was more like the colour of peapods, though still a long way from his usual deep green.

His wounds were no longer seeping blood through the bandages and he was resting fairly peacefully, though I wished he would wake up so he could tell us what had happened and who had taken Kayla. I would also be interested to hear how they had been ambushed: I knew from a past episode that her bodyguards would appear at the first whiff of danger, even waking from a deep sleep to protect their mistress. That at least one had sustained injuries whilst still in the bed was a mystery.

'He has shifted from unconsciousness into sleep,' Jinx said. 'A good sign.'

'How do you know?' I asked.

His eyes twinkled. 'I told you once before: sleep and being unconscious are all levels of death, and I'm an expert on that, if not anything else.'

'Oh good,' I said with a shiver, 'I'll sleep so much better for knowing that.'

By late afternoon we'd exhausted our search for clues in the house, Vaybian still slept, and our stomachs began to remind us that we hadn't eaten all day.

'Let's eat,' Jinx said, 'I'm starved.'

'Then you'd better go and get some food – we have none,' I reminded him.

'I don't like the idea of splitting up,' Jamie said.

'Well, we'll have to if we're going to eat. I'll stay to watch over Vaybian,' I said. 'Pyrites can stay with me.'

'Pyrites also needs to feed.'

'He can wait until we come back,' Jinx said. 'Unless of course you want to go and get the food with Pyrites while I look after sweet Lucinda?'

'I don't think so,' Jamie said.

Jinx smirked at him and I could almost see Jamie's hackles rising. 'Pyrites and I will be just fine until you get back, won't we boy?' I said, running my fingers over my little drakon's head. He puffed white smoke and rubbed his head up against my hand.

'We won't be long,' Jamie said, putting his hand on Jinx's back and pushing him towards the door.

Jinx winked at me over his shoulder, ignoring Jamie's scowl, and before they had even gone outside I could hear them beginning to argue. 'I think it's just as well Mr Kerfuffle and Mr Shenanigans will soon be here,' I said to Pyrites. He puffed steam, obviously thinking so too.

Three

I was worried about Kayla and the awful, heavy, sick feeling that had stolen over me when I first heard the news remained. Her guards had been slaughtered, which was terrible, but I took solace in Vaybian being alive as he would want to find her as much as I would; he would help us. Provided, that is, he hadn't orchestrated everything . . .

I found it hard to settle. I paced, stared into space, wandered around the garden and courtyard, but every time I ended my journey staring down at Vaybian's sleeping face. By my third circuit of the villa and its grounds I'd reached the stage where I was sorely tempted to slap the sleeping daemon very, very hard to try and wake him.

Fortunately for him, though not my frazzled nerves, Jamie and Jinx returned just as I was about to give in to the temptation. Jamie frowned at me and Jinx chuckled. I tried to appear nonchalant as I bent down to pull the blanket covering the patient up to his chin. I somehow doubted I carried it off, as Jinx began to laugh like a drain and even Jamie cracked a smile.

'Come on you,' Jamie said, 'we have lunch.'

I had been expecting fish or rabbit or something else that needed cooking. What they plonked down on the table was a basket full of bread, cheese and several flagons of what looked like it could be wine.

'Where did all this come from?'

'There's a village on the other side of the mountain,' Jamie said. 'Apparently Kayla's men shopped there regularly and,' he and Jinx shared a smile, 'they said that a group of riders passed through at speed one night ago, and came back through the village in the early hours of the morning. Some say they thought they heard a woman's cries.'

'Oh God,' I said, my heart dropping down into my stomach.

'When he says cries, what he means is they heard a woman shouting and swearing and cursing her companions with various anatomically impossible fates which would make a brothel keeper blush,' Jinx said, opening one of the flagons and sniffing the contents. He gave a contented smile and after glancing around the room strolled off to raid a cabinet for goblets.

In the meantime, Jamie disappeared into the kitchen and returned with knives, plates and a board on which to cut the bread.

'Here,' Jinx said, pouring out the wine, 'throw this down your neck. It'll make everything seem that much better.'

'Jinx, someone killed all of Kayla's guard,' I said.

'They did,' he paused as he passed Jamie a flagon, a resigned expression clouding his face, 'and there's not one thing we can do about it, so why waste emotional energy? Kayla and Vaybian are, however, alive and that is cause for celebration.'

'We don't know Kayla's alive.'

Jinx looked up from the wine he was pouring. 'She's not dead; I'm sure of it.'

'How could you be?'

'Do you feel deep inside that she's dead?'

'No, I feel sick with worry.'

'If she was dead you would know.'

'Would I?'

'Believe me,' he said, 'you, if no one else, would know.'

I must have looked confused as Jamie laid a hand on my shoulder. 'Jinx is right. You would. Remember how when the first time we entered court you were drawn to her?'

I did; it had been a very strange sensation. 'Yes, I could feel her before I saw her.' I accepted the goblet Jinx handed me. I would just have to trust that they were right.

'Though I must admit, I can't quite understand this connection the two of you have,' Jinx said.

Jamie took a sip of his wine. 'Nor I. I was going to ask Kayla, but never got the opportunity.'

'It's not a daemon sibling thing then?'

They both shook their heads. 'When we find her we'll have to ask,' Jamie said.

We sat on the floor around a small table close to where Vaybian was resting. The marble floor was cold and hard on my backside and Jinx very considerately went and collected some of the pillows off the bed for us to sit on.

The wine was thick and fruity and so dark a red it was almost black, though it wasn't heavy and actually slipped down the throat with an ease that had me accepting a refill, despite my not usually having a head for red wine. Jamie had cut the bread in thick wedges and slathered them in butter the colour of primroses. The bread was lighter than its texture promised and the cheese – the cheese was strong, creamy and made my taste buds tingle.

Pyrites accepted a couple of titbits, but it was too vegetarian for his liking and he soon disappeared to go hunting.

Despite everything, by the time we finished eating, I was feeling pleasantly mellow and when Jinx topped up my goblet of wine I didn't stop him. Jinx drained the last of the second flagon and rummaged in the basket for the third. He slopped some into Jamie's goblet and then into his own.

'Cheers,' he said and took a swig.

'Cheers,' Jamie said lifting the drink to his lips, but before he could sip, Jinx swiped the goblet from his hand sending it clattering across the marble floor. 'What the—'

Jinx turned his head away and spat on the floor. Once, twice and a third time. 'Drugged,' he gasped, getting to his feet and hurrying out into the courtyard as he began to gag.

Jamie picked up the last flagon and sniffed the contents. His lips twisted into a grimace. 'Now we know how they managed to attack Kayla and her guards as they slept.'

For a moment I was frozen in shock, then I put the goblet down gently. The sick feeling of fear returned full force. Jamie looked as ill as I felt.

Jinx staggered back into the room and flopped down beside us.

'You all right?' Jamie asked.

Jinx managed a sickly smile. 'I think I coughed it all up.'

'How did you know?' I asked.

'I could taste the death in it,' he said.

'It was poison?' I said, feeling sicker by the moment.

'No, drugged. Strong enough to make us all sleep, not strong enough to kill.'

'They obviously wanted at least one of us alive,' Jamie said, looking at me.

'So, the villagers were helping them,' Jinx said, his lips pressed together into a grim line.

'I doubt they had much choice, Jinx,' Jamie said.

Jinx pulled a face. 'I need some water.'

'Let me,' I said. I went to get the jug and a glass from beside Vaybian and poured Jinx a draught.

He rinsed his mouth and spat into the flagon that had held the drugged wine, then took a long slug of the water. 'That's better,' he said, wiping his mouth with the back of his hand.

'I think we should leave this place,' Jamie said, 'they must be coming for us.'

'We can't move Vaybian yet,' I said. I didn't want him slipping further into unconsciousness when we needed answers.

'Why do you think they let him live?' Jinx asked.

'Maybe they thought the thigh wound was enough,' I said. 'If they'd hit the artery he would have bled out.'

'But they didn't, and would've known it.'

'I suppose all will become clear when he wakes,' I said, voicing my thoughts.

'I'm not sure we can wait that long,' Jamie said. 'They attempted to drug us for a reason.' He tapped the drugged flagon with his finger. 'Maybe we should take another trip down into the village.'

'Maybe we should stay here and wait to see who comes for us,' Jinx countered.

'It's too dangerous for Lucky. They must have come armed to the teeth; they killed all of Kayla's guard.'

'Kayla's drugged guard.'

'I wish Vaybian would wake up,' I said, glancing at the sleeping daemon. Jinx got to his feet and wandered over to the couch and crouched down beside him.

'If he wakes up and finds *you* peering down at him you'll scare the shit out of him,' Jamie said.

Jinx glanced up and was about to make some comment but was interrupted by a loud thump, a flurry of wings and Pyrites skidding across the marble and screeching to a stop beside him.

'What is it lad?' Jinx asked.

Pyrites was jumping from foot to foot so fast he was practically tap dancing, his claws clicking away on the marble in an agitated *rat a tat tat*.

Jinx rested his hand on the drakon's head. 'Pyrites, calm down.'

Pyrites belched out black smoke and growled. Jinx jumped up and ran to grab his sword from where it lay on the floor.

Jamie was instantly on his feet, his own sword in hand. 'Fight or flee?'

'Aren't you interested to learn who is brave or foolhardy enough to risk the wrath of a Guardian and Deathbringer?' Jinx asked.

'Not at a risk to Lucky.'

'Pyrites, take your mistress to safety,' Jinx said.

'No way,' I said crossing my arms. 'I'm not going anywhere without you two. I did that once before and I don't think my nerves could stand doing it again.'

'Lucky, for goodness' sake, can't you for once in your life do as you're told?' Jamie said.

'Not if it means leaving you.'

'Jinx, tell her will you?'

Jinx put a finger to his lips then stretched out his hand in a 'wait' gesture. We all stopped stock still and waited, listening hard. From the courtyard came the tell-tale slap of leather upon marble. They weren't even bothering to keep quiet. Jamie and Jinx moved to stand either side of the entrance and motioned for me to sit down at the table. Pyrites got the idea. He immediately flopped down and stretched out as though asleep. I dropped down beside him and lay half across the table as though I had passed out, peering through the hair veiling my face.

Two grey-swathed figures appeared through the archway, their voluminous hooded robes hiding their faces in unnaturally dark shadows. They were followed almost immediately by two brown-robed daemons. I could see their faces, and it was their expressions not their daemonic features that gave me goose bumps. These daemons had ill intent on their minds. They stopped a few feet inside the doorway and formed a loose line.

'Where are the Guardian and Deathbringer?' a sibilant voice hissed from within one of the grey cowls.

'Find them,' the second grey figure ordered with a voice that sounded like he was gargling slime.

The daemons in brown marched towards the adjoining rooms, the smacking of the soles of their leather sandals upon the marble slabs incongruous when compared to the silent progress of the grey-robed figures gliding towards me. The daemons in grey were different, and I was in no doubt who were the more dangerous of the four.

'Stop!' Jamie said stepping out behind them, sword in hand.

The two lesser daemons whirled around to face him, whereas their leaders kept on moving towards me. Both held daggers in claw-like hands covered in skin that looked tight and bruise-blackened. There was something repugnant about them, and as I studied them through half closed eyes, I found myself mesmerised by a pulsating boil the size of a golf ball on the back of one of their wrists. The thing looked almost alive and an unbidden image of it bursting and spewing forth tiny spiderlike creatures flashed vividly into my mind.

'My fine feathered friend said stop – and that includes you, too, Sicarii,' Jinx said, and somehow he appeared to float down, as though descending an invisible staircase in between them and me. I snapped out of my trance, shuddered and had to swallow back bile, very glad that I couldn't see beneath the creatures' cowls.

The two figures stopped, one giving a malevolent hiss. Pyrites jumped to his feet with a long, low snarl and grew so he was shielding me with his body. I guessed the time for pretending I was unconscious was over, so I stood to peer over my drakon's back.

A shout went up from our robed attackers and more figures in brown came swarming in through the arched entrance, forming a barrier between us and freedom.

'James, my boy,' Jinx called as he moved forwards, and with a flap of his wings Jamie flew up and over the heads of the freaky grey daemons to join Jinx and Pyrites, putting all three of my guards between the intruders and me. It was now four against probably twenty or so – not good odds to my way of thinking, but Jamie and Jinx were unperturbed.

'I suggest you tell your guard to step down,' Jinx said.

'Give us the female and we will leave you in peace.'

Both Jamie and Jinx flexed their muscles and took a step closer to the two daemons in grey. 'Not on your nelly,' Jinx said.

'We will have her,' one of them said, gesturing to their brown-robed minions. They instantly surged towards us, swords in hand.

'Pyrites,' Jamie called as he stepped forward, his own sword at the ready.

My drakon understood immediately and he backed away, pushing me along with him. I heard the clash of steel against steel, and as soon as Pyrites came to a stop I stood up on tiptoe and strained to look over his back to see what was going on.

My men should have been overwhelmed by the sheer numbers, but with an ease that was bordering on magical Jamie and Jinx were holding their own. Several brown-robed daemons were already sprawled across the dark blue marble and several more were limping away clutching their wounds. Then three rushed Jamie, one from the front and one from either side, and another three ran at Jinx. Jamie and Jinx were good, but I wasn't sure they were that good.

'Pyrites – do something!' I said, though I had no idea what. Jinx and Jamie were between them and us, and if he let loose with a stream of flame he was just as likely to roast my men as the enemy.

Pyrites obviously thought the same as he immediately shrunk to the size of a very large bird and shot into the air leaving a trail of steam behind him. A yell of triumph went up from the minions upon seeing me apparently undefended and two came rushing towards me swords in hand.

I began to back away as I reached for the dagger tucked in my belt, but my fingers had barely touched metal when Pyrites let out a roar so loud that it reverberated throughout my body and left my ears ringing. He roared once again and before my attackers were even within a few feet of me, a spout of my drakon's fiery breath hit the first daemon and he erupted into a pillar of flames. The second skidded to a halt, but too late. Pyrites was not about to forgive a threat to his mistress and flew straight at him puffing black smoke. The daemon threw up his arms to cover his face and head, and was hit with a blast of fire that turned him into a screaming inferno of scarlet and gold.

The shrieking daemons careered around in a blind frenzy of panic and pain, clothing and flesh ablaze as their companions recoiled in the fear that their own robes might catch alight.

Taking advantage of the situation, Jinx shoved one of the two daemons he was fighting in the chest, sending him stumbling into his burning comrade. The back of his robe was a roaring sheet of flame within moments. Jinx's last opponent leaped out of the way, and only just avoided being turned into a fireball himself. With an anguished cry he rushed at Jinx, sword held high. It was a bad move; with a flick of his wrist Jinx sliced across the daemon's chest and the brown robe instantly turned to green as the thing sank to its knees.

Pyrites added to the chaos below him by letting rip with another long blast of flame, forcing our attackers to stop and retreat a step or two.

'Back off, we don't want to have to kill any more of your

people,' Jamie shouted as the last of his three opponents sunk to his knees with hands pressed to his stomach.

'Then give up the woman,' one of the grey-robed daemons called. The remaining brown-clad daemons spread out in a line behind him, their message clear: we're going nowhere.

'She bears my mark and that of my brother,' Jinx said with a gesture towards Jamie, 'do you expect us to give her up so easily?'

One of the creatures in grey gave a hiss, clutching his companion's sleeve with knobbly fingers, and moved in close so he could whisper to him.

'Is this the truth?' the other asked after a moment.

'It is,' Jamie said.

The two creatures huddled together and whispered some more, then one turned and dismissed the group of daemons behind them with a flick of a blackened hand, and several hurried forward to pick up their dead.

The bodies of the three who had been consumed by fire were still hissing, spitting and popping, and making other disgustingly indescribable sounds. They were far too hot to handle, but eventually the minions, after a lot of muttering and shaking of heads, brought in some sacking and with a bit of a performance, which would have been funny if it hadn't been so damned gross, dragged them away, leaving a greasy trail on the marble and the stink of burned flesh behind them.

'Our apologies,' one of the two grey-robed daemons said when the last of the minions had left. 'Your involvement in this matter wasn't explained to us.'

'Who sent you?' Jamie asked, sword still extended. Despite him telling them he didn't want to kill any more of their number, his expression said otherwise.

The creatures bowed. 'You know we can't disclose this to you.'

'In the circumstances, I think it would be understandable and indeed preferable if you did,' Jamie said. 'You've been sent here under false pretences.'

The two daemons whispered some more before turning back to

face us, though I couldn't see much within the cowls other than shadows, not even the gleam of hidden eyes. Judging by the state of their hands it was a relief.

'We were instructed by a third party, an emissary of a daemon of high standing,' one said.

'Do you know who?'

'The emissary is known to us, but whether he was acting for his master or another in this matter we're unsure.'

'The name of the go between,' Jinx said.

The creatures exchanged a look. 'You know we cannot—'

Jinx took a step towards them. 'You don't want to make me angry. You really don't.'

One of the creatures grabbed hold of the other's arm and they both recoiled from Jinx with a hiss. 'The law says—'

'The *law*?' Jinx took another step towards them. 'You scum dare to speak of the law to me?'

'Sir, we mean no offence.'

'No offence? *No* offence? At least six of the Princess Kayla's guard are dead, one lies injured, she's missing and you've attempted to abduct the bearer of my mark; I can tell you right now, I'm mightily offended, and if you don't give me a name I'll show you just how offended I can be.'

'Henri,' one hissed. 'His name is Henri.'

'Henri le Dent?' They both nodded, and to my disgust something black and crusty fell from within one of their cowls and floated to the floor. 'And was it he who instructed you to abduct the Princess Kayla?' Two heads bobbed and to my relief there was no more bodily debris; I was only just keeping my lunch down as it was. 'Where is she?'

'We don't know. We handed her over once her guard had been dispatched.'

Jinx turned to Jamie and never had I ever seen either of them look so grim and angry. Jinx's eyes almost appeared to burn, and his was an expression I would never want directed at me.

'Dispatched? Six fine daemons are rotting corpses,' Jinx said, his voice low and menacing, 'and you speak as though you had just sent them off on some errand.'

The two grey swathed figures began to back away.

'Jinx,' Jamie warned.

Jinx took another step towards the retreating daemons. 'Give me one good reason why I shouldn't "dispatch" you into the afterlife?'

'We acted in good faith.'

'You acted as assassins, as thieves in the night, as murderers and kidnappers. I hope you were paid well, as each coin you spend will bring you one day closer to your deaths and when the last is gone, the flesh will wither on your bones and your hearts will turn to stone.'

The creatures gasped and huddled together. 'No sir. No, kind sir.'

'Go now, before I decide to snuff out your miserable existences before you have the chance to make amends for past wrongs and put your affairs in order. That's more kindness than you deserve.'

The two backed away a few steps more then turned, and there was no more eerie gliding – they ran.

Four

'We have to wake him,' Jamie said, peering down at the sleeping daemon.

Jinx rested a palm on Vaybian's brow. 'Not yet. To wake him now would be a mistake. By morning he'll be fit enough to travel if we leave him be.'

'I doubt he can tell us anything we don't already know,' Jamie said.

'Other than how he survived when the others didn't,' Jinx said.

'It still worries you?' I asked.

He lifted his fist to his chin and stared down at Vaybian for a long time before answering. 'If it had been any of the others I'd have said they had betrayed her and were likely to betray us, but Vaybian . . .' he paused, the corners of his eyes wrinkling as he pondered Kayla's lover's peaceful expression, '. . . I'm convinced Vaybian would never deliberately hurt Kayla.'

'I don't know,' Jamie said, 'maybe if offered the right incentive he would.'

Jinx glanced his way. 'You think?'

'You can never tell what goes on between lovers. Jealousy can be a terrible thing.'

'Jealousy?' I said. 'Why would Vaybian be jealous? Kayla clearly cares for him.'

'She cared so much she left him for twenty-five years to be with you, and when she returned, would have let him die rather than give you up to her father,' Jamie said.

'She couldn't give me up; she didn't know where I was.'

'I know it, you know it, but would Vaybian believe it?' Jamie said. 'Then there was Daltas—'

'She loathes Daltas,' I said, crossing my arms and daring him to say otherwise.

'She allowed him to call upon her, and once again for you,' Jinx said.

'Only to save Philip.'

'Even so,' Jinx said and both he and Jamie looked grave, 'maybe it is enough to anger an ardent lover. He may see it as proof that she cares for you more than he.'

'But someone has taken her,' I said.

'Maybe in the knowledge that you'll try and find her.'

'He could have been threatened; told that he'll only ever see Kayla again if he leads you into a trap,' Jinx said.

'Would Vaybian risk upsetting you and Jamie? He's petrified of you as it is, Jinx.'

Jinx rubbed his chin. 'I think we should forget the conjecture until he wakes, otherwise we'll have tried and convicted him without hearing a word in his defence. It may be Baltheza's way but it's certainly not mine.'

I was silent for a moment. 'I still think that Daltas is behind all this. After all, it was Henri who paid those creatures to take Kayla and then me.'

'If they told the truth,' Jamie pointed out.

Jinx's brow furrowed in thought. 'I've never cared overmuch for Lord Daltas, but if it's he who is once again meddling in dangerous affairs, it may be I'll have to pay him some special attention.'

Jinx and Jamie's expressions were enough that I didn't ask what he meant. For once it was probably best I didn't pursue the matter.

None of us fancied sleeping on even the unbloodied side of the ruined mattress so we curled up together on one of the larger couches in the living room; close enough that we were within easy reach should Vaybian need us. I dozed, but couldn't get comfy, and after a lot of fidgeting and shuffling about, I gave up and was drawn outside to the large, ornamental pool.

The surface shimmered gold under the light of the two moons and was more than a little inviting. I resisted the temptation. If I went for a swim I'd never get back to sleep, though I did take off my sandals to sit on the edge with my feet dangling into the water.

It was a warm, balmy evening with a soft breeze that carried the scent of garden flowers and an underlying hint of the sea beyond, which coated my lips with its salty tang. It was hard to believe that such a beautiful, calm place could have been the scene of such violence. The thought made me shiver and any pleasure I might have had paddling my feet in the crystal water disappeared along with my optimistic mood.

'Ahhh – no, no!' I glanced back into the darkened chamber. I couldn't see Kayla's lover, but I could hear him.

I jumped up and hurried inside. Vaybian was still asleep, but his head was thrashing from side to side as he struggled beneath the blankets we'd laid over him.

'Kayla!' he cried. His face showed a grimace of desperation and perspiration beaded his forehead. I knelt down beside him, not knowing what to do.

'Hush now, brother,' Jinx said, appearing beside me. He rested a hand on Vaybian's brow. 'Hush now.' The daemon's body immediately relaxed and his expression became peaceful.

I pulled the blankets back up to under Vaybian's chin and got to my feet. 'He'll sleep easy until morning now,' Jinx said.

'He didn't sound like a man who'd betrayed his lover,' I said.

'No, he didn't,' Jinx agreed. 'He may not care much for you, but I truly don't think he'd risk losing Kayla by putting you in the way of harm.'

'Jinx, I'm scared for her.'

He took hold of my shoulders and turned me to face him. 'Kayla can look after herself.'

'But—'

'No buts,' he said with a smile. 'Whoever has taken her is probably wishing they hadn't. She's strong and she's tough.'

'No, if she thinks Vaybian is dead she won't be tough anymore. She'll be alone and hurting.'

He ran his thumb along my cheekbone and looked into my eyes. 'She's like you,' he said, 'she may be hurting, but she'll use her pain to fuel her resolve. She'll see those who've caused her pain repaid in kind.' Then he pressed his lips against mine in what was a soft, almost chaste kiss for Jinx. 'Come back to bed.' He took me by the hand and led me to the couch where Jamie still slept, and this time when I snuggled down between them both so did I.

Breakfast was a fairly quiet affair. Pyrites had gone hunting and Jinx had flown off somewhere on Bob before I had woken.

'Shouldn't Vaybian be awake by now?' I said glancing over at the still-sleeping daemon.

'Jinx reckons it won't be long,' Jamie said.

'Where's he gone, anyway?'

Jamie gave a shrug, but there was tightness to his expression that made me think there was something going on that was being kept from me. 'Where has he gone, Jamie?'

'Down to the village,' Jamie said reluctantly.

At last! He was finally learning that I wouldn't give up until he answered me.

'To do what?'

'Ask a few questions.'

Jinx going down to the village on Bob to ask a few questions. Great. The thought of it alarmed me, so heaven knows how the villagers felt with a Death Daemon on a black winged horse descending on them. 'Maybe you should have gone with him?'

'Trust me, Jinx knows what he's doing.'

'I don't for one moment doubt that he does. I'm thinking more of the poor villagers.'

'The poor villagers who sold us and Kayla's guard drugged wine?'

'You said yourself they probably had little choice.'

'Well, if they were coerced into doing it they won't have anything to worry about.'

'What if they weren't?' I asked.

Jamie sat back down and looked me in the eyes. In that moment, my gentle, angelic Jamie was gone; his expression became tough and uncompromising. 'You bear our marks and if we don't defend what's ours then we devalue ourselves and you.'

And we were back to the 'owning' thing again. I bit my tongue as now wasn't the time, but Jamie, Jinx and I were going to have to have a very long talk at some point. I did *not* belong to anyone; not even them.

'What will he do to them?' I made myself ask.

'Lucky, the villagers may have colluded in the deaths of Kayla's guard, her abduction and an attempt to abduct you. Do we not deserve some retribution?'

He stared at me and I stared back, but it was I who had to look away first. He was right, if they had willingly helped to drug Kayla's men, whether they knew what was to happen or not, there was blood on their hands. That I couldn't stomach any possible rough justice Jinx might hand out was probably my problem, not Jamie's or Jinx's. Even so, it didn't sit comfortably with me.

When Jinx returned he was grim faced and refused Jamie's offer of breakfast. I saw Jamie gesture with his head in my direction and heard Jinx murmur 'not now.' He then stalked out into the gardens and off towards the cliff. I watched him until he disappeared into the grove of trees.

I looked questioningly at Jamie.

'He'll no doubt tell us when he's ready.'

I frowned at him and glanced back to the grove of trees. I was fed up with waiting. Waiting for Vaybian, waiting for Mr Kerfuffle and Mr Shenanigans, waiting for someone to tell me what the hell was going on. I started off after Jinx.

Jamie grabbed me by the arm. 'I think it's best if you leave him alone for a while.'

'Best for whom?' I said, shrugging him away.

'Lucky—'

'Don't,' I said with a glare, then turned and strode out into the garden and across the lawn to the trees. The trail of carnage didn't look any better this morning than it had the day before. Trampled saplings and blood-splattered trees were the least of it. It crossed my mind that if ever I should see the spirits of those who'd lost their lives during violence it should be here. Then again, Kayla's men were soldiers and they knew about dying, it was usually only the spirits of those whose deaths had taken them by surprise, or who couldn't accept what had happened to them who lingered.

Jinx was sitting on the cliff's edge with his feet dangling above a hundred feet or more of emptiness. The very idea made me queasy and I did wonder whether that was why he had chosen this spot to be on his own. He was out of luck. I inched my way to the edge before kneeling down behind him, slightly side on so I could see the back of his head, but not out over the void. I was now within speaking distance.

'Are you all right?' I asked.

At first I thought he was going to ignore me as he was so quiet. I let him take his time; I wasn't going anywhere.

'Such a beautiful place and so much death,' he said eventually.

I swallowed hard. Was he saying what I thought he was saying? 'The villagers?' and I scooted forward as far as I dared so I could lean forward to catch a glimpse of his face.

He was staring out to sea, his lips pressed together, his forehead line-free. I couldn't see his eyes and I wasn't sure I wanted to. 'The villagers?' I asked again. He continued to contemplate the skyline. 'Jinx?'

He took a deep breath and let it out very slowly. 'Dead,' he said. 'All dead,' and even though I had half expected it, I recoiled back from him as if slapped.

'Jinx, you didn't? You couldn't?' I knew what he was. I knew he was one of the most feared of creatures in this world, but I hadn't wanted to believe; couldn't bear to believe that he could kill so easily. It made him no better than Henri le Dent, Lord Daltas' assassin of choice.

In the course of two days I had seen sides to both my men that

I'd never seen before: dark, vengeful sides. I didn't like it. I didn't like to think they could be anything but kind and gentle. They were what made this world bearable.

'Lucky,' I heard him say, 'Lucinda.'

He must have seen me recoil. I kept my head down. Surely he hadn't done this . . .

'Lucinda,' he said again, getting up onto his knees and gripping my arm to turn me towards him. I remained wooden, but he wrapped his arms around me and pulled me against his chest. 'Lucinda, will you listen to me?' His voice sounded so despondent and defeated that I stopped resisting and looked up.

He gave me such a sad smile that my horror at what he may have done began to wither away to be replaced by fear. 'Jinx?'

'The villagers,' he said, 'dead every single one.' Then he shook his head and pressed his lips together in a tight line.

'You—' I started.

'Slaughtered, even the children.'

'I don't want to hear.'

He looked back down at me. 'I'm capable of many things but . . .' He stopped for a moment as though he was finding it hard to speak; I know I was finding it just as hard to listen. 'In your world, death follows me everywhere; here a mere touch of my finger upon a person's skin can bring endless sleep, but I don't commit murder and I don't slaughter babies for my own ends.'

'What happened? How come they're all dead?'

'The Sicarii; the creatures in grey – they knew either Jamie or I would go to ask questions, so they made sure there was no one left to give us answers.'

'Oh, Jinx,' I said.

'I'm not a monster.'

I reached up and stroked his cheek. 'I know,' I said. And I did, but for a moment I had let my faith waiver. It wouldn't happen again.

'Do you?' and his expression was one of disbelief and such sadness I thought I could be losing him.

'Jinx,' I whispered and reached to kiss him. It was only meant to be a peck: short and sweet and comforting, but somehow his lips that had seemed so tight and unmoving when we first touched softened, and a hand crept up from my back to cup my head and his lips parted and so did mine and something deep down in my stomach gave a little flip and for a moment I felt like I was falling or I was floating or I was being swept away, I'm not sure which, only that I never wanted it to stop.

He pulled me so close I could feel his heart beating and the rise and fall of his chest. His other hand traced its way down my back until it rested on the curve of my bottom. He gently squeezed and pulled me closer, so close I could feel his body imprinted against mine, oh so hard. I stroked the back of his head and wondered what it would be like to unbraid his hair and set it free so it would hang down over me like a silken – shroud. My eyes sprung open and I started to pull away, but I was immediately looking right up into gold and green sparkling eyes and the thought of letting him go evaporated with any worry.

'Lucky Lucinda,' he murmured and ran his knuckles down my cheekbone. 'My lucky, lucky lady,' then he kissed me again.

'Ha hum,' someone coughed from behind me.

Jinx froze and let out a long, deep sigh before pulling back from me, although not letting go. He smiled down at me, still sad but wistful. 'Soon,' he said, then jumped to his feet holding out his hand to help me up.

I turned around expecting a glowering Jamie, but to my good fortune it was the smallest of my five guards who was waiting. 'Mistress, I've come to let you know we've arrived and the guard Vaybian is awake.'

'Mr Kerfuffle, how did you get here so quickly?' I asked, forcing a welcoming smile upon my lips. I wasn't at all sure whether to be relieved or frustrated by the interruption.

'We came by cart and when we reached the mountains Pyrites collected us.'

'Mr Shenanigans is here?'

'Yes mistress,' he said and gestured towards the villa with his oversized head that reminded me of a marshmallow.

Jinx took my hand. 'Come on,' he said leading me to join Mr Kerfuffle, 'let's see what the captain of Kayla's guard has to say about her abduction and the deaths of his men.'

'You still don't trust him?'

'I don't trust anyone when it comes to your safety.'

'Nor do I,' Mr Kerfuffle said, scowling up at Jinx then stomping off towards the villa.

Jinx put his lips close to my ear. 'Just as well it was Kerfuffle and not one of the others who disturbed us.'

'Just as well someone did,' I muttered to myself. He heard though as his eyes twinkled with laughter and he raised my hand to his lips and kissed my knuckles.

'Anticipation of delights to come can be almost as pleasurable as the actual act,' he said, 'and I shall enjoy the wait, though I'm hoping it won't be too long.'

'You are incorrigible,' I said, though my traitorous body gave a little shiver deep down, which was immediately followed by a warm glow.

Back inside Mr Shenanigans welcomed me with a shy smile. He was the largest of my guards at over seven feet tall with a bulky frame to match, and apart from Pyrites looked the least human. His skin was a lustrous emerald and probably the most attractive thing about him other than his kind and gentle nature. Large, white fangs hung down over thick, rubber-band lips, hiding a set of very impressive teeth. He also had a pair of ivory tusks; one sprouted from the centre of his forehead and the other from the top of his snout above two cavernous nostrils. In fact, the only thing about his face that was small was his eyes; little buttons hidden within his wrinkled, rhinoceros hide.

Pyrites appeared at my feet and rubbed himself around my ankles whilst making a weird purring sound, a bit like a cat. He didn't like being parted from me for too long and I did miss him when he wasn't about. I'd been told that now he had given himself to me he would pine away if I left him for too long. I tried to tell myself it wasn't true, but I wasn't so sure.

Vaybian was sitting up on the couch with a blanket wrapped around his shoulders and a goblet of something clasped between his hands. Jamie had pulled up a chair and was sitting opposite him and from his crossed arms and closed expression it looked as though Vaybian was in for an interrogation rather than a friendly chat from a concerned fellow daemon.

'I told you,' I heard Vaybian say as Jinx and I crossed the room, 'Kayla and I were outside when they came for her.'

'Doing what?' Jamie asked.

Vaybian scowled at him. 'What do you think?'

'*I'm* asking the questions: what were you doing outside with Kayla?'

Vaybian looked down into the goblet and took a swig. Jamie glanced at Jinx and raised an eyebrow. Jinx returned the look and went to stand by my angel's side.

'Vaybian,' Jinx said, 'I have just returned from a village where every living creature has been slaughtered; even the livestock. I have neither the time, nor the patience to play games.'

Vaybian took in a deep breath. 'We were spending a little time alone together,' he said. 'Probably like you were doing with her.' He scowled in my direction.

Jinx dropped down into a crouch in front of him and Vaybian jerked back in the seat. 'I'll ignore the slight to my lady,' Jinx said, 'for now. You were outside with Kayla?'

'We had spent some time together in the olive grove. We were just starting back when we heard shouting and Radnar came running our way, yelling that we were under attack. Then we were swarmed upon by brown-robed daemons. We fought our way through the olive grove and to the cliff where' – he looked up at us with haunted eyes – 'we were cornered. Both Radnar and I were wounded. We were going to take our chances and jump, but another two daemons in grey robes pushed their way to the front. They told Kayla . . .' he paused a moment, swallowing back emotion. 'They told Kayla that if she came quietly our lives would be spared. I told her we should jump, but they said that if she did they would go after her sister.' He glared up at me. 'That's you I believe.' His lips twisted into a bitter sneer. 'Of course, that was it: she agreed to go with them. The moment we'd thrown down our arms and they'd taken her away, they sliced Radnar's throat. It was so quick he didn't even have time to defend himself, then they turned on me. I had two choices: bleed out like a pig or jump and risk being swept out to sea. I chose the only way I'd have a chance of surviving – and eventually finding her.'

Jinx stood and wandered back to stand beside Jamie. 'A pretty story, brother.'

'It's the truth.'

'You should've been protecting her,' Jamie said.

'We were.'

'Then how did it happen?' Jamie asked. I frowned at Jamie; we knew how it happened.

Vaybian shook his head. 'I don't know. Radnar was the only member of the guard who made it outside and he was already wounded.'

'He didn't say?'

'There was no time. We were fighting for our lives.' He looked up at us, his expression pained. 'I can't understand it, they were all highly trained; the best.'

Jamie decided to put him out of his misery. 'They were drugged,' he told him, 'they tried the same on us. It was in the wine.'

'Kayla and I had supped on the wine.'

'Our wine was packed in a basket and it was only the bottom bottle that was tainted,' I said. 'I suppose they'd hoped that after two bottles we wouldn't realise the third was any different.'

'How did you notice?'

Jamie nodded Jinx's way. 'Who better than he who brings endless sleep to recognise a draught promising the same?'

Vaybian dropped his head forward until it was resting on the rim of the goblet still clasped between his hands. 'I can't believe they're all gone.' He looked up. 'Did none survive?'

'I'm sorry, brother,' Jinx said, and we all fell silent; I suppose each of us was thinking about the people who had died over the past couple of days.

I sank down onto one of the sofas, thinking hard. There was something about the murder of the villagers that was suspicious. 'Why did they kill the villagers?' I asked. 'Even if they did it to prevent us getting answers, it still doesn't make sense: the Sicarii had already told us what they knew, why then kill all those people?' I looked from Jinx to Jamie and back again.

Jinx rested his chin on his fist again, his forehead bunched into a frown. 'The Sicarii told us they handed Kayla over to Henri after they'd dispatched her guard, and didn't know where she'd been taken. If the villagers knew something the Sicarii didn't – such as who ultimately took Kayla – perhaps it wasn't the Sicarii who killed them, perhaps it was Henri and his men?'

We all showed our anger and worry in different ways: Jamie paced, Jinx leaned back against the wall and pondered, Vaybian slumped back on the couch glowering at anyone who dared to make eye contact, and Mr Kerfuffle and Mr Shenanigans, being the most practical, cooked lunch.

I couldn't stand the heavy, morose atmosphere inside the villa so wandered back to my spot by the pool and dangled my feet in the water. I felt like we should be doing something, anything, but as Jamie had argued, there was no point going off half-cocked. We needed a plan, which was difficult as we had no idea where they had taken Kayla.

When Mr Kerfuffle shouted that food was up we all wandered into the huge kitchen, though everyone denied being hungry except for Pyrites, who sat by my feet drooling. It was hardly surprising: the food smelled wonderful.

'They do say an army marches on its stomach,' Jinx said, unable to resist lifting the lids of some of the steaming dishes.

'We brought this food all the way from court. It would be a shame to waste it,' Mr Shenanigans said, piling up his plate.

Mr Kerfuffle gave a grunt of agreement through a mouthful of something, and Jamie joined Jinx in peering at the contents of the platters and bowls.

Jamie forked some slices of meat onto a plate and plonked it down in front of Vaybian. 'You,' he said, 'need to eat.' Vaybian looked down at the food and shook his head.

'You haven't eaten for over twenty-four hours and look like shite,' Jinx said. 'If you're to be any help to Kayla you'll need your strength.'

'I suppose,' Vaybian muttered in grudging acquiescence.

'So, what do we do now?' I asked. 'Do we go back to court as originally planned – now we have proof that Kayla isn't involved in a plot against Baltheza?'

'What plot?' Vaybian asked.

'There's been an assassination attempt on Baltheza. Kayla and all her guard disappearing into thin air had him jumping to all the usual conclusions,' Jamie told him.

Vaybian massaged his temples and picked up a fork, then prodded a piece of meat and dropped the fork back down onto the plate. 'Will he never understand?' he said, looking around the table at each one of us in turn, 'Kayla doesn't want the throne and neither do I, and if it wasn't for the fact he's madder than a hornet stuck in a jam jar, not many others would be trying to overthrow him either.'

'Daltas would,' Jamie said.

Vaybian grunted and picked up his fork again. 'I wouldn't trust Daltas as far as I could throw him, and I can't fathom why Baltheza can't see him for what he is.'

'Daltas certainly seems to be able to manipulate him,' Jamie said. 'Which is actually quite interesting: Baltheza's so paranoid I'd have thought he'd be looking to his lords as the first candidates to try and overthrow him.'

'And he's never liked Daltas,' Vaybian said.

'Even so, up until recently, he was an almost constant presence at court,' Jinx said, his voice quiet.

'What are you thinking?' Jamie asked.

Jinx tapped the table with a fingertip. 'Not sure. Everything points in Daltas' direction, which makes me suspicious. He's cleverer than that.'

'Maybe he's grown so arrogant he doesn't care,' Mr Kerfuffle piped up.

Mr Shenanigans leaned close to his friend and said, 'Would you risk the wrath of a Deathbringer and Guardian?'

Mr Kerfuffle gave a brusque shake of the head. 'No, and thinking about it, neither would Lord Daltas. He may be many things, but he's not stupid or suicidal.'

'Are you saying you don't think it is Daltas?' I asked. 'Henri's definitely involved.'

'The Sicarii said that, yes,' Jamie said.

'Sicarii?' Mr Kerfuffle said, his eyes wide.

Mr Shenanigans looked alarmed, too. 'The Sicarii were here?'

I stopped eating to look up. Clearly the Sicarii had a reputation. 'Who exactly are the Sicarii?'

Jinx took a swig of wine, but not before giving it a sniff. 'We brought it with us,' Mr Kerfuffle told him.

'The Sicarii?' I reminded them.

'They're a bunch of assassins, mercenaries and general fixers. If someone wants something dirty done they're the ones for the job,' Jinx said.

Jamie made an exasperated huffing sound. 'That is a bit of a simplification.'

'Sounds about right to me,' Mr Kerfuffle said through another mouthful.

Jamie gave him a look then turned back to me. 'The Sicarii are an ancient order of daemons who worship death and believe that the spirit of each life they take adds to their own spiritual wellbeing.'

'Death as in Jinx?' I said, glancing his way.

Jinx grimaced, his lips twisting in disgust. 'I have nothing to do with them and they have nothing to do with me. If it were up to me, their order would be banned and they'd all be rounded up and served a taste of their own medicine. However they try to pretty it up, they are nothing more than thugs who'll do anything for payment: murder, kidnap and torture being the least of it,' Jinx said.

'Torture?' I said; the mouthful of food I was chewing turned to sawdust as I thought of Kayla.

As usual, Jamie knew what I was thinking. 'They said they handed Kayla over.'

'But they handed her over to *Henri*, which doesn't exactly make me feel much better.'

'If Henri is involved, so is Daltas,' Vaybian said, 'he must be.'

'Maybe, maybe not,' Jinx said.

'We're going around in circles,' I said.

Jamie ignored me. 'Henri wasn't very happy with Daltas. Lest we forget: Daltas tried to get Henri to kill Lucky, omitting the fact that she was marked by us both, leading to her badly injuring him and Pyrites finishing off the job by giving him a light roasting.'

I remembered how Henri had so nearly snuffed out my life and rested a hand on Pyrites' head, stroking behind his ears and earning myself a puff of smoke.

'I'm actually surprised he's already up and about,' Jinx said, 'he was pretty burned up.'

'Do you think the Sicarii lied?' Jamie asked.

Jinx gave him a grim smile. 'There's only one way to find out.'

'We pay them a visit,' Jamie said, and his answering smile was cold.

'You know where to find them?' I asked.

'Oh yes,' Jamie and Jinx replied together, and for the second time in as many hours it was brought home to me that both of my men could be very dangerous indeed.

There had been some argument as to whether Vaybian should come with us or not. Jamie, ever the diplomat, suggested he may not yet be fit enough. Mr Kerfuffle was more forthright and told him he didn't trust him one bit, particularly where my safety was concerned. Jinx didn't say a word, but watched Kayla's captain from below lowered lashes with a half-smile playing about his lips. Eventually it was agreed that he would come.

I was informed that the order of the Sicarii lived in a series of caverns carved into a mountain to the north of Lord Baltheza's fortress. It was, I was told, a conveniently central location for them to ply their trade to any who required their services.

'How are we all going to get there?' I asked. I had Pyrites, Jinx had Bob and Jamie was pretty much self-sufficient, but Mr Kerfuffle, Mr Shenanigans and Vaybian only had leg power.

'Kerfuffle and Shenanigans can ride with you if Pyrites doesn't mind,' Jinx said, and Pyrites dipped his head.

'How about me?' Vaybian asked.

Jinx gave him a wicked grin. 'You, brother, can ride with me.'

Vaybian swallowed hard and Mr Kerfuffle giggled. Kayla's captain had been backed into a corner. He either rode with Jinx, who he couldn't bear to go anywhere near, or got left behind. He was clearly made of sterner stuff than any of my guard anticipated as he gave an abrupt nod.

'That's settled then,' Jinx said, his lips giving a little twitch as he fought back the urge to laugh.

I caught his eye and frowned, to which he replied with a self-satisfied grin. He knew I couldn't say anything without making it obvious to Vaybian that he was being played with, so I stalked off grumbling inwardly; humankind or daemon, men were all the same – puffed up with testosterone and ego.

As there was nowhere else inside the villa I could be guaranteed alone time, I started towards the garden, but then something made me pause mid-step and turn back towards the master bedroom. I'd thought I'd heard a voice or maybe a moan. I lay my hand on the doorknob and waited, my forehead resting against the door as I listened. Nothing. I turned the handle and pushed the door, letting it swing open.

I had wanted to be alone, but it wasn't to be. Sitting on the end of the bed was Diargo, one of Kayla's daemon guards. In life he had been third-degree-burn red and his hair had flowed down his shoulders in wave after wave of silken scarlet. In death he was more of a dusky pink. Upon seeing me he jumped to his feet, his hand reaching for a sword that wasn't there.

'Where is she? What've you done with her?' It must have been Diargo who'd died in the bed. He hadn't seen it coming and didn't realise he had passed over. 'Where are the others? Vaybian! Culpas!' he shouted.

I held out my hand to him. 'Diargo, Kayla has been abducted,' I paused, wondering how I was going to break it to him, 'and I'm sorry, but apart from Vaybian the rest of her guards are all dead.'

'Dead? How can they be dead?'

'The wine you bought from the village was drugged.'

His forehead bunched into a frown. 'I remember feeling woozy and coming in here to rest. I must've passed out.'

'You did, and I suspect the others did too, except for Radnar who raised the alarm.'

'Is he dead?' My expression must have given him the answer as he grimaced and was silent for a few moments. 'But Vaybian survived?' he eventually asked.

'Yes.'

'I must go to him,' he said, striding towards the door.

I followed after him. I knew what was coming and it was going to be heart-rending, but he would never believe me if I told him. Hopefully he would believe the reaction of his former captain.

Jinx glanced my way as I hurried into the room and did a double take. 'James,' Jinx said, touching Jamie's arm.

Jamie looked up and frowned, no doubt at Jinx's expression. 'What's wrong?' he said. Jinx leaned in close and whispered in his ear.

'Vaybian,' Diargo called. Vaybian didn't look up from the sword he was strapping to his waist – but why would he? 'Captain?' he asked again.

'He can't hear you,' I said.

Mr Kerfuffle glanced my way. 'Who can't?'

I ignored the question. 'Vaybian,' I called. 'A moment, if you will.'

Vaybian turned to me, though not with good grace. He didn't like me one little bit and it showed. 'Lady?'

'Captain,' Diargo said, stepping forward. Vaybian waited for me to speak.

Diargo turned on me. 'What have you done to him? Why won't he answer me?'

'He can't see or hear you,' I said, addressing him.

'What in the name of Hades is she talking about?' Vaybian said. 'Is she deranged?'

Jinx sighed. 'She is talking to your brother, Diargo.'

Vaybian began to shake his head. 'No, how can she? You told me they were all dead. You told me . . .' He stopped. 'Oh dear Lord of the Underlands. She's a Soulseer.'

'Say those words again and you'll say no others,' Jinx snarled at him.

'She can't be,' Diargo said. 'She *can't* be.' It was then that what I had told him began to sink in. 'He can't see or hear me?' he said.

'I'm sorry.'

'So I'm . . . I'm no more?'

'You need to move on,' I told him.

'But how?'

'I think he needs your help,' Jinx said.

'My help? How can I help him? I don't know how.'

'I thought you helped the dead move on in your world?' Jamie said.

'I've told them to move on and they either did or didn't; I'm not an exorcist.' I looked at Jinx. 'Can't you help him?'

'I bring death to the living, not peace to the dead.'

Diargo was standing in the middle of the room, fists clenched by his sides, head down, shoulders slumped. His fear was palpable, bringing a lump to my throat.

'I wish I could help him,' I said, and I did, with all my heart. Then I began to feel a little odd: a pinprick of warmth began to grow inside me and what I can only describe as a 'glow' formed in my chest. I began to feel a little lightheaded. I staggered slightly and Jinx went to grab my arm, but his fingers had barely touched my skin when he jerked away with a gasp.

'What . . .?' I started to ask him, but the room lurched and for a moment the air around me rippled.

My feet began to move, although I was sure I didn't want to move them, and my eyes were dragged towards the bedroom. It was like my body was no longer my own. The atmosphere around me was charged with some kind of energy; like static. Then, just in front of the bedroom door a small dot appeared and began to get larger, as though a tear had begun to form in the fabric of the world. The dot stretched into a line and then a gap, and through it a golden light began to seep and then pour as the tear grew longer and wider. Still my feet moved and I couldn't stop them. I began to walk towards it.

'Oh my,' Jinx said.

Diargo took a step towards the light then turned to me. 'I'm afraid,' he said.

'So am I,' was what I wanted to say, but instead I said, 'No need to be,' and gave him an encouraging smile. He looked back towards the light with a nervous expression and began to walk towards it.

'What's happening?' Vaybian said. 'I can feel something—'

'Your friend is finding peace,' Jinx said, and there was something in his voice that made me force my head to turn his way. He was watching Diargo with an expression of awe and wonder on his face.

As Diargo reached the tear he turned back to me. 'Thank you, Lady,' he said.

'You're very welcome,' I said. He gave me one last smile and stepped through the slit and into the light.

He stood there bathed in gold looking every bit like an angel. I saw him look down at himself then glance back at me and smile.

His lips moved, though I couldn't hear him. Through the shimmering light I saw hands reach for him and heard tinkling laughter as they drew him into their world.

I took one more step and another. I was beginning to panic. I was still walking towards the light – and I really didn't want to join him. By helping Diargo, had I sentenced myself to death, or even a fate far worse? I tried to speak, I tried to call for Jamie to save me, but it was like one of those terrible dreams when you're scared shitless and as much as you want to cry out for help you can't. The others were paying me no attention and Jinx was still riveted on the tear; I could have been all alone.

I was almost there. Surely Jinx would see me; surely he would realise something was wrong. Unbidden, my hand reached out towards the light. One step later the golden rays wrapped themselves around my fingers and the sound of laughter grew louder. Another step and my hand reached into the shimmering glow and hovered just on the edge of the tear. For one brief moment the light blazed so bright it dazzled, then the slit sprung together with an audible crack forming a long, dark line, which shrank from either end until all that remained was a mere pinprick; and it was gone – along with all my strength. My legs crumpled beneath me.

Jinx rushed to my side and helped me onto a sofa while the others remained standing, looking at me with shocked expressions. I was confused; for a few moments it had felt like I was no longer in control of my own actions, and it had scared me like nothing else. If I couldn't depend on my own body, what else was there to depend on?

Five

The atmosphere around the villa as we prepared to leave a little while later was very strange. There was a tension I didn't understand, although I realised it had something to do with me.

Vaybian had disliked me before, but now his default reaction was fear. Sadly, it wasn't only his attitude towards me that had changed; both Mr Kerfuffle and Mr Shenanigans regarded me with a certain amount of trepidation and even Jamie was on edge.

'Okay, I know that what just happened was . . . unusual, but why is everyone behaving so strangely?' I asked, looking around the room at each of the daemons in turn. 'What's going on?'

Mr Kerfuffle and Mr Shenanigans exchanged a sideways glance and kept their eyes firmly on their boots. Vaybian gave me a tight-lipped glare and Jamie stopped what he was doing and came to take my hand with an expression that gave me goose bumps.

'Now you're scaring me,' I said, trying to pull away from him. He wasn't having any of it.

'You carry on packing up,' Jamie said to the others and led me outside into the garden. Jinx followed us, and when we were out of earshot of the villa, Jamie pulled me down to sit beside him on one of the marble bench seats surrounding the pool. Jinx dropped down to sit in front of us.

'What's going on?' I asked. 'Have I done something wrong?'

'No, of course not,' Jamie said.

'Is it something to do with what Vaybian called me: a Soulseer?'

Jinx and Jamie gave each other sheepish glances. I rolled my eyes, I wasn't stupid enough to have missed all the hints and the expressions, and I'd been called a Soulseer twice now by Amaliel and Vaybian. I just didn't know what it *meant*.

'All right,' Jinx said, giving Jamie a sideways, narrow-eyed look. Jamie didn't quite smile, but it was plain he didn't care that Jinx would be the one to deliver the news.

I waited, but nothing was forthcoming. 'Enough,' I said, now so seriously grumpy I felt like smacking their heads together. 'What is a Soulseer? And what does it mean for me? Other than the fact my friends are suddenly scared of me.'

'The Soulseer is a kind of daemon legend,' Jinx said, looking to Jamie for confirmation. Jamie waved at him to continue, but his expression was very strange. 'And that's what most of us thought it was – just a legend.'

'So, what's this legend all about?' I asked, not sure whether I liked the idea of being the subject of a legend. It seemed to me, judging by most stories I'd heard, that legends ended up quite badly for someone; usually the one to whom the legend appertained.

They exchanged another one of their looks and I got the impression that it wasn't only Kerfuffle and Shenanigans who could communicate without saying a word. Something was certainly going on between the two of them.

I waited somewhat impatiently, but I kept my mouth shut. This time they would tell me even if I had to wait all day and all night. I think they must have seen from my expression that I wasn't about to let it go. Jinx hopped to his feet to sit down on my other side.

'It's years since I've heard the tale, and when I say years I mean like before the Aztec temples were under construction,' he told me, 'but then it's one of those legends that no one really wants to think too much about.'

Jamie sucked in air through his teeth and shot Jinx a look. Now I was really alarmed.

'This legend . . .'

Jamie took hold of my hand and started caressing my thumb with his. If it was meant to be comforting I had news for him; my anxiety levels were rocketing.

'Tell her,' he said.

Jinx swivelled around so he was looking at me. 'Now don't go reading anything into this because it is *just* a legend.'

'Jinx, you're scaring her half to death.'

'It's not my intention.'

'Just tell me why don't you?'

He looked away for a moment; staring into the distance as though collecting his thoughts. I shivered; despite the heat of the day I was feeling cold.

'It is said that a day will come when true evil will walk both the daemon and human worlds and then even the dead won't be safe from its devastation.' He turned his face to look me in the eyes. 'Legend says that it is then that a creature will be born who stands astride the worlds of the living and the dead; the Soulseer.'

'*Creature?*'

'Don't shoot the messenger!'

'Jinx . . .' Jamie warned.

'This *person* will bring comfort to the dead, seeing them on their way, and unite the guardian of life and the bringer of death.'

'You and Jamie?'

He and Jamie exchanged another of their looks. 'It would appear that way,' Jamie said.

'Is that it?' I asked, thinking it was probably more than enough.

Jinx took hold of my other hand, lacing his fingers between mine. 'The legend is by no means conclusive – but then that's the way of myths.'

'Jinx, I'm not stupid – what is it you're not telling me?'

He looked down at our laced fingers; his daemon maroon, mine very human pink. He raised our joint hands and rested them against his cheek and smiled at me. 'If we three *are* the creatures spoken of in the legend it will be down to us to save our worlds from forces that, if successful, will plunge both the Overlands and the Underlands into a darkness that will last for more than a thousand years.'

★

When we went back inside the villa my mind was reeling so it was of some small relief when it became clear that Mr Kerfuffle and Mr Shenanigans had been doing some talking. As soon as we stepped through the door they both came to greet us. Mr Kerfuffle gave me a tentative smile and Mr Shenanigans had his head bowed, giving the impression he'd rather be anywhere else than standing in front of us.

'Mistress,' Mr Kerfuffle said, 'we, that is, Mr Shenanigans and I, would like to take this opportunity to reaffirm our loyalty to you and, unless you would rather have us do otherwise, wish to remain in your service as two of your five guard.' He nudged Mr Shenanigans. 'Don't we?'

Mr Shenanigans gave me a sheepish smile. 'Yes,' he said, 'we do.'

'Are you sure?' I asked.

'Of course, mistress,' Mr Kerfuffle said, and after a nudge, Mr Shenanigans began nodding enthusiastically. 'If we appeared a little . . .' Mr Kerfuffle started before looking at Mr Shenanigans.

'Disconcerted?'

'Yes, disconcerted, it was just because we were somewhat taken aback by the recent developments. First the Sicarii and then,' he gave a little gulp, clearly still nervous, 'then finding you to be a hum, a hum, a—'

'A Soulseer,' Jinx said, putting the little daemon out of misery.

'Yes, quite,' he said with another tentative smile.

'Well thank you Mr Kerfuffle – Mr Shenanigans,' I said, giving them a big smile. I would have hugged them, but it looked like that might tip them both over the edge, given how nervous they were.

'I think mistress, that the time for formalities has passed – Shenanigans and Kerfuffle will suffice quite nicely,' Mr Shenanigans said with a shy smile.

'Why thank you gentlemen,' I said.

Pyrites chose that moment to come trotting over to rub himself around my ankles and it was true, if no one else, my drakon would always love me, Soulseer or not.

'Are we ready to leave?' Jinx asked, looking around at us. Everyone nodded or said 'yes'. 'Then let's be off.'

We all congregated outside and I looked over at Vaybian. He looked even paler when out in the sunshine.

'Do you think Vaybian is really well enough to travel?' I asked Jamie in a quiet voice.

Jamie glanced his way and his lips twitched slightly. 'I think his pallor has more to do with the prospect of being in very close proximity to the Deathbringer for the next few hours than his state of health.'

'Maybe I should ask him to ride with me and Kerfuffle go with Jinx?'

'And spoil all Jinx's fun?'

'That's cruel.'

Jamie grinned at me. 'No, it's Vaybian getting his comeuppance.'

'For what?'

'For being a rude and arrogant arse.'

I allowed a little smile to creep onto my own lips; Vaybian was rude and rather arrogant, but I still thought it was mean making him ride with Jinx when he was so visibly scared of him.

Pyrites trotted over onto the lawn where he had a bit of room to grow, while Kerfuffle and Shenanigans followed after him with our bags and started loading them into a saddlebag-type arrangement, which they threw over the drakon's back. If he minded he didn't show it and instead lay there on his belly waiting patiently.

Shenanigans gave me a leg up onto Pyrites and then helped Kerfuffle up behind me before climbing on himself. Once we were all aboard, Pyrites grew to his full size, which did nothing for my fear of heights. Funnily enough, the height didn't bother me at all when we were flying, which was totally irrational, like my stupid fear of driving.

Seeing we were all ready, Jinx put his fingers between his lips and gave a shrill whistle. Within moments a dark shadow passed in front of the two suns and before long the air reverberated with the thudding beat of powerful wings. Bob circled us, gradually getting lower and lower until he glided down to land a few yards away with a loud whinny and a thud of hooves.

Jinx sauntered over to his side, patted the creature's neck and turned to Vaybian. 'Coming?' he asked.

Kayla's lover looked from Jinx to Bob's massive head and had it not been for the rest of us watching I think he may well have bolted back inside the villa.

Jinx threw himself up onto Bob and trotted him over to stand next to one of the marble benches, his message to Vaybian clear. Vaybian licked his lips and then drew himself up to his full height – spine straight, shoulders back, head held high – marched over to Bob and hauled himself up onto the creature's back. He may not have been as graceful as Jinx, but he did it without the bench, and therefore without losing any dignity. Once up there, with no saddle or stirrups, he had little choice other than to put his arms around Jinx's waist. I had to suppress a giggle again. Vaybian's expression was one of tight-lipped fear, and it didn't help that Kerfuffle was sniggering away behind me.

Jinx glanced my way and winked. I tried to arrange my features into a disapproving frown, but my lips began to tremble where I was trying so hard not to laugh and I had to look away. Jinx knew though.

'Everyone ready?' Jamie asked, looking at us again. 'Then off we go,' he cried as he and Jinx took off together, leaving Pyrites to follow on behind.

We flew along the coast for about an hour before turning inland. The sea was the colour of lavender and so clear that in some places I could see the seabed below. On a few occasions I caught glimpses of huge, dark shadows moving beneath the surface and I wondered what manner of creatures lived in the oceans of this world. Although several of the silhouettes could have belonged to large sharks or whales, I did see one long, dark shape that reminded me of a recent satellite photograph taken from above Loch Ness. There was pause for thought: could the creature believed by some to be living in the depths of the ancient Scottish loch be an escapee from this world, rather than a relative of a species long extinct in ours? Daemons could travel via water, after all . . .

If nothing else, there was one thing I was certain of: there was no way on earth anyone was ever going to persuade me into or onto the water in the Underlands, and as for swimming – I was sticking to the pool.

We flew for another hour or so over rural areas punctuated by the occasional small village until tall, rusty eruptions of rock appeared in the distance. They looked different to the mountains at home; like giant shafts of stone that had forced their way upwards in pillars.

Jamie swooped down to fly beside us and pointed ahead. 'The middle pillar,' he said, shouting to make himself heard over the wind whistling past our ears, 'is Dark Mountain, the temple of the Sicarii.' It was the gloomiest of the five largest monoliths; tall and imposing and so dark it was almost a glossy black. At least, that's what I thought, until it became apparent that the mountain actually was more of a ruby red and slightly translucent; the suns sinking down behind it gave it a bloody halo that tinged the sky. I would have called it Blood Mountain, but as most daemons' blood was green, I supposed Dark Mountain was more logical to them. It then occurred to me the rock could actually be one great big ruby. Gold wasn't quite as precious here as it was at home, so maybe it was the same with some stones?

It got colder as we came closer, gradually flying lower and lower until we were only twenty or so feet off the ground, hidden from the mountain by a line of trees. Ahead of us Bob's wings stretched out to their full extent and he glided down until his back feet hit the earth with a puff of dust. He reared up for a moment, then his huge front hooves dropped to the ground.

Jamie glided down to join them as Vaybian half fell from Bob's back in his hurry to get away from Jinx, who slid off with his usual graceful ease. Jinx sauntered over to stand beside Jamie and they both looked up, shielding their eyes as they watched us coming in to land.

Pyrites took his time circling the waiting daemons, getting a little closer to the ground with each circuit until he touched down with hardly a bump. Almost immediately he began to shrink until he was small enough for Shenanigans to climb down before helping to lift Kerfuffle off and then me.

'From here on in it's best we walk,' Jamie said.

'Good,' I heard Vaybian mumble.

'Didn't you enjoy your trip, brother?' Jinx asked, the corners of his eyes crinkling with laughter. Vaybian glared at him, but kept quiet.

'Shall we have something to eat?' Shenanigans asked, probably trying to prevent an argument, although food was never far from his thoughts – unless he was thinking about his ladylove, Leila from the Drakon's Rest Inn.

'I'd prefer it if we were under the tree line at the foot of the range before we stopped to make camp,' Jamie said.

'We're not going straight to the temple?' Vaybian asked.

'We'll take a page out of their book,' Jinx said. 'We enter during the hours of darkness.'

'When we won't be able to see?' Vaybian said.

'When we can't be seen,' Jinx replied. 'We'll be exposed on the mountain path otherwise.'

Vaybian stared at him for a moment then gave an abrupt nod. 'I concur.'

Jinx looked surprised. 'You do?'

'If they don't see us coming they can't use my lady as a shield to deflect us.'

'Right then, let's head for the trees,' Jinx said, and we started to walk.

We made camp within the forest west of the Dark Mountain rather than directly ahead of it, where they were more likely to see the smoke from our fire.

'We could go without a fire,' I suggested.

'No need. I doubt they'll notice it, and if they do they'll just think it's travellers making their way to the village yonder,' Jinx said, pointing further to the west. I didn't argue. What did I know?

Pyrites lit the fire in one puff and Shenanigans had dinner cooking in no time. I wasn't sure how any of them could think of food; I was sick with nerves. Then Jinx broke open a bottle of wine.

'Should we really be drinking at a time like this?' I asked.

'Did you know that certain British regiments were given shots of rum before they went into battle?' Jinx said.

'Well, hopefully we aren't going into battle, but I still think it unwise to be swilling wine when we're going into a temple that's probably full of psychotic, bloody assassins,' I said.

'She has a point,' Jamie told him.

Jinx gave the wine a forlorn look and rammed the cork back into the bottle. 'You're probably right.'

Hence the meal was a fairly quiet affair and as soon we finished eating, Jamie suggested we should get some sleep. 'Shouldn't we have someone keep watch?' I asked.

'No need,' Jamie said with a smile. 'If there's danger we'll know it.' Even Vaybian didn't argue, so I snuggled down with my head on Pyrites' belly and soon Jamie and Jinx joined me with Kerfuffle and Shenanigans curled up together under the drakon's chin. Vaybian leaned up against a tree on the periphery of the group.

'I feel awful that poor Vaybian is all alone over there,' I whispered to Jamie.

'I think he's hurting a lot at the moment, he probably just needs some space — especially after a ride with Jinx.'

'You think?'

Jamie kissed me lightly on the lips. 'You are sometimes too good to be true.'

'I doubt it,' I said.

'I'm hoping she's not always so good,' Jinx said, snuggling up against my back and wrapping an arm around my waist.

'So am I,' Jamie said, but in a whisper only I could hear.

I closed my eyes with a smile on my face. Somehow they knew exactly what to say and do to chase away my fear, if only for a short time.

Six

'Vaybian's gone!' I heard Jinx say, and I was instantly awake.

'What's wrong?' I asked as I struggled to sit up.

'Bloody Vaybian,' Jinx said, and then added a few more choice words.

Instant anxiety that was fuelled by his anger flooded through me.

'He's not taking a piss is he?' Kerfuffle asked.

Shenanigans came lumbering out of the trees to the east of the camp. 'He's not back there,' he said gesturing with his head.

'He can't have gone far,' I said. 'We've only been asleep—'

'For long enough for him to get into the mountain,' Jamie said.

'Who in the whole of the Underlands does he think he is going off on his own crusade?' Kerfuffle grumbled.

'He must have a death wish if he's gone in there on his own,' I said, but I had a nasty feeling that he might have done: he hadn't wanted to wait, and in retrospect, had given in far too easily – it was probably also why he'd slept away from us, so he didn't wake anyone when he left.

'If we leave now we could catch up with him before he causes too much damage,' Shenanigans said. 'After all, he would've had to walk and we can fly.'

'He's had a head start of up to two hours. It wouldn't have taken a third of that to reach the bottom of the Sicarii stronghold,' Jinx said.

'So, at best it's all over, at worst he's dead and they're sitting there waiting for us,' Kerfuffle said with a scowl. 'Bloody upstart.'

'He was worried about Kayla,' I said.

'He'll get us all killed,' the little daemon grumbled.

'Pay him no heed,' Shenanigans said, 'he's fractious is all. Not much sleep and no breakfast always makes him like this.'

Kerfuffle scowled at his friend, then huffed. 'I'm sorry mistress.

I'm sure he is anxious about his lady, but going off poorly prepared is no help to anyone, least of all her.'

'If the Sicarii we questioned lied and they do have her, can you imagine what they'll do to him if they catch him?' Jinx said.

'I'd rather not,' I said.

'They won't be going for the quick slitting of the throat option this time, that's for sure,' Kerfuffle said. 'It'll be slow and they'll probably make her watch.'

'Shush,' Shenanigans told his friend.

'I will not shush,' Kerfuffle said, pursing his cupid bow lips, 'it's best she knows.'

'They won't waste a sacrifice,' Jinx said. 'If they think he's alone they'll use him for a ritual killing.'

'Lucky, I think you should stay here with Pyrites,' Jamie said. I began to protest when Jinx spoke up.

'No,' he said, with a shake of his head. 'If Lucinda is indeed the Soulseer, I think she should come to the Sicarii temple.'

'I don't agree. If they realise what she is—'

'She still is the bearer of both our marks.'

'Hey! I am here you know,' I interjected.

Jamie glanced my way, indecision written all over his face. I thought I'd make it easy for him.

'If you're going into that place, then so am I. And that's final.'

'Are you sure it's she who bears our marks, and not us hers?' Jinx asked with a grin.

'Come on,' I said, 'Vaybian may be in trouble, and I don't want to be the one to tell Kayla that we saved her captain only for him to get himself killed in some kind of Bruce Willis rescue attempt.'

'Bruce, who?' Jinx asked.

'He's an entertainer in the human world,' Jamie told him.

'Rescuing people is entertainment?'

'You really do not want to know.'

We flew to the base of the huge, ruby rock in a matter of minutes. The difficult and time-consuming part was finding the way in; it

was an almost sheer rock face with a surface like glass and therefore impossible to climb. We circled for a while before deciding
to land.

'There must be an entrance at ground level,' Jinx assured us. So
we began the long process of walking around the rock. It would
have been quicker to separate and go in opposite directions, but
splitting up was not an idea any of us wanted to contemplate –
especially in the dark.

'It's a bit rocky underfoot,' I said, as a lump of stone cracked and
crumbled beneath the heel of my boot. With the next step I stood
on something that felt like a branch; it rolled beneath my foot and
I almost went over.

'I can't see a thing. And what is that stench?' Kerfuffle grumbled. 'It smells like something died. How did we ever think we
could do this in the dark?'

'Well, unless we find Vaybian sitting on a log around the other
side of the mountain, he somehow managed it,' Jinx said.

'Yeah, when it was lighter,' Kerfuffle said with a snort. 'Or the
idiot got himself caught.'

'We're going to have to risk lighting torches,' Shenanigans said.
'The moonlight isn't enough for us to see by.'

'Pyrites, give us a quick blast of light will you lad?' Jinx said.

We all moved back so he was slightly ahead of us. He puffed out
a stream of fire that lasted a few seconds and instantly lit up the
landscape at the bottom of the monolith.

I let out an involuntary squeal, Jamie said, 'Oh shit,' and Jinx
and Kerfuffle came out with several more earthy expletives, followed by instant apologies to me.

The blaze of light faded away, but I could still see; the images
were imprinted on my retinas, and probably my memory, forever.
I had thought we had been walking on rock and other debris. Now
we knew differently.

Pyrites gave another little burst of fire. It lasted only moments,
but it was enough to prove to us our eyes hadn't been deceived.
The base of Dark Mountain was piled with the bones of the dead;

eyeless sockets peered up at us and fleshless jaws grinned, all cushioned upon a jumble of thigh, arm and other bones. We were surrounded by so many dead that it was impossible not to tread on their remains.

I took in one deep breath and then another. We were walking on the bones of the dead. I was walking on bodies. I could feel myself beginning to hyperventilate. *Get a grip Lucky, get a grip*, I told myself, and gradually my breathing slowed and the moment passed. For some reason I had closed my eyes. I had no idea why, as without Pyrites' blasts of flame I couldn't see much at all, only the dark figures of my companions outlined in the moonlight.

I opened them again and looked around to make sure I was close to the others. Jinx was slightly ahead of me, his hand resting on Pyrites' flank. Jamie was to my left and I could see Shenanigans' huge frame next to Kerfuffle's diminutive figure to the right of Jinx.

'We have to go on,' Jinx said, his voice trembling with anger, 'if for no other reason than to stop this.'

'We should look for a place where there are fewer bones,' Shenanigans said, 'or where they are crushed mainly to dust. That's where the entrance will lie.'

I took another deep breath. Jinx was right: these daemons had to be stopped, but to do that we would have to get inside. Then I thought maybe the spirits of the Sicarii victims could help us.

'Is there anybody there?' I asked inside my head, instantly feeling like a fool. It wasn't lost on me that I sounded exactly like the fake psychics I had spent so long trying to discredit.

I took a step towards Jinx, the crunching beneath my feet bringing bile to my throat. *Treading on their bones can't harm them*, I told myself.

'Please, is anybody there?' I tried again.

I took another step and their voices began to call to me.

'Milady, help us.'

Jinx's head jerked around to look at me, and I saw a flash of white as his lips curled back. 'Lucinda?'

'I can hear them,' I told him.

'Hear what?' Kerfuffle asked, and I saw Shenanigans bow down so he could whisper in his friend's ear.

The voices grew in number and in volume, and then wispy grey spirits began to rise up around us, though it was noticeable they shied away from Jinx, the ghostly figures parting around him as they glided towards me.

I went to greet them. Several dropped to their knees, their hands clutched together as if praying, others stretched out their arms to me. They surrounded me, some reaching out as if to try and touch me, though they couldn't; I slipped straight through their fingers.

'Help us, please help us.'

'Jinx, what should I do?'

'Ask them to show us the way inside,' he said.

'No, I mean for them.'

'If they show us inside it's possible we can stop Vaybian being added to their number. Once we've helped him, then we can help them.'

I turned back to them. 'Can you lead me inside?' I asked.

Their expressions became fearful. 'No lady, you mustn't enter,' one whispered, and then the others joined him until a chorus of whispering voices filled my head.

'Stop,' I said, 'please stop.' The voices continued for a moment or so then diminished into a soft moaning. 'I will help you, I promise, but first I must help the living and then deal with those who did this to you.'

'Sicarii, Sicarii,' they whispered.

'I know,' I told them. They began to drift away, and several turned and beckoned for me to follow. I let out a ragged breath. 'Come on,' I said to my friends, 'I think they're going to lead us to the entrance.'

We would have found the way in eventually. It was just as Shenanigans had said: there was a path up to the base where the bones had been either kicked aside or ground to dust. The entrance was a fissure in the side of the monolith, but at such an angle that rock overlapped rock, rendering the entrance invisible from where we were.

The spirits slipped inside and we followed. The fissure turned into a long and narrow corridor of glistening rock leading into the centre of Dark Mountain. It was dark, but not the pitch black I had expected. Light bled into the passageway ahead and after a few yards the confined space opened out into a huge high chamber, awash with light from dozens of flickering torches and lamps.

Vaybian was slumped, head in hands, at the bottom of a semi-circle of steps; his sword abandoned on the floor below him. At the top of the steps an altar carved out of the same red rock as the mountain had pride of place in the centre of a wide platform.

The spirits swarmed towards him, but it wasn't the captain they were interested in; it was the grey-clad figures hanging from two of the three crosses mounted at the back of the altar. Both dae-mons had been gutted, their entrails hanging down from their waists like ropes. Puddled beneath their feet were glistening pools of dark jade blood, together with other bodily fluids that tainted the air with their stink. The spirits roared their approval and my head felt like it might burst.

'Are you all right?' Jinx asked me.

I could only nod in reply. 'I need quiet,' I said, 'please be quiet,' but the spirits of the Sicarii's victims were enjoying their small moment of celebration too much to hear me.

'Lucinda?' Jinx said, and I must have staggered as he grabbed me by the arm and pulled me to him.

'I'm all right,' I said, but winced as my ears were ringing.

'Help her,' Jinx said, thrusting me into Jamie's arms. He strode across the cavern and, ignoring Vaybian, jumped onto the steps leading up to the altar. 'Desist,' he shouted, and when the spirits continued their roaring he ran to the top of the platform and put himself between the spirits and the dead Sicarii. The spirits drew back from him in fear. 'I said: *desist*,' and this time they quietened.

I walked across to the altar with Jamie holding my arm as if he was worried I might fall again. I climbed the steps until I reached Jinx and murmured a 'thank you.'

'I don't understand why there are so many,' I said to Jinx and Jamie, gesturing out at the ghosts. 'It was the same at the banqueting hall at court. They obviously know they're dead, so why are they still here?'

Jinx stared down at the spirits through narrowed eyes; apparently I wasn't the only one who thought it odd.

'Now you mention it,' Jinx said, 'I can understand why some may hang around, but in these numbers . . .'

Vaybian turned to glance up at us. 'Aren't you in the slightest bit interested to know what has happened to Kayla?' he asked.

'Yes, Vaybian, I am,' I said, more than a little irritated by his tone, 'but it's plain to see she isn't here.' The room only had one entrance as far as I could tell, which also served as the exit, and there was nowhere to hide. 'So I'm doing the best I can: looking for other clues.'

'She gave up everything for you,' he said, getting to his feet and glaring up at me. 'She left her home, she left me and how do you repay that loyalty? With indifference.'

'Now hang fire,' Jamie said, but I'd had it with Kayla's petulant captain.

I laid my hand on Jamie's arm. 'If you recall, Vaybian, I offered myself up in your place and was almost executed for it. I did that for her. I did that for you.'

'And your servant,' he said with a sneer.

'Yes, and for Shenanigans. I didn't want either of you to die because of me.'

'You should have stayed in your world.' The spirits began to moan and gather about him.

'I was given little choice,' I said.

'You were given the choice to return to your world and yet you came back to ours.' Some of the spirits plucked at his clothing and tried to shove him, but to no avail.

'I think you'd better leave this conversation until later,' Jinx said.

I glanced his way, and he gestured with his head at the ghostly figures surrounding us. Their expressions of anger were no longer directed at the two dead Sicarii, but at Vaybian. 'They can't harm him,' I said.

'I wouldn't be so sure,' Jinx said. 'They are getting rather het up.'

'Vaybian, come up here and stand close to Jinx,' I said.

The captain glared at me, then Jinx. 'And why would I want to do that?'

'Because you have seriously pissed off a cavern full of dead people,' Jinx said.

Vaybian swung around to look across the cavern, and several of the dead took swipes at him that would have knocked him flat had they been alive. As it was, their fists flailed straight through him, which didn't improve their demeanour any.

Jamie stepped down, took hold of Vaybian's arm and drew him up the steps to stand between him and Jinx. 'Can you see them?' Vaybian asked Jamie.

Jamie shook his head. 'No, it isn't one of my gifts, but I can feel them. I can feel their desperation. It permeates the air like a winter's chill.'

Shenanigans and Kerfuffle hurried towards us with Pyrites, now the size of a mastiff, padding along between them. A couple of times he paused mid-step, wrinkling his snout as he sniffed the air. He too could feel the spirits' presence.

'Did you kill the Sicarii?' Jinx asked Vaybian.

'No, more's the pity. They were dead when I got here.'

'There were no others at all?'

He gave a despondent shake of the head. 'I searched where I could,' he said, pointing across the cavern to steps carved into the rock, 'but the place is empty.'

I glanced around him: I hadn't noticed the steps, but I soon realised why; they were in the same colour as the rest of the rock, and once again cleverly hidden.

'Anything of interest up the stairs?' Jamie asked.

Again he shook his head. 'No, but they left in a hurry; I found half-eaten meals on a table up there.'

'Why did they kill two of their own?' I asked, glancing at the dead daemons with a shudder.

Jinx looked up at the bodies and walked over to take a closer look. When he turned back to face us his expression was grim. 'These are the two from the villa; I'm sure of it.'

'So?'

'They failed in their duty and returned marked for death. I suspect someone was very unhappy with them,' Jinx said.

''Tis true,' several of the spirits whispered.

I looked down on the mass of grey faces all staring up at me; their expressions imploring, pained and desperate. 'Why are you still here? Why don't you move on?'

'Cursed,' one said.

'Cursed,' said another.

'Cursed,' the word rippled throughout the crowd, growing from a single voice to a chant. 'Cursed, cursed, cursed,' until it sounded like the whisper of pebbles caught in a tide as it rolled up and down the shore.

'What do they mean?' I whispered to Jinx.

'I don't—'

'What do you mean?' I asked them.

One of them glided to the front and held up a hand to silence the others. In life he had been about seven feet tall, muscular, and from the look of the simple jerkin and pants he was wearing, probably a farmer or tradesman. His hair was long and tied back in a tail exposing pointed ears. Two small horns jutted out from just inside his hairline, and sharp pointed claws sprouted from his fingers and toes.

'It is all part of the ritual,' he said. The others all whispered 'yes' and 'ritual'. 'When we are right at the point of death, seconds away from freedom, knowing the pain will be over, they curse us. They curse us to remain in this world for all eternity so that they may feed on our pain. Our suffering.'

'Oh my God,' I said, and felt like crying.

'What?' Jamie asked.

Jinx's lips twisted into a grimace of disgust. 'When we find them, they die,' was all he said.

I paced back and forth in agitation. 'How do I release them from the curse?' I asked. 'I promised to help them and I don't know how.'

'It's a shame we didn't get here a little sooner,' Jamie said, 'before these two had died. Then we could have asked them.'

'Like they would have told us,' Kerfuffle said.

'They would've told us,' Jinx said, glaring at the two dead bodies. 'I would've made sure of it.'

'Well, we didn't and you couldn't,' Kerfuffle said, 'so get over it.'

Jinx turned on the diminutive daemon. 'What did you say?'

'Jinx,' I laid a hand on his arm, 'you're not the only one who's angry.'

He glowered at Kerfuffle, who put his hands on his hips and glowered back.

'When did you get so brave?' Jamie asked Kerfuffle.

'When I realised he was no different to the rest of us.'

'He's the Deathbringer,' Shenanigans said, his lips turned down in worry. He gave Jinx a sheepish look.

'I can bring death, you can bring death, even Mistress Lucky can bring death, just not in such large quantities,' Kerfuffle argued.

Even Mistress Lucky? I was about to say something, but thought better of it. The tension between my daemon guards was running high enough without me throwing in my two pennies worth. Instead, I said, 'Boys, this isn't helping.'

Jinx abruptly turned his back on Kerfuffle and went back to studying the dead Sicarii as though he was willing them into telling us their secrets.

'Maybe you can break the curse by opening the door to the world of the dead so they can pass through,' Jamie suggested, 'like you did for Diargo.'

'I could, except that was a total fluke,' I said, my voice low so the others and, more importantly, the spirits couldn't hear. 'It's never happened before, and I'm not sure I can do it again.'

'Well you managed it somehow.'

'Yes, I guess I did.' I thought for a moment, then walked to the front of the platform to look down on the waiting spirits. 'I'm going to try and help you, but you will have to be patient. It may be that this won't work, and we'll have to find the Sicarii to discover how to lift the curse.'

The spirits let out low moans. 'Help us, pleeease.'

'You,' I said, pointing to the spirit who had told us about the curse, 'what's your name?'

'Dreyphus,' he told me.

'Okay Dreyphus, we're going to try something. Are you willing?'

He pulled himself up straight. 'If it will help us to leave this place.'

I walked down the steps to stand beside him with Jamie following. 'Dreyphus, I want you to think of those you loved who moved on before you. Parents, grandparents, anyone you would love to see again in the afterlife.'

'My wife,' he told me.

'Think of your wife, picture her face and remember what it was like to hold her in your arms.'

He stood there, head bowed. We waited and I inwardly prayed this would work. Nothing happened. Then it occurred to me that last time, I had asked for help, or at least wished I could. I did the same again and this time I closed my eyes and concentrated on opening a doorway to the other side.

For a few moments there was nothing, and then the warm glow I'd felt before spread out from my centre and a low moan from the spirits made me open my eyes. I glanced around and there, a few yards to Dreyphus' right, a pinprick of bright golden light appeared and a split began to open, tearing downwards and allowing a swathe of gold to spill out. It grew longer and wider. Almost instantaneously I felt the pull of the gateway and my feet began to move.

Dreyphus looked up and saw the light. His eyes moved to mine and I forced myself to smile. I wondered what would happen if I got to the tear first. I gestured for him to go to it and he took one tentative step and another until he stepped into its glow, which turned him from grey to gold. He took another step and reached out, his fingers slipping into the split – and the light snapped off like someone had flicked a switch. The split slapped shut and was gone, leaving Dreyphus standing there staring at nothing, his hand still extended.

He slowly turned my way, his face crumpling into an expression of distraught disappointment and the other spirits wailed, joining him in his anguish.

'I am so sorry,' I said, reaching out a hand to him.

'The curse, it is the curse.'

I glanced over my shoulder to Jinx. 'I'm afraid he may be right,' he said.

The spirits of the dead slowly drifted away, knowing there was no help to be had from us. Not yet at least.

'We need to find the Sicarii,' I said.

'We'll find out how to break the curse before I send them all to oblivion,' Jinx said.

'Easier said than done,' Jamie said, sitting down beside us on the steps. 'We have no idea where they've gone.'

'I can't believe they'd abandon this place,' Shenanigans said joining us. 'It's been their temple for millennia.'

'And they'll probably return in another millennia,' Kerfuffle said, 'but for now they'll just make a temple somewhere else – if they haven't already got one.'

Jinx began to smile. 'Of course: they'll have another temple!'

'They have? Where?' Vaybian asked, his interest renewed.

'I have no idea, but it's just as Kerfuffle said: they will have one; a bolt hole for times like this.'

'It would make sense,' Jamie agreed. 'A sect like the Sicarii has a lot of enemies.'

'It could be anywhere,' Vaybian moaned.

'And we'll find it,' Jinx said.

'I wish I could be sure they had Kayla,' I said. 'I really want to make sure she's safe.'

'So now you care,' Vaybian muttered.

I ignored him. Jamie was right: Vaybian was a rude and arrogant arse. He was also petulant. But there must have been something about him that made Kayla want to keep him around.

'Well, one thing's for sure,' Jinx said, 'we won't find Kayla or the Sicarii sitting here all day.'

'I hate leaving them like this,' I said, glancing at the few spirits that remained in the cavern.

He reached out and brushed the hair back from my face. 'It's the only way.'

'I know, it's just so – awful.'

He put his arm around me and gave me a hug. 'You have a huge heart Lucinda de Salle.'

I gave her a weak smile. Maybe I had, I just hoped it wasn't going to end up broken.

Before we left I promised the spirits we would be back to release them. I'm not sure they believed me as they watched us go in a heavy silence.

'Where to now?' I asked.

'Jinx and I think we should go back to court,' Jamie said.

'What will that do, other than perhaps get me arrested?' Vaybian asked.

'One' – Jinx said, counting off on his fingers – 'if we tell Baltheza his daughter has been kidnapped and her guard left for dead, you will no longer be a suspect. He won't be happy someone has attacked a member of his family without his say so and may be more inclined to help us; he has spies everywhere and their knowledge could become our knowledge. Two: where better to pick up information than court and the Drakon's Rest?'

'Sounds like a plan,' Shenanigans said, and Kerfuffle nodded in agreement.

'Three: Shenanigans and Kerfuffle will get to see their lady-loves,' Jinx added with a grin in their direction. Kerfuffle's cheeks turned a funny shade and Shenanigans went all bashful. 'And four: Lucky will get a chance to check how little Angela is fitting in with her new family.'

'What about Philip?' I asked. Last time I had seen Angela's father he had looked half dead.

'What about him?' Jamie asked. Neither he nor Jinx were particularly sympathetic towards his plight. I couldn't blame them; Philip had betrayed me. Had things gone the way he'd planned, I would be on the end of a leash and the plaything of a daemon whose brain was located mainly between his legs. Still, I had to try and get Philip back to the Overlands if I possibly could. If I didn't, I'd be almost as bad as he.

If anyone was truly reluctant to go back to court it was me. Baltheza, the daemon who claimed he was my father, was a sadistic monster and I wanted nothing to do with him. But Jinx was right: he had a huge network of spies who could help us.

To everyone's surprise, Vaybian got up on Bob behind Jinx without any argument, although I suppose it was better than walking all the way.

We reached the fortress by early afternoon and it was decided, despite the sinking feeling in the pit of my stomach, that we should present ourselves at court immediately. We didn't want Baltheza to find out we were back via another source and risk him misconstruing our intentions. Similarly, we decided to go in through the front gate in full royal glory instead of through the tradesmen's entrance we normally used. This way we wouldn't look like we were trying to sneak in. I wasn't exactly dressed for the occasion in jeans, shirt, biker boots and black leather jacket, but I was astride a Jewelled Drakon, with a full complement of guards including the Deathbringer on his infernal steed, the Guardian, Shenanigans, Kerfuffle and one extra: Vaybian.

The royal palace – home to Lord Baltheza – was at the centre of

a small walled city, surrounded by homes, shops, an inn and everything else that one would expect to find, apart from perhaps a
church, which was to be expected; daemons didn't have much
truck with religion.

We flew in above the city streets and cobblestone alleyways,
making directly for the palace proper. The streets below us were
busy, and as we passed over the Drakon's Rest I caught a glimpse
of smoke spiralling up from the main chimney and a whiff of
cooking meat. They would be getting ready for the evening trade
and roasting several different joints on the huge fire at the heart of
the inn. I wished fervently I could be there; anywhere but heading
towards an audience with Baltheza.

All too soon we were dropping down to the palace entrance.
From the outside it looked like a castle from a children's fairytale,
or bearing in mind the occupants, an old Hammer House of Horror movie. Its heavily fortified walls with high battlements of
roughly-hewn grey stone, turrets, a moat, drawbridge and even a
portcullis, towered above the city.

The soldiers on duty cleared out of our path upon seeing us,
some with ill-disguised shudders as Jinx passed them by, and
nobody dared approach to arrest Vaybian. We dismounted outside
the main building. Jinx caressed Bob's snout and murmured a few
words into his ear before sending him on his way, while Pyrites
shrunk to the size of a pit pony and trotted along beside me, his
claws clicking against the cobblestones.

I entered through the huge wooden outer doors with some
trepidation. Once inside the castle, it wouldn't be so easy to leave.

Jamie beckoned one of the Royal Guard over and asked him to
inform Lord Baltheza of our arrival, and our request for an urgent
audience.

The guard looked from Jamie to Jinx, then to me, and decided
that arguing would be a mistake. With a nervous tic making his
right lower eyelid judder, he gave a small bow and requested that
we wait in a small antechamber inside the castle, then disappeared
in the direction of Baltheza's chamber. I would have preferred to

wait in the great hall, as it was there I would be able to see and question the spirits that haunted the rafters: I wanted to know why so many were still tied to the fortress. I knew they had been executed, so it should have come as no surprise to them that they were dead – and therefore they should have been able to move on. The violence of their deaths may have counted for some of them being unable to let go, but I felt that there was something I was missing. I had never liked mysteries.

'I want to take a look in the great hall,' I said.

'Yes,' Jinx said, 'I too would be most interested to learn what the spirits that loiter there have to tell you.'

'I think we should try and get through the audience with Baltheza without any mishap before worrying about the long dead,' Jamie said.

'Surely Baltheza isn't foolish enough to risk the displeasure of the Deathbringer or Guardian?' Shenanigans said.

'It didn't stop him trying to execute Mistress Lucky before, did it?' Kerfuffle muttered.

'In case you hadn't noticed brother,' Jinx said to Shenanigans, 'he's barmier than a scorpion trapped in a glass jar that's been left out in the midday sun. Who knows what he might do?'

'Thanks, boys. You're making me feel so warm and safe and cosy.'

'Just telling it as it is,' Jinx said.

Baltheza was apparently in no real hurry to hear what we had to say. He kept us waiting for so long that Kerfuffle nodded off and even Pyrites curled up at my feet, snoring. I was getting fidgety, and just wondering whether I should take the risk of slipping out to the great hall when the door to the anteroom swung open.

Two guards, both the size of hefty gorillas, stood in the doorway; one of them even looked like a large primate with a dark chocolate hairy coat and overlarge nostrils. It was he who stepped into the room and looked at us one by one, not bothering to hide his disdain. He wasn't one tiny bit in awe of Jamie or Jinx; though I think the words brawn and brains came into it somewhere . . .

'Lord Baltheza has agreed to see the Lady Lucinda, the Guardian and Deathbringer,' then he looked Vaybian up and down with a twist to his lips. 'He also wishes to speak to you.'

'Mistress?' Kerfuffle and Shenanigans asked.

'It's all right,' I said, 'take Pyrites and we'll meet you at the Drakon's Rest.' They both gave me relieved yet worried smiles.

'See you later,' Jinx said to them as we followed the soldiers out of the room.

The surly gorilla-like guard led the way while the other plodded along behind us. I began to wonder if this was how it felt to be under arrest.

I vaguely recognised the way we were going and thought we were being led to Baltheza's private chambers, which was comforting. Had we been going downwards I would have suspected we were being led to the dreaded Chambers of Rectification, and by all accounts that was a trip to be avoided. Even so, the sound of our footsteps echoing throughout the long stone hallways brought morbid thoughts of execution to mind.

We stopped at a huge, ironbound, wooden door I thought I remembered from before and the first guard knocked three times. I heard the word 'come' from inside and the guard opened the door, stepping back to let us to enter. I took a deep breath, plastered a smile onto my face and stepped inside.

Lord Baltheza was sitting on a small couch with a naked young woman curled up at his feet. She wasn't the same girl as the last time I'd visited, though she wore a similar collar attached to a lead looped around Baltheza's wrist. She was very pretty in a daemonic kind of way. A mane of white hair parted by a long unicorn horn fell to her waist and her skin was so pale I could see veins tracing the skin of her inner arms and wrists. She didn't look up as we entered, and instead rested her head against her master's knee. I did wonder how many girls he had as slaves; I now knew he had at least two – unless of course the first one had met with an unfortunate end. The thought made me shiver.

He hadn't grown any more attractive while I'd been away. Raven black curls framed a face only a mother could love. Two thick ridges of puckered skin ran from the bridge of his nose, forming reptilian eyebrows that continued up into his hairline where they met twisted, lethally pointed cornet horns. His skin was an opalescent white shimmering with green and blue, his jade lips were thin and cruel, and his nose long and narrow. These features made him ugly and scary enough, but it was his almond-shaped eyes that made him truly terrifying, particularly when the vertical slits of black surrounded by a blaze of dark orange were staring directly at me.

'Lucinda, my dear,' he said, with a smile that didn't reach those awful eyes.

I gave a small bow, but didn't speak. I wasn't sure what to say; last time I'd seen him he'd just ordered my heart to be torn out by the court assassin.

He glanced at my men. 'Gentlemen.'

'Lord Baltheza,' I heard Jinx and Jamie murmur from behind me.

Baltheza's eyes alighted on Vaybian. 'Give me one good reason why I shouldn't call for my guard and have you executed on the spot.'

'He's with me,' I said before Vaybian had the chance to speak and probably get himself into a whole load of trouble, 'and I'd be most upset if you did so without hearing what we have to say.'

'Perhaps you should prepare to be most upset.'

'Fine, if you don't want to help your daughter—'

'So you finally accept that you are of my blood?'

'I was talking about Kayla.'

His nostrils flared and his face twisted into a sneer of disdain. 'She betrayed me.'

'She has been abducted and her guard slaughtered,' I said. 'Or didn't you know?' I heard Jamie take a deep in-breath from beside me. Jinx being Jinx chuckled.

Baltheza's nonchalant indifference disappeared and a spasm of real, deep emotion briefly contorted his face. A forked tongue flicked from his mouth, licking his lips. 'Kayla has been abducted?'

I crossed my arms and stared at him, trying to figure out if he was acting.

He gestured for the girl sitting at his feet to pour him a drink. She raised her ice blue eyes to mine and slowly uncurled her legs from beneath her, then stood, her lips pressed into a line as though she was trying not to laugh. She turned away to get him some wine, leaving me feeling vaguely disconcerted.

'Tell me what has happened to my daughter,' Baltheza said, dragging my attention back to him. Any emotion I'd glimpsed on his face had disappeared to be replaced by a neutral mask. The only tell of his anxiety was in the constant twisting of his slave's lead between his fingers.

'She has been taken by someone, but we're unsure who. However, we know the Sicarii are involved; they tried to drug us,' I said.

'Sicarii?' Baltheza asked, as he took a goblet from his slave and gestured that I should sit. And for a second time in as many minutes his mask slipped, revealing a fear for Kayla I wouldn't have believed possible.

Then I told him everything we knew, with Jamie and Jinx adding the occasional detail. During our explanation, Baltheza's gaze fell upon Vaybian several times, and by the time we had finished he wasn't bothering to hide his feelings for Kayla's lover. So much so, I was beginning to worry for Vaybian's safety. To Baltheza's mind, he had failed in his duty to protect Kayla, which put him in a very precarious position.

'So the Sicarii told you they had been instructed by Henri le Dent to abduct Kayla?' Baltheza said at the end of our story.

'That is what they said,' Jinx agreed.

Baltheza handed his empty goblet to the girl to refill. 'They lied,' he said.

'You're sure?' Jamie asked.

Baltheza leaned back his chair and took a sip of his replenished drink. 'Henri has not left this castle since his little fight with Lucinda and her drakon,' he said, giving me a benign smile.

'He may have slipped out,' I suggested. 'Revenge could possibly be on his mind.'

Baltheza allowed himself a small chuckle. 'Impossible.'

I glanced at Jinx and Jamie. Both were looking as puzzled as I felt. 'So he is no longer in Lord Daltas' employ?' Jamie asked.

'Not at the moment,' Baltheza said. 'Maybe when he has recovered from his little stay below he might go back to Daltas, though I doubt he will ever be quite the same.'

I frowned, puzzled. Had Baltheza put him in the Chambers of Rectification?

Baltheza noticed my confusion. 'It was he who provided Daltas with evidence against you and your sister, which turned out to be false information – in fact, I would go as far as to say it was an outright lie.' He began to stroke his slave's silky white hair, and she looked up at me with a grin. 'One whose lies can slip so convincingly from the tongue should be punished, do you not think? Particularly when those lies could so very nearly have cost me my two most beautiful daughters.'

I glanced at my two men who were both staring at Baltheza with expressions of morbid fascination, which I guessed was a reflection of my own. He really was mad. I didn't dare look at Vaybian; I suspected his expression would be one of wide-eyed panic as he could well be next. So much for keeping our feelings to ourselves; Jinx and Jamie were no better at it than me.

Jinx pulled himself together first. 'Henri languishes in the Chambers of Rectification?'

Baltheza took a sip of his drink. 'I hope this meets with your approval, after all, his lies were told against the woman who bears your marks, and to make matters worse, he almost put us at odds with each other and that would never do.'

'So,' I said, 'the Sicarii were lying. That means they either still have Kayla, or they're working for someone else and used Henri's name to muddy the water.'

'Or to implicate Daltas,' Jamie said.

'We need to find her,' I said. 'We need to find them.'

'I'll send messages to some of my informants,' Baltheza said, 'and tomorrow we three will speak again, shall we say at mid morning?'

We bowed in acknowledgement.

'You will of course stay here in the palace. Your chambers are as you left them.'

'Thank you,' I said — I could hardly say no.

He fixed his gaze on Vaybian. 'Now, the question is: do you join Henri in the bowels of the palace, to be placed in the care of my Chief Enforcer?'

'He is Kayla's chosen companion,' I said. 'She would be very unhappy if anything were to happen to him.'

Baltheza regarded me for a moment. 'You're so very much like your mother. I'd forgotten how forceful and reckless she could be. How she would argue for lost causes even at personal risk to herself.' He glanced at my men. 'I would suggest you two gentlemen try and cure her of these particular traits. They can be very bad for one's health.'

He glanced back at Vaybian. 'Think yourself very fortunate that one of my daughters has a fancy for you, and the other cares enough for her sister to speak out on your behalf. But listen well: if Kayla isn't returned to me unharmed I'll have your head mounted on my wall — after you spend a considerable amount of time in Amaliel Cheriour's chambers. Are we clear?'

'Yes, My Lord,' Vaybian said with a bow.

We were dismissed, and I for one couldn't wait to get out of Baltheza's chamber. The slave raised her eyes to mine as I moved out, still smiling that disconcerting smile. I managed to control the fear until I was safely outside in the hallway and the door had closed.

'That went well,' Jinx said.

'Better than I could have hoped for,' Jamie agreed.

Vaybian was pale and tight lipped and strode away from us without a word. He was as eager to get out of the palace as I. He had very good reason. We found him waiting for us outside in the courtyard.

'Are you all right?' I asked. He nodded, though he didn't look it. In fact, he looked as though he was about to be sick.

He took a couple of deep breaths. 'Thank you,' he said, 'once again I probably owe you my life,' and from his open and not-quite-so-arrogant expression, I think it actually came from the heart.

'Kayla would never forgive me if I let anything happen to you,' I said.

All of a sudden, he dropped down to one knee. 'Until we find my lady I pledge to serve and protect you with all my heart, my life and my soul.'

'Thank you,' I said, not knowing quite how to respond to this development; it was unexpected and possibly a little awkward. Did this mean he would now pile into bed with the rest of us? He got to his feet and gave a little bow.

'Right,' said Jinx, who was eyeing Vaybian in a way that was not exactly friendly, 'let's get to the Drakon's Rest. I don't know about the rest of you, but I've a fine thirst that needs quenching.'

The inn was packed as usual, and the hubbub of conversation and laughter coming from within spilled out into the courtyard. As soon as we entered and the first daemon glanced over his shoulder to see us walk by, the voices faltered away into silence. I'd have thought they'd be used to us popping in by now. A corridor formed in the crowd of bodies, the daemons closest to us flinching away as Jinx passed.

Shenanigans and Kerfuffle had bagged our usual table right in the far corner, and as soon as we dropped down onto our seats the other customers relaxed and the burble of conversation resumed, albeit a little quieter than when we'd first arrived.

'You still here?' Kerfuffle said to Vaybian. 'I'd have put money on you spending time in the Chambers of Rectification.'

'It was a close thing,' Vaybian said. 'I've your lady to thank for keeping me out of there.'

I was finding this change in Vaybian a trifle perturbing, but thought that maybe this was the real Vaybian and the arrogance was a front.

'Do you want something to eat and drink?' Shenanigans asked, raising a hand and gesturing for service.

'I feel too sick to eat,' I said.

'You'll be fine when it arrives in front of you,' Jinx said, squeezing my knee under the table.

Pyrites appeared by my side and dropped his head onto my thigh with a purr, making me smile. I scratched his chin, earning more purring and a puff of smoke.

'What did Lord Baltheza say?' Kerfuffle asked. 'Did he know Lady Kayla had been abducted?'

'Nope,' Jinx said, 'it was a complete surprise to him. We're to meet with him tomorrow morning once he has spoken to his spies.'

'Any word on Daltas or Henri?' Kerfuffle asked.

Jamie was about to speak but was interrupted by Leila – Shenanigans' ladylove. 'What can I get you all?' she asked, leaning in between Jamie and Shenanigans to wipe the table and give us all a good look at her ample bosom.

'Ale all round?' Shenanigans asked, glancing around the table at us. We all nodded, and he turned back to address Leila. 'Two jugs of ale and six tankards, please.'

'You eating?'

Shenanigans again looked around the table and upon receiving more nods or 'yes's from all of us, ordered enough to feed a small army. Having taken the order, Leila stooped down low to whisper in our large friend's ear and he gave her a soppy smile. She whispered some more and his expression became more serious. She stood, squeezed his shoulder and then pushed her way through the crowd to get our order.

'Leila said that once we've eaten we can go up and see Angela if you want to,' he told me.

'I'd like to make sure she's all right and still happy here.'

'She seems contented enough,' Shenanigans said. 'She and

Petunia are best of friends and Leila thinks Odin has a bit of a crush on her.'

'Really?'

Shenanigans chuckled. 'He carries the girls' books to school. He never carried Petunia's before Angela arrived.'

'How does she like school?'

'Leila says she's doing well.'

I really couldn't imagine what it must be like for a young, human girl to go to daemon school, but as long as Angela was happy I knew that what I thought didn't matter.

'You were going to tell us if there was any word on Daltas and Henri,' Kerfuffle reminded us.

'Ah, now there's a story,' Jinx said with a grin, and gestured for Jamie to tell it.

'How the mighty have fallen,' Kerfuffle said with a smirk once Jamie had finished speaking.

'I wouldn't wish it on my worst enemy having spent a few hours down there myself,' Shenanigans said, 'but Henri – if ever there was a deserving case, it's him.'

Leila returned with a tray of drinks and started handing out the tankards; the one she plonked down in front of Shenanigans was half the size again of all of the others. I wasn't the only one who noticed.

'You're obviously in the luscious Leila's very good books,' Jinx remarked.

Shenanigans gave a toothy grin and Kerfuffle giggled. 'You wait and see how much dinner she serves him.'

'The way to a man's heart, so they say,' Jinx said, squeezing my knee again. 'Though I can think of better ways.'

'So can Leila,' Kerfuffle said, nudging Shenanigans in the side and causing the daemon to splutter his beer.

When the food arrived it was no surprise to any of us that Shenanigans' extra large plate was filled to overflowing. He beamed at Leila and she fluttered her eyelashes. 'To keep your strength up, my lover,' she said, before sauntering away with a provocative swing of the hips and a glance back over her shoulder to make sure he was watching.

Jinx was right: once the food was in front of me my appetite did return, though I had to feed Pyrites surreptitious chunks to finish it all. Despite the name of the inn, feeding drakons inside was no longer allowed after a rather nasty incident when one had nearly burned the place down.

When Leila came to collect the plates with another serving girl, she gestured for us to follow her. Kerfuffle stayed behind, his marshmallow cheeks glowing.

'That's Sybil,' Shenanigans whispered to me and gestured with his head towards the girl clearing the plates, 'she and Kerfuffle are courting.'

I glanced back to take a better look at the young woman. She was about the same height as Leila, but that was where the similarity ended. Whereas Leila was a buxom five feet in height, Sybil had a shapely hourglass figure and knew exactly how to show it off to her best advantage. Leila had porcelain-white skin, with long lilac curls, purple lashes and violet lips; Sybil was a rather fetching shade of baby blue, with long straight copper hair and eyes of the same shade. I had to admit I looked rather boring in comparison. *But this is not your true self*, a little voice whispered in my head. Despite not wanting to believe it, the image of my daemonic self I had seen in the mirror had been beautiful, if alien.

The stairs up to the children's room hadn't improved any. They creaked and cracked as we climbed the narrow staircase, and a couple of times they moved rather alarmingly beneath my feet.

Leila led us past the playroom and to a room at the end of the corridor. She rapped her knuckles against the door and called, 'Can we come in?' then pushed the door open and leaned inside. 'Go in,' she said to me, stepping to one side and gesturing for us to enter.

Angela and Leila's sister, Petunia, were sitting huddled together on one of the two beds. Angela had a book on her lap, which she closed as we walked in and passed to her friend. The two girls were as unalike to look at as they could possibly be. Angela was a human, fair-haired child who would grow up to be a heartbreaker, I was sure; she was already very pretty. Petunia, on the other hand, could be nothing other than daemon, and I had a feeling she would also have her fair share of suitors when she grew up. Her almond-shaped eyes were a beautiful liquid grass green; her skin a luminous moonstone white and her lips a pale lilac. Her hair was long and straight and the colour of heather, and hung in a thick braid that fell to her ankles.

'Hello Angela, hello Petunia. How are you both?'

They both stood and Petunia dropped a small curtsey. 'Very good, thank you,' Angela said.

'I hear you're doing well at school.' Angela's cheeks flushed pink.

'She's top of her class,' Petunia told me with a proud smile. 'If she's still doing so well by the holidays she'll move up into my class. That's why she's working so hard.'

'So, you're still happy here?' I asked.

'Oh yes,' Angela said, her light brown eyes looking at me with a wary defiance. 'I really love it. You're not going to make me go back, are you?'

'Not if you don't want to.'

She shook her head. 'No, never.'

'Never is a long time,' I said.

'You're still here,' she said, crossing her arms.

I had to smile; in less than two weeks she had grown from a frightened little girl to a confident young lady. 'Yes, I am,' I said.

She frowned, as if something was troubling her. 'Have you seen Daddy?'

'No,' I said, and to be truthful there had been so much going on I hadn't given him much thought. Then it suddenly occurred to me that last time I had seen him, he had been in Kayla's care. Did that mean his body was one of those thrown over the cliff at the villa?

'What?' she asked, her tone anxious. Whatever she might say, she still cared about her father. I forced myself to smile, but she wasn't stupid. 'Has something happened?' she asked.

'No, at least, nothing for you to worry about.'

'But what about Daddy?'

'I'll make some enquiries and see if I can bring him to see you.'

Angela shook her head. 'No, don't do that.'

'Don't you want to see him?'

She bit her lip. 'I want him to be all right, of course I do, but,' she gave a big angst-filled sigh that only pre-pubescent girls seem able to pull off, 'I really don't want to see him. He'll want to take me back home and,' another sigh, 'I really don't want to live with him anymore.'

I could understand that. He had betrayed her and her mother. In time she might forgive, but I doubted she'd ever forget. I glanced over my shoulder at Jamie who was standing behind me just inside the door. I could see Jinx out of the corner of my eye. He was leaning against the doorframe; half inside the room, half out. I guessed Shenanigans was outside in the hall with Leila. I didn't know where Vaybian was, but he and I would have to talk: if anyone knew where Philip was it would be him.

'We'll come back in a few days,' Jamie said to Angela, 'I'm sure we'll have news of your father by then.'

She gave him a shy smile. 'Thank you.'

'I'm taking it that Philip wasn't among the bodies thrown over the cliff?' I said as we descended the stairs back to the barroom.

'No,' both my men chorused.

'I would have told you if he had been,' Jamie said.

'I need to speak to Vaybian,' I said as I reached the bottom of the stairs. 'Where is he by the way?'

'I thought he was behind us when we left the table,' Jamie answered. We made our way across the bar to where Kerfuffle was waiting, but Vaybian was nowhere to be found.

'Where's Vaybian?' Jinx asked. His tone made me look at him; it hadn't been friendly.

Kerfuffle wasn't oblivious. 'I think he went for a piss. What's the problem?'

Jinx scanned the bar and Jamie followed his gaze. 'Not sure, but for someone who promised to protect Lucky with his life an hour or so ago, he is strangely absent.'

'I don't think you can read too much into him not being here, Jinx. Kerfuffle is probably right and he's gone out back,' Jamie said.

'I hope you're right.'

'What are you thinking?' Jamie asked. I saw the way his eyes were constantly moving as he looked around the bar and I began to worry. Although Jamie and Jinx were sometimes at odds with each other, when it came to my safety they were definitely as one.

Then a dark green figure appeared in the doorway and Vaybian pushed his way through the other customers with hardly a by-your-leave, his face back to its most arrogant. I cursed inwardly; I had so hoped we were over all this, and now, with my men all het up, I could see a confrontation coming on, which would end badly – and I doubted it would be my Guardian or Deathbringer who would come off worst.

'Where in the fires of Hades have you been?' Jinx asked as soon as Vaybian was within hissing distance.

Vaybian's lips curled into their usual pompous sneer. 'Doing my job, what do you think I've been up to?'

'Your job?' asked Jinx, clearly not impressed.

'Yes,' the green daemon said. 'My job.'

'Explain,' Jamie said, his tone no nicer than Jinx's.

'I swore on my life to protect my lady's sister and this is what I am doing.'

My two daemons crossed their arms and fixed him with stares that were so steely they were bordering on sword stabbing.

'While you were engrossed in feeding your bellies and visiting orphaned children, I was watching one who was watching us.'

'Orphaned?' I said, more alarmed by this word than any other danger. 'What do you mean by "orphaned"'

'Lucky, for goodness' sake,' Jamie snapped, 'Philip Conrad is not a priority here – your safety is.'

I glared at him.

'Perhaps a bad choice of words,' Vaybian said. 'But we cannot speak here. There are too many ears listening and too many eyes watching.'

Jamie and Jinx moved in close to him so they were huddled together. 'We are being spied upon?' Jamie asked, to which he received a curt 'yes' from Vaybian.

Jinx glanced over his shoulder towards Shenanigans who was making his way across the bar, and gestured that we were leaving with a jerk of his head towards the door. Kerfuffle hopped down off his chair and Pyrites padded out from beneath the table, growing to a size that meant my hand could rest comfortably on his head as he stalked along beside me.

Vaybian walked ahead, while Jamie and Jinx walked either side of me and Pyrites, Kerfuffle and Shenanigans followed behind. My guards were suddenly taking their duties very seriously.

Once outside the inn, Shenanigans and Kerfuffle took the lead and Jinx and Jamie dropped behind me, with Vaybian guarding my left and Pyrites my right.

'Where are we going?' I asked Jamie, glancing back over my shoulder.

'Out of the fortress and into the open,' he said.

'To somewhere Baltheza will have no ears,' Vaybian said.

'You think he's spying on us?'

'There was one in the inn who was taking more than a little interest in what we were saying and doing,' Vaybian said.

'You have a name?' Jinx asked.

Vaybian shook his head. 'No, he kept his face in shadows.'

'One of Amaliel's men?'

Vaybian glanced back over his shoulder at Jinx. 'I hope not,' and it wasn't just Kayla's green captain who had to suppress his fear.

Jamie and Pyrites ferried us over the fortress walls and out into the countryside, then we walked for a bit until we were in clear open space. Considering we were in a world where they didn't have directional microphones, spy satellites or any other technological wizardry, my men were mighty paranoid and it made me doubly so. I supposed people who could communicate by staring into bowls of water, or travel between worlds by stepping into a black void had equally strange ways of spying on each other.

When we reached a hill from where we could see for miles in every direction, Jinx flopped to the ground and the others joined him after having one final look around. Jamie took my hand and pulled me down to sit between him and Jinx with Pyrites lying across my legs.

'Right,' Jinx said and all eyes were on Vaybian.

'While we were eating,' Vaybian began, 'a figure slipped in from the back entrance and stood at the bar with his back to us. As soon as the small table next to ours became free he sat down, again with his back to us.'

'So?' Kerfuffle asked. 'The place was packed out.'

'When you went upstairs he called over a serving girl and they had a whispered conversation during which she glanced towards the stairs and then laughed, saying "no, those are the family quarters". He then paid her for his drink and left. I followed him out into the yard, but he had disappeared.'

'When you say disappeared, what do you mean?' Jamie said.

'Just that: I could only have been a few steps behind him, but he was nowhere to be seen.'

'He must have left the inn running,' Jinx said.

'Have you considered that it might be you who's being spied on?' Jamie asked Vaybian. 'Baltheza isn't at all happy with you, after all. He may think you've got something to do with Kayla's disappearance.'

'When I first spotted the spy, yes, I thought it was a possibility. But when you went upstairs, it was obvious it wasn't I who was under surveillance.'

'This isn't good,' Kerfuffle said.

'It may be Lord Baltheza is just keeping an eye on Lucinda . . .' Jinx said.

'Now say it as though you believe it,' Jamie said.

Jinx lay out on his side, resting on one elbow and plucking a piece of grass, tapped it against his lips. 'We're missing something, I'm sure of it,' he said.

'So, we know that Kayla may have been abducted in order to frame her for the attempt on Baltheza's life, but is there another reason anyone can think of?' I asked.

'They tried to take you too. Is that correct?' asked Vaybian.

I nodded.

'Perhaps they knew you would look for Kayla . . .'

'So, Mistress Lucky may have been the target all along? Although, it seems stupid to go after a woman marked by two such powerful daemons,' Shenanigans said.

'The Sicarii didn't know Lucky was marked by us,' Jamie said. Then he paused and added, 'You don't suppose this has anything to do with Lucky being a Soulseer?'

'No one knew,' Jinx said, then he and Jamie exchanged a very dark look. 'Amaliel Cheriour knew,' they said together.

That was a conversation killer; even Pyrites looked worried. 'Do you think he told anyone?' I eventually asked.

'He would have told Baltheza, surely,' Jamie said.

'I doubt it,' Vaybian said.

All eyes turned to look at him. 'Really?' Jamie said.

'Despite Amaliel providing the court with the entertainment Baltheza enjoys the most, there is no real love lost between the two of them.'

'And you know this how?' Jinx asked.

'Watching them when they're together, listening to what's said. General observations of Baltheza's body language . . . and if he did know Lucky was a Soulseer, I very much doubt she'd be welcome at his court.'

No one had to tell me why this should be, Jamie and Jinx had already explained: the voices of the dead could tell me secrets that some wouldn't want me to know. For a moment we lapsed into silence. We had got a bit further in our reasoning, but we had no hard evidence to back it up. The only thing we could do was return to court and hope Baltheza's spies would come up with something soon. However, before we headed back, I wanted the answer to another question.

'Hang on,' I said, as the others stood. 'Vaybian, can you tell me where Philip is?'

'Lucky,' Jamie gave an exasperated groan, 'Philip is not important.'

'Maybe not to you, but he is to Angela, even if she won't admit it,' I said, giving him a don't-you-dare-mess-with-me stare. 'Vaybian?'

'The last time I saw the human was at the villa, the night Kayla and I went to the olive grove. We left him in the corner eating.'

'And he definitely wasn't at the bottom of the cliff?' I asked Jamie again.

'No,' said Jinx and Jamie together. 'Although his body could have been washed away,' Jinx added.

'I don't think so. I wasn't unconscious the whole time I was on the beach. When I came to I crawled over to the others to see if any of them had survived,' Vaybian's voice cracked a little. 'I don't remember seeing him down there and I think I would've.'

'So they must have taken him,' Jamie said.

'But why?' Shenanigans asked. 'What good would he be to them?'

There was definitely more to this than a simple kidnapping, the troubling thing was we were scrabbling around in the dark while the enemy – whoever they were – marched ahead.

With that happy thought in mind we got up and made our way back to the very place I really didn't want to be, but we had little choice. Baltheza had welcomed me in his court and insisted I stay at the royal palace. To disobey would appear disrespectful – and probably land my guards and me in a whole lot of trouble. We were walking on eggshells with Baltheza's sanity as it was, all I could do was hope he didn't intend to have another of his banquets followed by his idea of 'entertainment'.

There was one good thing about staying in the palace — I might get the opportunity to creep into the great hall when no one was about, then I'd be able to question the spirits.

By the time we reached the fortress walls the light was fading and the two moons were beginning to rise above the horizon. The twin suns had almost disappeared except for the last few rays, which tinged the darkening sky.

I didn't want to cross those walls, and would have climbed up onto Pyrites and asked him to take me away if I could have, but it wasn't an option: I had to find Kayla, and now Philip. I had no idea what part he had to play in all of this, but the fact he was missing too worried me. I had a feeling I may find some clues to their whereabouts inside the palace walls.

'What are you thinking?' Jinx asked.

'She does have that look,' Jamie said.

'What look?' I asked.

'The "I don't care what they say I'll do exactly what I want" look,' Jamie said.

'Pyrites, be a good lad and take Shenanigans, Kerfuffle and Vaybian over the wall, James and I need a quiet word alone with your mistress.'

Kerfuffle and Shenanigans climbed onto Pyrites without comment. Vaybian didn't look very happy, but then he very seldom did, so who knows what he was thinking. As soon as they were gone both my men turned to look down at me; Jamie frowning and solemn, Jinx with crinkles at the corners of his eyes and lips twitching. Jinx could never stay serious for long.

'Out with it,' Jamie said.

'Out with what?'

'You know very well. I can practically see the cogs turning inside your head.'

'Strange choice of expression when you don't have anything mechanical in this world.'

'You do in yours so don't try to change the subject.'

I frowned up at him and he frowned down at me and when Jinx began to chuckle our frowns became glares as we both turned them on him.

Unperturbed, Jinx began to laugh out loud. 'My, my, my,' he said, 'I can't wait for you two to have a real barney; sparks will certainly fly.'

'Jinx, can't you be serious for once in your life?' Jamie said.

Jinx flashed teeth. 'You, James my boy, are serious enough for the both of us.'

Jamie closed his eyes and took a deep breath, I think counting to ten. Jinx gave me a nudge and winked, his expression slipping from devilish to innocence personified as Jamie's eyes opened again. He wasn't fooled so easily; he ignored Jinx and came straight back to me.

'Why do you want to find Philip so badly?'

'Well, it's the right thing to do—'

'Lucky, the man is a total bastard. Even his daughter wants no more to do with him.'

'I know what he tried to do was terrible, but sometimes people do terrible things for good reasons.'

'He manipulated you, lied to you and then betrayed you,' Jamie said.

'I seem to remember he wasn't the only one who manipulated me and told me lies.'

Jamie had the good grace to dip his head in agreement. He had lied to me; lied to me big time, all so that I'd invite him into my home. And I still couldn't quite believe he'd managed it so easily on the very first day I met him.

Jinx put his hands on my shoulders and turned me around so I was looking at him. His jovial smile had disappeared. 'Lucinda, believe me when I tell you Philip Conrad is not a good man.'

In my heart, I knew they were right. I just wanted to give Philip the benefit of the doubt. I wanted to believe he did what he did to save his daughter. Otherwise I would have to face the truth – I'd been gullible, naive and perhaps even a little bit stupid.

'I'll say no more,' Jinx said, 'other than I want you to promise me that if it comes to it you'll not risk yourself for Philip Conrad,' and Jamie gave a grunt. 'Please?' Jinx added, and his expression was so anxious that I heard myself saying, 'Yes, I promise.'

'Well, I'm glad we've got that settled,' Jamie said with a certain amount of sarcasm.

Jinx reached out to trace his fingers along my cheekbone. 'Yes, so am I. Though I must admit, I'd like to find out why Philip Conrad was of interest to the Sicarii, wouldn't you brother?'

Jamie opened his mouth to say something, changed his mind, then gave a slow nod. 'Yes, yes I would.'

'There might be some answers in the great hall,' I told them.

'That could be dangerous,' Jamie said. 'You really don't want anyone in the palace realising you can see the dead.'

'I thought maybe we could go and investigate when everyone's asleep.'

'I don't think there's ever a time in the palace when everyone is asleep. There's always someone up and about. Guards, servants and don't forget Amaliel; I don't think he ever goes to bed. Although, there might be a quieter time to go . . .'

'I'm with our lucky lady on this one, brother,' Jinx said. 'It is strange.'

Jamie thought on it. 'All right. Though I suggest we investigate at first light. Anyone who's about will be rushing around getting breakfast or changing shifts and we won't look like we're creeping around like thieves in the night.'

'Sounds like a plan,' Jinx said.

I agreed. I could wait just a little longer if it meant not bumping into Amaliel in the darkened corridors of the palace. The thought of it alone gave me the heebie-jeebies.

★

By the time we reached our room Shenanigans and Kerfuffle had already been on a raid of the wine cellar and we opened the door to the clinking of goblets and tankards.

'You timed that well,' Kerfuffle said, glancing up from the ale he was pouring.

'Here, take this, Mistress,' Shenanigans said, pouring a goblet of wine and handing it to me.

I sat down at the low table with the others as Shenanigans began to hand out more drinks.

We drank and talked and drank some more until, actually, I think we all became a little merry. Even Vaybian lightened up a bit. By the time we all started to fall onto the bed I could see our early morning mission being put off, or at least taking place a little later than we had planned. I went to get ready for bed.

When I came out of my dressing room all my guards were sprawled out and snoring; all but one – Jamie was waiting for me. As I stepped into the bedchamber he took me by the arm and pulled me back inside the dressing room, shutting the door behind us.

'What's up?' I asked frowning at him. His expression was serious; so much so I was instantly anxious.

'Lucky, I . . .' then he stumbled into silence and his eyes slid away from mine.

'Jamie?'

'What you said earlier; what you said about me lying to you – I wanted to say: I'm sorry.' He ran his hand through his golden curls in an agitated movement. 'I did it with the best of intentions, but I can see why you'd be angry.'

'I'm more disappointed than angry.'

He raised his eyes to meet mine. 'I think I'd rather suffer your anger than your disappointment.'

That made me smile a tad. 'I'm not disappointed in you Jamie. I'm disappointed in myself.'

His expression was puzzled. 'Why?'

'Why do you think? There I was believing I was a strong,

independent woman, confident that no one could ever put one over on me, and then along come two good-looking guys and any sense I was born with suddenly deserts me, and I let both of them manipulate me into doing exactly what they want.' It was my turn to look away. 'You and Philip completely took me in.'

'You never really trusted him.'

'No, but I did you. I believed every single thing you said to me.'

'Lucky—' he started to say, but I stopped him by placing two fingers against his lips.

'I understand why you did what you did and although I may not like it I can live with it.'

'But can you forgive me?'

I met his eyes. 'As long as you never try to deceive me again – whatever the circumstances. I'm not sure I could forgive you now we— Now we're so close.'

He brushed the hair back from my face. 'I won't,' he whispered as he wrapped me in his arms, pulling me close until his lips touched mine.

His kiss was soft and gentle, but there was a passion behind it that had my legs turning weak, and I'm sure it was only being held so close to him that stopped me falling to my knees. My body moulded to his, leaving me in no doubt my angel had some daemon in him after all.

My arms snaked around his neck and I returned his kiss, ignoring the little voice in my head telling me that this was neither the time nor the place.

He pulled away from me, his cheeks a little flushed. 'We should—' A *rat a tat tat* on the door interrupted him.

'Are you all right in there?' a muffled voice asked.

Jamie screwed his eyes shut and muttered an expletive.

'I'm fine thanks,' I called, unwinding my arms from around Jamie's neck.

The door opened a crack and Jamie and I jumped apart. 'Jamie seems to have gone missing,' Jinx said, and then poked his head inside. 'Oh – *there* you are.'

'Yes, here I am,' Jamie said, not bothering to disguise his obvious irritation.

'Something wrong?' Jinx asked with an overly sweet smile, which belied the glint in his eyes.

'No, we were just coming,' Jamie said and I had to press my lips together really hard to stop myself from laughing.

'Hmm,' Jinx said, pulling the door wide and stepping to one side. I went first, but I still heard him mutter, 'That's what I was afraid of,' as Jamie passed him.

I woke up in the wee hours to a pounding on the door and a wall of feathers and smoke as Jamie wrapped his arms around me and Pyrites stood in front of the bed with his wings drawn back tight against his body and head extended ready for a fight.

'Who is it?' I heard Shenanigans ask. There was a muffled reply and I heard the door open.

'I have a message for a Mr Kerfuffle,' a deep, rather grumpy voice said. 'There's a young woman at the palace door in a panic asking for him.'

'Did she say who she was and what she wanted?' I heard Kerfuffle ask.

'What am I, your personal messenger?' the voice said. 'I only came to get you as she was in danger of shrieking the place down and she said you were with the princess' guard.'

'I'll come with you,' Shenanigans said and glanced back at me. 'We'll be back shortly, Mistress.'

'Okay,' I managed to say, my thumping heart slowing a bit. Jamie released me and I struggled up into a sitting position. 'What do you think that was all about?' I asked once the door had shut.

'He didn't have a row with the lovely Sybil did he?' Jinx asked.

'They seemed to be getting on all right yesterday,' Vaybian said, 'though I was rather distracted at the time.'

'I doubt Shenanigans would've gone with him if that had been it,' Jamie said, to which we all agreed.

I got up and went to use the bathroom. I spent longer than

necessary sitting there, thinking about Jamie and Jinx and wondering what I was going to do about the two of them. They both meant more to me than I could ever have imagined and the thought of giving either of them up made my heart ache. But I would have to choose . . . or would I? They didn't seem to have a problem with the idea of sharing me, apart from the occasional episode of green-eyed-monster syndrome that emerged when one of them found me alone with the other. I yawned; I was too tired for all this.

I was coming out of the bathroom when the door to our chamber burst open and Shenanigans came lumbering in. He looked straight to me.

'It's Angela,' he said with no preamble. 'She's been taken.'

Seven

It had taken me only a few moments to throw on some clothes and run out of the door with my guard. We found Kerfuffle sitting on the steps to the entrance hall, his arm around the shoulders of the distraught Sybil while her head rested against his shoulder. As soon as he saw us he whispered in her ear and they both stood. Even in her distressed state she thought to bob a little curtsey to me, which made my chest ache.

Jamie and Jinx were all business. 'What happened?' Jinx asked.

'We'd been abed for about an hour when we were woken by the girls' screaming,' Sybil said her voice soft and shaky.

'You live at the inn?' Jamie asked.

She nodded. 'I share a room with Pammy, the other kitchen maid.'

'You say you heard screams?' Jinx said.

'Then shouting and the pounding of feet. Pammy and I ran upstairs to the bar and I could hear Barron and Celia up top shouting, then Leila came running down from the bedrooms and told me Angela had been taken and to come and get you.' She took a deep shuddery breath.

'She thinks Oddy's been hurt,' Kerfuffle said, giving her a hug.

We went straight to the inn. Lights were on and pouring out into the yard, but there was no drunken singing or hubbub of companionable voices. A silver-haired young woman I assumed was Pammy was waiting by the front door and if daemons could cry I'm sure she would have been crying. She and Sybil hugged and sank down together on a nearby bench. We left them there while we trudged upstairs to find out what happened.

Leila was at the top of the stairs outside an open doorway that led into a bedroom. Upon hearing our heavy footsteps upon the creaking staircase she turned to us and her face crumpled. Shenanigans took her hand and her lips pressed into a thin line of misery. 'Oddy's been hurt,' she said and looked away, back into the room. Shenanigans put his arms around her and she fell against his chest.

'Come on,' I said to Jamie and Jinx, and Shenanigans led Leila away from the door so we could enter.

A huge bed filled the centre of the room, and lying in the middle of it under a crisp white sheet and blankets was the forlorn figure of Odin. He looked so small in the oversized bed, his auburn hair too bright against his very pale skin. A white bandage stained by a circle of jade at its centre covered his right shoulder. The Innkeeper knelt on the floor, one trotter holding his son's, the other holding the hand of the woman sitting on the bed who I assumed to be his wife.

'He tried to stop them,' Leila said from behind us. 'His room is next to the girls' and when he heard them cry out he ran in to try and help them.' The last word was almost a sob.

Her parents looked up and the innkeeper, Barron, struggled to his feet and gave a small bow in my direction.

'Will he be all right?' I asked.

'He's a strong boy,' Barron said.

'But he's so young,' his wife said, reaching out to stroke her son's forehead, 'to survive so many wounds.'

'Wounds?' I said, my throat closing up. *Plural*.

'Petunia said he wouldn't stop attacking them even when he'd been stabbed in the shoulder,' Leila said. 'He just carried on fighting them so they skewered him,' and her voice broke.

Jinx stepped past me into the room.

'Please no, please don't take my baby,' Odin's mother said, stretching her arm out across her son and leaning forward so she was between him and the Deathbringer.

'I do not bring death this night,' he said, 'and I'll not have death's emissaries waiting in this chamber like carrion crows. Be off with you!' and after that, I'm pretty sure the room brightened just a little, and the air smelled that much fresher.

Jamie's hand found mine and gave it a squeeze. 'Don't worry, the boy's going to be all right now,' he whispered in my ear. As if to prove the point, Odin's eyelids flickered, he drew a soft breath and a smidgeon of colour returned to his cheeks and lips.

Jinx turned to the parents. 'We have to speak to your daughter,' he said. Odin's parents exchanged a fearful glance.

'We need to ask her a few questions so we can find who did this and get Angela back safely,' Jamie told them, and their expressions relaxed a little, though not a lot.

Barron gave Jinx a sideways look and then patted his wife on the shoulder. 'You stay with Odin,' he said and gestured for us to go out into the passageway. He led us to the room next to the girls' room. 'We've put Petunia in with Teasel,' he said. 'They're both scared to death and looking after him gives her something to do.'

The two children were huddled together in one small bed, their faces pale, their eyes huge and fearful. Teasel had his thumb stuffed in his mouth and actually cringed as we walked into the room. Petunia had a book spread out between them and it looked as though she had been trying to show him some pictures to keep them occupied. From their haunted expressions it didn't appear to be helping either of them. I gave them the best smile I could manage and sat down on the foot of their bed.

'Petunia, I need you to be very brave and tell me everything you can about the people who came and took Angela,' I said.

She glanced at her father. 'Go ahead Petunia, Mistress Lucky and her friends are going to get Angela back,' he told her.

'Is Shenanigans here?' she asked.

'He's out in the hall,' I said. 'Do you want us to get him?'

She bit her lip then gave a little nod.

'Shenanigans,' Jinx called, and then poked his head out of the door and held a muffled conversation.

I knew Shenanigans had entered the room behind me as both children sat up straight and Teasel wrenched his thumb from his mouth and held out his arms. Shenanigans picked up the boy and swung him around then hugged him close, kissing his mop of black curls before dropping down onto the bed next to Petunia. Petunia snuggled up against him and he put his other arm around her shoulders.

'Now then, now then,' he said. 'We're all safe here.'

'Is Oddy going to be all right?' Petunia asked.

'He's going to be as good as new in a couple of days, you'll see.'

'You sure?'

Shenanigans hugged them both to him. 'Of course I'm sure,' he said, looking up and over my shoulder. When I glanced back I saw Jinx give him a small nod. 'Now, let's tell Mistress Lucky and the Guardian all we know about the daemons who took Angela.'

'It was dark and I couldn't see very much,' Petunia begun. 'I woke up when I heard a floorboard creak and I saw someone leaning over Angela.'

'Is that when you screamed?'

'Yes. Whatever it was turned and hissed at me to shut up. It sounded like a snake.'

'Then what happened?'

'The door flew open and Oddy ran in and head butted it in the stomach. Then another one appeared from, like, nowhere and something glinted in its hand and I heard Oddy shriek, but he grabbed hold of it, then they were struggling and Oddy fell to the ground and it hit him again and again. Then they were jumping out of the window and Oddy was whimpering and Daddy came in with a lamp and there was blood; there was blood everywhere and I thought Oddy was . . . I thought he was . . .' her face screwed up and she covered it with her hands.

'There, there,' Shenanigans said, hugging her to him. 'Oddy's going to be all right and we're going to find Angela and bring her back home.'

'You promise?' she said, looking up at him with huge eyes.

'I promise,' he said and I did not doubt for a second that he meant it.

★

'Odin could probably tell us more when he's feeling better,' Shenanigans said as we walked back down into the bar.

'I don't think we have time to wait,' Jamie said.

'Nor do I,' Jinx said.

'But why would they want a little girl?' I asked. 'What possible use could she be to them?' Jinx and Jamie exchanged sidelong looks, as did Shenanigans and Kerfuffle while Vaybian suddenly found his footwear very interesting. I looked from one to the other. 'You know?' I said.

'We suspect,' Jamie answered me. 'The Sicarii are assassins who believe the souls of the dead make them strong, so one theory could be they think the souls of humans are special in some way,' Jamie said, 'and the soul of a human child doubly so.'

'But you don't believe that.'

He gave Jinx another sideways glance. 'No, I don't,' he admitted.

'So, what *do* you think?' I said, looking at Jinx.

'What do Kayla, Philip and his daughter all have in common?'

'I . . .' Then the penny dropped. 'Me,' I said with a sinking feeling.

It was well after dawn by the time we got back to the palace. I should have made straight for the great hall as we had planned, but I didn't have the stomach for it. My head was aching along with my heart and trying to think straight was becoming impossible.

'Would you like me to run you a bath, Mistress?' Shenanigans asked as he closed the door to our chamber behind us.

'Thank you, yes please,' I said and he and Kerfuffle trotted off, giving Vaybian a pointed look, which he ignored to slouch on the sofa instead. I assumed they were trying to give me some time alone with Jamie and Jinx.

I slumped down on the edge of the bed and Jamie dropped down beside me while Jinx pulled up a chair to sit opposite.

Jinx rested his elbows on his knees, intertwined his fingers, rested his chin on his knuckles and finally spoke. 'Someone is playing games. Very dangerous games.'

I looked at him. 'What are you thinking, Jinx?'

He kept his eyes lowered. 'It's bad enough that someone conspires against the woman who bears my mark, but to involve children,' he took a deep breath, 'that's unforgiveable – I can't get little Odin out of my head.'

'They will pay,' Jamie said. 'We'll make them pay.'

'Aye,' Jinx said. 'We will.'

It wasn't long before Shenanigans and Kerfuffle had the bath running and breakfast cooked, but our first meal of the day was a rather morose affair; even Shenanigans had lost his appetite and ate barely a plateful. The gloomy silence was too much for me, so I hid myself away in the bathroom for a good long soak. However, I soon found that being alone made me even more depressed and out of sorts. Eventually I climbed out of the bath, wrapped myself in a huge towel and stalked back into the bedroom.

My men were where I had left them and I almost ignored them and headed straight to the dressing room, but as I put my hand on the doorknob I hesitated and turned back to look. There was a heavy silence around the room and I knew them well enough to recognise when they were all angry about something.

Not one of them looked my way, which was a dead giveaway, and I wasn't in the mood for pulling it out of them, so after a moment of hesitation I opened the door to the dressing room – more of a walk-in wardrobe really – and went inside, leaving it slightly ajar.

After a few seconds I heard Jamie ask, 'So, what exactly was the plan?' his voice trembled with anger.

'Kayla thought she could keep her safe, and if it hadn't been for the two of you marking her, no one would have been any the wiser,' Vaybian said.

'Oh, so that would have made it all right then?'

'I knew we couldn't trust him,' Kerfuffle said.

'To be fair, this has Kayla written all over it,' Jinx said, but he didn't sound any less angry than the rest of them.

'Only yesterday you swore to protect her – is your word so easily broken?' Jamie said.

'Have a care Guardian.'

'James, Vaybian needn't have told us. He could have kept this to himself,' Jinx said.

'He didn't tell us this out of concern for Lucky's welfare. She should have let Baltheza send him down into Amaliel's workplace. This is a betrayal.'

'I've betrayed no one.'

'I wonder if she'll see it that way. I certainly don't.'

'Nor I,' Kerfuffle added.

I couldn't make head or tail of what they were talking about, other than that Kayla was somehow involved and none of my guard were happy about it. I continued listening.

'So, Kayla knew right from the start what Lucky was?' Jinx said.

'I think so,' Vaybian said, his voice suddenly weary. 'If I had realised she was a Soulseer, I'd never have . . .' He hesitated. 'I would've tried to talk my lady out of it.'

'So, it was Kayla's plan to eventually bring Lucky to the Underlands all along?' Jinx asked.

'Yes, but under her protection. In the Overlands Kayla found she could shield Lucky from the attention of our kind, and I suppose – now I know what she is – to a certain extent from the spirit world. She hoped to be able to do the same here.'

'For what reason?' Jamie said. 'I can't understand why she'd want to bring Lucky to our world.'

'Knowledge,' Jinx said, and I didn't have to see his face to know his eyes were glittering with dark intent. 'Knowledge is power and despite all of Kayla's postulating, that's what this is all about.'

'No,' Vaybian said. 'Power wasn't important, at least not to Kayla. She wanted to return to our world. She wanted to be with me, but she was worried Lucky would come to the attention of those who would use her for her power. Although I'm guessing she also knew that if she left her sister alone in the Overlands she would be swamped by every lost soul around.'

I sank down to the floor. They do say eavesdroppers never hear kindly of themselves, but this – this was something else.

'I believe the Sicarii somehow learned of Lucky and what she is. I believe this is why Kayla was taken.'

'To draw Lucky out into the open?' Jamie asked.

'I think so, but they didn't know she was marked by two such powerful daemons, if they had, they wouldn't have been so obvious.'

'Unless of course they want to control all three of us?' Jinx said. I heard several sharp intakes of breath. 'Imagine if the Sicarii had power over the three most powerful of Daemonkind.'

The three most powerful *Daemon*? *But I'm not totally daemon* . . . I glanced towards the mirror at the end of the room; the mirror that had revealed to me that daemon blood runs through my veins. I got to my feet and padded to the mirror. Lucky de Salle stared back at me – her human face, a little angry, a little scared, but human.

I glared at my reflection – the kid in me stuck out her tongue – then turned my back on it and marched along the rails of clothes to try and find something suitable to wear. I couldn't confront my men wearing nothing but a towel.

Usually I'm a jeans and T-shirt kind of gal, but in this world women were into long dresses and very little in the way of underwear, and I guess when I thought about it, Kayla had always worn dresses, although usually of the very short kind.

Kayla; my Kayla, five foot five with a perfect figure, dark blonde curls and a dazzling smile. Not the real Kayla, of course, she was over six feet tall with opalescent skin and venom green and scarlet curls that harboured a dozen or more writhing vipers. She had lied to me about who she was – everything she'd ever said had been a lie – but she was still my best friend and she *had* protected me from so many things, and I loved her.

'There must be something in here I can wear,' I muttered to myself as I padded along the corridor of soft velvets and shimmering silks and moved on to a rack of leather jackets and coats. Then a short, soft tan jacket caught my eye. 'This is more like it.' I pulled it out from amongst the others, wondering why it felt so heavy – and then I saw the reason. Underneath the jacket was a pair of leather fitted trousers. Kayla would have known I wouldn't want to wear dresses all the time. *Kayla*, I thought and let out a shuddery sigh.

I managed to find some under-things, which were more for entertaining than practical wear I was quite sure, but it was better than nothing. I slipped on the trousers and a linen shirt and finished it off with the jacket and a pair of boots. Fully dressed I ran my fingers through my hair and got ready to face my guards, hoping they hadn't murdered Vaybian during the five minutes I'd been changing.

I padded back to the door and listened through the crack I'd left open. It had gone very quiet. I moved a little closer, ear to the door – and it jerked open. I straightened up and inwardly cursed my reddening cheeks as I came eye to eye with Jinx.

'Ah,' he said. 'There was I hoping to catch you in the altogether, and instead I catch you fully dressed and snooping.'

'I was not snooping,' I hissed. 'I just wondered why you were all so quiet.'

'We need to talk,' he told me.

'Sounds serious.'

'Possibly.' He took hold of my hand and raised it to his lips then kissed my knuckles. 'You look very nice,' he murmured, 'but I preferred the towel.'

'Jinx,' Jamie called, his irritation obvious.

My maroon daemon winked at me then led me into the room still holding my hand and indicated the seat next to Jamie. Jinx dropped down onto the chair to my other side.

'You're all looking very grim,' I said as I made myself comfortable.

'We need to talk,' Jamie said, echoing Jinx.

'So I hear.'

'Vaybian has told us something of which we weren't aware.'

'Kayla knew I was a Soulseer,' I said. It was gratifying to see the surprise on all their faces.

'How— You didn't know you were a Soulseer, so how did you know she knew?' Jamie asked, flustered, which really wasn't like him.

'She's been with me for almost the whole of my life and knows me better than anyone. And if I can see ghosts in the human world, then why not here?' I bluffed, then turned to Vaybian. 'Why tell them this now?'

'I swore to serve you,' he said, casting an angry look in Jamie's direction, 'and as everything seems to point to you being the one the Sicarii want, I thought it could be important.'

Kerfuffle made a *harrumph*ing sound, but otherwise kept his thoughts to himself, as did the others. I stared at Vaybian for a very long time, but to his credit he didn't lower his eyes away from mine.

'All right,' I said at last, 'I'm a Soulseer, I get that.'

'*The* Soulseer,' Jamie said. 'According to legend there's only one, just as Jinx is "the" Deathbringer.'

'And James is "the" Guardian,' Jinx added.

'I thought there were other Guardians?' I said.

Jinx grinned at me. 'That was the lad being modest. There are lesser Guardians, who help monitor the interaction between the Under- and Overlands, but he is "the" Guardian.'

Jamie scowled at him, but all it did was make Jinx laugh and I must admit the mood around the table lightened a bit and even I began to feel a tad happier.

'So, I'm "the" Soulseer, which makes me dangerous in the minds of some, including the Sicarii, and they're hoping to draw me out into the open with Kayla, Philip and Angela. But it's not like they've made a ransom demand: give yourself up or they die. What are they expecting me to do?'

'They're probably hoping you'll risk yourself for them. You haven't made a move yet to rescue Kayla – maybe you would for a child you've rescued once before and have been keeping a watchful eye upon ever since,' Vaybian said.

'How would they even know about Angela?'

'There are a lot of things they know that could only come from someone who is close to you,' Jamie said, 'and I know each and every one of us is solid.'

'Too right,' Kerfuffle said. 'Though I'm still not so convinced about him.' He gestured with his head towards Vaybian. 'This could all be a plan to help him get back his *mistress*.'

'Don't think that because you're only knee high to a water sprite it won't stop me giving you the thrashing of your life, little man.'

'You and whose army?' Kerfuffle said jumping to his feet.

'Kerfuffle, sit down,' I said. 'And you' – I leaned over the table and poked Vaybian in the chest – 'if you can't say something nice or useful don't say anything at all.'

'He insulted me,' Vaybian mumbled, the teenage, sullen scowl back on his face.

'Suck it up.' I don't think any of them understood me, but Jinx chuckled merrily to himself. He never seemed happier than when there was a bit of confrontation going on.

'I hate to break up this happy little gathering,' Jinx said still smiling, 'but we've somewhere to be very shortly and I wouldn't want to keep the Lord of the Underlands waiting.'

'I suggest you stay here,' Jamie said to Vaybian. 'If he's had bad news about Kayla he could want to take it out on someone, and I suspect that someone would be you.'

'I won't argue with you on that,' Vaybian said. 'He doesn't like me one little bit.'

'I don't think he likes anyone overmuch,' I said, 'least of all me.'

'Oh, I don't know,' Jinx said. 'I think he quite likes that you remind him of your mother, despite all he says.'

'Hmm, and look what happened to her,' I said. I didn't actually know much other than that she'd died in mysterious circumstances. Perhaps the others knew.

'Do you think Baltheza really had her killed? Only, that's what he's hinted on a couple of occasions.'

'She disappeared after returning from a long absence,' Jinx

said, 'possibly followed by a short stay in the Chambers of Rectification.'

'He had her tortured?' I asked, aghast at the thought. 'He had his own lover tortured?'

'Possibly,' Jamie said.

'Probably,' Jinx corrected.

'Almost definitely if the rumours are true,' Vaybian said.

The thought made me infinitely sad, but I reminded myself that this was still all hearsay, perhaps later I could find out what actually happened to her.

'Come on,' Jinx said, bouncing up onto his feet, 'we don't want to be late.'

I got up, but it was with a feeling of impending doom. I really didn't want to see Baltheza right now and I suspected if he did have any news for us none of it would be good.

'Chin up,' Jinx said, his lips close to my ear. 'Once we've seen him we can leave and go in search of Kayla.'

'But where do we start?'

'Hopefully that's something Baltheza may be able to tell us. There's not much that goes on in this world he doesn't know about.'

The same two guards from the previous day were standing to attention on either side of the door to Baltheza's chamber. Upon seeing us one knocked three times, opened the door and gestured for us to go inside.

Baltheza was not alone. As we walked in a figure swathed in black who I knew only too well glided towards us. His face was, as usual, hidden within the shadows of his hooded robe, his only visible features were his eyes, which glowed with infernal fire: Amaliel Cheriour. For a second fear stopped me dead before we moved to one side to let him pass.

'Brother,' Jinx murmured.

'Deathbringer,' Amaliel said and then acknowledged Jamie, 'Guardian.'

I could feel the court enforcer's eyes on me, but he didn't say a word, instead he gave a small bow before drifting past us and out into the hall.

Baltheza watched Amaliel leave in silence and it wasn't until the door had closed behind him that his attention turned to me. 'Lucinda, gentlemen.' He beckoned me forward and stood to kiss me on both cheeks. It was something I would never get used to no matter how hard I tried. Each time his lips touched me I had to force back a flinch.

'Sit,' he said, gesturing towards the other end of the couch as he settled down. 'A drink?'

'No, thank you.'

He waggled his fingers at the same white-haired girl at his feet, then leaned back in the seat as she got up to get it for him, then handed it over. He crossed his leather-clad legs and fixed his eyes on me. 'I hear you had a disturbed night,' he said.

I shouldn't have been surprised that he'd heard about Angela, but it still took me aback. 'Yes, I'm afraid so.'

'The Sicarii?'

'We think so.'

He tapped a pointed fingernail against the rim of his goblet. 'I wonder why they'd want the human child?'

'We don't know.'

'Most odd,' he said, his eyes on mine. I was finding it hard not to fidget under his intense scrutiny. It was like he was waiting for me to do or say something, but I didn't know what. 'I hear the innkeeper's son was hurt.' I nodded, my mouth too dry to speak. I wished I had accepted the offer of a drink. 'Brave boy to try and fight off two attackers.'

'Very.'

He sipped from the goblet, still watching me while the girl at his feet once more rested her head against his knee and smiled up at me – that same knowing smile as before. If the pair of them wanted to make me feel uncomfortable they had succeeded.

He took another sip of his drink. 'And now to business. The Sicarii temple at Dark Mountain remains empty apart from the rotting corpses of two of their number. Strange they should execute two of their own.' He tapped his bottom lip with his fore-finger, a gesture very reminiscent of one of Kayla's. 'Though I suppose nobody likes failure.'

'Have you any news of Kayla?' Jamie asked, probably hoping to move things on a bit.

Baltheza's eyes remained fixed on me and he almost had to force himself to look up at Jamie. 'I have spoken at length with Daltas and he is unaware of her current whereabouts.'

'Daltas is here?' Jamie asked.

Baltheza's answering smile was chilling. I glanced at Jamie and Jinx, and both had non-expressions plastered on their faces. It was something I was going to have to practise.

'He is presently residing in quarters next to his favourite servant Henri le Dent.'

I just about managed to stifle a gasp, not that I cared overmuch about Lord Daltas; he and Henri deserved each other, but it was fast becoming clear that Baltheza was teetering on the brink of madness and had possibly lurched right over it.

'And he doesn't know where Kayla is?'

'He'd have told me if he did.'

Both Jamie and Jinx could have been carved in stone. I felt like the air had been sucked out of the room and I was glad I was sit-ting, as I'm sure my legs would have been shaking.

He reached out and stroked his slave's snowy white locks like she was a dog – no, a cat: her smile was definitely feline. 'No one is above a trip to the chambers below this palace; no one.'

Jinx's lips formed a tight line. I was unsure whether Baltheza was threatening just me or all three of us, but even if no one else found it amusing, his slave did, as she had to turn her head against his leg to hide her laughter.

'So, from all of this we must reach one conclusion.' Baltheza placed his goblet upon the table by his right hand. 'Kayla has certainly been abducted by the Sicarii. However, I have been unable to find out where she has been taken, and I've no idea why they would wish to incur my wrath.' He ran the nail of his forefinger down the slave's shoulder leaving a trail of green. She snuggled against his leg even more. 'Have you been down to the Chambers where Amaliel plies his trade?' he asked.

'No,' I just about managed to croak.

'It's worth a visit. He has a remarkable gift when it comes to the infliction of pain. He can take a creature apart until all that remains is a beating heart and yet it still lives. He can make a daemon scream until his lungs bleed without causing a single bit of permanent damage.' He dipped his finger in the beads of blood oozing from the scratch on his slave's shoulder and raised it to his lips. His forked tongue flicked out to lick it from his finger.

I had a flashback to Henri licking my face in the boarding school. I was beginning to feel quite ill. And what on earth was Baltheza getting at? His thoughts were erratic and jumping all over the place. I couldn't follow their thread.

'Well then,' he said, 'I suggest the three of you go and start looking for my daughter – and you can take her fancy, the green captain, along with you. I haven't yet forgotten his part in this whole sorry affair and nor am I likely to.'

I started to rise and hoped my legs wouldn't give way beneath me; I was eager to be out of the room and away from Baltheza's growing insanity.

'Oh, and Lucky,' he said just as I reached the door, 'it is not only Vaybian who will be enjoying a spell in the depths of the palace dungeons if Kayla is not returned to me safe and sound. So, if a choice has to be made forget the human child.'

I span around to face him. 'She's just a little girl.'

'A human and of no consequence to me.'

I was about to say something I probably shouldn't, and certainly not to a lunatic, but Jamie grabbed hold of my arm, bowed in Baltheza's direction and dragged me through the door Jinx was holding open. He too gave a bow and pulled the door closed.

'Come on,' Jamie said, marching me along the corridor and out of earshot of the two guards.

I tried to shrug my arm out of his grasp, but he was having none of it.

'Ouch,' I said. He ignored me and I heard Jinx chuckle from behind us.

As soon as we entered our room and the door was shut Jamie swung me around to face him. 'Are you completely mad?'

'She definitely is,' Jinx said with a smile.

Jamie turned his displeasure upon Jinx. 'This is serious.'

'Life is serious, and that is why we have to make light of it when we can; to do otherwise is to live a half-life full of gloom and pessimism – and what's the point in that?'

Jamie opened his mouth to reply then shut it again. 'We were that close to having to fight our way out of there . . .' He turned to me. 'You do realise he's becoming completely unhinged?' I was about to say that I wasn't stupid when Kerfuffle interrupted us.

'Shush,' he said, then both he and Shenanigans glanced around the room as though there may be someone listening in on us.

'I must admit, he has gone a little too far. He can't be thinking rationally,' Jinx said in a quiet voice.

'What's happened?' Shenanigans asked.

'Daltas is residing in the Chambers of Rectification with our old pal Henri,' Jinx said.

Shenanigans and Kerfuffle exchanged a glance and the little daemon moved closer to us to speak in a low voice. 'If this is true—'

'We heard it from the horse's mouth,' Jinx told him.

'Oh dear, oh dear, oh dear,' Kerfuffle wagged his head from side to side, his marshmallow cheeks bouncing and swinging so hard I had to stifle a giggle that was more than a little hysterical. 'If word gets out, there's no telling what the other lords will do.'

'No one will feel safe,' Shenanigans agreed.

'What do you think tipped him over the edge?' Jinx asked Jamie.

Jamie blew through pursed lips. 'He was always bordering on bonkers, and arresting Henri was a surprise; I always thought he was fireproof. But Daltas?' He sunk down onto the edge of the sofa. 'His arrest is downright alarming.'

'One thing we can be sure of,' Jinx said, 'neither Daltas nor Henri have anything to do with Kayla's abduction. If they had they would have told Amaliel.'

All my guards nodded, their expressions very grim indeed.

'Surely to admit to it would make things even worse for them?' I said.

Six pairs of eyes turned to look at me and Pyrites made a mewing sound and wrapped himself around my ankles. 'Lucky, what Baltheza told you about Amaliel's methods was the truth. Amaliel has made torture an art form.'

'So, you really don't believe Daltas and Henri can have had anything to do with Kayla's abduction?'

'They would have admitted it,' Jamie said. 'No question.'

I blew out a breath. We were basically back to square one. 'Well,' I said, 'for all his spies and contacts he couldn't tell us where the Sicarii are now. So, where do you suggest we start looking?'

'The Drakon's Rest is usually a good place for rumours, and if you were indeed followed there by a Sicarii spy, then it might be the place to find him again,' Shenanigans said.

'Will they be open for business?' I asked.

'Of course,' Kerfuffle said, 'Barron loves his work and it'll keep his mind off worrying about Odin and Angela.'

'He needn't worry about Odin,' Jinx said.

'You're sure?' I asked.

'A perk of the job, I know when someone who is sick or injured has the shades of death waiting at their shoulder and sometimes, particularly when it's a child, I can shoo them away. Odin wasn't so close to death I couldn't change his fortune.'

'But he would've died?'

'His life was in the balance, it wasn't a foregone conclusion. If it had been I wouldn't have been able to help him. Don't go thinking I can work miracles.'

'No miracles required. A little push in the right direction is enough,' I said with a grateful smile.

'I'm not so sure,' Kerfuffle said, 'we could do with a miracle if we're to find the Lady Kayla.'

'Then let's hope we find one at the Drakon's Rest,' Jamie said.

Eight

The inn was busier than ever, though the clientele were a little more subdued than usual, but I guess word had got out about the events of the morning. Once again, as soon as we walked through the door the chattering stuttered into silence and a passageway formed in the crowd leading to the corner table we normally used.

'Nice one, Deathbringer,' a voice said as we passed.

'Aye, good on yer,' another voice added. Then another, and another as we passed. They didn't go quite as far as patting him on the back, but it was clear word had got around about what Jinx had done for Oddy.

'This hasn't done your street cred a terrible amount of good,' Jamie murmured as he pulled out a chair and gestured for me to sit.

Jinx looked at him in puzzlement. 'Street cred?'

'It means reputation,' I explained.

'What can I say,' Jinx replied, 'I am one seriously misunderstood individual.'

We had hardly dropped into our seats when Leila appeared by the table.

'How's Oddy?' Shenanigans asked, getting back onto his feet.

She held a hand level and tilted it from side to side. 'In himself much better, but he's distraught about Angela.' She turned to Jinx and gave him a shy smile. 'Me and the family, we'd like to say thank you, you know, for Oddy.'

'Leila my darlin', you know I would do anything for you,' Jinx said and winked.

Leila's cheeks glowed lilac as she laid her hand on Shenanigans' arm. 'You should have thought of that before.'

Jinx gave a dramatic sigh, got to his feet and gave her a low bow. 'My loss is my fine friend's gain.'

'Hmm,' she said, clearly not impressed. 'What can I get you all?'

Shenanigans dealt with our order while Jamie, Jinx and Kerfuffle surreptitiously looked around the crowded room. Vaybian got to his feet as he too scanned the faces of the occupants. Kerfuffle, not to be outdone, jumped up onto his chair to get a better view, his head turning this way and that. He must have glimpsed someone he knew as, with a satisfied, 'He'll do,' he hopped down from his perch and waddled off, pushing his way through the wall of bodies. Shenanigans saw him go, and after a few words to Leila, who sashayed off to the kitchen, followed after the little daemon.

'Where are they going?' I asked.

'Kerfuffle must have seen someone he thought could give him reliable information,' Jinx said.

Vaybian slumped down onto his chair. 'Let's hope they can help us,' he said, his voice weary.

'We will find her,' Jinx said.

'It's taking too long and who knows what she's going through.'

'Knowing Kayla, she's probably making their lives as difficult as possible,' Jinx said. 'Anyway, I'm sort of thinking it may not be all that hard to find them.'

'What makes you say that?' Vaybian asked as Leila returned with a tray of tankards and several jugs of ale together with a goblet of wine for me.

Jinx filled one of the tankards and pushed it across the table to the other daemon before filling one for himself, while Leila served the drinks for the rest of us. 'I'll be back with the food shortly,' she told us.

Jinx took a slurp of his ale and when Leila was out of earshot leaned back in his chair and returned his attention to Vaybian. 'If the whole idea is to lure Lucky into a trap, it won't work very well if we are unable to find them.'

'If Baltheza's spies couldn't, I doubt anyone else can.'

'The Sicarii might know how to evade Baltheza's spies,' Jinx said. 'After all, they do have spies of their own.'

I sipped on my goblet of wine as I glanced across the room,

hoping to catch sight of my other two guards. They were nowhere to be seen.

'If they're obtaining information they've probably gone out back,' Jamie said, seeing me scanning the bar.

'You think?'

He took another swig of his drink. 'If you're asking questions about the Sicarii you don't do it in a crowded bar.'

'And if you did you certainly wouldn't expect any answers,' Jinx said, 'not unless your informant has a death wish.'

'Why is it they've been allowed to get away with this for so long?' I asked.

'Think on your world. How many times have there been cults, regimes or even nations that have killed and tortured in some religious fervour? Besides which, Baltheza, who is really the only one with enough power to do anything, has his own motivations. There may be a reason he hasn't yet confronted them,' Jinx said, and if I had to describe his expression I would say it was pained. He may be the bringer of death and destruction, but it was pretty damn obvious violence and cruelty filled him with sadness and anger.

There wasn't much more I could say to that. I was beginning to realise that humans and daemonkind weren't much different; some were kind, some were cruel and some were downright nasty.

We all sat there staring into our ale, or in my case wine, in silence. We were at a loss and unless Kerfuffle and Shenanigans came up with something, we still had a lot to do before we had any chance of finding the Sicarii and hopefully Kayla.

The food arrived, but Kerfuffle and Shenanigans didn't. 'Shouldn't we try to find them?' I asked.

'All the more for us,' Jinx said, piling food onto his plate. 'With the big guy out of the way we'll get double portions – at least.'

I picked at my food, not having any appetite after my conversation with Baltheza, much less coming face to face with Amaliel Cheriour. I wondered what he had been doing in Baltheza's chambers – reporting back after questioning Henri or Daltas perhaps? I put down my knife and fork; I didn't like either Henri or Daltas, but the thought of what they may be enduring pushed all desire to eat right out of my mind.

Pyrites laid his head on my lap and gazed up at me with his beautiful emerald-amethyst-sapphire kaleidoscope eyes and fluttered his eyelids, which made me smile. His love was unconditional and although he'd been mine for only a short time I couldn't imagine what it would be like without him. He knew when I was happy and when I was sad, and somehow he knew instinctively what to do to make me feel, if not better, at least loved.

'Guardian,' Vaybian said, leaning across the table and keeping his voice low. 'The one in the dark, hooded cloak standing at the counter; I'm sure it was he who was spying on us yesterday.'

Jamie looked across to the bar and Jinx turned in his seat, raising his hand as though calling to Leila for service. The daemon was leaning on the counter, with one hand resting next to a tankard of ale. His body was angled so he was half turned away from us, but it would only take a slight movement of the head for him to keep an eye on what we were doing.

'I think I need a piss,' Jinx said, getting to his feet as Leila appeared by the table.

'You wanted something?'

Jinx leaned in close to her. 'The gent at the bar in the hooded cloak – do you know him?'

Leila immediately got the gist of what was going on. She laughed as though Jinx had said something incredibly funny. 'You are a one,' she said then lowered her voice, 'he's been in a few times over the past couple of days. Has one ale, makes it last and usually doesn't finish it. Keeps his head down so I've never had a look at his face.'

'Would you keep an eye out for him – and anyone he meets with – in future?'

She laughed again. 'I'll be back with your ale,' she said as she turned and walked away. Jinx glanced Jamie's way and made for the backdoor.

Jamie got to his feet. 'Pyrites,' he said, and my drakon popped out from under the table, 'keep an eye out for trouble.' Pyrites puffed steam and sat to attention. Satisfied my drakon was on the case, Jamie followed Jinx outside.

Vaybian made a pretence of eating his meal, but his eyes were constantly shifting towards the cloaked figure. 'Who do you think he is?' I asked.

Vaybian glanced my way and for once he wasn't scowling. 'If I had to guess I'd say he was one of Baltheza's spies, but he could be Sicarii.'

I pushed my plate away. I was in danger of getting serious heartburn if I tried to eat anything. Pyrites put a claw on my knee and puffed a bit of steam. I took the hint.

'It's all right boy. I hadn't forgotten you,' and, after taking a quick glance around to make sure no one was watching, took a few pieces of meat off my plate and dropped it into his open jaws. 'Was that good?' I asked. He licked his lips and I passed him another titbit.

One of the other serving girls appeared with two more flagons of ale and plonked them on the table, then leaned in close to Vaybian and whispered something in his ear. His eyes narrowed and he turned to me as she walked away.

'What's going on?'

'Apparently we're to drink up and then leave by the back door.'

'Who says?'

'Leila.'

I glanced across to the bar where she was filling some tankards and tried to catch her eye, but two rowdy customers were keeping her occupied with their order and continuous banter. I noticed she had to bat away their wandering hands a couple of times. It was probably just as well Shenanigans wasn't about.

'Right,' I said, knocking back the last of my wine.

Vaybian threw some coins onto the table and stood. As soon as I was on my feet he guided me towards the back door, Pyrites trotting along behind us – though I did notice my drakon paused long enough to take a surreptitious swipe of my plate with his long tongue.

We passed right by the cloaked figure at the bar and it took all my self-control not to sneak a look at him, then once he was behind us I was sure I could feel his eyes on my back. Pyrites made a low rumbling sound in the back of his throat. He didn't like the daemon either.

As soon as we were outside Vaybian drew his sword and grabbed my right hand. 'Stay close to me,' he said, leading me across the courtyard towards the gate.

Behind us I heard the backdoor slam shut and we both swung around; Vaybian with his sword at the ready, but it was only Barron putting out an empty barrel. We hurried on across the yard, dodging crates of empty bottles and stacks of barrels until we reached the gate where Vaybian released my hand to reach for the catch. The door behind us slammed again and I glanced back over my shoulder.

'Vaybian,' I hissed grabbing his arm.

'What?' he hissed back. Then he saw: standing outside the back entrance to the inn was the figure in brown. Vaybian stepped past me and pushed me behind him while Pyrites began to grow. 'Where are the others?' Vaybian muttered under his breath. I was wondering that too.

The brown-clad daemon advanced towards us. 'Fight or flee?' I asked.

'Fight,' he said, striding towards the centre of the yard.

I followed for a couple of steps and then there was a *thwang*-ing sound that made the air vibrate followed by another and another. Pyrites let out a high-pitched wail and collapsed onto his forelegs.

'Pyrites!' My drakon made a mewing sound as three more arrows whistled past my head, hitting him in the back and sides. He swung his head around, snapping at the shafts and breaking several, but the heads remained embedded in his scales.

I looked around, searching for where the arrows were coming

from. Three archers in brown stood on the roof of the inn. I dropped to my knees beside Pyrites, and took his head in my lap. He made a small mewing sound in the back of his throat that had me fighting back tears; they'd hurt him, they'd really hurt him. I wanted to hug him to me and tell him everything would be all right, but I wasn't sure it would be and as if to prove it, the back gate burst open and three daemons dressed in grey robes glided in, followed by five or six of their minions.

'Bastards!' I yelled at them and they laughed, damn them, they laughed.

They moved towards me and two of them grabbed hold of my arms and dragged me to my feet. I struggled and kicked as I tried to get back to Pyrites, my rage driving me beyond reason. Even as I fought them I couldn't tear my eyes away from him and the liquid gold bleeding down his scales to puddle on the ground.

When I couldn't bear the sight any more I looked for Vaybian. He had also been overpowered and was kneeling with his hands on his head.

I couldn't understand what had happened: my men were always vigilant. They could only be yards away – unless they were . . . I couldn't even think it. Could the Guardian and the Deathbringer die? The bringer of eternal night surely wouldn't succumb to an arrow or blade? And Jamie; my beautiful angel, he couldn't be dead, he just couldn't. What if I had lost them all: Shenanigans, Kerfuffle, Pyrites? Only sheer willpower stopped the tears of pain and desperation from flowing. They wouldn't want me to weep for them, not now. They would want me to survive. *Don't get mad, get even*, and I would.

The spy walked across the yard towards us, his hood still pulled forward hiding his features. I wanted to see, damn him. I wanted to see him so I would know who I was going to kill, because kill him I would, no doubt at all.

He stood in front of Vaybian looking down for a few moments, but then passed him by to stand over Pyrites. My drakon had stopped growing at the size of a baby elephant. Whether or not being shot had something to do with it I had no idea, but he didn't look good. His flank shuddered with every breath and his eyes were closed. I was very much afraid I might be losing him. I couldn't understand it: Jamie had told me drakons were virtually indestructible and that their only vulnerability was the soft scales beneath their chin.

'I am so looking forward to this,' the spy, assassin – murdering scumbag – said as he reached up with dark red scarred hands to pull back his hood. 'How lovely to see you again, Lucky de Salle,' Henri le Dent said.

I just about managed to bite back a gasp, though it was hard. I knew Henri had been burned by Pyrites, but I hadn't realised how bad it had been. The right side of his face was a shiny, dark pink expanse of scar tissue matching his right hand. His right shoulder looked odd beneath his robe and I guessed it hadn't fared too well either beneath Pyrites' fiery breath.

He stood above Pyrites looking down with a distorted smile upon his misshapen lips; the right side frozen in a rigour grimace while the left curled into a manic joker grin. 'I am going to enjoy this so very much, just as I am going to enjoy watching you being slowly taken apart piece by piece,' he said, and with that he pulled a sword out from within his robes.

He looked up at me and licked his ruined lips. 'Say goodbye to your drakon Lucky,' he said, and gave Pyrites' head a nudge with his boot, exposing his vulnerable throat.

'You touch him you bastard and I'll—'

'You'll what?'

'I'll kill you.'

He gave me another distorted, revolting grin. 'You tried; you failed. It's my turn now, and I will not fail.' He gripped the sword between both hands and lifted it up above Pyrites' neck.

'No!' I shouted. One of the Sicarii holding me laughed, letting go of my right arm. I glanced sideways and to the daemon on my left, reached back, pulled his sword from its sheath and threw myself away from him, wrenching my other arm from his grasp. I ran – no – bounded forwards, screaming my lungs out: a war cry, a death cry – a daemon cry – and I felt myself change. Long mahogany and aubergine-coloured hair flew around my face and the hand holding the sword glowed a shimmering pink.

Henri, on hearing and seeing the daemonic me, recoiled back in surprise and must have skidded in Pyrites' blood as he slipped and fell backwards, his left hand reaching behind him to break his fall, his sword arm reaching up to defend his exposed head.

I am not a swordswoman, I have no idea how to handle something so large, heavy and ungainly, but I was incandescent with rage, sorrow, horror. I was not going to let him slaughter my faithful drakon. I went in at him slashing wildly, there was no finesse about it at all. I hit flesh and the sword slipped through it as though cutting tender steak, didn't even waiver at the bone and went right through to the other side. Henri shrieked, clutching his severed stump, as his right hand, still clutching the sword, flew across the yard spraying green across the paving slabs in a spattered arc.

I wasn't finished. I leaped over Pyrites, sword raised, and would have kept on slashing, but the Sicarii, having gathered their senses, clutched at me, pulling me off him with warnings of terrible consequences if I didn't stop fighting them. Fat chance, I knew they were going to do terrible things to me whatever, so I fought them: biting, scratching, kneeing, kicking and gouging.

Henri's screaming went from ear-piercing to ear-bleeding, and even if I could have put him out of his misery I wouldn't have; I'd rather put up with his screams. They were worth it.

Then I looked at Pyrites and wanted to kill Henri over and over again and I would have if I could have fought free of the daemons clinging onto me, but they were too strong. It didn't stop me from elbowing one in the guts and stamping on another's instep before they finally restrained me.

'Well, well, well,' the first Sicarii hissed from behind me, 'aren't you full of surprises.'

'What do you want us to do with this one?' one of the minions asked, his sword pointed at Vaybian's chest.

'It would be a waste to kill him here,' one of the three said, his voice a sibilant hiss.

'I agree,' another said, his voice several tones higher but just as eerie.

'Tie him up and bring him,' the third said.

'What about him?' the minion asked gesturing with his head at Henri, who had stopped screaming and was trying to prise the fingers of his severed hand from the hilt of his sword. Having only his left hand to work with, he had the top end of the blade wedged between his knees as he struggled to free his right.

The third Sicarii gave a sigh that sounded like he had lungs full of phlegm. 'Bring him and his hand along. The healer may be able to do something with it.'

Two of the minions wrestled Vaybian to his feet, but when they tried to tie his hands he fought against them, which earned him a vicious blow to the head with a club that knocked him back down onto one knee. Then another hit him and another as I screamed for them to stop, but they kept on until he was sprawled out on the floor unconscious.

The three Sicarii turned as one towards the gate and I was frog-marched behind them, held in the vicelike grips of two of the minions. I tried to struggle, but it was useless – they weren't going to let me get loose again.

As they hauled me away I strained to look back at my fallen drakon. He puffed out a small cloud of steam, like a vapour trail of raindrops or maybe tears, and his tail gave a limp flap against the flagstones. His flank shuddered and then – he was still.

My chest felt like it was being crushed. 'No,' I murmured, 'no.' I had lost Pyrites, my faithful Jewelled Drakon – and with him a huge piece of my heart.

Nine

Once outside of the yard I was whisked along the side street at almost running speed. I had tried to pull back, but they just lifted me up so my toes weren't even trailing the road beneath them.

At the corner a cart was waiting. They threw back the rough, woven cover and jumped on the back to manhandle Vaybian in and lay him down amongst assorted sacks and barrels. Then it was my turn. I struggled as they tried to bind my wrists, earning myself a hard slap. A minion raised his stout club, but one of the grey-robed Sicarii stopped him and leaned close to whisper in the acolyte's ear. I saw a flash of white teeth from within the shadows of the brown cowl and suddenly I was plunged into darkness as a coarse sack, smelling of rotten vegetables, was thrown over my head and hauled down to my waist. Ropes were then wrapped around me and I knew I had little chance of escaping; even breathing was going to be difficult.

I felt myself being lifted and then I was dropped down with a thud that rattled my teeth and sent a lightning bolt of pain through my spine. I knew I had just reverted to my human self. I didn't feel so strong; I didn't feel so powerful.

'I advise you to keep very quiet,' a voice hissed. 'Your guard's surplus to requirements and if you don't behave he may not make the journey in one piece.'

Then it got a whole lot darker and the sound from outside the cart became even more muffled and I assumed the cover had been replaced, hiding us from view.

The cart rumbled along the cobbled streets, bouncing my already bruised body up and down on the unforgiving floor of the cart. I think I may have cried a bit. Not for myself, but for Pyrites, for Jamie and Jinx, for Shenanigans and Kerfuffle. They were usually by my side at the first whiff of danger, so if they hadn't turned up I knew one of two things: they were incapacitated – or they were dead. But crying would help no one, and if I wanted revenge I was going to have to make sure I stayed alive long enough to get it. And by God I wanted to see Henri go down.

I rolled to one side and my forehead hit solid wood – a barrel or crate. I rolled the other way and again there was a solid mass. I raised my knees as best I could and pushed against it. Something gave. I moved closer. It was hard to tell wrapped up inside a sack, but it felt like I was pressed up against Vaybian's muscular back.

I pushed forward with my foot and ran it up and down against what I guessed was a calf, the soft leather of my boots allowing me to feel through them. My hands were tight against my hips, but with a bit of wriggling I managed to inch them to in front of my crotch and slowly pull the fabric of the sack up between my fingers until they were free, and yes, I could feel smooth skin beneath my fingertips.

'Vaybian,' I said in a quiet voice, and again a moment later: 'Vaybian.' Nothing. He was out cold.

I poked him hoping to wake him, but he was unresponsive as a sack of spuds. I tried again, but I didn't think bagpipes and a military brass band were going to wake Kayla's captain. I wasn't surprised; he'd taken a beating that would have killed a mere mortal.

I rolled onto my back and wriggled some more, trying to loosen the ropes wrapped around my shoulders, arms and waist. I sucked in breath and hunched my shoulders forward as much as they would go; the ropes didn't feel so tight. I shrugged my shoulders up and down, up and down. The rope slipped up until it was high on my right shoulder. I wriggled and jiggled and squashed myself up as small as I could be and the rope slipped up a bit further until it was balanced on the last bit of my arm before it rounded into shoulder. I pushed out hard, straining against the ropes and then sucked in as far as I could and gave my shoulders an almighty shrug and – there the first loop was gone. The rope had slipped over my shoulder, loosening the rest of the coils wrapped around my chest by a good few inches.

I wasn't out of the woods yet. I started to inch the sack up my body, taking the ropes with it, all the while bouncing around as the cart bucked and jumped over every stone, rut or clod of earth. My backside felt as though it had been pummelled with a tenderising hammer and every jolt had my vertebrae begging for mercy.

I lost all sense of time. All that mattered was each millimetre of sack that had rolled upward and each extra bit of space between me and the rope. My body was drenched with sweat, making the sack stick and chafe against my skin, and my hair was stuck to my face, getting in my eyes and mouth.

Every now and then I kicked Vaybian in the back of the legs hoping for some sign that he was still alive. He'd probably be black and blue, or whatever colour bruised green people go when knocked about, but I didn't care; if I got free and he was awake I could take him with me. If he wasn't, I'd have no alternative - I'd have to go it alone.

I was getting tired. There was no way I was going to give up out of choice, but I was sweating buckets and dehydration would get me if exhaustion didn't. Every muscle in my body was aching, my throat felt like I'd gargled with glass and I was finding it hard to swallow. I'd have killed for a glass of water.

'Vaybian,' I managed to croak one last time and I heard him groan. *Thank you God*, I thought, at least he was alive. 'Vaybian, can you hear me?' There was no answer. He was alive, though not alive enough to be receptive.

I rested for a couple of seconds, building myself up to one more massive effort to break free, then I was off again, tearing at the ropes with ragged nails and bleeding fingertips. Then the coils of rope slipped over my boobs, went slack and with a couple more shrugs slipped up to my neck and I dragged them up over my head.

I pulled the sack off and gulped in air. It was fetid but by no means as bad as what I'd been breathing for the past few . . . was it hours?

Now in the gloom I could see Vaybian lying beside me. I pulled on his shoulder and rolled him over onto his back, laying my fingers against the artery just below his chin, hoping daemons were the same as us. Apparently they were; a steady throb against my fingertips confirmed he was alive and healthy enough.

Even though I felt mean doing it, I slapped his cheeks a couple of times trying to wake him, but to no avail. There was no way I could carry him – I was going to have to leave him, we'd just have to find him and Kayla before the worst happened. I didn't allow myself to think that I may not find my other guards, or that they might not be alive when I did.

I rolled Vaybian back on his side and wedged a sack of something behind him. After surviving so far I didn't want him choking on his own vomit. Then I crawled to the back of the cart. I didn't dare lift the edge of the cover, but instead tried peering between the planks of wood making up the backboard of the cart. It was a good decision; two daemons were following on behind. Crap – what was I going to do now?

I pressed my cheek up against the back of the cart trying to make the most of my limited field of vision. It didn't help that the light was going.

There were definitely two riders, but that was as much as I could see. It didn't make much difference – two riders or twenty – I still didn't stand a chance of getting past them.

I scrabbled about a bit trying to get comfortable then pressed my eye back to the crack. All I could do was watch and wait and hope that an opportunity would arise for me to make a run for it – with or without Vaybian if he ever woke up.

With nothing better to do I did a bit of mental arithmetic in my head. There had been three grey-clad Sicarii and three archers, plus five or six others. The waiting cart had probably already had a driver aboard, so that meant there would be at least eight or nine Sicarii on horseback including the two who were giving me a problem. Then of course there was Henri, but I wouldn't have thought he was in a fit state to ride. Maybe he was sitting at the front of the cart?

None of this really mattered if I couldn't get past the two back riders and by the looks of them they weren't going anywhere. I peered out at them willing them to disappear off somewhere. Then, as if in answer to my prayers, they fell back a bit and moved slightly closer together. I pressed my face so hard against the wooden boards I'd probably have imprints of the grain etched into my cheek. They *were* slowing. Then they swung their beasts around to trot to the side of the road.

I risked pulling the cover back a bit and sticking my head out into the blessed fresh air. The feel of a cool breeze against my face was almost worth the chance of getting caught. I peered back down the road. The two daemons were dismounting. Then I got it; they had stopped to take a piss.

I got up on my knees and pulled the cover back a little to take a look around. We were on a gloomy road surrounded by tall trees, and I could just see two robed heads at the front of the cart. I got up into a crouch. Up ahead at the edge of the forest, I could see a black, glossy coach flanked by two riders outlined in grey light. Henri was probably in there . . . and that was what gave me the push I needed to risk the jump off the moving cart: the thought of getting away, and later, getting revenge.

I peeped back under the cover one more time, hoping beyond hope that Vaybian was waking up, but it wasn't to be. I knew I had to leave him, if I didn't there was no way I could get help, but this didn't make me feel any better; I could be sentencing him to death. I took a quick look back down the road. The two daemons were still watering the shrubbery, mainly hidden by their two steeds. I had only a matter of moments and couldn't wait any longer otherwise I might not get another chance.

'Sorry Vaybian,' I whispered. 'I will find you, I'll find you and Kayla.'

I sat on the edge of the cart, flipped my legs over the side and dropped down onto the ground below, hitting it with a bone shaking thump and jarring my ankles and knees. Then I was up and running off the road and into the lines of close-packed trees. I tried to keep the road in sight to my right. Having escaped, I didn't now want to become lost in a forest. It was bad enough I was all alone and had no idea how to get back to the palace.

After a few minutes I slowed to a jog rather than risk poleaxing myself by running into a tree. The gloomy light was fast fading and I suspected it was almost dusk. I shivered; I really didn't want to be wandering around in a forest in the dark. Sadly, I didn't have much choice – being on the road would mean the Sicarii would see me. I'd have to go through the trees and hope the Sicarii wouldn't notice I was missing before I'd found open ground.

Of course, jogging through the forest in the half-light, scared and lost, gave me time to think. First I worried about Vaybian and what would happen to him when they found me gone. I forced myself to think of something else, and immediately Pyrites' forlorn figure appeared in my mind and my spirits plummeted even further. Then I thought of Jamie and Jinx and I felt like curling up at the side of the road and dying.

'Don't you dare,' I told myself swiping away tears. 'Don't you bloody well dare. You will find Jamie! You will find Jinx! And you will avenge P—' I swallowed a couple of times, took a deep breath and pulled myself together, calling Henri le Dent a few choice names under my breath, which actually did make me feel a smidgeon better.

In amongst the trees, night came quickly and with no moons to light my way it was hard to see a yard or so ahead of my nose. I was about to make my way back to the road, where I could at least move a little more swiftly, when I saw a light up ahead and to the right: a glow amongst the trees. *A fire.* I slowed down; stealth being the sensible course of action. I was lost in a strange world and had no idea how to tell a friend from foe.

When I grew level with the fire I stopped to peer through the trees. Should I investigate, or keep on going?

'And what have we here?' a voice said from behind me. I swung around to find myself facing three shadowy figures. There was a flicker of light and then the glow of a lamp as one of the daemons lifted it up to get a good look at me.

The one holding the lamp was the most human in appearance. He was tall, with unkempt long dark hair and eyes that looked like beads of jet in the flickering lamplight. His nose was long and narrow; his lips thick, brown and moist. His skin was a weathered walnut in colour and texture. He grinned at me showing long canines.

His two friends could have been twins. They were shorter than him, and probably only an inch or two taller than me. Both had glowing red eyes, scaly grey skin and were bald except for a quiff of white hair on the top of each of their heads. They looked me up and down very slowly. I didn't like the expressions in their eyes one little bit.

'Well then, popsy, what are you doing in our forest?' Dark Eyes asked.

'I'm travelling back home,' I said.

'And where might that be?'

'The Drakon's Rest,' I said, thinking quickly. I doubted saying the palace would have been a particularly brilliant idea.

'The Drakon's Rest? The inn in the fortress of Lord Baltheza?' Dark Eyes said, glancing at his mates.

'The same,' I said. 'Now, if you'll excuse me.'

I turned to walk away and a hand shot out and grabbed my arm. I froze, and forcing myself to keep calm, turned back slowly. I stared down at the claw on my sleeve for a count of two then raised my eyes to meet those of the daemon touching me.

It was one of the twins, who obviously saw something in my eyes that he didn't like as his claw dropped away. Dark Eyes was made of sterner stuff.

'Pathetic,' he sneered, handing the other twin the lamp and grabbing hold of my arm. 'You're coming with us to sit by a nice warm fire, to have a nice strong drink and then to have a fine old time.'

'I don't think so,' I said, trying to shrug his claw away.

'Well, I do,' he said, licking his lips with a very pointed black tongue, and began to march me off the road and towards the campfire.

Panic began to bubble up inside me. If there were only three I was in trouble, if there were others at their camp I was well and truly stuffed.

'I don't know, Pablo,' the pathetic twin said, 'she looks like trouble to me.'

His twin gave a snort. 'Duffus, Pablo's right, you are pathetic.'

Duffus' lips curled down into a pout. 'Something about her isn't right. Look at her.'

Pablo stopped pulling on my arm and took the lamp from Duffus' twin, lifting it up to peer at me. 'Her clothes are pretty fine,' he admitted. 'Though she looks like she's been dragged through a corn field backwards.'

'Maybe she was thrown from her steed?' Duffus said.

His twin fingered his chin, contemplating me with a frown. 'Makes sense. Why else would she be out here all alone at this time of night?'

'Well, she's here, she's alone and we're in need of a bit of company. So, let's get back to camp,' Pablo said and began to pull on my arm again.

Company! I struggled against him. 'Let go of me,' I said.

'You going to make me?' Pablo said with a grin.

I punched him hard on the upper arm and stamped down with all my strength on his foot. He let go of me with a yelp and I was off and running as fast as my legs would take me, praying that none of them had wings.

Feet pounded behind me. The widening road was ahead of me, and as I broke out of the trees I could see the night sky. I was nearly out of the woods, but not out of trouble. In the human world I had gone running most nights, now I was glad of it. Even so, they were gaining on me; I could hear them getting closer. One of them was so confident he was whooping.

I reached the tree line and was out into the open countryside. Decision time: did I keep to the road or veer off? Then my head snapped back and I was yanked backwards by my hair. A pair of arms was wrapped around me and I was turned to face the way I'd come. In a moment, Duffus had caught up, with Pablo lumbering on behind.

'Got ya.'

'Let me go,' I said, struggling like a wild creature, all tiredness forgotten in the panic.

'After making us work up an appetite, you've got to be joking,' the cocky twin whispered in my ear.

Pablo had slowed down to a stroll now he knew I was well and truly caught. 'Well done, Dags.'

'You lay a finger on me and you'll be really sorry,' I spat at him.

'Really?' Pablo asked, and lifted his claw and extended a talon, 'Like this you mean?' He leaned towards me and tapped the end of my nose with the nail. 'Or like this?' He grabbed hold of my chin and pulled my face to his, planting a wet kiss on my lips and pressing his body against mine so I was sandwiched between him and his mate. I gritted my teeth together and squeezed my lips shut as I tried to twist my head away. He clasped the back of my head, holding me still, his tongue trying to push its way into my mouth.

Then he froze. His claw dropped from my head and he took a step away from me. Eyes wide and staring into mine. 'Let her go,' he said.

'What?'

'I said, let her go.' The arms dropped away from around me. Pablo's nostrils flared and his eyes narrowed. 'What are you? Who are you?'

'What?' Dags repeated.

'She's marked,' Pablo said.

'I told you – I told you she was trouble,' Duffus said.

'Shut the fuck up, you idiot.'

'Who do you belong to, popsy?' Pablo asked and reached out to touch my face again. He laid his palm against my cheek and I let him, hoping that if they knew who I was marked by, it might save me. This time he jerked away. He ran his tongue across his upper lip. His hand went to his belt and he pulled out a dagger.

'What are you doing?' Duffus asked.

'She's marked by someone powerful. She is someone powerful.'

'Then leave her be,' Duffus said, glancing from Pablo to me and back again, 'before any harm's done.'

'Too late. No higher daemon will allow this discourtesy against him to go unpunished.'

'You kill me and they will hunt you down.'

The twins exchanged worried looks. 'Come on Pablo, leave her be. We've committed no offence as of yet. Hurt her and she's right, they will hunt us down.'

'Not if we kill her and burn her body. Then there will be no trail to us.'

'So you say,' Duffus said.

'Just shut your flapping chops.'

'If we let you go will you promise to leave us be?' Duffus asked.

'I said shut it,' Pablo snapped at him. 'When will you learn that you can never trust a woman – whatever they say?'

'Sexist dick,' I muttered.

'What?' Pablo glared at me.

'If you let me go, those whose marks I bear won't come after you. For one thing they've better things to do,' I said.

'Those? You are marked by two daemons?' Dags said.

'I thought as much,' Pablo said.

'That's not possible,' Dags said.

'Seems it is,' Pablo said as he lifted the knife to my throat. 'Now you understand why we have to kill her?'

'No,' Duffus took a step away from me, palms raised. 'Then we'll have two daemons wanting our heads and the law says they can take them.'

'We can't just let her go.'

'Why not?' I asked.

'Well,' Dags said ignoring me, 'if we're going to kill her and risk the wrath of two powerful daemons we might as well have some fun first to my way of thinking.'

'Have you got shit for brains?' Duffus said.

'Better than piss for courage and balls so small you can't see them.'

'There's nothing wrong with my balls,' the daemon muttered.

'Then prove it,' Dags said with a nod in my direction. Duffus backed up further, shaking his head as he went. If I shouted 'boo' I was sure he'd bolt.

Pablo grabbed hold of my arm. 'You're coming back to camp with us. We'll have a nice drink and an even nicer time while we decide what to do with you.'

'Yeah, right,' I said. 'You expect me to let you take me back to your camp so you can have your fun and kill me? I don't think so.' Then I wrenched my arm up and bit into the soft bit between his thumb and foreclaw very, very hard.

He shrieked, let go of my arm and I turned, kneed Dags in the groin and pushed him away from me, then ran like hell, expecting a knife between the shoulder blades at any moment. I could hear someone coming after me, though I doubted it was Dags, he had crumpled into a moaning heap. I guessed it was Pablo: the dangerous one with the dagger.

A cloud passed across the moons and for a moment or two I could hardly see the road ahead. I tripped on something, staggered, thought I was going to regain my balance and then was thrown forward as someone barrelled into me.

Lying face down in the dirt I felt him drop down astride me. 'Bitch,' Pablo said, grabbing a fistful of my hair, pulling my head back and pressing his dagger to my throat.

I tried pushing down with the palms of my hands to lever myself up, but it was no good. I was well and truly trapped.

'Give us a hand,' I heard Pablo say, and to my relief the knife left my throat. The feeling was short-lived. Pablo shifted his weight to roll me over and Dags dropped down, his knees either side of my head as he grabbed my wrists and held them against his chest.

'We'll forgo the comfort of the fire and a nice drink to get you in the mood,' Pablo said ripping open my jacket, pulling my shirt out of my trousers and wrenching it apart, sending buttons flying.

I tried to struggle, but Dags' grip was so tight I was in danger of losing the blood flow to my hands and Pablo had shifted down my body so he was sitting on my thighs.

'Interesting,' he said, looping a claw under the front of my bra, giving it a tug and then letting it go with an elastic twang. It was obviously too much like hard work for him to deal with as his attention wandered down to the button on my trousers. He leered down at me as he undid it.

'No!' I cried. 'You do and you'll be sorry.'

'Yes,' he said, undoing another button and another.

'They'll kill you for this,' I spat.

'They'll have to find us first.'

'They will.'

'Maybe,' he said, 'but who's to say that when they do, we won't kill them first?'

I struggled beneath him and managed to wrench my right wrist free. I clawed at his face. I'd have done anything for my daemon self's sharp pointed nails, but my own found their mark and I felt flesh give as I raked them down his cheek.

'Bitch!' he half screamed, and grabbing my chin smashed my head back down against the earth hard enough that I saw stars. 'Hold her for fuck's sake,' he said to Dags.

Another cloud skittered across the moons so that all I could see was his teeth as he grinned down at me and opened another button. His weight shifted again as he grabbed the waistband and started to pull.

'No, don't!' I said.

'Gonna beg? I like it when they beg, don't you Dags?'

'Yeah, and I think we should make this one beg a lot after what she did to my janglers.'

'Go on, beg,' Pablo said and I clamped my lips tight shut. I was not going to give him the satisfaction.

Another cloud blotted out the moon and a breeze disturbed the air as he lifted himself up again and tugged at my trousers. I clenched my eyes tight shut. I didn't want to see his face. Didn't want to see his expression as he did this to me.

And suddenly Pablo was gone.

'What the . . .' Dags said letting go of my wrists. 'Pablo? Pablo!' and then there was a grunt and so was he.

I lay there on the road for a few moments, eyes still tight shut. It was a trick. It must be a trick. I thought I heard a soft moan from somewhere far off to the right of the road, though it could have been the wind. I opened one eye and then the other. I was alone. I slowly sat up and looked around. I was totally alone. Where had they gone? Did I care?

I got to my feet and pulled my trousers back into place, buttoning them up tight and tucking in my ruined shirt. To stop my shirt gaping open and exposing my bra I did up my jacket all the way to my throat.

Then I began to shake and I could feel tears welling up.

'Get a grip, Lucky,' I told myself, 'get a grip.' They hadn't taken from me what I had promised to two others. They hadn't managed to violate me or murder me, or even really hurt me . . . but they so very nearly had and it scared me and I felt sick and lightheaded and I didn't know what to do. I squeezed my eyes shut. I had to keep going, I just had to.

I started to trudge along the road, but my boot kicked something that slid across the ground with a metallic rasp. A dagger. I crouched down and picked it up: Pablo's dagger. I didn't know what had happened to Pablo, but a weapon was good, so I shoved it into my belt. I'd come a long way from the woman – no, girl – I had been when I'd refused the dagger given to me on my first day in the Underlands.

I had to get back. I had to get back to my men. I had to get back to Jamie and Jinx . . . and then I did begin to cry. What if I'd made them wait too long? I could so easily have lost what I'd been saving for them and what if they were dead? What if I'd lost them? What if we never shared that special moment together?

I stopped, screwed my eyes shut and hugged myself as my shoulders began to heave. I had lost Pyrites and it could be I'd lost them all. What other reason could there be for them not coming to save me?

'Lucky,' I heard a voice say from behind me. I stiffened. 'Lucky?'
No, it can't be. It must be my imagination. It sounded like Jamie. I
opened my eyes and turned back.

And then I was in his arms and he was holding me tight and
kissing me. 'I thought I'd lost you, I thought I'd lost you,' he said
and his kisses were no longer the gentle comforting kisses of an
angel, but those of a red-blooded man who wanted me as much as
I wanted him. And then, as if by divine intervention, it began to
rain; not a splattering of raindrops, but a stair-rod downpour that
had the pair of us soaked to the skin within seconds. Even my
leather jacket was soaked through.

He looked down at me, his arms still around me, the rain drip-
ping off his hair and nose and gave a ragged sigh. 'I thought I'd lost
you forever.'

'What happened, Jamie? How come neither you nor Jinx came
to save me at the inn?'

'We heard Pyrites yell and you scream, but before we could
move we were surrounded by a crowd of armed Sicarii and however hard we fought and cut our way through, more appeared. I
didn't want to leave Jinx and the others, but it got to the stage that
I had no choice if I was to find you. Jinx made me go, he made me
leave them.'

'Will they be all right?' I asked through chattering teeth.

Jamie hugged me to him, trying to keep me warm, though his
skin felt just as chilled as mine. 'I hope so.'

'Pyrites,' I said, and my eyes filled with tears. 'Pyrites is dead.'

'Are you sure?'

'They shot him Jamie; they shot him full of arrows,' and I went
on to tell him what happened in the yard at the back of the inn.

By the time I had finished the rain had stopped and I was shivering with the cold.

I wanted to ask what had happened to Pablo and Dags, but I
didn't have the heart . . . and I wasn't sure I cared.

Jamie saw me shivering and hugged me closer. 'I need to get you
back to the palace and out of those wet clothes.'

At any other time I would have made some smart alec comment, but my heart was too heavy and I didn't think I would ever be able to smile again. I wrapped my arms around Jamie and in a moment we were in the sky and heading back to the palace.

We flew back to the fortress and landed outside the back entrance to the palace.

'Will Jinx and the others be here?'

'If they fought the Sicarii off I'd imagine they'd be either in your chambers or at the inn. Or searching for us,' he said as an afterthought.

Then something occurred to me. 'Why didn't Jinx just do that freezy, freezy thing that he does?'

'He told you before. When Jinx calls upon his skills to bring a layer of death to our world anyone nearby who is ill or injured could bear the brunt. We were right outside the inn and he didn't dare risk Odin.'

It was very quiet in the corridors of the palace, but then it would be: it was the middle of the night. We passed a couple of guards, who watched us with bored eyes, and a few servants walking the hallways, but they were the sum of it. When we reached the room it was empty and I could tell by Jamie's expression that this wasn't a good thing. He tried to get me to take a bath, but I was having none of it. I needed to find Jinx, Shenanigans and Kerfuffle. He didn't put up much of a fight; he wanted to find them too.

I rubbed myself down with a towel and changed as quickly as I could, catching one brief glimpse of myself in the dressing room mirror. I wished I hadn't: I could have been a corpse, my skin was so pale and my red-ringed eyes were underlined with purple smudges. My arms were covered with bruises and there was a dark patch on my right temple where I must have thumped it at some point. I almost wished my daemon self would appear; she could only look better than I did.

The inn wasn't in darkness, for which I was grateful, as we could hardly wake Barron and his wife in the middle of the night.

Jamie knocked on the door and after a couple of seconds a deep voice I recognised as Barron's asked who was calling so late.

'It's me: James,' Jamie said.

There was the sound of bolts being drawn and a key being turned and the door opened a crack and Barron's face appeared. His worried expression relaxed and he pulled the door open and beckoned for us to come inside. 'This way,' he said, leading us out to the back room. He pushed the door open and gestured for me to go in first.

'Mistress,' Shenanigans said and would have got up, but Leila pushed him back onto his chair.

'You stay put,' she said and dabbed at his forehead with a piece of white cloth that was fast turning green.

'Shenanigans!' I said, hurrying around the table to take a good look at him. 'You're hurt.'

'Only a scratch,' he said.

Leila gave a tut. 'Only a scratch to his face. I've spent an hour or more patching up the rest of him.'

'Are you all right?'

He gave me a toothy smile. 'Better than the other fellows.'

'Where's Kerfuffle?' I asked.

'He's downstairs in the kitchen getting more hot water,' Barron said. 'He's got a few lumps and bumps but not too much to worry about.'

'And Jinx?' Jamie asked.

'Combing the countryside on his black beast looking for you two,' Leila said. 'I wanted him to let me take a look at his wounds, but he wouldn't wait.'

'Wounds?' I said, my voice coming out an octave too high.

'Lucky, Jinx is the Deathbringer, a couple of wounds won't kill him,' Jamie said.

I sank down on the chair opposite Shenanigans. 'This is such a mess. Now they have Kayla, Angela, Vaybian and Philip.'

'We should never have left you on your own with Vaybian,' Jamie said.

'I wasn't. Pyrites was with us,' I said, and my eyes started to fill up.

'He'll be so pleased to see you,' Shenanigans said. 'He blames himself for you being taken.'

'He was full of arrows and he couldn't . . .' Then I realised what he'd said. 'What do you mean?' I asked, looking up at Shenanigans.

'Pyrites; he's blaming himself because he couldn't defend you. We've tried telling him it wasn't his fault but he won't listen.'

'But I thought . . .' I glanced up at Jamie who was beginning to smile, his first since finding me. 'I thought he was dead.'

'Of course not. It would take more than a few arrows to kill a Jewelled Drakon,' Shenanigans said.

'But he'd collapsed and was barely breathing.'

'Drakon's Bane,' Shenanigans said. 'They'd coated the tips of the arrows with Drakon's Bane.'

'It's an herbal fusion that puts drakons to sleep. It's the only way to catch one who doesn't want to be caught,' Jamie explained and with that the door opened and Kerfuffle came trotting in carrying a steaming jug. Pyrites padded along beside him, head down and favouring his front right foot. His back right leg had a drag to it and puffs of grey mist followed in his wake.

'Pyrites,' I said. His head jerked up and his eyes began to glow, then he was scrambling across the floor to bounce around my ankles and up onto my lap where he licked my face like an over-excited puppy. I hugged him to me and buried my head in his neck, 'I'm so glad you're all right.'

'He will be now,' Kerfuffle said, 'he was getting right despondent.'

The hours ticked by and dawn was on the horizon and yet Jinx still hadn't returned. I don't think I was the only one who was worried, either. Well, maybe I was.

'He's the Deathbringer,' Kerfuffle said. 'He's darn near fireproof.'

'Do you want me to go looking for him?' Jamie asked, albeit reluctantly.

'Great idea Guardian,' Kerfuffle said, 'you go off and he comes back and then he'll go looking for you and you'll come back and then it'll all start over again.'

'Lucky's worried about him,' Jamie said.

'Mistress, the Deathbringer will return shortly,' Shenanigans said.

I guessed he was right. I just didn't like us being separated. My run in with the Sicarii and then Pablo and his mates had rattled me more than I could say. 'Jamie, what happened to Pablo and Dags?'

Jamie glanced at me, his expression very dark indeed. 'You ask, but you don't really want to know,' he said.

I looked at him for quite a long time and he stared back. He was right; I probably didn't. I was about to ask about Duffus, but thought better of it. Then the door opened and any thought of what might have happened to my three assailants flew straight from my mind. Jinx had returned.

When he strode through the door his expression was bleak, then he saw Jamie and he immediately glanced around the room and as soon as he saw me a huge smile lit up his face.

'You found her then brother.'

'Just in the nick of time as it happens,' Jamie said and Jinx gave him a quizzical look.

'Later,' my angel said and then I was in Jinx's arms being hugged so tight I could hardly breathe.

If I'd had my way we would have stayed at the inn until we were ready to leave and begin our search for the Sicarii. Jamie and Jinx thought differently.

'How long do you think it will be before Baltheza hears of our being attacked? If we don't present ourselves before him with this news his paranoia will get the better of him and before we know it we'll all be on his most wanted list,' Jamie said.

'Anyway, I want to know how Henri is walking around free and almost certainly in the employ of the Sicarii,' Jinx said.

Maybe Baltheza was barmier than we suspected and he'd set

Henri on us? Though he had been pretty convincing when he'd told us Henri was being held in the Chambers of Rectification, but if it was the case that Baltheza had set him on us, how come Henri had been spying on us for several days? It didn't make any sense at all. Was Baltheza playing some sort of game?

So we went back to my room in the fortress and, as I knew all my friends were safe and Jamie and Jinx were deep in conversation, I decided to have that bath.

The bath was filling slowly as there were no taps in the Underlands – only hand pumps – and the water was, at best, tepid. I wondered how Shenanigans and Kerfuffle usually got it so hot and I was beginning to think I should have accepted their offer to run the bath for me.

A knock on the door made me jump. I really was unsettled. 'Are you decent?' a muffled voice asked.

'Come in.'

Jinx poked his head around the door and upon seeing me sitting fully clothed on the edge of the bath, came in with Pyrites limping along behind him.

'Do your stuff, lad,' Jinx said and Pyrites flew up above the bath and shot a sharp burst of flame down onto the water. Jinx trailed his fingers across its surface. 'Once more,' and Pyrites obliged with another puff. 'Perfect,' and Pyrites dropped down to the floor, rubbed himself around my knees then padded back outside.

Jinx closed the bathroom door behind him and sat down on the bath edge beside me. Being alone with him in a bathroom was not something I'd usually encourage. Not because I didn't want him, but because I did, and that was the problem. His sparkling gold and green eyes and irreverent sense of humour could easily be my undoing, and actually I quite *wanted* to be undone, especially after the events of the last few days. Then, why was it a problem? It was twofold: I wanted Jinx and I wanted Jamie: socially acceptable in their world, but not in mine.

Jinx gave me a smile, but it was the sort of smile I would have expected from Jamie and it put me on the wrong foot straight away. Laughing, teasing Jinx I could put up with; tender Jinx was another thing altogether.

'Jamie told me what happened.'

I poured some scented oil into the bath and swished it about with my hand making bubbles. 'Nothing happened.'

'It nearly did.'

'But it didn't.'

He took hold of my hand and raised it to his lips. 'I promised to protect you. We promised to protect you and we so nearly let you down.'

'Jinx, it wasn't your fault. We were played.'

'We should never have left you alone. All four of us leaving you with Vaybian and only Pyrites as guards was a mistake.'

'Jinx, it's over. Done with. All five of you are safe and so am I. I'm now more worried about Vaybian. I think the Sicarii have him lined up for ritual slaughter, so we haven't much time. Another reason I didn't want to come back here. I really can't be doing with another "interview" with my . . . with Baltheza.'

'Maybe not, but I'd be interested to find out whether or not he knows Henri is no longer languishing in the palace dungeons.'

'I agree, I'm a little puzzled as to Henri's involvement in all this.'

Jinx looked into my eyes and stroked my cheek with his thumb. 'I thought I'd lost you,' he said echoing Jamie.

'And I you,' I said and had to look away.

He wasn't having any of it. He caught hold of my face and turned me back to face him. 'It's lucky James found you first.' He didn't have to tell me what he meant. I shivered, whatever Jamie did to my assailants was probably ten times kinder than any punishment Jinx would have handed out. Then he kissed me, and although there was always a passion to Jinx's kisses, this kiss was *the* kiss and I knew, although he may never say the words, that I wasn't the only one who had lost their heart.

He pulled me into his arms and his lips moved from my lips to my neck as he lifted me up and onto his lap. 'Lucinda, my lucky,

lucky lady,' he whispered and his lips were back on mine and I could have died there and then and been happy.

A knock on the door saw us pull apart. Me gasping for breath; Jinx smiling his sexy smile. 'I'm thinking that'll be the Guardian making sure I'm not taking advantage of you.'

I slid off Jinx's lap and walked around to the other side of the bath, putting some distance between us. 'Come in.'

It was as Jinx surmised and I wasn't at all surprised when Jamie's head popped around the door. 'I'm not interrupting anything?' he said, his slight frown saying 'if I was – good'.

Jinx looked down at the floor with a smile.

'Nope,' I said, 'but you both will be interrupting me soon. I'd like to get into my bath while the water's still hot.'

'Don't let us stop you,' Jinx said. 'There's plenty of room for three.'

'Jinx,' Jamie said, 'now is not the time. Lucky was nearly . . . she nearly . . .' and when he glanced my way his anguish was palpable.

I went to my angel and rested a hand on his shoulder. 'Jamie?' He looked away. I glanced at Jinx expecting a nonchalant shrug, but for a split second a similar pain was etched onto his face before he had a chance to hide it. *Okaaay* – this was different – and for once it felt like I was going to have to be the strong one. 'Boys, listen to me. True, it wasn't exactly the best night of my life, but I'm fine. The worst didn't happen, Jamie saved me.'

'Only just.'

'And I didn't,' Jinx said, 'I wasn't even there.'

Wow. This was more serious than I thought. 'Jamie, Jinx, listen to me. What happened last night wasn't your fault. If you're going to blame anyone blame Henri, blame the Sicarii, but don't blame yourselves. I'm alive, I'm unhurt and we're all here together.'

They both looked up at me, and not for the first time I thought that for all their differences, they were very much the same, and maybe that was what made it so easy for me to love both of them. And it was true: I did love them both.

Jinx stood up, came to me and took my hand; Jamie took the

other. 'Why is it sometimes it is I who feel marked by you?' Jinx said, studying my face.

Jamie squeezed my fingers. 'I feel the same.'

I lifted both their hands to my lips and as their fingers touched while held in mine I felt a surge of power shoot upwards to my head and downwards into the tips of my toes.

'Hells bells, and buckets of piss, what was that?' Jinx said and although his hand had jerked in mine – both of their hands had – neither of them pulled away.

'Oh wow,' Jamie said looking at me.

'Bloody hell,' Jinx said giving Jamie a sideways look.

There was a knock on the door. 'Are you all right in there?' I heard Kerfuffle call.

'Fine,' Jamie said. 'We're fine.'

'Mistress?' Shenanigans asked.

'Honestly, we're all fine,' I said.

There was some muttering from the other side of the door. 'Well . . . if you're sure.'

'I think we'd better let them come in,' I said. Jamie and Jinx exchanged another look. 'For goodness' sake, what is it?'

Both my daemons led me across the bathroom to the washbasin. Jinx's lips twitched into a smile and he gestured with his head towards the mirror. My heart began to pound in my ears and there was a solid lump of anxiety in my diaphragm. I took a deep breath, exhaled slowly and looked. My daemon self gave me a tentative smile back.

'This has happened before,' I told them, not wanting them to read too much into my transformation.

'Not like this,' Jamie said.

'Yes, just like this.'

'When? Your reflection has changed, but we've never seen the daemon you in person,' Jamie said.

'Yesterday,' I said, 'when Henri tried to kill Pyrites.'

'Hang fire, you never told us this,' Jinx said, which was true, I hadn't; too much had been going on – and I'd been too embarrassed.

I could feel my skin flushing. 'He wanted revenge on Pyrites and me for slashing and burning him. He was going to stab Pyrites in the throat and I sort of lost my temper.'

'Pyrites wouldn't have survived a slit throat,' Jamie said.

'I know, that's why I attacked Henri with one of the Sicarii's swords,' I explained, then told them how I had hacked off Henri's right hand. At the end of my story they both looked at me in open-mouthed amazement and I was way past embarrassed.

'You cut off Henri's hand?' Jamie asked and Jinx began to laugh.

'It's not funny, Jinx,' I said.

'I think it is. Henri's going to have to have a change of career.'

'The Sicarii seemed to think their healer might fix him.'

'Let's hope not,' Jinx said and as uncharitable as it might seem, I agreed with him.

This time I didn't change back, at least not straight away. I shooed the boys out so I could take my bath and examine my new body. It actually didn't look a lot different except my skin was a shimmering rose pink. My hair was no longer chestnut, but a glistening mahogany and aubergine. My nails were sharp, pointed and maroon and my eyes a kaleidoscope of glowing violet and garnet. I was still about five foot five; I had no horns, wings or a tail and, thank the lord, no third or fourth boob, though rather disappointingly they weren't any bigger either.

I sank down into the bath to contemplate looking like this forever. It was a possibility; I certainly hadn't felt any surge of power when I'd changed before. Last time I had felt stronger, faster, tougher and more powerful, but not like I'd been plugged into a mainframe.

My long, hot soak lasted little more than five minutes before there was a knock on the door and a message that Daddy Dearest wanted to see me. That I didn't want to see him, and certainly not looking as I did, didn't come into it. I had been summoned. I wrapped myself up in a towel and walked into the dressing room to find something to wear. I hoped that somewhere amongst the rails and racks of clothes I'd find another pair of trousers. The pretty frocks would no doubt look good on me in my daemon form, but I was happiest in a pair of jeans. Leather trousers would do if there was nothing else.

Kayla came up trumps. Under another leather jacket, this time in a rather fetching oxblood red, was a pair of black leather trousers. They laced up at the front, but were actually quite comfortable.

Suited and booted I returned to my men. 'How do I look?' I asked.

'Like a real daemon princess,' Kerfuffle said and Shenanigans nodded enthusiastically.

Jinx licked his lips and winked, which made me laugh and Jamie mouthed 'you look beautiful'. Why he couldn't say it out loud I don't know, but that's men for you.

'Why does he want to see me now?' I grumbled with ill-disguised bad grace; I'd been looking forward to a long hot soak.

'He probably expects to hear about what happened yesterday as soon as possible,' Jamie said as we strode through the passageways leading down to the great hall.

'How does he know about that already?'

'I suppose the piles of dead Sicarii lining the streets may've been a bit of a giveaway,' Jinx said.

'Oh.' I'd never given them a thought. 'Why do you think he wants us to meet him in the great hall?'

'Ego trip,' Jinx said.

''Scuse me?'

Jamie made a huffing sound at Jinx. 'He's handing out sentencing this morning to convicted felons,' he said.

'As I say – ego trip,' Jinx said. 'He loves his power over life and death.'

'And you don't?' Jamie asked. I don't think he was being mean, just curious.

'No, brother, I don't. I have no choice, it's my role in life.'

'So, if you did have the choice would you be a farmer or a baker or a cabinet maker?' Jamie asked with a chuckle. Jinx, of course, didn't get that very human expression.

'Hmm,' Jinx said, 'I think I would be a reprobate, with nothing better on my mind than wine, women and song.'

'Not very much different then?' I said.

Jinx grinned and addressed Jamie. 'But what about you? If you weren't the Guardian, how would you spend your days?'

'I think I would join you, making love to a beautiful woman in the sunshine with a bottle of red at my elbow.'

'Let's do it,' Jinx said. 'When we've done with this latest challenge, let's find some exotic beach and spend our days eating and drinking and making love to our lucky, lucky lady.'

'I'm game,' Jamie said.

'Lucinda?'

I smiled at my two men. I knew what they were doing and appreciated the gesture, but nothing was going to abate the nerves I felt every time I went into Baltheza's company. I didn't tell them this, instead I said, 'I'd like that very much.' And then we reached the entrance to the great hall; Jamie lost his smile, Jinx plastered on a devil-may-care smirk and I held my head up high and entered the chamber doing my best power strut.

Baltheza was seated on his ornate throne on a dais towards the back of the hall. A line of daemons stood before him; bedraggled, pathetic-looking creatures weighed down with heavy chains around their wrists and ankles. Amaliel Cheriour stood in front of the dais slightly to the left watching the proceedings. There were a few onlookers, mainly bored soldiers, who were scattered around the back of the hall.

Baltheza saw us arrive and if he was surprised by my appearance he didn't show it. We stopped halfway across the hall behind a rope barrier spread across the width of the chamber, and used to separate the members of the court from the criminals awaiting sentencing. I had a feeling I'd been summoned here for a reason, probably to see more of Baltheza's vile justice in action. I hoped the sentences would be carried out at one of his after-banquet entertainment sessions and not now. I certainly didn't want to see it. Once had been enough.

Baltheza gestured to a guard in shiny dress uniform to proceed. They had apparently been waiting for our arrival. I clenched my fists; if that were the case, I knew things were about to get bloody. Baltheza enjoyed seeing my reaction to his excesses, I'd learned that much.

'Here we go again,' Jinx muttered under his breath. 'Time to put an "I don't give a shit" smile upon your face and hope you can keep your last meal down.'

'You think?'

''Fraid so,' Jamie answered for him.

The guard read out what I imagined was a load of ceremonial blather about the court of Lord Baltheza and its legal processes then proceeded to walk along the line of miscreants stopping at each one to list the crimes for which they had been found guilty. He then climbed up upon the dais and handed the parchment to Baltheza who made a great show of looking at each individual in turn and running his finger down the scroll reading their crimes.

While this was going on, grey spectres drifted down from the high beamed ceiling above and moved around the condemned, touching their arms and patting their backs; offering unnoticed sympathy. One daemon, larger than the rest and not so under-nourished, started at such a touch and looked this way and that. A sensitive I assumed. He wasn't like the others. When I caught a sideways glimpse of his face he appeared alert and intelligent. He reminded me a bit of Shenanigans, although to look at he was completely different apart from his size and brawn.

His torso could have belonged to a Greek god, though he was a strange orange brown that reminded me of earthenware pots; he even had the same semi-glazed look. His sandy hair was short, curly and also had the Grecian look. His features were almost human apart from a short tusk between his eyebrows. I don't know what it was about him, but I had this feeling that he was here, not for a crime he had committed, but because someone wanted him gone. He glanced back over his shoulder and looked straight into my eyes. It only lasted a moment, but it was enough. I wasn't sure how, but I had to help him.

The restless dead began to drift my way as I studied the prisoner. They reached out to me, imploring me. To do what, I had no idea.

Baltheza got to his feet and the spirits whirled around to face him, but not before I saw their expressions, and I was left in no doubt that if they could have become whole again he would have suffered their wrath.

'I've considered your crimes and have found that some of your sentences should be carried out immediately.' The spirits moaned and held their heads in their hands. Some shook their fists; some threw ineffectual punches at the guards although none approached Baltheza and his pet executioner Amaliel.

'Kubeck Vansk,' Baltheza said and the sandy-haired daemon stood to attention, 'you've been convicted of crimes so heinous I'll not see you live another hour let alone a day.' The spirits groaned. 'You will pay for your felonious and treasonous acts in flesh.' The spirits turned to me, some dropping to their knees. 'I sentence you to be flayed from your toes to your neck, then to be drawn and quartered and your entrails drenched in boiling oil.'

Amaliel gestured with a wave of the hand to two guards standing by the back entrance, who opened the door for a large, wooden table to be wheeled in. The wood was dark, but it couldn't hide the many jade and maroon stains that blemished the wood. Leather straps hung at the corners with more stretched across its width. Deep channels were carved around the edges and cut into a cross shape in the centre. I didn't need an explanation of them, I'd seen similar in paintings of mediaeval torture chambers. Kubeck Vansk did not utter a word, but stood there, head held high as the table rumbled across the stone floor to stop directly between the dais and where he waited.

The spirits were not so quiet; they wailed at the sight of the table, and a small apparition I had seen on several previous occasions floated over to stand directly in front of me.

'Save him,' his voice a plaintive whisper. 'Please save him.'

'There's nothing you can do,' Jinx said to me from the corner of his mouth as he stared straight ahead.

'There is a law,' the little ghost said, and other spirits took up the cry.

Amaliel glided across the chamber to stand beside the table and gestured for two guards to bring the unfortunate Kubeck across.

'What law?' Jinx whispered.

The little spirit ignored him. I lifted my hand to cover my lower face and asked, 'What law?'

'A princess of the blood may claim his life.'

I glanced at Jinx. He lifted his fist to his chin, frowned into space and took a step back to whisper in Jamie's ear.

Kubeck had been led to the table while all the other prisoners had been taken to the side of the hall. They were to witness Kubeck's fate, probably in anticipation of their own executions. 'Hurry up and think of something,' I muttered.

Jamie and Jinx both stepped back to my side. 'Baltheza won't like it, but the law says that a blood royal can claim the life, body and soul of a convicted felon,' Jamie told me.

'What does that mean?'

'You will save his life, but he's yours forever or until you tire of him.'

'He'll be your slave,' Jinx said, 'but he'll be alive and I can't imagine being your slave would be a bad thing. In the old days sometimes a felon would rather accept the death penalty than be owned by a blood royal as the torture could go on forever.'

'Nice,' I said with a sigh.

'Get on with it,' I heard Baltheza say.

'Get on the table,' one of the guards grunted as three others stepped forwards, their swords raised.

Kubeck hesitated by the table, his shoulders sagging. He knew it was useless to fight and he was about to die horribly.

'For the record,' he said, giving Amaliel a pointed look, 'I'm not guilty of the charges made against me and I'll see he who has spoken falsely against me in the afterlife.'

'No afterlife for him,' the small spirit cried and the others chanted, 'No afterlife.'

'What do they mean?' I asked.

'No time to ask,' Jinx said, nodding towards Kubeck who was being forced up onto the table.

I strode forward and Jinx lifted the rope so I could pass underneath. 'As a princess of the blood, I claim this daemon's life.'

'My Lord,' Jamie whispered behind me.

'My Lord,' I repeated louder.

Amaliel turned around to face me, not that I could see his face, just those awful red, burning eyes.

Baltheza sat up straight in his throne. 'Why would you want this creature?'

'I need a servant.'

'You've five guards.'

'It's become apparent I need more.'

'Sire,' Amaliel hissed at Baltheza, moving to his side to whisper in his ear.

An expression of irritation passed across Baltheza's face and he waved his Court Enforcer away. 'You realise he will be totally your responsibility?'

'I do,' I said.

Baltheza, to my complete surprise, smiled an almost affectionate smile at me. 'You are so much like your mother,' he said. 'How could I not grant you your request?' He flapped a hand at the guards. 'Release him into her custody.'

A ghostly cheer rose up from the surrounding spirits and the little ghost punched the air, while others whooped and clapped.

'Lord Baltheza,' Amaliel said, 'I must protest.'

Baltheza's smile slid from his face to be replaced by a cold and arrogant glare which he turned upon Amaliel. 'Am I not the Lord here? Am I not your ruler? Is it not for me to say who should live and die?'

'My Lord, I—'

'Enough! Kubeck Vansk is now the property of my youngest daughter. Keep him here while I speak to Princess Lucinda in private.' He rose and beckoned for me to follow him out into the smaller dining chamber. I glanced back at my men and they both were right behind me as I walked across the hall.

Baltheza went straight to the table and poured himself a goblet of wine from the waiting flagon. He gestured at a second goblet and I shook my head, 'No, thank you.' I needed to be able to think clearly when I was talking to him.

He leaned back against the table, crossed his ankles and looked me up and down. 'I see you're settling into our world in more ways than one.'

'You wanted to speak to me?'

He took a sip of his drink and studied me over the rim of the goblet. 'I understand you were attacked yesterday.'

'Yes, as were my guards.'

'They let you be taken,' he said, casting a look in Jamie and Jinx's direction. 'What possessed them to leave you under Captain Vaybian's protection I cannot fathom.'

'What I don't comprehend,' I said, cutting to the chase, 'is how Henri le Dent was able to follow us for the past couple of days when it was my understanding he was a guest of Amaliel Cheriour's?'

Baltheza's smile froze and the knuckles of the hand holding the goblet grew pale. 'What?'

'Vaybian noticed a daemon watching us a couple of days ago. The same daemon was in the Drakon's Rest yesterday and revealed himself to be Henri,' Jamie told him.

'Impossible.'

'I saw him with my own eyes,' I said.

'No,' Baltheza said with a determined shake of his head. 'No, you are mistaken.'

'Well, next time you see him ask him how he lost his right hand,' Jinx said.

'The Sicarii said their healers might be able to fix it,' I said.

'If they do it'll never be the same,' Jamie said. 'It's not like they can stitch it back on as they would in the Overlands, reconnecting each tendon and blood vessel.'

Baltheza looked at each of us in turn then stood up and strode to the door, flinging it open. 'Someone get me Amaliel. I want to see him now. And tell him to bring Henri le Dent with him.' He closed the door and leaned back against it. 'It cannot be, it cannot be,' he muttered almost to himself.

I felt my men move close behind me. They were obviously of the same opinion as me: Baltheza looked like he had gone fully over the edge.

He pushed himself away from the door and stalked back to the table, then poured himself another drink with shaking fingers, spilling a drop on the cuff of his sleeve. For a moment he appeared mesmerised by the growing spot of red on the snow white fabric, then he knocked back the wine in one and poured himself yet another before turning back to me.

'Why did you want the miscreant Kubeck?' he asked.

'I told you I need a servant.'

'But why him?'

'He looks strong and tough.'

'A bit of rough for your bed?'

I heard Jamie suck in air through his teeth. Baltheza didn't appear to notice. I gave him what I hoped was a pleasant smile. 'I have that taken care of, thank you,' I told him. 'I need a loyal servant who will help me find my sister. I have an inkling he will fit the bill.'

'Really?'

'Yes, really.'

'Hmm.' He took another swig of his drink and his expression changed, purple smudges colouring his cheeks. 'Where is he?' he said, slamming the goblet down and sending a shower of wine across the table. He strode back to the door and threw it open again. 'Where is Amaliel? Bring him to me now.'

This time he left the door open and began to pace. 'Why is he not here?'

'It must be quite a walk from the dungeons,' I said, though why I was trying to defend the revolting creature I don't know.

Baltheza stopped his manic pacing and turned to me. 'Have I told you how like your mother you are?'

I had to force my expression to remain smiling and friendly, but not because I concerned for my own safety; something wasn't right. Baltheza had always been borderline insane, but this behaviour was bizarre.

'I think I will join you in a drink,' I said.

'Good girl,' he said. 'Like mother like daughter.' And then he frowned, 'Should be like father like daughter.'

'That's me; a chip off the old block.' I poured myself a drink and wandered over to stand next to Jinx. 'Could you hold this for a sec,' I said, passing him the goblet and giving it a pointed look. He frowned at me and I mouthed *smell it*.

His eyes narrowed as I turned away to distract Baltheza. 'We hope to leave this afternoon,' I told him. 'I don't want to delay any longer. Have your spies had any news of the Sicarii's whereabouts?'

I glanced back at Jinx and he didn't need to nod, his expression told me all. Someone was poisoning my father.

I had never even remotely thought of Baltheza as my father, preferring to hope he was mistaken. Finding out he was being poisoned didn't exactly change that – I still thought him cruel and wicked – but if he was my father and he was being poisoned I wanted to know by whom and why.

I took the goblet from Jinx, pretended to take a sip and pulled a face. 'My Lord, don't you find the wine a bit tart?'

'What?'

'The wine,' I said. 'Is it from your cellar?'

He gave a distracted wave of the hand. 'Where is Amaliel?'

'We'll go and find him,' Jinx said.

'Will you?'

'Of course, My Lord,' Jamie said, taking the goblet from me and taking a surreptitious sniff at the wine before placing it on the table next to the flagon. 'We'll be back in a few moments.' He placed his hand on my back and guided me towards the door.

'Find him and bring him to me,' Baltheza said draining the wine. 'And bring me another flagon.'

As soon as we were outside Jinx let rip with several earthy expletives. 'Just as well you never accepted the wine he offered you before,' he said when he had calmed down a bit.

'Do you think it would have killed me?'

'Not necessarily,' Jamie said. 'You are one of us.'

'So it won't kill him?'

'The poison he's being fed isn't to kill, it's to befuddle the senses,' Jinx answered. 'To drive him mad – and succeeding rather well judging by the display we just witnessed.'

'It would explain why he's been so erratic of late.'

'I want to know who and why,' I said. Both my men looked at me and Jinx began to chuckle. 'What?'

Jinx clasped his hands together beneath his chin and fluttered his eyelashes. ' "He's not my father. Baltheza can't possibly be my father",' he said in a high pitched soprano, then his voice dropped back to normal, 'but as soon as he's in danger you become like an avenging angel.'

I glared at him. 'This isn't funny Jinx.'

'No, it's not. Someone is causing harm to our monarch, which isn't funny at all. Your reaction to it, however, is hilarious.'

'Well, I'm so glad I keep you amused.'

I was about to say more when two guards came striding across the great hall. Upon seeing us their relief was palpable – they clearly had bad news and would rather give it to us than Baltheza.

'Lady Lucinda,' one said and they both gave brief bows of their heads, 'we think you should know Amaliel Cheriour is no longer in the palace.'

'And neither is the prisoner Henri le Dent,' said the other.

'You're sure?'

'Amaliel was seen leaving directly after being called to present himself before our lord.'

'Thank you,' I said. They both gave deeper bows and then hurried away.

'Great, now *we* have to break the bad news to him,' Jamie said.

'Do I tell him he's being poisoned?' I asked.

'I think maybe I should do it,' Jinx said. 'He can't question my motives.'

I re-entered the chamber with some trepidation. Telling Baltheza Amaliel had run off and that Henri was no longer in custody, and also 'by the way you're being poisoned', was never going to go down well.

As it happened it went better than I'd have expected, but I think this was more down to Jinx's acting abilities than anything.

'My Lord,' he said, dropping down onto one knee and bowing his head, 'I have grievous and disturbing news.' He then went on to tell Baltheza in quiet and shocked tones how it would appear Amaliel had allowed Henri to go free and was himself involved in some nefarious conspiracy.

A couple of times Baltheza began to work himself up, but Jinx somehow managed to calm him. By the time we left he had surrounded himself with guards, and the daemons he had condemned to various horrible deaths less than an hour before had seen their sentences commuted to lifelong servitude as food and wine tasters to their monarch. Unfortunately, we were none the wiser as to where we should be searching for the latest Sicarii hideout.

I also had a new servant to deal with.

When I went back to find him, he was still in chains and kneeling between two guards who were even bigger than he was. He was obviously still considered dangerous.

'Unchain him,' I said to them.

'Milady?'

'You heard her,' Jinx said.

'He's convicted of treason and crimes against the monarchy.'

'So was I a few weeks back,' I said, 'so we should get along just fine.'

Kubeck climbed to his feet while the guards unlocked the shackles. 'Should I be thanking you?' he asked me. 'Or am I in for worse than what was destined for me in Amaliel's care?'

'Who did you upset?' I asked. 'You must have upset someone quite a lot for them to want you executed in such an awful way.'

He gave a wry smile. 'You didn't save me to learn this.'

'No, but I'd be interested to know.'

'Who wields the real power in this court?' he asked.

'Amaliel,' Jinx said.

'Amaliel had you arrested on trumped up charges? Why?'

'It isn't something we should speak of here,' he said.

'He's right,' Jamie said. 'Just because Amaliel has disappeared doesn't mean he hasn't left some eyes and ears behind.'

'I'm with the Guardian on this one,' Jinx said.

'Right then,' I said, 'let's get the others and leave.' Then I looked up at the ceiling. 'Though, before we go, I'd be most interested to find out why so many spirits linger here.'

Kubeck shot me a surprised look. 'Get used to it,' Jinx said. 'You ride with three very different kinds of daemon now.'

Jinx excused the guards and closed the doors, leaving us alone.

I walked to the centre of the hall and looked up at the shadows clinging to the rafters. 'Come speak to me,' I said. 'Let me try to help you,' and the ghostly figures of those executed at Lord Baltheza's pleasure began to descend.

Jinx walked to my side and they shifted away, forming a circle around us. The small spirit who had begged me to help Kubeck earlier glided to the front. As he came closer I could see he wasn't a child, as I'd at first thought. He had wrinkles around his eyes and his face could have been human had it not been for two short horns on his brow. He had short, tight, curly hair and when I looked down he had small hooves instead of feet, like those of a goat, and fur-covered ankles that poked out beneath his trousers.

'Soulseer,' he said, his voice melodic and low, 'you have returned to us.'

'Why do you remain in this place where you were caused such pain?' I asked. 'Why don't you move on?'

'We cannot. We don't want to stay but we can't leave.'

'Why?'

There was a low groaning wail from the other spirits. 'Cursed,' they chorused, 'cursed.'

'Who by?' I asked, though I had a sneaking suspicion.

'The executioner, Amaliel,' the small spirit said to more groans from the others. 'He cursed us at the moment before death, tying us to this place forever.'

'This is getting weird,' I said.

'Help us, help us,' the spirits whispered, their voices sounding like dead leaves rustling in the breeze.

'Where have I heard this before?' Jinx said.

'The Sicarii,' I said.

Jinx let out a long deep breath. 'I am beginning to think there is a lot more to all of this than we at first thought.'

'What's your name?' I asked the spirit.

'Clement.'

'Clement,' I said, 'I can't help you until I find a way of breaking the curse,' the spirits groaned, 'but I promise I will find out how to do this and I'll return as soon as I can.'

'Be careful,' he said. 'He wants your power.'

'Who wants my power?'

'Amaliel. He wants all your power.'

'I don't understand; I don't have any power.'

'The power over the living and the dead,' Clement said. 'If he captures the trinity he will have it all.'

'I—' Then the door at the back of the hall opened and the spirits began to float back up into the rafters as two servants came out carrying trays.

'Be careful,' Clement said as he drifted away. 'You are our only hope of salvation.'

Jinx touched my arm. 'Come on,' he said, 'there's nothing else to be learned here.'

Back in our room Shenanigans and Kerfuffle had been getting ready for us to leave and had laid out several changes of clothing on the bed for me. It was apparent they'd got to know me very well – there wasn't a single dress. There was also no underwear, but this wasn't an omission, Shenanigans explained in embarrassed, hushed tones, it was just that neither he nor Kerfuffle thought it seemly that they riffle through my under-garments.

'This is Kubeck,' Jamie told them. 'He's the newest member of Team Lucky de Salle.'

Kerfuffle looked him up and down, hands on hips. 'Can you handle yourself?'

'Aye, little man, I can.'

'I'll be *Mr* Kerfuffle to you,' he said with a haughty look.

'I'm Shenanigans,' my largest guard said, ignoring his grumpy friend, 'and this is Pyrites.'

Pyrites grew to the size of a mastiff and gave Kubeck a dainty sniff, then sat back on his haunches with a puff of steam.

'Okay Kubeck,' I said. 'Tell me why Amaliel wants you out of the way.'

'He had my cousin convicted of treason, a charge that was untrue. I was heard to complain, next thing I know I'm arrested and accused of the same offence.'

'And there was no truth in it?' Jamie asked.

Kubeck laughed. 'No, the most my cousin was guilty of was having a flapping jaw when in his cups and my only crime was supporting him. If you look at the records of execution, you'll see that there have never been more poor souls executed for "crimes against the state".'

'That could be because Lord Baltheza is madder than a cat in a sack,' Jinx said.

'But we know he was being pushed over the edge,' I said, turning to Shenanigans and Kerfuffle to explain. 'Baltheza was being poisoned.'

'With verillion most probably,' Jinx added.

'That'd do it,' Kerfuffle agreed. 'He's always been a bit crazy – the verillion would have been able to do its work easily.'

I took a deep breath and went on to tell them what happened in the hall.

'Now I think about it,' Jinx said, 'it does explain why the spirits of the dead are so grey.'

'Grey?' Jamie said.

'Yes, the spirits in the great hall are just like the ones at the Sicarii temple – grey, like they've been drained of all colour.'

'I thought it was a daemon thing,' I said, then thought on it. 'Though Diargo was still colourful.'

'His soul hadn't been drained,' Jinx said, his eyes glittering and angry.

'The question is: why would Amaliel do all this?' Jamie asked.

'Power,' Jinx rested his chin on his fist, 'he loves the power.'

I flopped down on the bed. 'But why all the executions?'

'Because he's a sick, psychopathic monster?' Jinx suggested.

'I think it's more than that,' I said. 'Clement said he wanted the trinity for power over the living and the dead – what did he mean?'

Jinx's brow furrowed. 'If he means what I think he does, Amaliel is punching well above his weight.'

Then it finally sank in – the trinity; three; power over the living and the dead . . . 'It's us, he doesn't just want me, he wants the three of us . . .'

'Amaliel must be in league with the Sicarii,' Jamie said.

'Not good, not good,' Kerfuffle said.

'Where to now?' Shenanigans asked.

'We have no idea where to start,' I said.

'Yes we do,' Jamie contradicted me. 'We know the direction they were taking you. And it could be there are Sicarii scouring the countryside trying to find you; if we find them, we find their hideout. So we make for the Forest of Dignus – the place where I found you.'

I shivered, painful memories returning that would have

overwhelmed me if I'd let them. I pushed them away; I was safe, my men were safe, that was all that mattered. 'Sounds like a plan,' I said. This was a lot more positive; now we had somewhere to start.

'I don't want to piss on your bonfire,' Kerfuffle interrupted, 'but aren't we playing straight into their hands?'

'What choice do we have?' I asked. 'I have to find Kayla and Vaybian, and Angela's just a little girl.'

'Mistress, I don't wish to upset you, but they might already be dead,' Kerfuffle said.

'I think Lucky would know it if Kayla were,' Jinx told him.

'Until I know for sure, I can't give up on her or Vaybian.'

'Then it's agreed,' Jinx said. 'We make for the Forest of Dignus.'

Ten

Pyrites seemed none the worse for his being shot with arrows and, except for one sore-looking patch on his flank, all of his wounds had healed. If he was bothered by having me and two large daemons on his back he didn't show it.

Kerfuffle was another matter. He didn't like sitting on Bob behind Jinx one little bit. It was actually quite funny considering how he'd sniggered when Vaybian was in the same position.

'If you don't hold me around the waist you will fall off,' Jinx said.

'Then I will fall.'

'Don't be so stubborn.'

'I'm not going to hug you. I don't even like you much.'

'It's not hugging me, anyway how do you think I feel?'

'I don't care.'

'By Beelzebub's bollocks you are the most cantankerous little sod I know.'

'Sticks and stones.'

'For the love of Mephistopheles, will someone tell the halfwit that if he doesn't hold onto me he'll fall?'

'He'll soon grab hold of you once you take off,' Jamie said.

'No,' I said, as I had a feeling Kerfuffle was just as likely to let himself tumble to the ground to prove a point. I stroked Pyrites head and whispered in his ear, 'Sorry boy but I'm afraid I'm going to have to fly with Jinx, otherwise Kerfuffle is going to end up getting himself splattered all over the countryside.'

Pyrites gave a little purr; I think he knew it too. He laid down on his belly so I could slide off and I stalked over to Bob who was snorting and stamping his feet, eager to get going.

'Off you get,' I said to Kerfuffle. 'You go and ride on Pyrites.'

Kerfuffle didn't need telling twice. He hopped down and hurried over to Pyrites, where Shenanigans gave him a hand up.

Jinx grinned down at me. 'Now this is more like it,' he said.

Jamie very gallantly linked his hands together to give me a lift onto Bob's broad back, but he wasn't quite so happy about the situation. 'I could always carry you,' he said.

'I know,' I told him as I made myself comfortable, 'but that would be silly when I can ride on Bob.'

'You're not going to argue about putting your arms around me are you?' Jinx said with a chuckle when Jamie had moved away.

'Not on your nelly,' I said, wrapping my arms around his waist.

He gave a big sigh. 'I'm in paradise.'

I leaned my head against the back of his shoulder. 'This is rather nice,' I whispered so only he could hear and then we were off to the pounding of hooves and the beating of powerful leathery wings.

It was a completely different sensation to riding on Pyrites. My drakon was softer and although warm, was not hot. Bob was hot, and I could feel his solid muscles moving beneath his taut flesh. Of course, I was also holding on tight to Jinx, and I was thinking that 'rather nice' had been an understatement. His back was pressed against my chest, my cheek resting against his shoulder, and the feel of my arms around his waist did things to my insides that had nothing to do with accelerating through the air, no matter what I might try to tell myself.

It didn't take too long to get to the forest – probably less than half the time it had by rickety, horse-drawn cart. We followed the road until it disappeared into a sea of scarlet and rust-coloured pines, and continued flying above the forest until it came out the other side. The road was winding, but there were no branches off of it for miles and miles. When we did come to the few side lanes they all led to small villages and not much else.

'You all right back there?' Jinx called over his shoulder.

'Fine thanks.'

'You comfy?'

'Lovely.'

'Yes you are,' he said.

I kissed him on the apple of his shoulder. One of his hands closed over mine and I hugged him a bit tighter. This was one journey I would be sorry to see the end of.

After a while two mountains rose up ahead of us. These were regular mountains and nothing like the Sicarii's ruby red Dark Mountain. The road twisted around to go in between them until we were travelling through the top of a narrow pass flanked on one side by a roaring amethyst river.

Jinx urged Bob to fly lower so his hooves were almost skimming the foaming water and spray wet our faces and hair. Jamie dropped down beside us. 'It can't be much further,' he shouted to Jinx over the pounding of wings and thunder of the river. 'We've travelled what would be a day's journey by cart.'

Jinx pointed down to the road below and Jamie gave a nod of understanding and accelerated ahead to glide down, with us following.

'Hold on tight,' Jinx said over his shoulder as the ground rushed towards us. Bob spread his wings out and slowed us down for the last few yards until his hooves hit the earth at a canter. He slowed to a trot, to a walk and then stopped.

I rested my head against Jinx's back for a couple of seconds with my eyes closed. 'Hmm, that was wonderful.'

'Almost as good as sex,' he whispered, 'but not quite.'

'Here, let me help you down,' Jamie said, giving Jinx one of his disapproving looks, which I guess meant Jinx hadn't whispered quite quietly enough. If Jinx cared he didn't show it, he just jumped down from Bob with a grin.

Pyrites' shadow passed over us as he came in to land a few yards away. His back feet hit the ground first; his front claws dropped down with a puff of sand, then he shrank down a bit for the boys to climb off.

'Why have we stopped?' Kubeck asked.

'We thought we ought to have a little talk before we go much further,' Jinx said. 'Once we've passed through the mountains I should think we'll be getting close to wherever it is they've holed up and they're bound to have lookouts. They'd be fools if they thought we weren't coming.'

'And they probably think we're fools if we do,' Jamie said.

'I'm afraid you're right there brother.'

'So what do we do?' I asked.

Jinx rested his chin on his fist and stared along the road. 'Maybe we make them think we're more foolish than we are,' he said.

'I'm listening,' I said.

'No, absolutely not,' Jamie said a flush of dark pink creeping along his cheekbones.

'They won't expect it and it'll throw them off guard,' Jinx said.

'You are making too many assumptions.'

'It's not as risky as it sounds.'

'Not for you perhaps. For Lucky it is.'

'I have sworn to protect her and I will.'

'Sending her into a den of psychopaths on her own is protecting her? I'd hate to think what it'd be like if you had it in for someone.'

'If you can think of a better way to find their temple and get inside, I'm all ears. Anyway we'll be right behind her.'

'I'll do it,' I said, cutting through the crap.

'No,' Jamie said.

'It's too dangerous, mistress,' Shenanigans said.

'I agree,' said Kerfuffle. 'Apart from anything else, Lady Kayla will have our guts for garters if she finds out we let you do this.'

'Three against two,' Jamie said.

'It's a bold move, but it could work,' Kubeck said.

'Who asked you?' Kerfuffle asked, glaring up at Kubeck, hands on hips.

'They'd be stupid to believe Mistress Lucky would attempt to find the Sicarii temple without us,' Shenanigans butted in.

'Look, why don't Pyrites and I just fly ahead for a few miles to see if there's anything that looks like it could be their new temple. Then I come back and we make a decision.'

'Why don't we all just carry on together?' Jamie said.

'Because they will see us coming.'

'Surely the Deathbringer, Guardian and Soulseer will be the match of the Sicarii,' Kubeck said.

'Hmm, normally I would say yes,' Jinx said, 'but we were nearly overcome by sheer numbers alone back at the inn.'

'How come there are so many of them?' Shenanigans asked. 'They always used to be a rather small sect.'

I turned to Jinx. 'What you said before about Amaliel wanting power,' I said. 'Could it be that he's been planning this right from the start? Maybe he's built the sect up over the years. Maybe he thinks that with enough followers he can seize the Underlands for his own?'

'And what a happy place this would be then,' Jinx said.

'No one would be safe,' Jamie said.

'Think of all the souls he would collect,' I said. 'If this is his plan, it has changed things. This is no longer about saving Kayla and Vaybian or even Angela.'

'It's about saving the Underlands,' Jinx said.

Despite the higher stakes, we still argued. Jamie, Shenanigans and Kerfuffle wanted us to stick together. Jinx thought I should allow myself to be used as bait – and as scared as I was of what they might do to me I thought he was right, and Kubeck very sensibly kept quiet after Kerfuffle's outburst.

'How about if Pyrites shrinks down to bird size and takes a little look around?' Shenanigans asked.

Jinx's eyes met mine. 'I have a better idea.' He patted Bob on the head then threw himself up onto his back. 'I'll be back in a couple of ticks.'

'Where are you going?' I asked, laying my hand on his knee and squeezing.

'To gather my spies my lucky lady, to gather my spies,' and with a slap to Bob's rump he was off into the sky.

He didn't go far, just up onto the peaks above us. Once there he leaped off his steed and strode along the ridge until he was standing at the highest point. He threw back his head, stretched out his arms and stared up at the heavens. Within moments the sky darkened with the shadows of birds: ravens, his harbingers of death, his spies. Soon he was surrounded and all sight of him was lost behind their flapping wings.

Even from so low down we could hear the birds' chorus as they massed about Jinx. Then all became quiet as they drifted down to land on the rock around his feet, turning the surface black.

For about five minutes he stood there speaking to his audience. A single bird cried out, then another and another until the mountain echoed with their calls and the blanket of feathers rose up, blotting out the suns and turning the sky black, before breaking into hundreds of fragments as they spread out and flew across the countryside.

Jinx raised a hand in farewell then lowered it to shield his eyes from the sun as he watched them go.

'I hope they can find out what we need to know,' Jamie said as Jinx climbed back on Bob.

'I doubt they'll be watching out for birds,' Shenanigans said.

He was right. Why would they?

Bob circled the two mountains and then powered down towards us, his hooves hammering the air as though he was galloping even as he flew. He touched down at a run, stopping a few yards away from us. Jinx jumped down and ran his hand down the creature's glossy neck and I saw his lips move, 'good lad' I think he said.

'Now we wait,' Jinx said. 'My feathered friends won't take long. They already have an inkling of where there may be a large gathering of daemonkind.'

'Really?'

'Not many pass this way, at least not on a regular basis. But they tell me that recently there has been a steady trickle of travellers through this pass to and from the west.'

'How many?' Jamie asked.

'They were unable to tell me,' Jinx said.

'Not good, not good,' Kerfuffle said.

'I was hoping we'd finished off a large proportion of their membership outside the inn,' Jamie said. 'Looks like they were the cannon fodder.'

'So it could be ten, twenty, a hundred . . .' I said.

'Or a thousand,' Kerfuffle said.

'Is it being so cheerful that keeps you going?' Jinx asked him, and Kerfuffle scowled.

'Shall we carry on?' I asked.

'Best we continue on foot once we get to the end of this pass. There's more chance we'll be seen in the air.'

Jamie helped me back up behind Jinx and we all set off again, this time flying low between the mountains. When the rock faces on either side of us began to get lower we landed and started to walk.

The landscape on this side of the mountain was a dark red expanse of rock and sand – not the rusty red I had grown to expect, but blood red. There was very little in the way of plant life and the temperature out in the open was several degrees hotter than it had been in the pass, and it was in this inhospitable place that the road ended.

'I think this is where we should wait for the ravens,' Jinx said.

So that was what we did.

The waiting made me nervous and gave me time to think. I wanted to get on with it and have it over and done with. Of course 'it' was no longer just a matter of rescuing Kayla, Vaybian, Angela and possibly Philip, but the whole of the Underlands from Amaliel's twisted ambitions. My heart was pounding, and my chest felt like it was encased in an iron bodice.

The enormity of the task ahead of us wasn't lost on my men and they were in similar moods to mine. Even Jinx wasn't his usual jovial self.

Shenanigans and Kerfuffle were handing out skins of water when the first of the ravens returned. Three of the creatures landed a few yards from where we were sitting. Jinx got to his feet and moved towards them, holding out his right hand. The largest of the birds cawed twice and with a flap of wings flew up to land on Jinx's outstretched fingers.

Jinx cocked his head to one side and the bird did the same, and for a moment bird and daemon looked very much alike. The creature cawed again and was joined by a chorus from his friends. Jinx frowned and they cawed some more.

Jinx reached out and stroked the creature's head. 'Thank you,' he said at last, and the bird fluttered down to join the other two. All three gave one more cry and then launched back into the sky.

'Good news I hope,' Jamie said.

'Could be better, could be worse,' Jinx said, dropping down to sit cross-legged beside me. 'The Sicarii have set up in the caverns below this wasteland.'

'Below it?'

'If we travel due north we will come to a ring of stones; in its centre there is a slab of rock that once served as an altar and beneath the altar there should be a flight of stairs leading down into the caverns. Millennia ago it was a temple to the Fallen One. Now the Sicarii have resurrected it as their own.'

'Where better to hide than a place that is shunned by all daemonkind?' Jamie said.

'Why is it shunned?' I asked.

Shenanigans gave a shudder, which was mirrored by Kerfuffle. 'The worshippers of the Fallen One were creatures of the night,' Kerfuffle said. 'The nightwalkers believed in blood sacrifice. On the day they were finally outlawed and put to the sword, it was believed that their blood turned the earth surrounding their temple black and the plains were forever cursed.'

'Superstitious hogwash,' Jinx said.

'In the tale I heard, it was the Deathbringer that led the royal soldiers against them,' Kerfuffle said.

'I wouldn't believe all you hear,' Jinx said.

'Still—' Kerfuffle started to say, then saw Jinx's narrow-eyed stare and shut up.

'I'm actually wondering whether maybe the Sicarii and the nightwalkers are one and the same,' Jamie said.

'We saw them during the daylight hours,' Shenanigans said.

'They were creatures of the night only because they chose to be so,' Jinx said. 'Don't go believing all this nightwalker rubbish.'

Shenanigans and Kerfuffle exchanged a glance. 'Are you saying absolutely, categorically that the stories weren't true?' Kerfuffle asked.

'I am,' Jinx said.

Kerfuffle squinted at Jinx and Jinx looked straight back. 'Well, I've heard many stories about the Deathbringer and so far none of them have lived up to the myth, so I'll take you on your word.'

'So, it is possible that the Sicarii could be either survivors from the previous cult or have chosen to continue some of its practices?' I said.

Jinx rubbed his chin. 'The more I think on it, the more likely it seems.'

'The only difference is the Sicarii marketed themselves as assassins to make themselves appear more respectable,' Jamie said.

'Being an assassin is respectable?'

'Come on, Lucky. In your world there are contract killers who are considered, if not respectable, then certainly glamorous because they work for government agencies. Look at James Bond,' Jamie said.

'He's a fictional character.'

'Yeah, right. A fictional character allegedly based on the author's experiences within a government agency.'

'Hype, pure hype.'

'Do you understand what they're talking about?' Kubeck asked Shenanigans from behind his hand.

The huge daemon shook his head. 'Not a clue.'

'Now we know where their temple is, what's the point of Lucky leaving herself open to capture?' Jamie asked.

'Come now, wouldn't you be interested to find out why they're so keen to get their hands on her and what they intend when they do?' Jinx asked.

'It could be their intention to kill her slowly and horribly,' Kerfuffle said.

'But we won't let them. We'll be right behind her.'

'Jinx, what exactly has come over you? Why are you suddenly so willing to risk the life of one marked by both of us?' Jamie asked.

Jinx reached out and lifted my hair in his palm. 'She's daemon now. She's stronger, tougher, more powerful.'

'And scared shitless,' I said.

'Yet you say you will do Jinx's bidding and not mine,' Jamie said.

Typical that he should make this into some kind of macho one-upmanship thing. 'I'm not going to do anyone's "bidding" ' – I made quotation marks with my fingers – 'I'm going to do what-ever I think will get Kayla and Angela back safely, and – not to put too fine a point on it – save your world from Amaliel Cheriour.'

'Oh, so you're Superwoman now?'

I was very tempted to tell him to go forth and multiply, but he was an angel, whatever he might say. Anyway I didn't want Jinx thinking he'd scored points. He was far too confident that he could twist me around his arrow point tail as it was. 'Let's get moving,' I said getting to my feet.

'Perhaps we should camp here so we arrive at the temple in the full light of day?' Kerfuffle suggested as they all stood to join me.

'Still scared of nightwalkers?' Jinx asked with a smirk.

'No, I just want to make sure I can see my mistress if she follows your counsel and walks into the Sicarii stronghold alone and unprotected.'

'I won't let anything happen to your mistress,' Jinx said. 'She means more to me than you can possibly know,' and suddenly all eyes were on him and his expression became sheepish.

'Jinx?'

He ignored me, clearly embarrassed that he'd said more than he'd meant to. 'Come on,' he said as he started to walk away. 'Let's make for the ring of stones and see if we can find a good spot from where we can keep watch.'

We could see the circle of stones a good few miles before we reached them. Not only were they huge monoliths upon a mainly flat although rocky landscape, but they and the ground about them were death black, as the legend said.

Slightly to the east there was an outcrop of red rock, which was close enough for us to keep watch from, but not so close that we would be at risk of discovery. We circled around so we came at it from behind. That way, in the fading light, we wouldn't be seen from the temple if they had lookouts.

The outcrop was a good place to hide. It was actually three or four huge lumps of rock that had erupted out of the earth and plenty of nooks and crannies where we could lay in wait. The best hidey-hole was a large wedge-shaped crevice that directly over-looked the ring of stones below. It was large enough for all of us to sit quite comfortably, and had an overhang above so that we were sheltered from the elements.

Jinx had sent Bob off when we had started walking up from our landing site, so it was just the seven of us.

The two rising moons allowed quite a clear view of the circle of monoliths and I could see how abruptly the earth around them changed from blood red to black. It was most strange, as though someone had drawn a circle around the area.

'The whole place looks cursed,' Kerfuffle said with a shudder.

'It is rather creepy,' I agreed. 'How do you think they turned the earth and rock black?'

'I don't know, but it's a good way of scaring superstitious folk into keeping away,' Jinx said.

'I'm not superstitious, but even I'd think twice,' Kubeck agreed.

*

Darkness fell and the two moons rose fully into the sky, casting their orange glow across the rugged terrain. The circle of stones could have been huge lumps of coal bathed in fire. I glanced across at Jamie and Jinx. They were sitting side by side, staring out across the landscape, their expressions unreadable, which set me to thinking about what Kerfuffle had said. Had Jinx led the slaughter of the people who had worshipped here? He'd denied it, and although he could be mysterious and secretive, I didn't think he'd ever lied. But maybe he would about this? He'd seen my reaction to the massacre of the villagers, when I'd thought he might've done it. But the villagers had been innocent, and by all accounts the creatures who had worshipped beneath this plain had been anything but.

Then I thought about Kayla and the leaden feeling in the pit of my stomach got heavier and the steel corset about my chest grew tighter. Was she alive? Was she hurt? Was she scared? Then there was Angela, the poor little thing was probably terrified. And Vaybian: were they using him to control Kayla, or was he already dead; sacrificed to whatever deity they worshipped? Would I see his washed-out grey spirit when I entered the underground caverns? A ghastly thought crossed my mind. What if we were sitting here waiting for dawn while Vaybian was being horribly murdered? Panic surged through me and I could no longer sit and wait, I had to do something; anything.

I took quick look around me. Kerfuffle and Shenanigans were curled up with their heads resting on Pyrites' belly; Kubeck was sprawled out on his back and snoring; but Jamie and Jinx were both still awake and they were the ones I had to worry about. Jinx said he thought I should go in alone, that was his plan; his very odd plan, though I could see the method in his madness. I don't know why but I thought it was like he was testing me and, call me proud, I didn't want to be found wanting.

I climbed to my feet trying to appear nonchalant, but my heart was hammering so hard I was surprised they couldn't hear it.

'Where are you going?' Jamie asked as I walked to the ledge leading down to the ground below.

'Comfort break.'

'One of us goes with you.' He went to stand, but Jinx beat him to it.

'I don't need a babysitter, thanks.'

'You're not going anywhere on your own.'

'I'll avert my eyes,' Jinx said with a grin.

I gave an over-the-top sigh, said, 'You'd better mister,' and stalked off, guessing he would be right behind me.

When we had got almost to the ground and well out of Jamie's earshot I turned to face him. 'I'm going in now,' I said without any preamble.

'Why?'

'They could be murdering Vaybian as we speak.'

'When did he become so important to you?'

'He isn't, but Kayla is. Even so, I wouldn't want to find he'd been tortured to death overnight and we'd missed being able to help him by a few hours.'

'I can't let you go.'

'Why not? I thought that was the plan.'

He looked at me, his eyes sparkling gold in the moonlight, and I suddenly had another thought, 'Or were you just messing with Jamie's head?'

'It is – was – the plan, and my head tells me that it's the best way to get in there and find out what's going on, but my heart tells me something else completely.'

'I don't understand.'

'When we marked you we didn't realise what you were.'

'The Soulseer?'

'That's right. We are meant to be together. Together we are more powerful than you can possibly imagine, but you, you're powerful in your own right and we need to let you come into that power. We can't always protect you and I doubt you'd want us to. You're strong and independent and I want you to stay that way, because that's what makes me . . .' He stopped and looked down at his feet.

'Makes you what?'

He started fidgeting. 'If I let you go down into the Sicarii temple and it all goes wrong and you never come back, James would never forgive me.'

'Would you care?'

'Yes, because I'd never forgive myself.'

This was getting confusing. 'But you were all set to let me go before, what's changed your mind?'

'James changed my mind.'

'Jamie? How? I didn't see you talking.'

'We didn't. He did.'

'What did he say?'

Jinx shook his head. 'I can't tell you.'

'Shall I go and ask him?'

'Maybe you should.'

'Jinx, why must you *always* talk to me in riddles?'

He took a quick peek at my face then looked away. 'He said that if I didn't love you enough to keep you safe, I should let you go. And when I thought about that and letting you be his alone, I knew I couldn't do it.'

'So this is all about you not wanting Jamie to have me to himself?' I said in exasperation.

'No,' Jinx said, his voice barely a whisper. 'It's about me being *unable* to let you go – it would suck the warmth from my soul, and my soul has been so cold for so many years. I couldn't bear for it to be that cold again.'

I think my jaw dropped open. 'I don't know what to say.'

'Say you'll let us protect you,' he paused, his eyes searching mine, 'and promise me you'll never ask me to let you go.'

'Oh, Jinx,' I said, resting my palm against his chest. So warm, so solid; his heartbeat so steady.

Then my fingers were on fire and Jinx went rigid beneath my hand. Something warm and sticky ran down my wrist as Jinx sank to his knees. I looked at my hand, blood was pumping out from between my fore and middle finger and my palm was slick with blood; Jinx's blood mingling with mine.

'Jinx,' I whispered as he crumpled onto his side, an arrow sticking out of his back. 'Oh my God,' and I was about to scream Jamie's name when the back of my head exploded in pain and the whole world went black.

Eleven

I woke up to the Royal Marine Military Band marching up and down and round and around inside my head, banging the biggest drum I could possibly imagine. The right hand side of my face felt cold and numb and for one horrible moment the word 'stroke' floated through my mind and then I remembered Jinx collapsing to the ground and my heart froze.

I struggled to sit up and the world gave a lurch and began to spin. 'Oh God,' I groaned and then threw up. I kept on retching long after I'd emptied my stomach and until I was sure I was going to rupture something.

When I eventually stopped and managed to sit up straight, I wasn't particularly surprised to find myself in a black stone cell with wrist irons hanging from the wall. The solid, wooden door was banded with iron and had a small grill at about head height for someone a good few inches taller than me. *Well*, I thought, *I suppose this was Jinx's original plan*, and then my eyes filled up. He couldn't be dead, he was the Death Daemon for heaven's sake; you surely couldn't kill a Death Daemon. I'd been wrong about Pyrites; he'd been alive and well, and Jinx would be too.

Then I looked down and saw the cut in between my fingers and the blood on the palm of my hand and my eyes filled up again. I brushed the tears away, they wouldn't help anyone, least of all me. Anyway, I was a daemon and daemons didn't cry, at least not in this world. I looked at my hand again, my pink, human hand. Typical – now I needed to be strong and powerful I'd reverted to my puny human self. I took another look at the cut between my fingers where the arrow had pierced my skin. It was only a nick, yet it was still bleeding. Red blood; it was bleeding red blood and it had been bleeding red blood when Jinx had been shot. If I was Baltheza's daughter it would be blue.

'Oh crap,' I muttered to myself. Could my life get any more complicated?

I managed to crawl into the corner as far away from the pile of my vomit as I was able and wished I had some water to wash my mouth out – and wash Jinx's blood from my hand.

I slumped back against the wall. He would be all right. He would be. He had more or less just told me he loved me. Why hadn't he said the words damn him, then I would at least have that; the knowledge that he and Jamie loved me. Oh shit, this was such a mess.

The pounding in my head gradually subsided to a steady hangover throb and I built up the courage to touch the back of my skull, hoping it wasn't soft and squishy. It wasn't, and there was no more blood, so I supposed that was something.

With nothing to do but wait I began to mope and worry. What had happened to the rest of my friends? Were they locked up too? Were they dead? No, that wasn't an option. Wherever they were they were still alive. And how about Vaybian? I'd promised I'd come and find him. Being locked up *near* him was no help to him whatsoever. I wondered whether Kayla was in a similar cell to mine. Maybe it was she who was in the cell next door?

I lost all track of time, then dozed a bit – probably thanks to the head wound – and each time I opened my eyes I was disappointed to find it hadn't all been just a bad dream. Then I heard the slap of leather on stone as several pairs of feet approached, followed by the rattle of a key in the lock, and the door swung open.

Two brown-robed minions came in first and stood on either side of the door to allow a Sicarii in grey to enter. I didn't bother to get up.

'Awake, I see,' he said. I ignored him, and instead studied my hands that rested in my lap. 'Take her up.'

The two minions grabbed me by the upper arms and hauled me to my feet. The room shifted alarmingly and I would have fallen if they hadn't had such a tight hold on me, but the moment passed and my legs started working again as they marched me out of the cell. We walked along black stone passageways and up a flight of narrow stairs where I was sandwiched between the two minions at the front and back. As soon as we reached the top they grabbed hold of me again. They certainly weren't taking any chances.

The end of the final passageway opened up into a large cavern. Red light glowed from twelve braziers, which cast black flickering shadows, reminiscent of Native Americans doing a war dance, on the walls. At their centre was an altar similar to the one above ground, though set on a circular plinth and with two smaller braziers placed at either end. From the various implements plunged into the burning embers, I guessed these weren't for decoration.

Behind the altar stood six huge wooden crosses, very much like the ones the two Sicarii had been crucified on at Dark Mountain. I couldn't help but wonder who had thought up this method of execution first, and it struck me again that, whether man or daemon, both were capable of cruelty.

I had taken only a few steps into the chamber when the first of many spirits began to drift towards me. They moaned in desperation when they saw I was a prisoner. Several plucked at the sleeves of the two Sicarii holding me, their grey fingers passing through the material. Others threw punches at them, although they must have known it was useless.

The Sicarii in grey led the way, oblivious to the souls surrounding us. Or he may have been ignoring them, I supposed – they were nothing more to him than cattle to be drained of their essence. I wanted to tell them to be patient; I would help them when I could, but until I was absolutely sure the Sicarii knew I was a Soulseer I didn't want to reveal myself. I raised a finger to my lips, which was the best I could do without drawing my guards' attention.

To my relief, the two Sicarii led me past the altar and the

braziers to a room at the back. The grey-robed Sicarii opened the door and glided inside and I was forced to follow. Once in the chamber I wondered whether I should've just taken my chances with the braziers and the red-hot torture utensils, because, sitting behind a desk that filled half the room, was Amaliel Cheriour.

As if this wasn't bad enough, my other least favourite daemon Henri le Dent sat in the corner nursing his bandaged stump. Gone was his usual sneer. When he looked at me it was with undisguised animosity, his grotesque lips twisted in hatred. For the moment he didn't warrant my attention; Amaliel was another matter.

Red eyes burned from within his cowl and I shuddered inwardly, hoping I would never see what was hidden within the shadows of that hood.

'So nice of you to join us at last,' his voice brought to mind a snake slithering through autumn leaves. 'Having you brought here has proved to be more than a little tiresome.'

'You shouldn't have taken so much trouble. You knew we'd come anyway.'

'Hmm, I couldn't be too sure. You and the Lady Kayla aren't the friends you once were. Though I did hope you'd come, if not for her then for the child.'

'What do you want with me?' I could see no point in playing games.

'Leave us,' he said to the Sicarii.

'But, My Lord,' the Sicarii in grey said, 'surely it's not safe to leave you alone with this creature?'

'We have her sister, and I give you leave to put out the Lady Kayla's eyes with red-hot irons if this one tries to cause me harm.'

The Sicarii gave a little bow. 'My Lord,' he said and backed out of the door, followed by the two minions.

Once the door had closed behind them Amaliel gestured to the vacant chair opposite him. 'Please take a seat.'

I was about to refuse, but the old adage about cutting off one's nose to spite one's face came to mind, and as my head still had a couple of Royal Marines stomping around in there, I decided to accept the offer.

'After all this time I feel we should celebrate, but that will come later. Do you know how long I have been waiting for this moment?'

I crossed my arms and leaned back in the chair.

'Twenty-five years. From the moment you were born.'

I frowned at him. How . . .?

'The Soulseer: I never believed for one moment she would come, she was a creature of legend. Then you were born and your coming sent a shockwave from the human world into ours . . .'

Kayla had said much the same thing the day she had told me she was a daemon. I didn't say a word, I didn't want to distract him from this story – maybe I would finally get the truth.

'. . . Even so, I couldn't quite believe it. That you had been born into the human world was a surprise and made me doubt it could be true. I decided to see for myself, but as I have no jurisdiction in the Overlands I had to find a different way to you. Unfortunately, the Lady Kayla took things into her own hands. She shielded you – no sooner had I found you, than you were gone.'

'Did she know what I was?'

'Maybe, but she was probably more concerned that she had an illegitimate sister, then she took everyone by surprise and grew to care for you.'

Henri gave a derisive snort. 'She cares for no one but herself.'

'I think you have already been proven wrong on that.'

'We'll see.'

Amaliel's attention returned to me. 'I had to change my plans, so that when I eventually found you, I could bring you to the Underlands. Unfortunately, fate conspired against me and some-how the Guardian and Deathbringer became involved.'

'It was you who set up Philip Conrad.'

'So ambitious, so greedy; he was perfect. But he failed and I couldn't afford for him to be traced back to me, so I implicated the idiot Daltas. It wasn't difficult – he is always plotting and planning. All I had to do was say a word here, a word there, whisper suggestions in his ear; before long even *he* believed he'd been conspiring to bring Lady Kayla and her sister back to the Underlands.'

'So this has been your doing all along?' I said. 'And I suppose I needn't ask who's been poisoning Baltheza?'

'That imbecile,' Amaliel spat. 'He was slowly getting out of control, I just made sure it happened a whole lot quicker.'

'So, how was it going to work – you drive him mad, and then what? I don't know much about daemon royalty, but I'm pretty sure you're not in line for the throne.'

Amaliel chuckled, a disgusting, gurgling sound. 'With Baltheza declared insane and locked up for his own good, his legitimate daughter missing presumed dead, and his illegitimate daughter having also disappeared, the throne would be up for grabs.'

'And you'd be the one grabbing it?'

'The Sicarii would take control with me at their head.'

'So, I'll ask the question again – what do you want with me?'

'There is no place for the Soulseer in our new world.'

'Then why bring me back to the Underlands?'

'I had to be certain. At first, when I saw you, I was convinced I'd been mistaken. You were weak and puny. You appeared human. There was no possible way you could be the Soulseer of legend. Even so, I thought it best that you die. Then I touched you and I felt your power: your power, not just that of the Guardian and Deathbringer whose marks you bear, your power; the power of the Soulseer.'

There was a knock on the door: three short, sharp raps and I heard it open behind me.

'We're ready,' a voice said.

Amaliel bowed his head and the door closed. He laid the palms of his yellowed, skeletal hands on the table and pushed himself up from his seat. Henri also stood. I stayed where I was. I didn't want to go anywhere with either of them.

'You can come with us by your own volition or I can have my guards drag you.'

I hesitated a moment then got to my feet. If I was being held fast by two burly Sicarii I had no chance of escape, or cutting off Henri's other hand. Unescorted, I had a chance of eluding them both and trying to find Kayla and Angela. Henri opened the door and Amaliel gestured to me that I should go first.

I heard Kayla before I saw her. If she was hurt, it wasn't so badly that she couldn't berate her captors. She was letting rip with a steady stream of abuse that would probably have made a Chatham dockworker blush.

'You'll be sorry, you little shit, I'll make sure each and every one of you is sorry. I'll have your bollocks for bed socks and your dicks for doorstops.'

'Lady Kayla,' Amaliel said gliding past me, 'in fine fettle I see.'

I followed on behind him, desperate to see my friend. Until I saw the position she was in: both she and Vaybian were hanging from the crosses at the back of the chamber, and as I moved closer I could see she hadn't been tied there. Streams of blue ran from the centres of her palms and from her feet. I bunched my fists to my sides and clenched my teeth together. Somehow I was going to make Amaliel pay for this. I wasn't sure how, but I would. I glanced around the chamber, counting up the number of Sicarii present. There were three in grey close to my friend and her lover, plus five in brown in fairly close proximity to the altar; that was all, but it was enough, even if Vaybian and Kayla had been free and armed.

Kayla fell silent, looking around as she felt my presence and then saw me. 'Lucky?' she asked, and her face crumpled for a moment; then she began to fight against the nails holding her to the cross.

'Lady Kayla, please desist. You'll only hurt yourself,' Amaliel said, but I could hear the laughter in his voice, and if I'd still had my dagger I would have plunged it into his cold, black heart; no problem.

'Not as much as I'm going to hurt you, you putrid bag of pus,' she said, still struggling.

'Slit his throat,' Amaliel said, gesturing to Vaybian.

'No!' Kayla shrieked.

'Then behave.'

Kayla glared at him but stopped fighting against the nails pinning her to the cross.

I couldn't see her legs for her skirt, but I could see Vaybian's, and his feet were pushed flat against the posts, forcing his legs to bend outwards into what must have been a tortuous position, not forgetting the pain from the nails in his feet.

'Now then,' Amaliel said, 'we're going to play a little game. It's called truth or pain. The rules are simple: I will ask one of you a question and you'll give me a truthful answer. If you lie I'll inflict pain upon the other party. Understood?'

'Cretinous maggot,' was Kayla's reply.

'Lady Kayla,' Amaliel said, 'who do you love most – your sister or your lover?'

The snakes in Kayla's hair hissed and spat at Amaliel. 'I love them both, but the love I have for each of them is different. There can be no comparison.'

'I think there is. Who do you love most?' he asked and gestured with a nod towards the grey-robed Sicarii standing to Vaybian's right. The daemon glided over to one of the small braziers on the altar and selected a long, straight, poker-like utensil; its tip glowing almost white. Kayla watched him glide back to Vaybian and her lips pressed together into a thin line.

'I'm waiting.'

'My sister,' she whispered.

'I'm sorry?' Amaliel said, raising a hand as if to his ear. 'I didn't quite hear.'

'My sister.'

'Lucky?'

'Yes.'

'Is that true?'

'Yes.'

'You love her more than the Captain of your guard?'

'Yes,' she said, risking a glance Vaybian's way.

He gave her a smile. 'It's all right, I've always known it to be so.'

'Interesting,' Amaliel said, gesturing to the Sicarii holding the poker.

'It's the truth,' Kayla blurted out as he approached Vaybian, the poker extended towards her lover's exposed abdomen.

'So, Vaybian,' Amaliel said. 'If I asked who you'd rather suffer the pain of white hot metal upon flesh – you or your mistress – who would you say?'

'Me,' he said, without a moment's hesitation.

'How about you?' Amaliel asked, turning to me. 'Whose skin would you rather see sizzle and pop?'

'You are so totally disgusting I'm surprised you don't make yourself puke,' I said.

'That doesn't answer my question.'

'I'll answer yours when you answer mine. What do you want from me? It's clear you want something, otherwise you'd have killed me already.'

The spirits surrounding us moaned; some pressed their hands to their mouths, others wrung their hands.

'Do you want to hear your sister's lover scream and beg for mercy?'

'He won't,' I said.

'You think not? Maybe we should have a wager as to how long it would take until he pleaded for me to end his miserable existence?'

'You are vile.'

'Henri, maybe you would like to give me a hand with this?' The assassin glared at him. 'Sorry, that was insensitive of me, though I'm sure you would welcome a chance to exact a little revenge for your suffering.'

'Let me have her,' Henri said, gesturing towards me with his stump.

'Maybe later, but first things first.' He turned back to me. 'Who out of your sister and her lover do you want to see burn?'

'Neither.'

'You have to make a choice or I will scar them both.'

'I guess you never knew your father,' I said.

Red eyes blazed at me. 'Scar them both.'

'If you hurt either of them, I won't do whatever it is you want from me.'

He laughed out loud and Henri sniggered. 'My dear girl, of course you will,' and with that he strode across to the Sicarii holding the poker, snatched it from his hand and pressed the length of glowing metal across Vaybian's stomach. Kayla screamed, but Vaybian didn't. He screwed his eyes tight shut and his lips twisted into an agonised grimace, but not a sound came from him other than the sizzling of his skin. If I hadn't already thrown up the contents of my stomach the stench of burning flesh and the awful spitting sound of his searing skin would've had me vomiting again.

'Stop it,' Kayla cried out, 'stop it!'

Amaliel continued to press the metal against Vaybian's skin. 'Next time I will use the tip, and I will not stop until it has burned through flesh and muscle and has made a hole all the way through his torso and out the back.' Kayla let rip with another string of foul-mouthed abuse.

Amaliel looked up at her, laughing, and ripped the poker away from Vaybian's skin. This brought a little 'err' sound from the back of the green captain's throat. Amaliel handed the poker to the Sicarii. 'Bring me another,' he said, 'and let's see if the Lady Kayla can suffer in as much silence as her captain.'

'No,' Vaybian gasped. 'You hurt her and I'll—'

'You'll what?' Amaliel said, and Henri's mutilated lips twisted into a sneer.

I glared at the pair of them, thinking fast. Amaliel held all the cards and I had nothing to bargain with. Or did I? If nothing else, maybe I could cause a little mischief by playing the divide and conquer tactic. 'Why didn't you warn the Sicarii who came to take me that I was marked by the Deathbringer and Guardian?' I asked.

Amaliel stopped very still and the Sicarii standing beside Vaybian swung around to face him. 'What?' it hissed.

'I don't suppose he mentioned that I'm the Soulseer, either.'

Another hiss and this one was echoed by several of the other Sicarii spread throughout the chamber.

Amaliel strode around the altar and grabbed hold of my arm, his fingertips digging into me so hard I knew I'd have bruises where each of his fingers had been. 'You little bitch,' he said, his voice low so the Sicarii couldn't hear. 'When I've finished with you I'll have your tongue, but not before I've made you suck on a white hot ball of iron.'

Henri drew closer to Amaliel's side and peered at me over his shoulder. 'Perhaps you could stitch her eyelids together so she is forever in the dark.'

'Even better: cut them off so she can't shut out the torments I shall inflict upon her sister and the captain.'

I started to struggle, trying to pull out of his bony grasp, but it was impossible. 'See how she squirms,' Amaliel said.

'Maybe we should put her up there with her sister,' Henri said, gesturing with his stump towards the cross to Kayla's left.

A Sicarii appeared beside Amaliel and leaned in close, cupping his hand to whisper to him. Amaliel took a deep gurgling breath. 'Are you sure?'

'Yes Lord.'

His blazing eyes looked straight into mine for so long, I thought that if I closed them I'd still see his burned onto my retinas. 'Take her back to the cells.'

'What about them?' the Sicarii asked, jerking his head towards Kayla and Vaybian.

'Put Lady Kayla in my chamber of fun. He can stay where he is; I haven't finished with either of them yet.'

The Sicarii beckoned for two of the minions to come forward and Amaliel thrust me into their arms. 'Prepare her for a visit from me. I want to see if she is so brave without an audience.'

'No!' I heard Kayla cry, and although I struggled to look back I was marched away without being able to catch a glimpse of her.

Twelve

I think I would have preferred to have been taken back to the cell with the pile of vomit in the corner. My new accommodation had all the accoutrements of a torture chamber and I was shackled by both wrists to a chain hanging from the wall. The chain was long enough that I could sit on the floor, but kept me just far enough away from anything that could potentially be a weapon – like the very sharp-looking knives, metal pincers and long-handled branding irons lying on a solid wooden bench on the other side of the cell. There were other instruments that were even more scary, and I was rather glad I had no idea what they were for, although my overactive imagination was having a field day.

I sat down and waited, not knowing which was worse: wondering what was happening to Kayla and Vaybian, or hearing the sound of footsteps in the corridor.

I was cold and uncomfortable, but there was nothing to be done. The shackles were solid and uncompromising. They weren't locked by a key; instead a nut and bolt held each cuff together. I tried again and again to undo the nuts, but they were too tight. The Sicarii had tightened them with pliers, and if they could hold a fully-grown daemon the size of Shenanigans or Kubeck, what chance did I have?

I waited and waited, but nothing happened. Then, just as I was on the verge of dozing off through sheer exhaustion, Kayla screamed. Not out loud – I'm sure she didn't give Amaliel the satisfaction – I heard her inside my head. Again and again she screamed, and each time a little piece of me died, because that was how she was feeling: that a little piece of her was dying with each scream. I didn't know what it meant. But I did know that if I had the chance I was going to do serious damage to Amaliel Cheriour.

Once again I started to work on the nuts and bolts holding my shackles together. I worked on them until my fingers were slick with blood and I had to give up as I couldn't get a firm grip. So I tried making my hands as small as I could and forcing them out of the cuffs, but there was no way this was going to happen. I have small hands, but the cuffs were even smaller. It made me wonder whether sometimes they kept children in this awful place; I guessed they probably did.

Kayla's screams stopped. She was distraught; I could feel her pain, but I'm sure that wherever she was she was holding it in, too proud to let Amaliel see. Unfortunately it didn't stop me feeling it.

Footsteps in the corridor that stopped outside my room announced a visitation, *my turn?* I wondered. The door opened and two brown-robed Sicarii entered followed by another in grey. Once he was inside he waved for the two minions to leave.

He stood looking at me for what seemed an age. I couldn't see his eyes or other features; like Amaliel, the Sicarii in grey kept their faces bathed in shadows and I suspected there was good reason for this. Any creature so evil they could torture, murder and then curse their victims with an eternal half-existence must have their awful cruelty etched upon their souls, so it wouldn't surprise me if their faces were similarly marked.

'So,' he said with a voice like he had a wet fur ball stuck in his throat, 'the rumours are true.' I leaned back against the wall and ignored him. 'You've been marked by both the Deathbringer and Guardian.' Again I ignored him. I'm a firm believer in the old adage 'if you haven't anything sensible to say, keep quiet', perhaps it was a tip I should share with him.

He wandered over to the bench and stared down at the various pieces of metalwork. If he thought this would scare me he was right, but I set my expression into what I hoped was a nonchalant, disinterested look.

'And you say Amaliel knew this before he sent us to capture you?' Now he had my attention. This wasn't about me; this was to do with Amaliel.

I looked up at him. 'Of course he knew. Everyone at Lord Baltheza's court knew.'

He let out a low hiss and I wondered what would happen if he removed his hood; perhaps it would reveal the countenance of a snake? I rather hoped I'd never find out.

'And you are the Soulseer?'

'So I'm told.'

'You have seen the dead here?'

Now I was puzzled, but I tried not to let it show. 'Of course.'

Another low *hiss*. 'Tell me, how do they appear?'

'Vulnerable, scared and angry – very angry.' I'd let him stick that in his pipe and smoke it. Let him be afraid for once.

He gave a snort that sounded more like a whistle through congested sinuses. 'Angry, but unable to act.'

I curled my lips into a half smile. 'Maybe, maybe not.'

Hiss. 'What do you mean?'

I looked away and began to fiddle with the cuffs of my shirt. 'In my experience the dead can sometimes make their presence felt.'

'No, not these dead,' he said, but he didn't sound so sure.

'We'll see,' I told him.

'Amaliel said,' he hesitated and took a few steps towards me, 'Amaliel said you were lying.'

'About what?'

'Being the Soulseer.'

'Why would I do that?'

'He said you were trying to cause disquiet amongst us. He said you were trying to make us distrust him.'

I let out a small ripple of laughter. 'He seems to be doing a pretty good job of that all by himself.'

Another *hiss*. 'I think you're dangerous.'

I looked up at him and gave him a full-on bitch smile. 'You'd be right, and sadly for you I'll apparently be even more dangerous when I'm dead.' I didn't want him getting ideas when he had so many sharp instruments close to hand.

'How *sssso*?' It sounded like I'd rattled him.

'I'm the emissary of the dead, you figure it out.'

There was a noise in the corridor outside and his head snapped around to face the door. Keys rattled in the lock and the door swung open, revealing a brown-robed Sicarii. He held the door wide, his message clear; get out now. The Sicarii in grey gave me a brief backward glance and left, the door shutting with a solid clunk behind him. The keys rattled again and I heard the drawing of bolts. They were certainly taking no chances with me, and it did make me wonder – not for the first time – if being the Soulseer was a bigger deal than I'd thought. Jinx *had* been on the brink of telling me something before he . . . Before he'd been shot.

I closed my eyes and took a deep breath. I couldn't think about that, I just couldn't, not now. I had to concentrate on the problem at hand, which was getting myself, Kayla and Vaybian out of this bloody place and to safety. And where was Angela? I had to find her too. All well and good in theory, but being shackled in irons, chained to a wall in a double-locked cell did limit my options somewhat. Though, if the Sicarii were at odds with Amaliel maybe I could use this to my advantage – if I got the chance.

First things first: what I needed was something to help me get the bloody metal bracelets off my wrists. I glanced across at the wooden bench and got to my feet to take a better look. I crossed the room as far as the chain would let me, but the bench was well out of reach and my hands were being pulled to one side and back behind me. I tried stretching out one leg, but even standing on tiptoe with my leg extended as far as it would go I was nowhere near. I wasn't sure even Shenanigans could have reached if he were here, and he was a good foot and a half, maybe even two feet taller than me.

I slumped down and leaned against the wall – back to square one. I made another half-hearted attempt to undo one of the nuts from the bolts connecting the shackles, but only made my fingers bleed again – red blood.

I fell back to contemplating my alleged heritage. I wasn't bleeding blue blood, like Kayla would. And her blood was truly blue, a

deep sea blue. And this was the thing: if I was her sister and
Baltheza's daughter, my blood would also be blue. It put me in a
rather precarious position. One: Baltheza would be pissed. Two:
Kayla would probably be pissed, meaning that two of the most
important people in the Underlands could become my enemies.
Baltheza might, because he had probably been cuckolded and I
couldn't imagine that would go down well – even though my
mother wasn't his wife – and Kayla might because she had believed
me to be her sister and loved me accordingly. Then again – Kayla
must have known my blood was red – we'd grown up together. Of
course, I had been disguised as a human – maybe red blood was
part of the disguise?

All this conjecture was making my poor head ache even more. I
couldn't worry about things that wouldn't be important if I didn't
manage to get myself out of this mess. And sister or not, I had to
get Kayla and her green captain out of it with me.

I doubt that even ten minutes went by before I heard someone
coming. Probably a couple of the minions; Amaliel and the grey
Sicarii glided everywhere they went and didn't make a sound . . . I
wondered whether this was something they practised or whether
it was a skill awarded to you upon joining the Truly Evil Club.
'You are now pronounced Truly Evil and may you forever glide
from place to place'. Then, as the key turned in the lock, I wondered if I was finally losing it.

The door opened and Amaliel entered. Two daemons built like
sumo wrestlers – and wearing as little clothing – were with him.
Both were a fake suntan orange and their skin glistened as if freshly
oiled, and both had jet black hair tied in a single braid that almost
reached their hips; I would have said waists, but they were far too
rotund to have them. There, the similarities ended. One had
almost no nose, just two nostrils in a pig-like stump, and beady
little eyes. The other had a Harris Hawk beak and eyes to match.
He even had a smattering of feathers across his cheeks and where
his eyebrows should have been.

As mesmerising as they were, it was Amaliel who had my

attention as he moved straight to the wooden bench, his right hand hovering over the utensils as if trying to make up his mind which to pick up first. Fear shot through me and I prayed that I'd be brave, though in my heart I knew I could never be as stoic as Vaybian. Amaliel would only have to squeeze my fingers in on themselves and I'd probably yelp. If he had a red hot poker in his hand I'd tell him anything he wanted to know – and probably make up stuff to make him go away. Fortunately they hadn't brought a brazier with them, but I wasn't holding my breath that one wouldn't be rolled in if he wanted.

'Unchain her.'

Hawkman pulled a pair of pliers from the belt of his loincloth and began to work on undoing the bolt through the cuff on my right hand. Once he had freed it, he started on the other.

I resisted the urge to rub my wrists when he had finished. Instead, I crossed my arms and tried to look badass.

'Bring her here,' Amaliel commanded and both daemons grabbed me by the upper arms and forced me over to the bench. He gave a nod towards the daemon to my left. Pigface grabbed hold of my wrist and held my hand out in front of me. Amaliel's palm moved across the bench and then stopped above a double bladed instrument similar to a pair of small agricultural shears.

'Do you play a musical instrument?' he asked. I shook my head. I couldn't speak. If I'd tried it would have come out as a squeak. 'Pity,' he said, taking my hand and rolling my fingers into a fist except for my little one.

I tried to pull away from him, but the two daemons could have been blocks of stone. He moved the shears until the blades were positioned just below my finger nail and above the first knuckle. I knew what was coming and I steeled myself. I wouldn't scream. I would *not* scream.

He reached out and took hold of my chin and raised my head so he could look me in the eyes. 'Now, listen to me very carefully. I want you to remember how this feels. I want you to remember the pain. Do you understand?' He made that awful gurgling sound I now knew to be laughter, paused to study me and then said, 'Yes, I think you do.' He moved my head again so I was looking down at my hand. 'Keep your eyes open. If you don't, I will work my way through each of your digits until you do.'

I stared at my little finger and the two blades surrounding it. He wasn't going to do it, was he? Of course he was. He loved this. It made him feel powerful.

I didn't scream, but my legs gave way beneath me and I would have fallen if it wasn't for the two daemons holding me. As it was I watched in awful fascination as the tip of my finger dropped to the floor and blood pumped from where it had once been. Then it began to hurt and I only just managed to hold back the whimper building up at the back of my throat.

'Hmm, interesting,' he said, bending down to pick up my fingertip and examining it. 'I think I'll give this to Henri. It mayn't be as satisfying to him as your hand, but perhaps I can oblige later – with your head.'

He pulled a piece of linen out of his robe and handed it to me. 'You had better staunch the blood; I don't want you bleeding to death. Where would be the fun in that? Now, I am going to take you to see your . . . I would have said sister, but I'm wondering now if this is the case. You're certainly no child of Baltheza's.'

I clutched the linen to my ruined finger and wrapped it around the bleeding end the best I was able. I didn't dare look at it, as I knew without a doubt that if I saw the bone sticking out I would either faint or be sick. Both probably.

They marched me along the corridor and through another couple of doors until we reached a door with a grill at the top. Amaliel peered inside and laughed again.

'Now, remember the pain of losing the tiny little bit of flesh and bone at the tip of your finger and the pain you are feeling now.'

I licked my lips. What was he trying to tell me? What had he done to Kayla? Oh God, what had he done to her?

He opened the door and gestured for me to go in first. It was very similar to my cell except the chamber was divided in two by iron bars stretching across its width. Behind the bars there was a bed, and huddled up in the corner of the bed was a figure.

My heart was hammering, what had he done to her?

'Lady Kayla, I have brought your sister to see you.'

She stiffened and then gradually raised her head. 'Oh my God,' I murmured to myself and took a step towards her.

'Lucky?' her voice was a tremulous whisper.

I took another step toward the cage and she got to her feet and walked towards me to grip hold of the bars. She lifted her chin up high as she glanced Amaliel's way.

'Oh, Kayla,' I said, and my voice broke. Now I knew why he had cut the tip off my finger. He had shorn her head. Her beautiful locks were now messy clumps of green and red interspersed with the limp bodies of the vipers that had grown from her scalp. Blue blood still leaked from the lifeless stumps staining what was left of her hair.

I crossed to her and she took hold of my right hand through the bars. I kept my left hidden behind my back. I didn't want her to see; compared to what he had done to her it was nothing.

'I'm all right,' she said, 'it'll grow again.'

I wanted to ask, 'what about the vipers?' but I didn't. I didn't want to hear she had lost them forever. It would have been too hard for both of us.

'Now,' Amaliel said, 'this is how it will be. You' – he pointed a bony finger at my chest – 'will do whatever I say, whenever I say it, or your sister and her lover will pay in body parts. Do you understand me?'

I nodded.

'Do you understand?'

'Yes. Yes, I understand.'

'Good.'

'Vaybian,' I said. 'Can I see him?'

'If you wish,' and he gestured for me to leave the cell.

I squeezed Kayla's hand and mouthed the words, 'I'll be back to get you.'

She mouthed back, 'be very careful.'

Then I left her and it had never been so hard.

Vaybian was in the next cell, an identical one to Kayla's. He was sprawled out on his back across a bed in the corner of the room. As soon as we came in he swung his legs off the bed and got to his feet.

'What did you do to her you *bastard*?' Vaybian said. 'I know you did something.'

'She's all right,' I said, but as soon as he saw my face he knew I was lying.

'What did he do to her?'

I felt my eyes filling up and brushed the tears away with a swipe of my hand. I had to be strong. I just had to be. 'He cut off her hair.' I took a deep breath. 'You know.'

The look on his face was awful, and if I hadn't known it before I knew it now: he loved her with all of his heart. The pain he was feeling for her was palpable.

'One day I am going to kill you,' Vaybian said to Amaliel.

'You'll have to join the queue,' I said.

Amaliel only laughed. 'I very much doubt you will leave these caverns alive. For one thing, your wellbeing relies on this one,' he said gesturing to me. 'Every time she disobeys me or displeases me, you or Lady Kayla will pay in blood, and I'm a very exacting master – it won't be long before there'll be a pile of the bloody bits and pieces I'll take from you.' Vaybian looked at Amaliel with the same disgust and hatred as I was feeling towards him.

My finger was throbbing, I was tired, I was scared and my heart ached; for Kayla, for Vaybian, and most of all for my men. I wondered where they were. Was Jinx all right? And if so, would he and the others be coming for me soon? If they weren't then there was no help to be had and it was down to me, Kayla and Vaybian to save ourselves and Angela. As for Philip, I'm afraid he was on his own. As Jamie had pointed out, I wasn't Superwoman.

Hawkman and Pigface led me from the cell and we followed Amaliel back along the corridors – passing my last room – until we reached the huge main chamber. Amaliel glided to the centre and climbed up onto the plinth supporting the altar. Except for the four of us the hall was empty.

'Tell me, Soulseer,' Amaliel said, raising his hands and gesturing around the chamber, 'what do you see?'

As tempting as it was to make some flippant reply, I didn't dare. I didn't want any of us to lose any more body parts. I glanced around me. 'I see a large empty hall.'

'No spirits?'

'Not at the moment, but no doubt they'll come when they realise I'm here.'

He turned to face me, his red eyes burning into me. 'You seem very sure of yourself.'

'If I know nothing else, I do know the dead. They've been around me since the moment I was born.' And sure enough, the first of the spirits began to drift out from the shadows as I spoke.

'You must escape,' they whispered.

'I think you can let go of me now,' I said to the two sumo wrestlers, 'I won't be going anywhere.'

They both glanced at Amaliel who gestured with a wave of his hand for them to release me. I took a step away from them and turned so neither Amaliel nor his two stooges could see my lips and mouthed the words 'Can you help me?' to the spirits.

'Help you, help you,' their voices chanted, but could they?

I mouthed something again. 'Can you leave this place?'

'Never, never, never,' reverberated through my head.

'What do you see now?' Amaliel asked, jerking my attention back to him.

'The dead.' I could see no point in lying.

'And what do they tell you?'

'That they want to be free.'

He laughed and I felt something deep inside of me stir and my body began to warm as anger coursed through me, making my chest and throat ache with the tension of holding it in.

'They'll never be free. They'll remain here for all eternity until they're barely more than a puff of breeze on the air.'

The spirits moaned, but none approached him. Even in death they feared Amaliel, though I had no idea what else he could possibly do to them. Several drifted towards me, but stayed out of reach. I tried to smile at them to put them at their ease, but I found it very hard.

'You mustn't give up,' one said. She was tall and slight with horns on her brow and a severe overbite caused by a top jaw of very sharp, pointed teeth. Then she added, 'We will never give up.'

And then it hit me. That was what I was doing: I was letting my despair sink into my heart and bones. It was going to be hard, no doubt about it, but if I gave up Amaliel would win.

I closed my eyes and inside my head I whispered, 'talk to me.'

And they did.

As soon as Amaliel realised something was happening over which he had no control he dragged me from the hall. But it was too late. I now knew the way out of the temple and why my men had not yet come to save me: they thought the way in was through an entrance beneath the altar up top. The Sicarii had destroyed that doorway a very long time ago after carving other passageways beneath the plain. Those passageways exited outside the black circle surrounding the monoliths. When they had taken me, they had dragged me into such a passageway directly beneath the rock where we had set up our camp. Even though my guards would have acted immediately, it would have still been too late; I'd already gone.

Communing with the spirits had been a weird sensation. At first it had felt like a soft breeze was caressing my skin, then as though that breeze was passing through my flesh and bones and swirling around inside me. Then came the knowledge. I saw through their eyes and their memories. As well as showing me the way out, they'd shown me where Amaliel rested his head. They'd also told me something very interesting: although the Sicarii had cursed the dying, binding them forever to the temple, they couldn't see the spirits all the time, only when they performed their rituals to consume power from the captive souls.

The spirits had also told me why the Sicarii harvested that power. At first they had used it to gain the ability to walk unseen among the living. Then they began to believe that one day, when they had absorbed enough energy, they would have power over death and the ability to cross over from this world to the hereafter at will.

'And will they?' I'd asked, but I'd been dragged away before they could answer.

They put me in a new cell, which was slightly more comfortable in that I had a thin mattress to lie on. The toilet was a deep, black hole in the corner that stank to high heaven. It was covered by a grating, but I don't think even the most desperate of souls would have used it as a route for escape.

The only light came from a torch outside in the passageway, so once the door slammed shut behind me I was in almost total darkness – apart from the small patch of light coming through the grill at the top of the door. There was no mention of food or water and, as I guessed it wasn't his intention that I starve to death, I reckoned something would be brought to me soon.

I slumped down on the mattress. I was going to have to free myself in order to follow the spirits' escape route. At least I knew where Kayla and Vaybian were; I had no idea where Amaliel was keeping Angela and neither did the spirits, which made me wonder – was she here at all?

Sitting alone in the dark with nothing to think on but the fates of those I loved and how inadequate I felt was not conducive to bucking my ideas up, and my brief period of gung ho 'I'll show Amaliel bloody Cheriour' was dwindling away fast.

I got to my feet and walked over to the door to peer out of the grill. I had to stand on tiptoes and grip onto the bars, which was difficult when my throbbing left hand screamed for mercy every time I tried to flex it. It was hardly worth the effort. As far as I could tell the passageway outside was empty, though my arc of vision was pretty limited. I dropped down and leaned back against the door. The inactivity was driving me nuts. I needed to be doing something – anything.

They do say be careful what you wish for.

There was a creak of the door along the corridor and a thud of footfall, which had me immediately wishing I'd be left alone.

I shifted to one side of the door, pressed myself flat against the wall and waited. The footsteps stopped, keys clinked, bolts were drawn and the door swung open with a squeal of hinges. A Sicarii stepped inside, lamp held high. I glanced out through the open door. Two minions waited outside, backs to the door. I risked them turning and seeing me as I moved across, reached out and pushed the door shut. The Sicarii turned on me with a hiss.

I leaned back against the door. He lowered the lamp slightly, but not before I saw a glint of something within his cowl; his eyes maybe.

'What do you want?' I said.

'I had to leave before I got my answers.'

'Scared Amaliel might catch you talking to me?' I was goading him, but if I riled him enough he might let something slip, or make a mistake I could use to my advantage.

'I do not fear him.'

'Yeah, right.'

He took a step towards me. 'Your life hangs in the balance – to have me as an enemy could tip the scales.'

'Do you really think that killing the Soulseer with all these spirits hanging around would work out well for you? I don't think so.'

'You're talking in riddles.'

'No, I'm telling it how it is.'

'With you dead there'll be no one to thwart our plans. There'll be no one to release them.'

'So why is Amaliel planning on keeping me around?' I asked, forcing a sunny smile onto my face. He lifted the lamp slightly to study my expression. 'Well?'

'He said . . .' he hesitated.

'He said what?'

'He said you were to be sacrificed.'

'Then why did he go to such great lengths to threaten me?' I said, lifting up my left hand wrapped in the bloodstained linen.

'Show me,' he said, taking a step closer.

I hugged my hand to my chest. 'No thanks.'

'I said show me,' and a dagger appeared in his hand.

I took a deep breath and extended my hand, but not by far; if he wanted to look at it he could come to me. He took another step, and with the tip of the dagger lifted the edge of the material encasing my hand.

'Unwrap it.'

'No, it's stuck to the wound and I don't want to make it start bleeding again.'

He gave a *hiss*, put the lamp down onto the floor and reached out to grab my arm. As he did I grabbed the wrist of the hand holding the dagger, stepped in close and kneed him as hard as I could through his flowing robe.

He grunted, doubling up as I took a firmer grip of his knife arm with my other hand and brought his forearm down hard across my knee with all the force I could. He yelped and the knife dropped to the floor. I let go of his arm and, putting a hand on each of his shoulders, pushed down, bringing my knee up and straight into his face. There was a crack and I felt something give, but I couldn't be squeamish. This was my one and only chance and I had to finish it before the boys outside realised something was up. If they'd heard anything at all they'd hopefully assumed it was me being beaten. I brought my knee up again and he collapsed on the floor with barely a groan.

I glanced around looking for the dagger and snatched it up, then pointed it at his prone body. If I was in his position I would play dead, so I wasn't taking any chances. I gave him a hefty kick and he didn't make a sound.

Now came the nasty part. If I were to get out of the cell and past the two minions, I'd have to be in disguise, which meant removing his robe and seeing what was underneath it. I took one deep breath, two deep breaths, then bent down and began to search about his robes for a fastening. It was easier said than done: it had no opening down the front and had to be lifted up over his head.

I gripped the hem and began pulling at it until I got it to his armpits at the front, then grabbed an arm and rolled him onto his side, pulling it up at the back. To my relief he was wearing an undershirt and knee length breeches underneath. Even so, I saw more of him than I wanted to. Desiccated flesh the colour of ashes covered his skinny arms and legs, and scabby patches of what looked like blackened mould clung to his skin. I really so did not want to have to look at his face. When I had the robe off his arms and rolled up to his neck I hesitated. I took two more deep breaths then heaved the robe up over his head. I tried not to look, but at the same time found it hard to keep my eyes from wandering up to his face.

I pushed the knife into my waistband, picked up the robe and, despite not wanting anything that had touched his skin resting against mine, pulled it over my head. He wasn't much taller than me so the hem skimmed the ground, and I thought by taking small, quick steps I could maybe give the appearance of gliding. Hopefully the minions wouldn't be watching me too closely. I turned to pick up the lamp and as I straightened I caught a glimpse of the back of his head. The thought of what the hood I was wearing had so recently rested against made me shudder: his scalp was completely hairless, and like his arms and legs a wrinkled grey. A large patch of the mouldy substance covered the crown of his head and just above his collar was an open sore, shiny and yellowing. It was almost as though he was rotting. I turned my head away; I didn't want to see anymore.

I walked to the door and, keeping my head down, pulled it open and closed it behind me, hoping the minions wouldn't look inside. One immediately stepped forward with the keys while the other threw both the bolts across. I walked away taking quick baby steps and hoped it was giving the appearance I was looking for.

I heard the minions following behind me, and if they noticed anything out of the ordinary they didn't say. When we reached the cavern containing the altar one of the minions called to me.

'Master, do you need us any longer?' I turned so I was sideways on to them and shook my head.

They both gave small bows and hurried off, leaving me alone. It was then that I began to tremble. I gripped my hands together, remembering my mutilated finger too late. I winced and it began to throb again.

I had no time to dawdle. I glanced around to make sure I was alone and hurried across the chamber to the passageway Kayla and Vaybian were imprisoned within.

I went straight to her cell, almost running through the empty corridors. The outer door wasn't locked; there was no need for that as she was behind bars within the cell. She looked up as soon as I walked in, but didn't move from where she was sitting on the bed. I threw back the hood as I hurried towards her.

'Lucky?'

Where's the key?' I asked, looking around the room.

'Amaliel has it.'

'Damn and blast.'

'Where did you get the robe?'

'Off a Sicarii who was stupid enough to try and question me on his own.'

'Did you kill him?'

'I don't think so.'

'You should have.'

'He's unconscious.'

'But probably not for long. You've got to get out of here.'

'Not without you.'

'Well, unless you can find a way of getting the key off Amaliel you're going to have to.'

'I know where he sleeps.'

Kayla laughed. 'I don't think he ever does.'

'I can search his room for the key.'

'Don't be stupid, you'd get caught, and anyway he keeps it on a chain around his neck.'

'Crap.'

'Lucky, you must go – now, while you have the chance.'

'If I leave you and Vaybian he'll kill you.'

'I doubt it. He'll be needing us for if he catches you again.'

'He'll hurt you.'

'And when you come and get us with your Guardian and Death-bringer you will hurt him.'

'I will kill him.'

She gave me a smile. 'No you won't.'

'I will,' I told her, 'I bloody will.'

She reached out through the bars and took my hand. 'I want you to be safe,' she said. 'That's all I've ever wanted.'

'Kayla,' I said, knowing there wasn't time for questions but having to ask anyway, 'when you came to me, when I was a child, did you know I was the Soulseer?'

A strange expression passed across her face. 'No, I had my suspicions, but no, not at first.'

'Why did you come? Was it to protect me or was it to kill me?'

She met me eye to eye. 'You were so very little, not big at all really. I towered over you in my full daemonic glory waiting for you to recoil in horror, waiting for you to scream. Do you know what you did?' I shook my head. I couldn't speak, she *had* come to kill me. 'You reached out with your chubby, little arms and smiled up at me. Really smiled. I picked you up and held you, knowing I should crush the life out of you. And then you put your head against my shoulder and your arms around my neck and snuggled up under my chin. From that moment I was smitten and I knew I had to protect you from the others who would no doubt come for you.'

'Kayla,' I said squeezing her hand.

'Now, you must go.'

'I can't.'

'You can and you must. Don't you see? This isn't about me and Vaybian, this is about saving our world. Imagine what it would be like if Amaliel became ruler. My father is barbaric and cruel, but it's what Amaliel has made him.'

'In more ways than you know,' I said.

'Lucky, please go. Please do this for me.'

I nodded, my heart aching. She was right. 'I will go, but I'll be back and then together we are going to kick Sicarii butt and send Amaliel somewhere he can never hurt anyone again.'

Thirteen

It had been so hard walking out of the chamber and leaving her behind. I'd looked back as I'd opened the door and she'd given me a big smile, and even with hair shorn in messy lumps she was still beautiful.

I'd hurried along the corridors expecting a hand to reach out and grab me by the shoulder at any moment, but I'd reached the main hall without seeing a single daemon. This changed before I had even taken two steps into the main cavern: two brown-robed minions were at work by the altar, filling the braziers with charcoal from hessian sacks, but they'd only glanced up briefly before returning to what they were doing. I'd held my head up, pulled my cowl forward and walked across the cavern hoping my quick, little steps were doing the business. I'd waited for the shout of 'stop!' and the sound of pounding feet as they'd chased after me, but none had come, and then I'd been surrounded by spirits hurrying along with me, guiding me to the passageway.

'Through here, through here,' they'd called and I was out of the hall and in the narrow passage to freedom.

As soon as I stepped out into the fresh air I realised why there weren't many Sicarii about: judging by the positions of the two suns it was mid-morning. I threw the grey robe over my head and to the ground, hoping I hadn't picked up some disgusting disease from the putrefying creature I had stolen it from, then glanced around looking for a landmark I recognised. Over to my right the blackened monoliths rose up out of the landscape and beyond them the red stone rocks where we had hidden. I doubted my friends would still be there, but it was a good place to begin.

I started across the plain hoping I would quickly find my friends and they'd all be well. I didn't dare let myself think otherwise.

Then, in my head I saw Jinx sinking to his knees and keeling over to one side, an arrow in his back, the tip protruding through his chest. I raised my right hand. The nick between my fingers from the arrow tip had crusted over and I could still see traces of his blood ingrained into my skin. He had to be all right.

I was out in the open with little shelter and nowhere to hide, expecting the alarm to be raised at any moment and a swarm of brown-robed minions to appear from beneath the plain. Then a shadow passed above me and one of the two men I now knew I loved dropped down in front of me, his wings spread wide.

'I do so wish you would stop doing that,' he said.

'What?' I said, confused.

He didn't reply. Instead, he pulled me into his arms and wrapped his wings around me, making me feel safe and protected.

'For the second time in only a few short days I thought I'd lost you,' he said, his hand cupping the back of my head and his lips grazing my hair.

'Jamie,' I said and I had to swallow back tears, 'Jinx? Is he – all right?'

Jamie leaned back to look at my face. 'If it hadn't been for the arrow through his chest I would have killed him myself for letting you be taken again.'

'He's dead?' I said. I didn't think I was capable of drawing another breath.

Jamie smiled, showing teeth. 'Don't be silly. He's probably very sore, not that he'd admit it, but he'll be back to normal in a day or so. Maybe even sooner now we have you back. We've all been beside ourselves.'

And suddenly I could breathe again. 'You couldn't find the way in?' I managed to say.

He shook his head. 'The old entrance had been completely blocked.'

'We have to get back inside,' I told him, 'they have Vaybian and Kayla and I'm scared of what Amaliel might do to them.'

'Come on,' Jamie said, 'I'll take you somewhere safe where we can make plans.' Then he kissed me, a soft chaste kiss on the cheek, wrapped me in his arms and took me up into the sky.

As I had thought, they had moved camp. This time to a higher rock a lot further from the Sicarii temple; there was no way they could creep up on us here, and I doubted they had tunnelled this far out. Shenanigans and Kubeck were on guard duty, and upon seeing me both their worried frowns were replaced with relieved smiles.

'Mistress, I am so pleased to see you safely returned to us,' Shenanigans said.

'I'm glad to see you too,' I told him.

Jamie showed me inside what was to be our temporary home, and before I had hardly taken a couple of steps Pyrites, the size of a large dog, wrapped himself around my ankles and puffed steam in excitement, pushing his head up under my hand to be petted.

'He's been moping,' Kerfuffle said, 'and he's not the only one.' He jerked his head towards the back of the cave.

I gave Kerfuffle's shoulder a squeeze as I passed him to go to where Jinx was lying down, stretched out on a bed of pelts and skins.

'You found her then,' Jinx said to Jamie, and his face creased into a huge smile.

I dropped down onto my knees beside him. 'Are you all right? I thought you were dead. You looked dead. I was so—' I stopped and drew breath before I made a complete fool of myself.

'He'll be fine in a day or two,' Jamie said from behind me.

'I'm fine now,' Jinx said, 'especially since you've come back to us.'

He pushed himself up into a sitting position and in doing so the covers slipped, showing his muscular chest wrapped in a white bandage, stark against his shiny, maroon skin.

'I think the patient deserves a kiss,' he said, puckering his lips and pointing to them. I shuffled on my knees to get closer and leaned in to kiss him. I had been planning on a gentle touching of lips – I should have known better. Before I knew it, I was wrapped in his arms and he was giving me a full-on kiss which involved tongues and set my heart pounding and the rest of my body quivering.

'Jinx,' I heard Jamie say and I didn't need to see his face to tell he was getting pissed off.

Jinx's lips stayed locked on mine for a few moments longer and I'd started to see stars and feel very light-headed before he let me go. 'Keep that thought,' he whispered in my ear before kissing me on the cheek.

'You're obviously feeling better,' Kerfuffle said with a huff.

'Our lucky lady has returned to us, of course I'm feeling better.' Then his brow creased into a frown. 'Did something happen to your hand?'

'What?'

'I . . . I felt . . . I felt,' he frowned at me and looked downwards at my fists. 'Something *did* happen to your hand.'

I put it behind my back. 'Nothing,' I said. 'It's nothing really.'

Jamie dropped down to his knees beside me and gently took hold of my hand, lifting it up so he and Jinx could see. The linen was no longer white. Large blotches of red stained the fabric along with smudges of grime. 'It looks worse than it is,' I said.

'Let me be the judge of that,' Jamie said as he began to unwrap the material.

'Don't,' I said, 'you'll only make it bleed.'

He glanced up, his blue eyes staring into mine. 'Kerfuffle,' he said. 'Bring me a fresh bandage and some of that gloop you made up for Jinx's chest.'

The little daemon peered over his shoulder and down at my hand and made a tutting noise as he hurried away.

'It's nothing to worry about.'

'It will be if it gets infected.'

'There's an awful lot of blood for "nothing to be worried about",' Kerfuffle said, putting a jar of something down on the floor beside Jamie.

When Jamie unwrapped the final fold of material exposing my

little finger, he sucked in breath and Jinx leaned forward to see. 'Who did this?' Jinx asked, his eyes glittering.

'Amaliel,' I said. 'He did it so I would know how much Kayla had suffered,' then I told them what he had done to my friend while Jamie bathed my hand and applied the surprisingly cool and soothing cream. He then bandaged my hand so my little finger and palm was covered, but nothing else. While this had all been going on, Shenanigans and Kubeck had joined us, their expressions growing as grim as my other guards'.

'I always had an inkling the day would come when I would purge our world of Amaliel's existence,' Jinx said. 'But never before did I think it would bring me so much pleasure.'

'I have to go back for Kayla and Vaybian,' I said. 'I don't like to think what he might do to them if I don't. And I have to find Angela. Heaven knows where he's keeping her.'

'You are the last person who should go into that place again,' Jamie said. 'It's you he wants.'

Jinx rested his chin on his fist, a small frown creasing his forehead. 'He didn't kill you while he had the chance, which means he needs you badly, but for what?'

'He was very interested in what I could do as a Soulseer,' I told them, then briefed them on the conversations I'd had with Amaliel, and told them how I'd escaped. When I got to the bit where I'd kneed the Sicarii in the groin, disarmed him and then smacked my knee into his face, Jinx and Kerfuffle had burst out laughing and Jamie put his arm around me and hugged me to him.

'I told you Mistress Lucky was a force to be reckoned with,' I heard Shenanigans whisper to Kubeck.

The other huge daemon nodded. 'Who would have thought it? She's such a little thing.'

'What does size have to do with anything?' Kerfuffle said, sticking out his chest and staring up at the two daemons.

'Nothing,' Shenanigans said with a sheepish smile, 'nothing at all.' Kerfuffle gave a harrumph and turned his back on the pair of them.

'So,' Jinx said, 'Amaliel is keeping secrets from the Sicarii?'

'It would appear that way,' I said. 'And we know what the Sicarii think they're getting from their rituals – power and the ability to move between life and death – but what I don't yet understand is what Amaliel wants to use me for.'

My daemon guard all went quiet as they thought on it.

'Hell's bells and buckets of shite,' Jinx murmured almost to himself.

'What?' Jamie asked.

'What is it?' I asked, almost at the same time.

Jinx breathed in deeply, his expression troubled. 'If the Sicarii can really drain power from the spirits of the dead, imagine how much stronger they would become if they could draw on the souls of, not only their victims, but all those who have passed on to the other side for time immemorial?'

Jamie sucked in air through his teeth. 'They would gain the power of everyone who has ever died, but also those who have yet to die. No creature would ever be able to rest in peace again.'

Jinx nodded and we all fell silent.

Pyrites took Shenanigans' place on guard duty while Kerfuffle and Shenanigans joined us to give some thought to this latest development.

I was all for launching an immediate attack on the temple, even if we were terribly outnumbered. I was worried about my friend and her lover. Jamie wanted to carefully plan and Jinx wanted to be fully fit.

'But surely the living cannot enter the afterlife?' Shenanigans said after much pondering. 'Not without dying first?'

'He has a point,' Jamie added. 'Just because Amaliel and the Sicarii think it's possible doesn't necessarily mean it is.'

Shenanigans passed me a goblet of wine. 'It could be that if they try to pass over they will have to die first.'

'As in – you think it will kill them?' I asked for clarity.

Shenanigans shrugged. 'Just thinking out loud.'

'If that's the theory – do we dare let them try to cross?' Jamie asked.

Jinx accepted a tankard of ale from Kerfuffle but put it to one side untouched. 'I think you and me, brother, need to pay the Sicarii temple a visit.'

'Not without me you don't,' I said.

'Lucky, it's too dangerous for you to return there.'

'It is for you too,' I said folding my arms.

'We're immortal.'

'Apparently I am too.'

'We don't actually know that,' Jamie said.

'I'm at least half daemon,' I said.

'Though not the royal we thought you were,' Jinx said and that made us all pause for a moment.

'Does it matter?' I asked eventually.

'Not to me,' Jinx said, and Jamie shook his head.

'I never liked the royal family that much anyway,' Kerfuffle mumbled.

'Me neither,' Shenanigans agreed.

'I suspect Baltheza may be a little – shall we say – upset,' Jinx said.

'What about Kayla?' I asked.

Jamie smiled at me. 'I suspect Kayla already knew.'

'But why would she let me and, more importantly, her father believe it?' I asked.

'Because she wanted you with her,' Jamie said. 'For all her faults I really do believe she cares for you.'

'You've changed your tune,' Kerfuffle said with a snort. Jamie glared at him. 'Just saying.'

'Well don't.'

'This isn't helping,' I said. 'Kayla and Vaybian are in serious trouble and need our help.'

'We need some time to think of a plan,' Jinx said and gestured for me to sit down beside him. I moved over and he lifted up the cover so I could slide in next to him.

'I'll take the next watch,' Jamie said and got to his feet.

'No need,' Shenanigans said, 'we've got it covered between the four of us.'

'Are you sure?'

Shenanigans and Kerfuffle both nodded. 'Get a few hours sleep and when you're refreshed we'll talk strategy,' Kerfuffle said.

'Now Mistress Lucky is back you'll both think more clearly,' Shenanigans added.

'I was thinking clearly,' Jamie protested. Shenanigans and Kerfuffle shared a look. They obviously didn't think so.

When they had gone outside to organise shifts with Kubeck and Pyrites, Jamie got under the covers beside me. 'I was thinking clearly,' he repeated.

'Then you're a better daemon than me brother,' Jinx said, lifting his arm to put it around my shoulders with a care that told me he was hurting no matter how hard he tried to deny it. 'I couldn't sleep, couldn't think; I was going as mad as Baltheza. Well, maybe not quite that mad.'

'You were injured. Of course you couldn't think straight,' Jamie said.

Jinx gave him a surprised look. 'Since when have you had anything nice to say about me?'

'I wasn't being nice, I was telling it how it how it is.' Jamie went quiet for a moment. 'Anyway, I guess I felt the same, I just didn't dare let you and the others see.' Then he smiled at me. 'I should have known you'd escape. I should've had more faith in you. Like Jinx has.'

Jinx looked around me to Jamie who was staring straight ahead, a frown lining his forehead. 'I fear for her, just like you, but we have to give her a chance to use her wings and fly.'

'But I haven't got wings,' I said with a mock sigh. 'I wish I had, they could come in really useful.'

Jinx flapped a hand at me. 'You don't want wings. Just think of all that preening you'd have to do.'

'I don't preen,' Jamie said.

'Feathers don't stay that white and luxurious without a bit of titillating,' Jinx said.

'I do not titillate,' Jamie said, his lips turning down into a very unangelic pout.

'Do so.'

'Do not.'

'I think you do,' Jinx said with a grin.

'Nope,' Jamie said, but his lips began to twitch.

'Not even for our lucky Lucinda?'

'Especially not for Lucky.'

I thumped him on the arm. 'That's plain mean.'

'No,' Jinx said and his smile turned sad. 'No, it just means he cares too much to admit it.'

'And you don't?' Jamie asked.

'I think I've already laid my cards on the table,' he said.

We all went quiet. The tension between us was unsettling, as it had nothing to do with danger, at least not the physical kind, though a broken heart was probably what was utmost in our minds.

When I couldn't stand the brooding silence any longer, or worrying about the relationship between the three of us, I said, 'I wish I knew where Angela was.' Jamie lifted the coverings and we all slid beneath the skins to lie down together. 'The spirits didn't seem to know anything about her.'

'Maybe Amaliel decided not to keep all his eggs in one basket,' Jamie said.

Thinking about it, that made sense – if we stormed in there and rescued Kayla, Vaybian and Angela, he wouldn't have any hostages to use as bargaining power. If she was somewhere else and his position looked precarious—

'I'm going to kill him,' Jinx muttered.

'I hate to ask but, did you find Philip?' Jamie said.

'No, I didn't manage to do anything other than get Kayla and Vaybian tortured and my fingertip cut off. It was a total disaster really.'

'You escaped.'

'But not with Kayla and Vaybian.'

'Don't beat yourself up over it,' Jinx said rolling onto his side to face me. 'You did all you could, and when we wake in a few hours time, the seven of us will do more.'

'We're going in tonight?'

'If it's going to stop you being cranky,' Jamie said, also turning onto his side to face me.

'Now, will you get some sleep?' Jinx said.

'I'm not tired,' I said, crossing my arms.

Jinx reached up and laid his palm on my forehead. 'I think you are,' he said, and it was as though someone had pulled a plug on my energy reserves: my strength drained out of my body and limbs, my eyes drooped shut, my brain filled with smoke and I was gone.

'Shh, you'll wake her,' a hushed voice said.

'Are you willing to risk doing this without her? I'm not sure I am,' Jinx whispered.

At least Jinx was willing to argue for me. I struggled into a sitting position. 'What are you two up to?' I asked the two shadows at the foot of our makeshift bed.

'Now you've done it,' Jamie said, and there was a flare of light and Jinx lifted up a lamp.

'Just getting ready for our little escapade,' he said.

'You weren't planning to go anywhere without me?' I asked.

'Nooo,' Jamie said.

'Not on your nelly,' Jinx said, both of them with guileless expressions plastered onto their faces. Even if I hadn't overheard their conversation the looks they were giving me would have left me immediately suspicious.

'Hmm, why am I not convinced?' I said, getting up to join them.

'So, she's coming then,' Kerfuffle said as he walked into the cave.

'Of course she is,' Jamie said. 'Why wouldn't she be?'

'I wish you two would make up your minds,' Kerfuffle said as he picked up a short dagger and stomped back outside again.

''Fess up,' I said. 'You were going to sneak off without me.'

'No, not at all,' Jamie said. 'We were just letting you have a few minutes more sleep.'

'Does this mean me and Pyrites are coming with you?' Shenanigans asked from the cave's mouth.

'So, you weren't going anywhere without me?' I said, giving them both killer looks. Shenanigans pulled a face and backed out of the cave.

'We just thought that having been through so much we should let you rest,' Jinx said, his tail creeping around his thigh to waggle at me.

I stood up, took a step towards him and prodded him in the middle of the chest. 'What about you? You had an arrow right through you, mister.'

Jamie took my hand. 'We worry about you.'

'And I don't about you?' I asked, pulling my hand from his. 'I spend most of my time worrying whether you've been killed or not.'

'That's different,' Jinx said.

'Why?'

'Well, you're —'

'I'm what?' I said glaring at him.

'Um.'

'I hope you weren't about to say it's because I'm a woman.'

'Well, no, not exactly,' he glanced at Jamie for support, but found none there; Jamie was too busy smiling down at his boots. 'Some help here, brother,' Jinx muttered out of the corner of his mouth.

'Jamie, I know both you and Jinx want to look out for me, but I want to be with you. *That's* why I came back to the Underlands, and if it means sometimes being in danger, then so be it.' I took both of their hands. 'In this instance I have no choice, I have to go back. I promised to find a way to release the spirits from the curse and if I don't then I'm not doing my duty as the Soulseer.' Both Jamie and Jinx bowed their heads. 'Do you understand?'

Jamie looked up and nodded.

'You're right,' Jinx said. 'All three of us have obligations and we should be grateful that they bind us together.' He lifted my bandaged hand to his lips and kissed my knuckles.

'Let's do this thing,' Jamie said.

'What's the plan?'

'Buggered if I know,' Jinx said. 'Rescue the fair damsel and her knight and anyone else who needs to escape I suppose.'

'You lead us to the entrance,' Jamie said, resting his hand on the hilt of his sword, 'and we'll do the rest.'

'Can I have a weapon?' I asked.

'What would you like?'

'I suppose a 44 Magnum would be out of the question?'

''Fraid so,' Jamie said, so I had to make do with a dagger.

Fourteen

I led them to the second entrance, used when the Sicarii were transporting victims or provisions by cart to their temple. The spirits had shown it to me when sharing their memories. By entering here, it meant we didn't have to go through the main cavern, which was fraught with danger, but it was a convoluted route to where the prisoners were held.

At first I worried I wouldn't find it in the dark, but after trudging back and forth for about five minutes between two familiar landmarks, we stumbled across a slope in the ground and the gully where the entrance was located.

'We'll go in first,' Jamie said, indicating him and Jinx, 'then Kubeck, Lucky and Pyrites next, and Kerfuffle and Shenanigans last.' He addressed the last two: 'If it all goes terribly wrong, you make sure Pyrites gets Lucky out of there,' he turned to my drakon, 'and if that means roasting a few Sicarii you do it – understand?' Pyrites bowed his head.

'I smell death,' Jinx said as soon as we stepped inside, and it was true: an odour of decay mixed with the aroma of hay and animal manure scented the air.

After a few yards we stepped into a well-lit cavern with a paddock to one side. Four creatures grazed on hay hanging in baskets from the rails of their compound; other than cursory glances they paid us no heed. Despite the danger, I was fascinated. I had assumed the cart and carriage had been pulled by horses, but these beasts were bovine and bore a similarity to oxen. Their coats were a glossy, chocolate brown, their eyes of a slightly darker shade and framed with long black lashes. Each had a double set of long handlebar horns plus a tusk mid-snout for good measure.

Behind the paddock there were entrances to two more gated caves and I assumed that was where the Sicarii housed their other animals. I was sure some of my captors had been riding animals very similar to horses – more similar than these bovines, at any rate.

We hurried on and into another passageway hewn into red rock. The animal smells faded, but the stench of decay grew stronger until it was almost overpowering. Then the corridor we were following forked into two.

'Wait here,' Jinx said and strode off to the left.

Jamie and I exchanged a glance and he went after Jinx.

'Wait here,' I told the others and then jogged after my two men.

'Bollocks,' I heard Jinx say.

'Oh shit,' Jamie's voice echoed along the passageway, then I was stepping into another large cavern and the smell was so terrible it made my eyes water and bile rise into my throat. I clasped my hand over my nose and mouth to try and shut it out, but it was impossible.

Jamie saw me first and went to stand in my way. 'Don't look,' he said, putting his hands on my shoulders and trying to turn me back.

I put my hand on his. 'Jamie, you can't protect me from everything.'

'Let her see,' Jinx said, his voice cold.

I went to stand by his side. He didn't look at me. His jaws were clenched and his eyes narrowed. He was angry, angrier than I had ever seen him; angrier even than when he had seen the severed tip of my little finger. I followed his gaze and God help me, I wasn't even surprised; disgusted but not surprised.

In the centre of the cavern there was a hole, a chasm really, that could have gone down into the centre of the world as far as I could tell. In that hole, discarded like pieces of rubbish, were the broken bodies of the Sicarii's victims. Rotting corpses, some not much more than denuded bone, were heaped in a nightmarish jumble of rags and body parts.

'There must be hundreds,' I whispered.

'Could be thousands,' Jamie said his voice bleak.

Then I saw something move amongst the dead. A body shifted and a head fell back revealing deep, empty eye sockets and a skeletal grin. Images from every zombie apocalypse film I had ever seen flashed through my head, and if I could have got my legs to move I would have run. Instead, frozen to the spot, I clasped onto Jinx's arm and fought back the scream building up inside me.

Down in the pit an arm flopped to one side and a skull toppled over, tumbling down the pile to rest against the rock face. Another body shivered and its chest began to move.

'My God,' I whispered, 'he can't be—' and the flesh burst outwards as a gore-covered snout forced its way through the ribcage and I began to gag.

'Filthy creatures,' Jamie said, his lips twisted in disgust.

'Nature's cleaners,' Jinx said.

'Let's get out of here,' Jamie said, taking my hand and leading me back out into the corridor.

Jinx held my hair out of the way as I threw up while Jamie put his arm around me to stop me falling.

'It's okay,' Jamie kept telling me, but it wasn't; nothing was ever going to be okay again, not while creatures like the Sicarii and Amaliel Cheriour remained in this world.

When I eventually finished making a fool of myself we followed the passageway back to the others. 'I wish I had a packet of peppermints right now,' I said.

'If you're asking for wishes to be granted I'd stick with the 44 Magnum,' Jamie said, 'we could certainly do with one.'

A thought occurred to me. 'Why are there no spirits here? At the other temple there were some spirits outside, where their bodies rested.'

'Maybe they are otherwise engaged,' Jinx said.

'What do you mean?'

'Maybe Amaliel is conducting a ritual tonight.'

'I do hope you're wrong,' Jamie said, but his expression told me he didn't think so.

When we joined the others they didn't ask us what we had found; they knew. We followed the right hand corridor; dark shadows between red walls. Then, as though a line had been drawn, the rock to either side of us, below our feet and above our heads turned black as coal, and ahead of us was a blackened brass-bound door.

'It's probably more to do with keeping the smell out than blocking intruders from entering,' Jinx said. 'It should open easily enough.' Sure enough, when he turned the handle and pushed, it swung open without a sound.

We all hurried through, and with the door closed behind us the smell lessened, though I was sure it had permeated into my clothes, skin and hair, like smoke would when you're close to a bonfire. I scrubbed at my lips with the back of my hand, scared of licking them in case they tasted of death.

Four steps into the corridor I felt Kayla's presence, and like the first time I had entered the great hall after arriving in the Underlands, I felt myself being drawn to her. Forgotten was the smell of death lingering on my body, forgotten were the heaps of putrefying bodies and the horror of the rats scavenging amongst them.

'I recognise this passageway,' I murmured to myself, but when I reached the door to her cell I didn't stop; I knew she wasn't there.

I opened the door to Vaybian's prison, but the gate to his barred enclosure was wide open and he was nowhere to be seen.

'We have to hurry,' I said to no one in particular as I pushed my way past Jamie and then Jinx.

'Lucky,' Jamie hissed. 'Jinx, stop her.'

A hand encircled my arm and tried to hold me back, but I forged on. I had to find Kayla. I had to get to her before Amaliel sacrificed her in one of his terrible rituals. I tried to shake off the hand gripping onto me so tightly. Jinx spun me around to face him.

'Lucinda, stop it.'

'I have to get to her, I have to find her,' I said, trying to pull away.

He grabbed me by the upper arms and shook me and I began to fight him. Why wouldn't he let me go? I needed to get to Kayla.

'This is going to hurt me more than it will you,' he said, and let go of my arm, drew back his hand and slapped me hard around the face.

I glared at him, lashing out with my fist. His hand closed around my wrist. 'You can hit me later,' he said, and the anger drained out of me along with the compulsion to find Kayla – whatever the cost.

'Are you all right?' Jamie asked me. Then he turned to Jinx, 'Did you have to hit her so hard?'

'I pinched her arm and she didn't even feel it,' Jinx said. He was right: I hadn't. 'I think this was more than Lucinda being drawn to Kayla, I think this was Amaliel using their connection to compel Lucinda to go to Kayla.'

'In other words, he knows we're here,' Jamie said.

Jinx gave a nod. 'You can count on it.'

'So much for the element of surprise,' Kerfuffle said.

'What do we do now?' Kubeck asked.

'What we need to do,' Jinx said, 'is march right in there and rescue Kayla and Vaybian. We knew they'd be expecting us to do something, maybe they won't expect us to be so bold.'

'You do realise there could be hundreds of them in there,' Jamie said.

'There isn't,' I said.

'How can you be so sure?' Kubeck asked.

'There are five grey Sicarii and twelve minions,' I told them, 'plus Amaliel and possibly Henri.'

'How do you know this?'

'The spirits told me.'

Kubeck's brow bunched into a thoughtful frown. I wondered

whether he had a problem with me and what I was, but then he said, 'That is eighteen against us seven,' and grinned. 'I like those odds.'

'Particularly when we have a drakon as back up,' Shenanigans said.

'Don't get too confident,' Jamie said, 'Amaliel is bound to have something up his sleeve; he knows what he's up against.'

'Come on,' I said, setting my shoulders and looking towards the main chamber. 'Let's do this thing.'

We started down the corridor again, moving at speed now, making hardly a sound; even Pyrites somehow managed to pad along without the telltale click of claws on rock.

Then the chanting began, or rather a cacophony of voices: at first a low rumble echoed through the mountain, then it got louder with every step we took until I doubt they would have heard us above the roar of their discordant cries.

'By Beelzebub's balls,' Jinx said with a wince. 'What a racket.'

'It's like fingernails down a blackboard,' I said, my front teeth feeling like someone had set about them with a metal file.

The jarring hubbub abruptly ended and silence reigned for a few seconds before they began again, this time with a chant: regular, rhythmical, and it could have been in time with the beating of my heart.

I couldn't make out the words, but they were probably in Latin or some other long-dead language. Strangely enough, nearly everyone in the Underlands spoke in the language of humans; or maybe it was that we spoke in theirs?

This chant rose, though at least it didn't have me gritting my teeth. Then a drum started to beat and, in a most ridiculous moment of mind babble, I had a vision of the actor Danny Kaye being marched around in a scene from a very old film as he tried to remember whether it was the vessel with the pestle that held the brew that was true.

I nearly giggled, but it was a hysterical giggle, the type that probably came before you got yourself killed, so I sucked it back, stood tall and thought serious thoughts, like: let's hope I'm not about to get myself and my friends slaughtered within the next few minutes.

The corridor widened and then there we were moving into the sacrificial cavern. There was no point stopping on the periphery and waiting to see what was about to happen. We were about to happen; and they were clearly waiting for us.

Amaliel was up on the dais behind the altar, Kayla pressed back against his chest with a very sharp blade to her throat. Vaybian was hanging upside down by the ankles from a rope above the dais, blood leaking from cuts sliced into his chest, legs and arms. None of them were life threatening, but the steady patter of blood upon the stone below him was forming a shimmering jade pool.

'How nice of you to join us,' Amaliel said, his voice a slimy gurgle of phlegm, which made me want to puke all over again.

Kayla's eyes were immediately on me. Her lips moved, 'tell him to go fuck himself,' she mouthed, and she meant it – I knew her better than I knew myself. She saw my indecision. 'We're dead already. Save my world and save yours.'

I started to shake my head. No, I couldn't lose her. I couldn't let this monster take her away from me. Then she smiled, and I knew she was right; This was bigger than both of us. We had to stop Amaliel because once he ruled the Underlands and the afterlife, what was there to stop him looking further? But that didn't mean I wouldn't try and save her if I could.

'Lucky,' Jamie whispered and I glanced his way, 'look.'

Rising up out of the black rock floor and floating down from the high vaulted ceiling were hundreds of spirits; their faces contorted with misery. 'Help us!' they cried.

'You can see them?' I asked. Jamie nodded.

'So can I, mistress,' Shenanigans said.

'And I,' Kerfuffle added and Kubeck muttered, 'yes.'

'They've started the ceremony,' Jinx said.

'They say the true Soulseer can open the door between this

world and the next. Do it and I will let the Lady Kayla live,' Amaliel said.

'Do it and he'll have his way into the afterlife,' Jinx whispered, his mouth close to my ear.

Well, I thought, Jinx's guess had been right: Amaliel wanted me so he could get to the other side. And now we knew what he wanted, once and for all: he didn't just want the Underlands, he wanted to rule everything – the living and the dead. 'Maybe,' I said, 'but maybe not.'

His forehead creased into a frown. 'What are you thinking?'

'The doorway into the next world, when opened, doesn't necessarily let everyone enter. Remember Dreyphus.'

'But he was cursed.'

'It's like Shenanigans said: do you think the door would remain open for the living? I'm not sure it would.'

'Willing to risk it?' Jamie said.

'If I can get Amaliel to free these souls, I might.'

Jamie and Jinx exchanged a look. 'Do it,' Jinx said.

'I'm waiting,' Amaliel interrupted, 'and I think I've been more than patient.'

'To open the doorway there needs to be souls waiting to pass. Free them,' I said, gesturing to the spirits surrounding us, 'and I can open the door.'

'No, Lucky, don't do it,' Kayla said.

'Shut up or I will open your throat like a second mouth,' Amaliel hissed.

'Free them,' I said, trying to distract him.

Amaliel's red eyes bored into mine. 'If this is an attempt to trick me – she dies.'

'Do you want the door open, or not?'

He stared at me for a few moments more then turned to the dais where the five Sicarii waited. 'Release the souls.'

'My Lord?' one said.

'Do it, they can always be replaced.'

The Sicarii bowed, then he and the four others gathered behind the altar and began to chant. At first nothing happened and then a couple of the spirits brightened, then a few more and a few more.

Amaliel turned back to face me, still holding Kayla tight against his chest. 'Your turn,' he said.

I took a deep breath and walked forward. 'Are you ready to leave?' I asked the spirits.

'We are free to go?' the tall, slim daemon I had spoken to before asked.

'When you're ready,' I told her.

'Nothing's happening,' one of the Sicarii hissed.

'I'm waiting,' Amaliel said.

I ignored both of them. 'Please welcome these poor souls into the afterlife,' I whispered to myself, hoping that some divine being could hear me.

The spirits who had been whispering excitedly to each other fell silent and the atmosphere changed. There was a weight in the chamber. I wasn't sure whether it was our tense anticipation of what was about to occur, or the door itself opening, until a warm glow filled my chest and a pinprick of light appeared just in front of the altar. Like before, the small dot lengthened into a glowing slit and began to open, golden light spilling out across the blackened floor, and again I felt an overwhelming urge to walk towards the light.

I gestured towards it. 'You can go now,' I said.

A couple of the long dead stepped towards it, but then hesitated. 'Is this the way?' one asked.

'Yes,' I told them as my right foot took an unwanted pace towards it, 'it is the way.' One of them stepped into the light and was instantly transformed from a grey wraith into a bright gold creature of beauty.

'Ahh!' he cried. 'It's so warm!' and he stepped through the widening slit. From the other side I could hear tinkling laughter that sounded so beautiful I wasn't sure I wanted to stop my feet from taking me there.

It was enough for the others. Those who had hung back surged forward; some going straight through into the unknown while others stood, bathed in the golden light for a few moments before taking that final step. A steady stream passed through the gateway until at last they were all gone.

'Now you,' Amaliel said.

I turned to face him. 'It's not a doorway for the living, it's for the dead,' I told him even as my feet betrayed me by taking a couple of steps more towards the light.

'That can be arranged,' he said.

I glanced at my two men. Jinx gave a tiny nod, though Jamie didn't look so sure. As Jinx was the expert on death I'd have to hope he knew more than the rest of us. My feet didn't need telling, they continued to move even as I worried about the implications; I just hoped they weren't about to get me killed.

I stepped into the light, fists clenched tight by my sides and, as the golden rays caressed my skin, all my troubles and fears disappeared, and a wonderful warmth seeped into my bones, leaving my body fizzing like a fine French Champagne.

I walked on until I was standing in the entrance between the two worlds. Through the doorway I could see golden figures and could hear laughter and singing. If this was what came after death I was no longer afraid; it was a beautiful, joyful place.

I stepped inside and two figures who could have been Jamie's brothers walked to greet me.

'Welcome Soulseer,' one said.

'Though, sadly for us it's not your time,' said the other and gestured with his hand that I should leave.

'But—'

The first angel lifted his hand and waggled his forefinger from side to side. 'No buts. Return to your world; you have much work to do.'

Hoping they knew what they were doing, I gave them a small smile and stepped back out through the slit and onto cold, black stone. Any warmth and sense of wellbeing I'd had was instantly sucked from my bones, leaving me feeling almost bereft.

The five Sicarii were grouped around the entrance waiting for me to return. 'She survives,' one hissed, turning to Amaliel.

'Then it is safe for us to enter,' Amaliel sneered. And it hit me: he didn't know I'd been turned away at the gate; he thought I'd gone in and come back safely. He gestured to the Sicarii. 'Go then brothers,' Amaliel said. The Sicarii hesitated, standing just outside the pool of light. 'Go forth into the new world.'

One, braver than the others, or possibly more stupid, walked forward and into the light.

'It feels warm,' he hissed as he glided towards the slit of light. He reached out his hand and passed it through the opening – then the light changed.

The golden rays flared for a moment before burning a bright orange, turning to scarlet then darkening to purple.

'What's happening?' the Sicarii said, snatching his hand back from the light and stumbling backwards away from the gateway.

The lamps around the cavern flickered and flared as a swirling breeze surrounded us and a weird crooning noise spilled out from inside the slit, getting louder and louder until I felt like covering my ears. The sound stopped as quickly as it started, but it was the lull before the storm; black shapes began to slip out from the now almost black hole. As sinuous as shadows, they slid towards the nearest Sicarii, engulfing him within moments. When the Sicarii had all but disappeared amongst the shadowy mass, he began to scream – and it was a scream more awful than anything I had ever heard.

The other four Sicarii backed away, then one's nerve broke and he turned to run. Before he had even gathered speed, he too was surrounded by the terrible chattering shadows and began to scream as they pulled him into their midst.

I felt hands take mine; Jamie to my left, Jinx to my right. I was glad of the comfort; I didn't think things were going to get any better, at least not for the Sicarii, as more of the dark phantoms poured from the entrance and overwhelmed the remaining grey-clad assassins and their screams joined the echoes of their comrades.

The minions had seen enough – they all bolted this way and that, making for the nearest exits to the cavern. They needn't have worried; the shades had got what they had come for. They began to retreat back through the hole, taking their captives with them. Once or twice a grey-covered head, foot or arm erupted out of the shadowy masses, but they were soon re-submerged beneath a blanket of pulsating black and hauled through the entrance into the world beyond. As soon as the last shadowy mass had disappeared inside the hole it snapped shut into a thin line and receded at either end until all that was left was a small dot of black, and then it was gone.

I swung around to face Amaliel Cheriour, but he too had lost his nerve. He was stumbling backwards towards the main exit, Kayla still in his grasp. She was kicking and struggling against him to no avail.

Jinx and Jamie started after him just as he reached the passageway. 'Stop right there,' Amaliel shouted.

'Release the Lady Kayla,' Jinx said, 'and we will give you a chance to do the honourable thing rather than face your execution in shame.'

'Fool,' he spat. 'You're a fool if you think this over: I still have the child. This one, however, is no longer of any use to me.' He put a palm on Kayla's forehead and pulled back her head. 'Say goodbye Lucky,' he said, and drew the blade across my friend's throat.

A blue band that for a second could have been a sapphire necklace instantly appeared across her neck. Amaliel shoved her towards us then turned and ran. Jinx was after him in a heartbeat.

'No!' Vaybian shouted, struggling against the ropes with the little strength he had left.

'Kayla!' I screamed, sprinting across the cavern to drop down beside her crumpled body. I lifted her head onto my lap as she clutched at her ruined throat, trying to staunch the gush of blood flowing between her fingers and saturating the front of her gown. 'Kayla, don't leave me. Please don't leave me.'

Her lips moved and blood seeped out of the corners of her mouth. 'Keep you . . . safe,' they said, though she didn't utter a sound. 'Never leave you.' Her eyes fluttered shut. 'Never leave . . .' and with one final, harsh breath, she did just that.

Fifteen

I was past tears, and unaware of everything except for her. I sat stroking her hair while Jamie cut Vaybian down and sat with the both of us as we mourned our loved one.

Kayla, my constant companion for most of the past twenty-five years, was gone, and as her heart had fluttered to a stop, I could swear I had felt her physically wrenched away from me. Inside I was numb, cold and empty like there was a void where my heart should be.

Jinx and the others returned. Jamie looked up at him and Jinx shook his head. My pain was compounded: they had been unable to catch Amaliel.

'We'll take her back to the palace,' Jamie eventually said, 'it's only right she has the state funeral she deserves.'

'We will find him, won't we?' I said. 'He will pay for this?'

'He will pay,' Jinx said, putting a hand on my shoulder. 'And then some.'

'I wonder where Henri was while all this was going on – do you think he's got the child?' Kerfuffle asked.

'Poor little thing,' Shenanigans said, 'she'll be scared to death as it is, let alone being left alone with that creature.'

'We'll find her, but first we need to take Kayla's body back to her father,' Jamie said.

I nodded in agreement. Jamie was right; Baltheza deserved that at least.

We laid Kayla out gently in the back of the cart and covered her with skins while Vaybian followed. He was barely able to walk or concentrate. Shenanigans and Kubeck harnessed up two of the bulls and tied the other two to the back of the cart.

'We couldn't leave the poor creatures to starve,' Shenanigans said.

They had also saddled up the four horse-like creatures from the stalls behind the paddock. 'There were at least two others stabled here,' Kerfuffle said.

'Amaliel probably made his escape on one,' Jamie said, 'and Henri would have taken the other.'

I eyed up the creatures. They were a lot bigger than the horses we had at home and each had a short, stubby horn on their snout.

'Me, Vaybian, Kubeck and you will get up on these beasts,' Jinx said, 'if you think you can manage it,' he added gently to me. 'Shenanigans and Kerfuffle will ride on the cart.'

'I keep telling you, I can't ride.'

'Yes, but you have since ridden on Pyrites and Bob, and this is not so different.'

'I was with you on Bob.'

'Well, today you can have your first solo riding lesson.'

I shrugged; I would try it. I had faced too much to be afraid now. As it happened, the gentle warmth and the trotting gait of the huge beasts wasn't so bad, and staying in the saddle kept my mind off Kayla for a while. The distraction was probably why Jinx had insisted I ride the creature rather than Pyrites, who padded along beside me. Kayla was always there though; as soon as my mind wandered for even a second, she was back and the pain of losing her washed over me, filling me with despair.

Jamie had been right, I thought. If Kayla had died before I'd got to her, I would have known it. I certainly felt as though a part of me was missing. Maybe it was a bit like Peter Pan losing his shadow? I had heard the expression that someone was 'heartsick', and it was a pretty good description of how I felt: tired, beaten and drained of any emotion other than misery.

We made camp just outside the Forest of Dignus. I soon discovered that, after all that had happened – the highs, the lows, me lost and found twice, and Kayla's murder – we were all more than a bit overwrought, and in my case the numbness I'd been feeling immediately following Kayla's death and most of the day was turning into a bitter anger: Amaliel hadn't needed to kill her. It was pointless, so fucking pointless.

Of course, then Vaybian just had to open his big mouth.

We were sitting around the fire when I asked how long it would be before Kayla's funeral took place.

'It'll be a big affair so a few days, possibly a week,' Jamie told me.

'That long? We need to find Amaliel,' I said, massaging the bridge of my nose.

'So that's that then,' Vaybian said with a sneer. 'Kayla's dead so we can forget her?'

'That's not what I said, Vaybian.'

'That's exactly what it sounded like.'

'You know something? You can be a complete arse at times,' I said.

'And you can be an unfeeling bitch.' The words were hardly out of his mouth before Jinx had his hand twisted in Vaybian's long green hair and was glowering into his face.

'Take that back,' Jinx said, his voice low and mean.

'Jinx, it doesn't matter. Forget it,' I said, sick of the whole thing.

'I said, take it back,' Jinx said, ignoring me.

'Or you'll do what?' Vaybian said, glaring back at him. 'Kill me? Do it, go on, do it. You might as well; I've nothing left I want to live for.'

I laid my hand on Jinx's arm. 'Please, let him go. He's hurting too.'

Jinx gave me a snarly look and then, with an angry grunt, let go of Vaybian and pushed him away. 'You disrespect Lucinda and you disrespect me – remember it, because next time I will not be told to leave you be,' then he gave me another angry look and stalked off.

I watched him go off into the dark, then I started to get upset and angry, and the tears I'd been bottling up started to flow and then I really lost my temper and jumped to my feet to go after him.

'Lucky—' Jamie said as I went to storm off, then he saw my face and went quiet. Just as well.

I grabbed one of the lamps hanging from the side of the cart and walked into the trees after Jinx. At first I thought I'd lost him, then I saw his back as he strode away from me.

'Jinx,' I called but he ignored me. 'Fine,' I said to myself and carried on after him.

He was walking fast so I started to run. He was angry, but I was angry too, and like him I wanted to take it out on someone. Quite how him defending me from someone else's insults had suddenly become a fight between the two of us I had no idea, but then I guess neither of us was thinking rationally. I know I wasn't.

He disappeared into the forest again, but I wasn't about to give up, and then I burst into a clearing. Jinx was sitting on a fallen log at the far side.

I slowed from a run to a march and walked around the log to confront him, placing the lamp on the floor beside us.

'What was that all about?' I said, impatience tingeing my voice. He gave me a narrow-eyed look and turned away to stare across the clearing. 'For goodness' sake!' I shouted.

He very slowly turned his head until he was staring me right in the eyes. 'How many times must I tell you what it means to be marked by me?'

'Jinx, this is a crock of macho shit.'

'Really?' he said, jumping up so we were face to face.

'Yes, really. And I don't need it right now . . .' My voice cracked and I had to look away.

'Lucinda,' he said, more gently.

'Lucky – I prefer Lucky,' I said.

'I prefer Lucinda,' he said, putting his hands on my shoulders and turning me to face him.

'I don't want to fight with you,' I said, all my anger draining away. I fought to control my feelings. Kayla was gone; Kayla was really gone.

He reached out to brush the hair off my brow. 'Do you know I've never been involved with a woman who can stir up my emotions so easily?'

'Well, I guess it must be a two-way thing, because sometimes you make me so angry I could thump you, and at other times . . .' I trailed off. Telling him that sometimes I wanted him so desperately it physically hurt wasn't going to do much for my dignity.

'Do you want me to let you go?' he said, and his eyes dropped away from mine as he stared at the forest floor beneath our feet.

'What! I thought you asked me never to do that?' He looked up at me and I felt sick. 'Do you want me to? Do you want to be free of me?'

He took a shuddery breath and looked up at the sky. 'I don't want to, but what I want doesn't really matter.'

I was confused. Was he dumping me? Was he telling me I was too much hard work? 'Jinx,' I said. 'Tell me what you want. Tell me how you feel, or how can I make any sort of decision?' I really did not want to be having this conversation right now. I'd lost my best friend and now it looked as though I could be losing a lover before we even took that first step.

He kept his eyes looking down away from mine. 'I . . . I find myself in a most peculiar circumstance.'

'Speak bloody English why don't you,' I said getting angry again. 'Are you telling me you lied before? Are you telling me you don't want to be with me?'

His head jerked up. 'No. No. What I said before was true. I . . . I—'

'You what, Jinx?'

'I . . .' he turned his face away, his lips tight, then looked me in the eyes and took hold of my hands. 'I cannot bear to lose you, and I'm scared that I will because of who I am.'

'What? Why would you think that?'

'I am the bringer of death and darkness and endless night. All the things you fear. Why would you want to be consort to a creature such as me?'

'You're also kind, gentle and funny and I . . . I love you far too much for it to be good for me,' and I had to look away as I couldn't bear to see his expression.

He was silent for a few moments. 'And what about James?' he asked, his voice low and gentle.

'That's the problem,' I said with a hysterical half sob, 'I love him too. I love you both. I love you both so very much.' There, I'd said it. I'd actually said it.

A hand rested on my shoulder and squeezed before lips touched my neck and a second body pressed up against my back and encircled me.

'Well,' Jinx said, his voice a breathy exhalation, 'I'm glad we've got that sorted out.'

'So am I,' Jamie whispered. I glanced to my right and got a face full of blond curls as Jamie nuzzled between my head and shoulder.

We stood for a few moments in the silence, and it felt as though a little piece of my heart had healed, then Jinx shifted.

'I suppose I'd better get back to camp and apologise to that jackass Vaybian,' Jinx said.

'I wouldn't,' Jamie said, coming up for air, 'I gave him a talking to as well and I'm certainly not going to apologise.'

'He's hurting Jamie. Just imagine it were me who had died.'

'Don't,' Jinx said, 'I can't allow myself to even think of it.'

'Nor I,' Jamie said, and I could feel my eyes welling up again at the thought of losing either of them.

'When we find Amaliel I'm going to kill him,' I said.

'Leave that to me,' Jinx said as he turned to walk back to the campsite, 'I bring death, you look after the dead and dying.'

When Jinx had gone, Jamie turned me around to face him. 'It's all right to cry you know.'

'I didn't see her spirit, Jamie. Why didn't I see her leave?'

'Maybe because you were too close to her. Maybe it's different for you when it's your own loved ones.'

'He didn't have to kill her. Why did he do it?'

'To hurt you. To hurt us. Amaliel likes to cause pain, and as he couldn't hurt you physically, he hurt you in the only way he could.'

'I hate him,' I said resting my head against Jamie's chest. 'I hate him so much.'

When Jamie and I got back to camp we ate, but not a lot, and drank maybe a bit more. Shenanigans apologised for having no wine and only ale, but it was probably just as well; I'd only get maudlin if I had too much wine. No one spoke much, and when they did it was in hushed voices – although most of my guard hadn't particularly liked Kayla, none of them would have wished her dead. It was a relief when we all curled up to go to sleep. For me though, sleep was elusive.

In the end I gave up and went to sit on one of the logs by the dwindling fire, feeding it with a couple of small branches Kerfuffle had collected earlier.

As I stared into the flames with nothing else to do but think, I thought of Kayla. I glanced towards the cart where she lay and felt the anguish building up in my chest again. I had to take a few deep breaths – I didn't want any of my friends to wake and find me sobbing my heart out, not that they would think badly of me if I was, but I just didn't want them fussing.

I poked at the fire with a stick, causing orange and red sparkles to fly up, and remembered how, as children, Kayla and I would curl up together on the sofa in front of the hearth, and she would tell me wonderful stories of dragons and their treasure, and dwarves mining for jewels in deep and dangerous caverns. I loved those stories.

'Well,' said a voice. 'Here we are once more.' It was a voice I knew; it was a voice I loved, and I had thought I would never hear again. I nearly cried out, but swallowed it just in time – I wasn't ready to wake the others.

There she was, sitting on the log next to mine. 'Kayla!'

She gave me a smile. 'Ironic don't you think? For all those years I pretended to be a ghost and now I truly am one.' She wound one of her long green curls around her finger. 'How fortunate that I won't have to spend eternity with a shorn head,' and the vipers in her hair hissed their agreement.

'Oh, Kayla,' I said, shifting over to sit beside her and wishing with all my heart I could give her a hug. 'Why haven't you moved on?'

'I said I wouldn't leave you, silly, and that's a promise I intend to keep. Anyway, I want to see that snake Amaliel get his comeuppance.'

'You're not alone,' I said. 'We'll go after him when we know where he's gone – and we'll make sure he gets what he deserves.'

'Where do you think I've been? I wasn't about to let the scumbag out of my sight.'

'You know where he is?'

'Hiding out in the last place anyone would expect. He's gone back to the palace.'

'Is he mad? Baltheza wanted his head on a plate before and when he finds out what he did to—' I bit my lip.

'Hey,' she said, 'I'm here and I'm not going anywhere soon.'

'But one day I'll have to . . .'

'But not yet,' she said. 'I'll be here as long as you need me.'

'But I can't touch you; can't hold you,' and my voice broke as I knew deep down one day I would have to let her go.

'If you recall, for the last twenty-five years you haven't touched me or held me. You thought I was a ghost, remember?'

I knew she was right, but a mere few weeks of knowing she was alive had changed all my expectations – the fact that we had been at odds for most of those few weeks broke my heart.

'I'm sorry we fought.'

'And I'm sorry that I didn't tell you the truth before.'

I gave her a watery smile and we both sat there for a while staring into the fire like we'd used to when I was a child. 'So, Amaliel is back at the palace?' I asked eventually.

'Hiding beneath the Chambers of Rectification with Henri. There's a warren of tunnels and passageways to all kinds of hidden rooms under there – it's where he carries out the worst of his work. Nasty stuff he wouldn't even want the palace guards to see. And he's got the child – Angela – with him.'

That made me look up. 'Is she all right?'

'Scared senseless,' Kayla said, 'but she is one tough little girl.'

'I have to get her away from him.'

'Lucky, there's something else . . . Amaliel has Philip.'

'You saw him?'

Kayla nodded. 'Yes, but you're not going to be happy . . . I think he's made himself Amaliel's little pet human.'

'What do you mean?'

'You know it was Amaliel who was using him in the Overlands? Well, Amaliel must think Philip can still be useful to him, because he's given him a second chance. Philip's had a wash and brush up, and he's looking quite well; at least better than he did when I rescued him from Daltas' slimy claws.'

'What could Amaliel possibly want with Philip?'

Kayla's dark eyes glittered and she appeared so real she could have been alive. 'I don't know, but whatever his intentions, I would wager they are going to be very bad news to somebody.'

After we'd put that aside it was like old times; we talked away most of the night. The only time we both found it hard was when she asked after Vaybian. 'He's really hurting,' I told her. 'I think he blames himself because he was unable to protect you.'

'How is he with you?'

I pulled a face. 'But I don't blame him. He thinks you put me before him.'

'I did,' she said, 'and I would do the same again.'

'Don't you love him?'

'Apparently not as much as he loved me,' she said, but her tone was wistful and I had the feeling she was kidding herself.

When I eventually slipped back in between Jamie and Jinx the twin suns were beginning to cast a pale glow over the edge of the horizon and there was no point trying to sleep; my men would be waking within a matter of minutes.

We had decided Kayla was going to stay out of the way for a while until I'd had a chance to speak to Jinx and Jamie. Although Jamie wouldn't be able to see her, Jinx certainly would and we didn't want him saying anything to alert Vaybian to her presence. His feelings were raw wounds, and knowing she was there for me to see when he couldn't would hurt him more than any red-hot iron.

'You seem a bit brighter this morning,' Jamie said as he helped me up onto Dobbin; I had to call my steed something and it was the best I could think of when there was so much other stuff floating around inside my head – and it was definitely better than Bob.

'I need to talk to you and Jinx alone,' I said, leaning down to whisper to him. He gave me a puzzled frown. 'It's important.'

'When we stop mid-morning?'

'Okay,' I said, but wished it was sooner. Kayla was riding in the back of the cart with her body and wasn't particularly keen on it. Despite what she'd said, I think her love for Vaybian was part of the reason she was prepared to do it.

After almost a full day's travel, and when we were about an hour away from the palace, we stopped for what Jinx called a 'piss stop' and it was on the way back from taking the aforesaid 'piss' that Jamie drew him to one side.

I watched them from my place beside the cart and waited. Jamie talked; Jinx listened and then looked across at me. Jamie spoke some more and the pair of them started to walk towards me, heads down, still talking. It made me wonder what they were talking about – it shouldn't have taken that long to tell Jinx I needed to speak to them in private.

'What's up?' Jamie asked as he stepped up to the cart.

I had a quick look around to see that Vaybian was a little way away, kneeling down by a small stream washing his face and taking a drink, his back to us. 'You can come out now,' I said, lifting the corner of the sturdy material that covered the back of the cart.

'Thank goodness for that,' Kayla said, poking her head through the gap I had made. 'It's blooming creepy riding around with a corpse.'

'Hell's bells and vats of pus, what the f—?' Jinx said.

'What?' Jamie said. 'What is it?'

Jinx gestured with his head towards Kayla still kneeling in the cart. 'Kayla.'

'What about her?'

Jinx gave an exasperated snort. 'Lucky Lucinda is the Soulseer, so what does she see?' he waved his hand in a rolling motion.

'Souls,' Jamie said, giving us both a blank look, and then it dawned on him. 'Kayla's here?'

'In the willing spirit, but not the rather unwilling flesh,' she said.

'Yes,' Jinx said. 'She's back.'

'Why didn't you say before?' Jamie asked me.

'You were all asleep and this morning I didn't want one of you saying something in front of Vaybian; he's having a rough enough time as it is.'

'Why haven't you passed over?' Jinx asked Kayla.

'Lovely to see you again too, Deathbringer,' Kayla said with a huff.

'You have no reason to stay.'

'Actually, I have. I promised Lucky with my dying breath that I would protect her and wouldn't leave her and I won't.'

'She's safe with us.'

'Let me be the judge of that. Anyhow, I want to see that glob of slime called Amaliel Cheriour meet his end, and the bloodier and stickier the better.'

'Fair point,' Jinx said.

'Er, could someone translate?' Jamie asked. 'Or at least tell me the gist of what she's saying?'

'The Lady Kayla promised Lucky she wouldn't leave her – and there is the small matter of revenge tying her to this world.'

'I'm not tied to anything or anywhere,' she said with a pout, 'I'm just not ready to go yet.'

'Is that how you could follow Amaliel?' I asked.

Kayla smirked at me. 'I've never been a conventional spook, have I?'

'No,' I said with a laugh, then saw Vaybian get up and walk towards the cart and the smile dropped from my face. 'Vaybian mustn't know,' I told Jamie and Jinx.

'He won't hear it from me,' Jinx said, 'he's already crankier than you on a really bad day.'

'Thanks.'

'You're welcome,' he said with a Cheshire-cat grin. I wiped the smile from his face by telling him and Jamie what Kayla had said about Philip.

'Of course it could be Philip's just doing whatever he can to survive,' I said, though I was beginning to think I was kidding myself.

Both my men gave derisive snorts of disgust and Kayla slapped her forehead. 'Lucky, when will you learn that Philip Conrad is nothing but trouble?

'I can't believe you're still defending him,' Jamie said.

'The man's a total scrote,' Jinx said.

'He won't have any if I get hold of him,' Kayla said.

'You,' I pointed out, 'can't get hold of anyone.'

She gave me an over-the-top sweet smile. 'Then I'll have to leave it to the Deathbringer.'

'Fine by me,' he said.

'What?' Jamie asked.

'Come on,' Jinx said, throwing his arm around Jamie's shoulders. 'I'll explain on the way back to my steed.'

'I'll ride with you,' Kayla told me. 'At least I know how to ride a shavna.'

'Is that what they're called?'

'Hmm,' she said, 'I'm glad they gave you a docile one; they can be a bit of a handful.'

As I'd had years of practice, it wasn't so hard hiding the fact I was talking to Kayla when we spoke, though Vaybian gave me odd looks once or twice; of course, this could have been because he really didn't like me. I had thought that when he pledged himself to me our relationship would get a little better, but obviously not.

By the time we reached the road leading to the fortress my anxiety levels had risen to boiling point. Telling Baltheza Kayla was dead was not going to be an easy conversation, and it could mean that both Vaybian and I would be heading straight down to the Chambers of Rectification. Although this was to be my first destination after seeing Baltheza, I'd hoped it would be under my own steam.

We entered through the front gate and Jamie called to the guards. He requested they go straight to Lord Baltheza to tell him we had grave news, and to ask that we be granted an audience. Put that way, I supposed Baltheza would at least have an inkling we weren't about to make his day. Within ten minutes we were being ushered up to his private apartments.

He was seated on the couch with his pet slave at his feet. She smiled as we entered; he did not. We had left Vaybian with Kerfuffle, Shenanigans and Kubeck; I hoped being out of sight would keep him out of mind. Baltheza had made it quite clear what would happen to Kayla's green captain should we return without her.

Kayla came with us, and I hoped that with her guidance I might be able to quell Baltheza's volatile temper, though now he was no longer being poisoned perhaps he would be a little calmer.

'Where is my daughter?' he asked.

'My Lord,' Jinx said and he and Jamie bowed their heads.

'I said, where is my daughter? Deathbringer.'

'I am very much afraid I have the worst of news,' Jinx said.

Baltheza pressed his lips together into a tight line. He tapped the slave on the shoulder and gestured to the flagon of wine on the small table by his side. She uncurled her legs from beneath her and stood, smiling that unpleasant smile. There was something about her that made me want to shudder. I wasn't sure if she reminded me more of a big cat or a snake.

'Kayla is dead?' Baltheza said.

'I'm sorry, My Lord,' Jinx said.

Baltheza's blazing orange eyes turned on me. 'Yet you are not.'

'It was a close thing,' Jamie said.

'You no doubt saved she who bares your mark over my daughter?'

'Here we go,' Kayla said, 'same old papa working himself into a right royal strop.'

I wanted to ask her what to do to defuse the situation, but talking to his dead daughter, whom he couldn't see, would hardly help.

'Amaliel killed Kayla during our rescue attempt so he could escape us,' I said.

'There was nothing to be done,' Jinx said.

Baltheza's lips curled into a sneer. 'Only a few short days ago you managed to save the innkeeper's son from imminent death. You did this and yet you couldn't save my daughter?'

'Odin's life was in the balance; Kayla's was not.'

'How so?'

Jinx glanced my way, or he may have been looking at Kayla, I wasn't sure. 'He slit her throat. She bled out before anything could be done.'

'You must have been able to do something?'

'I am the Deathbringer, not a miracle worker,' Jinx snapped.

Baltheza raised an eyebrow. 'Have a care Deathbringer.'

'No, Baltheza – you have a care. I am sorry for your loss, I truly am, but if you want to point the finger of blame, point it in the direction of Amaliel Cheriour. He murdered your daughter and would have killed your other one had he half the chance.'

Both men glared at each other for a few moments before Baltheza took a swig of his drink. 'Bring another flagon of wine,' he said to the slave, unclipping the lead from her collar and waving her away.

She strolled out of the room. It wasn't until she closed the door behind her and I let out a long breath that I realised I'd been holding it in.

Baltheza's eyes fixed on me over the top of the goblet before he took another slug. 'Last time you came before me it was as your daemon self; why has she gone to be replaced by this pale human imposter?'

Kayla choked back laughter. 'Light the blue touch paper why don't you?'

'What you see is what you get,' I said.

'Today I do not see my daughter, therefore I shall not treat you as such,' Baltheza said, looking down his very aristocratic nose at me.

'Well that's just fine with me,' I retorted.

'Lucky,' Jamie murmured a warning.

'Give me one good reason why I shouldn't send you down to my Chambers of Rectification for some correction.'

'Maybe because you no longer have a court torturer?' I said, giving him a bitchy smile.

He glared at me. 'Amaliel can be easily replaced and don't you forget it. Now,' he said, getting to his feet, 'I wish to see my daughter.'

'I think it would be better if you didn't, My Lord,' Jamie said.

'Why ever not?'

'Surely it would be preferable for you to remember her as she was in life?' Jinx said.

'Amaliel had tortured her?' Jinx nodded. Baltheza slammed his goblet down onto the table. 'I will have his hide decorating my wall along with his balls!' he said, and strode to the door. 'Take me to her.'

Jamie opened the door for Baltheza to leave and we all filed out behind him. Jamie moved forward to fall into step beside Baltheza and take him to Kayla's body.

'This is so not going to go well,' Kayla said to me as we followed her father along the corridor.

'At least he hasn't mentioned Vaybian yet,' I said, keeping my voice low.

She glanced at me in alarm. 'You won't let my father hurt him?'

'Not if I can help it.'

'I couldn't bear it if he had him executed.'

'I suppose you'd be together, at least.'

'I'd rather he had a long and happy life.' I knew she meant it, but I didn't think it was going to happen; he was miserable without her. I held my tongue; I'd let her find this out for herself.

The cart was in the entrance courtyard where we had left it, with Kerfuffle, Shenanigans and Pyrites on guard. Vaybian was nowhere to be seen, which was probably just as well.

'You brought my daughter back to her home in a vegetable cart?' Baltheza said, his lips curling in distaste.

'It was either that or fling her over the back of a shavna,' Jinx said.

Jamie quickly stepped in between the two of them to lift the cart's cover, and Shenanigans hurried forward to give him a hand in pulling it out of the way.

Baltheza moved closer as Jamie let the back down. 'Are you sure you want to see her?' he asked.

Kayla's father nodded and Jamie lifted the skins that were covering her and pulled them down to her shoulders. Baltheza's lips stretched into a tight grimace and he raised a clenched fist to his chest.

'He did this to her? He cut her beautiful hair?'

'Yes,' several of us murmured.

He turned to my two men. 'You will find him and you will bring him to me.'

'Alive?' Jinx asked.

'Yes, I want to keep him alive for a very long time. In fact I intend to think up a particularly special fate for Amaliel.'

I suppressed a shudder, but I couldn't help thinking Amaliel

Cheriour would deserve every single torment he got. Not just for what he had done to Kayla, but for all the other poor souls he had tortured, killed and cursed.

'Have you any idea where to find him?' he asked.

Jamie and Jinx exchanged a glance. 'We think we may have a lead,' Jamie said. 'With your leave we would start by searching his chambers below the palace.'

'Searching for clues?'

'Something like that.'

'Good,' he said and went to walk away, but then turned back to me. 'Captain Vaybian is conspicuous by his absence. You didn't manage to get him killed as well?'

'No,' I said, 'although he was also tortured by Amaliel.'

His nostrils flared. 'If he helps you bring Amaliel to me I may spare his life. I will think on it.'

'You do that,' I said.

'I will also think on what I am to do with you. Perhaps if you return looking like you could be a daughter of mine I will consider letting you live.'

'He doesn't mean it,' Kayla said. 'He was always saying stuff like that to me.'

'I'll bear that in mind,' I said to him.

He glared at each of us one more time and strode off.

'That went better than I expected,' Jamie said. 'Though you two weren't much help. When are you both going to learn to control your tempers?' He pulled the covers back up over Kayla's face before turning back to us. 'I suppose we should be thankful the effects of the verillion have worn off a bit. Otherwise we may have all ended up in the dungeons.'

'He disrespects us,' Jinx said.

'Don't take it so personally,' Jamie said, 'he disrespects everybody. Anyway, when did you start getting so precious?'

'When he threatens our lady.'

Jamie glanced my way. 'When it comes to Lucky, I don't think he means it.'

'See,' Kayla said wafting around us.

'Where is Vaybian anyway?' I asked Shenanigans and Kerfuffle.

'We sent him to the Drakon's Rest to wait for us there,' Shenanigans said. 'We thought it safest.'

'Good call,' Jinx said. 'I'm pretty sure Baltheza means every word he says when talking about Vaybian.'

'I hope not,' Kayla said, 'but dear Papa did always have a soft spot for me.'

'I think we should go straight down to the Chambers of Rectification,' I said.

'What do you expect to find down *there*?' said Kerfuffle.

Jinx glanced around us then gestured for the others to move in close so we couldn't be overheard.

'Lady Kayla told us that Amaliel and Henri are hiding out in the tunnels underneath the palace. She says that's where they're keeping the child.'

'Lady Kayla?' Kerfuffle said, glancing towards the cart where her body rested. 'When did she tell you this?'

'How would she have known?' asked Shenanigans.

'What is it exactly you lot don't understand about Lady Lucinda being the Soulseer?' Jinx asked in exasperation.

'You mean Lady Kayla is here? Now?' Shenanigans asked, glancing around us.

'Yes,' I said, 'but you mustn't tell Vaybian. It will only upset him.'

'Why hasn't she passed over?' Kerfuffle asked.

'She didn't want to leave me,' I said.

'Trust her,' Kerfuffle said. 'She always had to be difficult.'

'I heard that,' she said.

'But he can't hear you, Kayla. It's not like when we were in the Overlands.'

'Well, I suppose I wasn't really a ghost then,' she said.

'This is weird,' Kerfuffle said with a scowl, 'I'm never going to know if she's talking to us or not.'

'This isn't getting us anywhere,' I said, turning towards the palace entrance. 'Let's get down to the dungeons.'

Jamie grabbed me by the arm. 'Are you sure?'

Jamie and Jinx exchanged a glance.

'I'm not certain you want to see what goes on down there,' Jinx said.

'I shouldn't think much is going on at the moment.'

'Just because Amaliel is no longer Court Chief Enforcer, it doesn't mean there aren't others down in the Chambers of Rectification carrying out punishments,' Jamie said.

'Then I will just have to try and not look.'

'You know you don't have anything to prove,' Jinx said.

'Maybe not, but we have to find Angela, and I have to find out how to release the spirits in the great hall and at Dark Mountain from the curse.'

'We know how to release them,' Jinx said, surprised.

'We do?'

'The Sicarii chanted the words.'

'I didn't understand a thing they said.'

Jinx grinned at me. 'I did.'

'Can you remember it?' He gave me a you-cannot-be-serious look. 'Well I suppose that's something.'

'So can I,' Jamie said. 'It wasn't that difficult actually.'

Now they were making me grumpy. 'All right, all right, I'm the idiot that flunked Latin at school.'

'It was ancient Egyptian actually, a bastardisation of spells from the *Book of the Dead*,' Jinx said. Now *that* I had heard of.

'So – no arguments – I'm coming with you.'

'I suppose we could tie her up,' Jinx said, resting his chin on his fist, 'but then she'd be really cranky when we got back.'

'Hmm,' Jamie said, mirroring Jinx, 'she probably wouldn't talk to us for hours.'

'You tie me up and we're talking weeks, maybe months,' I told them.

'We'd have to toss her for who got to sleep in the bed and who got the floor.'

'No argument,' I said, 'I'm the princess – I get the bed.'

'I think being the Deathbringer and Guardian outranks royalty.'

'She is the Soulseer,' Jamie said.

'True,' Jinx said. 'I suppose there's no way round it; she'll have to come with us. But,' Jinx raised a finger, 'if you start spewing you hold your own hair.'

I flicked him the V, and when he looked perplexed I stuck out my tongue. Why Jinx sometimes made me act like a small child I had no idea, but for whatever reason it usually made me feel better.

'We'll be going with you,' Shenanigans said.

'Aye,' Kerfuffle said, 'we *will* be going with you.'

Jamie and Jinx exchanged a glance. Jamie nodded. 'Your choice,' he said.

'I will join you in this,' Kubeck said.

'And don't forget me and the drakon,' Kayla said, 'I'm really looking forward to seeing Amaliel get his just desserts.'

'Why don't we sell tickets?' Jinx said.

'The way people feel about Amaliel you'd probably make a fortune,' Kerfuffle mumbled and with that we set off.

Sixteen

Everyone grew quiet as we descended the stairs towards the dreaded Chambers of Rectification. Shenanigans and Kubeck had both spent time in its depths; I hadn't, yet I still felt cold inside.

The steps were wide; wide enough for a large daemon to be escorted either side by two even larger daemon guards. There was no decoration here, just broad stone steps flanked by grey stone walls, and once we had descended below the ground floor the air grew colder until our breath left plumes of mist every time we exhaled.

Down here dark patches, reminiscent of the mould-like blemishes upon the Sicarii's skin, stained the walls. There was even a slight scent on the air of something having turned bad.

Then we reached the corridor leading to the Chambers of Rectification. No one had to tell me we had reached our destination. I could feel it, I could smell it and I could hear it. Cells lined each side of the passageway and from inside them I could hear low moans and sobbing. Pyrites shrank to the size of a bird to perch upon my shoulder and Jamie took hold of my hand; as usual they both knew how I was feeling.

'Let's get this done with and get out,' Jinx said, 'this place makes me want to puke.'

'Well, if you do you can hold your own hair,' I told him, which brought a small smile back to his face.

We didn't look in the cells. If we had it would have been so very hard not to set the occupants free and, if we did, this could take us to a very bad place indeed; probably the very same cells we had emptied.

The corridor opened out into a large chamber, and again, no one had to explain what this was used for. A large crocodile-skinned daemon was washing blood off a huge, wooden butcher's table in the middle of the room, while a smaller daemon with long dreadlocks and a boar's snout mopped the floor.

The larger daemon paused to look up at us. 'Can I help you?' he said.

'We're looking for Amaliel Cheriour's private quarters,' Jinx said.

The smaller daemon leaned on his mop and eyed us up and down. 'You can't go in there.'

'Why not?' Jinx asked.

'The clue's in what you said. Amaliel Cheriour's *private* quarters.'

'Do you know who you're talking to?' Kerfuffle said, marching up to the daemon and scowling up at him.

'Well, I know at least two of you have spent time in these chambers, and I wouldn't be surprised if you did so again,' he said, plunging his mop back into the bucket and splashing Kerfuffle's boots.

'Bloody upstart,' Kerfuffle said.

'Want to make something of it?' the daemon said, brandishing his mop.

'Now then, now then,' the other daemon said, 'we don't want any trouble here. What is your business?'

'We have been ordered by Lord Baltheza to find and arrest Amaliel Cheriour. We need to take a look at his private quarters to see if there are any clues to his whereabouts,' Jinx said.

'So, it's come to that, has it?' The daemon threw his scrubbing brush down onto the table and lumbered towards a doorway at the back of the room. He opened the door and beyond it was another corridor.

'His chamber is the last door on the right. The one opposite goes through to where he plies his trade.'

'Not here?' Jamie asked, gesturing to the room behind us.

'Nah, this is where the ordinary felons are questioned and punished: common thieves, poachers, murderers and the like. He looks after the important inmates: insurgents, daemons guilty of treason and crimes against the state, that sort of thing.'

'I see,' Jamie said.

'Don't mess up his room and don't break anything, just in case Baltheza has a change of heart,' the large daemon said, going back to the table.

'I don't think that's likely to happen,' Jinx said, 'Amaliel murdered Baltheza's daughter.'

'Lady Kayla?' the daemon with the mop said.

'I'm afraid so,' Jamie said.

The large daemon picked up his scrubbing brush again. 'In that case, I wouldn't want to be in his shoes.'

'Nor I,' said his mate and they both got on with their cleaning, leaving us to investigate on our own.

'Which room first?' Jamie said when we reached the end of the corridor.

'His. I doubt he'd leave anything incriminating in his torture chamber; too many others might see it,' Shenanigans said.

'We don't need proof he's bad, we just need to find the way down to the underground tunnels,' I said, turning to Kayla. 'I don't s'pose you know?'

'The entrance is beneath his bed,' Kayla said. 'There's a trap door leading onto some stairs.'

Jamie paused, hand on doorknob. 'Why do I feel like I'm about to enter the depths of hell?'

'If there is a hell, it's where he should be,' Jinx said.

'You don't know whether there's a hell or not?' I asked.

Jinx tapped the side of his nose with a forefinger. 'Trade secret.'

'Judging by those things that carried of the Sicarii, I'm guessing it's not much of a secret anymore,' Kerfuffle said with a shudder.

'True,' Jinx said and gestured for Jamie to open the door.

I had expected a dark, tomb-like chamber. I wasn't disappointed; the decor was either black, or shades of it. A large, black desk littered with scrolls, books and papers filled one end. On the other side of the room was a narrow bed, but it had no pillow or covers.

'It appears he really doesn't sleep,' Shenanigans said as he followed us in.

Jinx lit a lamp, but if anything it made the room look even creepier. Lines of shelves filled the wall behind the desk and in between leatherbound books there were shiny glass jars of varying shapes and sizes that reflected the lamplight, giving the impression they were filled with flickering flames.

'Might be worth taking a look to see if there's anything that might give us a clue to what he's likely to do next,' Jinx said as he wandered around the desk to take a look at the shelves lining the walls behind it. Jamie began to paw through the papers and other bits and pieces while Kubeck stayed in the doorway and Shenanigans waited just inside. Kerfuffle joined Jamie at the desk picking up and discarding scrolls and manuscripts.

'Nothing much of interest here,' Kerfuffle said.

'What's in the jars?' I asked Jinx.

He turned to me with a grimace. 'You really don't want to know.'

Jamie looked up from the desk and joined Jinx in front of the shelves. 'That is so disgusting,' Jamie said, and when he turned I could see his face had gone very pale.

'The trapdoor is under the bed,' I told them.

Shenanigans and Kubeck lifted the bed and moved it to one side. 'If there is one, I can't see it,' Kubeck said, looking down at the stone slabs.

'Kayla?'

She knelt down on the floor and ran her fingers over the stone. Out of habit I guess – if there was anything there she wouldn't be able to feel it. 'It's here somewhere.'

'Did you see how he opened it?' I asked.

She shook her head and the vipers in her hair hissed. 'No, he had his back to me, but he touched or pressed something around here somewhere,' she said. Jinx got down on one knee beside her and drew his finger along the join between the wall and the floor.

'If there is an entrance here I'll find it.'

'Well there is, so you'd better,' Kayla said.

'Even in death you're bossy,' he said, concentrating on the floor, his hands gliding back and forth.

'We could always take a hammer and chisel to it,' Kerfuffle said.

'Very subtle,' Jinx said.

'Just saying.'

'If we can't find the way in we'll have little choice,' Shenanigans said.

'One: he will hear us, and two: so will half the palace,' Jinx said. 'Ah ha! Here we go,' and there was a click and a grinding sound as a slab slid back under the wall leaving a rectangular hole in the floor. Jinx hopped to his feet. 'Pass me the lamp, brother.' Jamie handed it to Jinx, who peered down into the dark. 'I'll go first,' Jinx said.

'I'll be right behind you,' Jamie said.

'Shenanigans and Kerfuffle, you come next and Kubeck – you watch Lucky's back. Pyrites, stay where you are,' Jinx said and Pyrites puffed warm air against my neck and snuggled down upon my shoulder.

I shivered as I watched Jinx and then Jamie disappear down into the hole. There was something very disturbing about seeing them descend into the darkness; like the way they sank into the ground was some ill omen. I immediately wished I hadn't thought of this; as though my thinking of it might make something bad happen.

I wanted to hurry down behind them and be next to them, but Shenanigans and Kerfuffle were having none of it. 'We are to go next, mistress,' Shenanigans said, and I couldn't argue with him, he was doing his job.

'I'll go ahead and make sure they don't get into any trouble,' Kayla said. As Kayla and trouble usually went together hand in hand this didn't offer me any comfort. I didn't try to dissuade her though; she probably needed something to do as much as I did.

The stairs led down to a long, narrow corridor. Jinx and Jamie could probably just about walk side by side, but Shenanigans, and

I guess Kubeck, who was behind me, filled the space. Shenanigans' broad shoulders were almost brushing the walls on either side of him and he had to stoop down to keep his head from scraping the ceiling.

Our breath smoked the air and our footsteps echoed, bouncing off the grey stone walls. I wished I had a hand to hold. Pyrites knew how I was feeling and nestled close against my head.

No one spoke and the tension was palpable as we crept along the passageway, our shadows dancing against the walls as the flame in the lamp Jinx was carrying flickered and leapt. Kerfuffle had drawn his dagger and Pyrites sat up, alert upon my shoulder. Kayla wafted past Jamie and Jinx; I hoped she would warn us if there was trouble ahead.

We came to another door. Jinx and Jamie waited until we were right behind them before Jinx reached out to turn the ringed handle. The door swung open with a gentle swish.

The room beyond was large, dark and empty, just four grey stone walls, a ceiling and a slab floor. A door beckoned from the opposite wall. Jamie exhaled as Jinx moved across the slabs and we all followed. Again, Jinx waited until we were all ready. This door also swung open with a soft whisper and led onto another corridor, this one lined with open doors on either side.

Jinx paused by the first doorway and lifted the lamp to see. I moved forward past my guards to peer inside. It was a prison cell that probably doubled up as a torture chamber. An overturned brazier lay in the corner along with a haphazard pile of iron-mongery; long pointed pokers and pincers were only the half of it. Jinx lowered the lamp and moved on to more of the same.

Each time he paused I expected a Sicarii, or one of the brown-robed minions, or even Henri to appear, a lethal weapon raised above their heads. By the last open doorway I was ready to jump three feet in the air if someone so much as coughed.

Vaporous figures began to drift out of the open doors, watching us pass in silence. How many hundreds or maybe even thousands had Amaliel executed and murdered over the years? He had probably been alive a very long time, so it could even run into tens of thousands, and the thought of all the terrible suffering he had inflected made me want to kill him even more.

The final door was at the end of the passage. This was where we would find trouble; I could feel it. Jinx reached for the door handle.

'Wait,' I said, and although I whispered, my voice sounded too loud in the confined corridor. Jamie and Jinx turned to look at me, their eyes glittering in the lamplight, lips tight; they were feeling the tension too. 'Let Kayla go first.'

'Good thinking,' Jinx said, his voice a soft murmur.

Kayla grinned at me and wafted past them and through the door. She was gone for less than a second.

'It's a torture chamber,' she told us, 'full of really nasty stuff, but no sign of Amaliel or Henri.'

'Any other doors?' Jinx asked.

'Two,' she said, holding up a thumb and forefinger, 'one on the far side, the other to the left.'

'Want to see what's behind each of those doors?' he asked.

'Too right,' she said and was off through the door again while we waited. When she came back her good humour had disappeared. 'The door straight ahead leads to another chamber like Amaliel's room upstairs: books, papers and jars full of body parts,' she said. 'Amaliel is through the door to the left with Henri, Philip and Angela. He knows you're coming. He has a knife to the child's throat, and from experience I'm guessing he's quite prepared to use it.' Her hand rose to her own throat as she spoke.

'What do we do?' I asked.

'Wait,' Kayla said, putting a finger to her lips and passing back through the door.

I repeated the instruction and what she'd told me to the others.

'Philip's coming,' Kayla said as she reappeared through the door. 'Don't trust him.'

Jinx and Jamie took a step back from the door as the handle slowly began to turn and the door opened a crack.

'It's me – it's Philip,' a voice said and he stepped through, both hands raised as though he was in an old western movie.

'What do *you* want?' Jamie asked with undisguised animosity, and he hadn't even heard Kayla's warning.

'He has my daughter and says he'll kill her if either you or him' – he gestured at Jinx – 'enter the next room.'

'What about me?' I asked.

'You, he wants. It's always been you he wanted.'

'Figures,' Jamie said.

'You'd better go back to your master and tell him that where Lucinda goes, we go,' Jinx said, 'because there is no way in the whole of the Underlands I'm letting her anywhere near Amaliel Cheriour or Henri le Dent on her own.'

'He'll kill my daughter,' he said and turned to me. 'Please Lucky, there's no time. Come with me.'

Philip grabbed hold of my arm and two blades instantly appeared at his throat and another at his crotch.

'Just give me an excuse,' Kerfuffle said, pushing the point of his blade against the seam of Philip's breeches.

Philip gasped, letting go of me, but Jamie's and Jinx's blades stayed put; one resting against his Adam's apple and the other just below the left side of his jaw.

'One nick and you'll bleed out all over the floor, so I suggest you stay very still,' Jinx murmured in his ear.

'Lucky,' Philip said, his eyes very wide and his lips hardly moving at all. 'Please,' he gasped. 'Help me.'

I looked from Philip's desperate expression to Jamie and Jinx. If they were moved they didn't show it. I glanced at Kayla; her hand was still resting against her throat. We both knew Amaliel would do it.

'I have to go with him,' I told them.

'Lucky—' Jamie started to say, but I held up a hand.

'I have to. No ifs no buts, I have to.'

I beckoned to Shenanigans to follow me down the corridor a few feet putting him between me and Philip while I made sure

Pyrites was secure and well hidden beneath my hair. This was something I didn't want Philip to see. Pyrites was my secret weapon.

'All right Philip. I'll go with you,' I said when I was done and gestured for Jamie and Jinx to lower their weapons.

'No mistress,' Shenanigans said.

'Don't worry,' I whispered to him, 'I'm going in to try and get Angela back.'

Shenanigans and Kerfuffle both glanced from me to my two men who, with a certain amount of reluctance, moved their daggers away from Philip's vulnerable throat.

I gestured for Philip to open the door and enter. I followed after him, pulling the door closed, but not before exchanging one last look with my two men. Both were grim faced, but Jinx's expression was not as worried as Jamie's; he had faith in me, probably more than I had in myself.

Philip hurried across the room and paused outside the other door, waiting for me. 'Go on,' I said, and he reached out and turned the doorknob.

'It's me,' he said, before pushing the door wide open and turning to me. 'After you.' He couldn't quite keep the expression of smug triumph from curling his lips.

'Little shit,' Kayla said, 'I told you he couldn't be trusted.'

I stopped dead and stared him out. 'Not a chance in hell.'

His smug smile turned into more of a grimace, but when he saw I wasn't about to move anywhere he made a disgruntled sound and went inside.

I straightened my back, held my head up high and followed him into the room where Amaliel and Henri were waiting. Amaliel had one arm wrapped around Angela's chest and a knife pressed against the artery just beneath her chin. Her eyes were red-rimmed and her face pale, but even as frightened as she must have been, it didn't stop her giving her father an adolescent-girl glower.

'How nice of you to join us,' Amaliel said, gesturing with his head to Philip who disappeared behind me. Then I heard bolts being drawn on the door. Kayla was right, Philip was a little shit. 'Come,' Amaliel said, but he wasn't speaking to me. Philip hurried to his side and took hold of Angela's arm. Amaliel lowered the dagger, handed it to Henri and rested his palm on Philip's shoulder. 'I am very pleased with you.'

'I'm not,' Angela muttered under her breath and tried to shrug her father's hand from her arm. If anything, he gripped it even harder. She winced. 'You're hurting.'

'Then be a good girl and keep still.'

Amaliel turned his red glowing eyes on me. 'You, Lucky de Salle, are becoming more than a minor irritation.'

'Good,' I said, crossing my arms and trying to appear relaxed and nonchalant even though my heart was pounding.

'Tell me, what happened to the Sicarii at the temple? Did you orchestrate their disappearance?'

I laughed. 'I really wish I did have the power to blast you and your mates down into hell, but apparently there are those in the afterlife who are more than happy to take the truly evil – whether it's their time or not. Your friends tried to enter a place where they would never receive a welcome and they forfeited their lives.'

'Can you open the doorway again?'

'Not unless there are souls waiting to pass over. Of course, if you're willing to risk going the same way as the Sicarii, I'll give it a go,' I said with a bright and bitchy smile.

'It appears you have underestimated her,' Henri said with a sneer.

'I recall it was you who said she was little more than a frightened child,' Amaliel said.

Henri's disfigured lips twitched. 'That was before she had been marked by two so powerful daemons, *and* I knew she was the Soulseer; I recall this snippet of information you saw fit to keep from me.'

'Let's cut to the chase,' I said. 'What do you want of me?'

'If you cannot give me safe passage back and forth between here and the afterlife I'm not sure there is anything you can do for me, other than perhaps die.' He gestured to Henri with a careless flick of his hand, 'Over to you.'

'Shit,' Kayla said and disappeared as Henri took a step towards me.

'Pyrites!' I said, and I felt my little drakon drop down from my neck and in a whir of wings he flew around to hover in front of me and began to grow – fast.

Henri recoiled, his burned face a mask of horror, and threw up his arms to protect himself.

I heard Amaliel move, taking my attention off Henri, but before I could do anything he'd grabbed Philip's shoulder, pulled him and Angela back against the wall, and there was a sound of grinding rock. In a moment, Amaliel, Philip and Angela were gone, and I was left staring at a blank expanse of grey stone. For a moment I was dumbstruck, but needed to move quickly to have any chance of catching them – I took action.

Henri was huddled down on the floor with Pyrites above him, holding him down with a clawed foot. 'How do I open the secret door?' I snarled at Henri and pointed to the wall.

Fists began to hammer against the door behind me. 'Lucky!' I heard Jamie shout.

'Henri?'

'I don't know. I truly don't know,' he gasped, not taking his eyes off Pyrites.

'Pyrites,' I said, pointing at Henri. 'If he moves, torch him.' Then I hurried to the door and began to draw the bolts. Kayla materialised through the dark wood as I did so.

'Where's Amaliel?' she asked.

'Secret passage,' I said, gesturing to the wall as I stooped to pull the bottom bolt.

'Bugger,' she said and disappeared through the wall after them.

The door flew open and Jamie was through it in an instant. 'Where is he?'

Jinx strode past us followed by my other three guards. 'Not here by the looks of it.'

'Secret passage,' I repeated. 'Kayla's gone after him, but it's this way – we need to find out how to open it.'

'Kayla said Henri was going to kill you.'

'Pyrites wasn't about to let that happen,' I said.

My drakon had shrunk to a smaller though no less impressive size while Jinx took hold of Henri and dragged him to his feet. 'Give me one good reason why I shouldn't let the drakon roast you to a crisp and then gnaw on your bones.'

'I'd let him if I were you,' Kerfuffle said.

'He left me. He left me behind for the human,' Henri said in disbelief.

'Why is the human important to him?'

'He left me.'

'Henri, if you don't answer me I'll see you in hell.'

'I don't know. I didn't know he was until now. I thought he was only using him to manipulate the woman.'

'Where's Kayla?' Jamie asked.

'Following Amaliel,' I said.

'There must be a hidden mechanism somewhere,' Shenanigans said, running his fingers across the stone work. Kerfuffle stooped down to examine the crack between the wall and the floor, his back almost bent double.

Kayla appeared through the slabs of stone. 'Come on,' she called, making for the door, 'you'll have to hurry, he's on a staircase leading up into Baltheza's private dining chamber beyond the great hall.'

'We'll go ahead,' Jinx said, running after Kayla, 'Shenanigans, Kubeck – follow Lucinda and bring Henri with you. If he gives you any trouble at all, kill him.'

'I'll give you no trouble, I'll give you no trouble,' I heard Henri say as I ran out of the door behind Jamie.

Once we got into the main corridor, Pyrites whizzed over our heads to fly at the front. He no doubt would have forged ahead, but he had to wait for doors to be opened. When we reached the stairs up into Amaliel's chamber he was up through the hole like a shot with Jinx pounding up the steps behind him.

By the time Jamie and I had run up the stairs, Jinx and Pyrites were gone, the sound of their passage echoing along the hallway. We raced past the two daemons in the torture chamber who had moved on from washing away blood to polishing up equipment. They watched our passing with no comment and little interest.

Then we were charging up more stairs onto the ground level of the palace and along wide passageways leading to the great hall. Several guards had gathered outside, but it was clear from their fearful expressions that they weren't planning on getting involved.

'If you're not going to help us arrest Amaliel at least make sure he doesn't leave,' Jamie shouted at them. Their response was to push the doors closed behind us.

By the time we skidded to a halt the confrontation between Jinx and Amaliel had already begun.

'Let the child go and I will make your passing quick and pain free, that's the best and most generous offer you're going to get from me,' Jinx said. His back was to us, and I could see his tail was moving in agitated flicks from side to side like that of an angry cat. Pyrites was by his side, dwarfing Jinx and Amaliel. The clicking of his claws as he paddled the stone and the small puffs of black smoke and flame showed he was as unhappy as the Deathbringer. Kayla hovered by their sides, the hissing and spitting vipers in her hair letting her feelings be known.

Amaliel once again had Angela pressed against his chest, a blade to her throat. If Philip was worried about his daughter's wellbeing he didn't show it. His lips were curled into an arrogant sneer and I wondered at the man's sanity. Was he willing to give up his daughter for whatever favours Amaliel had offered him? If so, he must be mad: I wouldn't trust Amaliel to keep a single one of his promises, other than the promise he'd made to see me dead.

The pounding of more feet upon stone and the door being yanked open announced the imminent arrival of the rest of my guard. They piled into the hall and spread out beside us, forming another barrier between Amaliel and freedom.

'There's nowhere to go Amaliel,' Jamie said. 'Give yourself up.'

'I have considered you many things Guardian, but never before an idiot.'

'Let's just cut him to ribbons and be done with it,' Kerfuffle said.

'Willing to risk the child, little man?' Amaliel sneered.

'Willing to risk your life?' Kerfuffle answered.

'According to the Deathbringer and Guardian it's already over, so what have I to fear?'

Kerfuffle glowered at him, but Shenanigans' expression was murderous. If we managed to get Angela away from Amaliel there was no doubt in my mind he would instantly be on the receiving end of Shenanigans' rough justice.

I laid a hand on his forearm. 'Easy,' I said, but was interrupted by grey spirits rising up out of the stone beneath our feet and floating down from the rafters. There were more than ever before, and I guessed the apparitions of those executed in the great hall had been joined by those tortured and murdered in the chambers below.

'Save the child,' they called.

'Jinx, say the words that will release the spirits from this world,' I said.

Jamie moved to Jinx's side. 'On three,' Jinx said. 'One. Two . . .'

'Three,' they said together and began to chant.

Amaliel hissed. 'Fools, do you think by freeing them you will stop me? I will rule the Underlands and when I do, it will not end there. Next I will take control of the Overlands and when I have gathered the millions of souls that can be had from that over-bloated world of self-serving imbeciles I will take the afterlife as well.'

'He's more bonkers than Baltheza ever was,' Kerfuffle said.

'I heard that,' Kayla said.

I ignored them as I closed my eyes, took a deep breath, and with a ripple of warmth, I felt myself change. This time I felt more confident in my ability. I visualised the spot of light that preceded the opening of the door to the other side, and when I opened my eyes a small glowing tear was appearing between us and Amaliel.

'Oh my life,' I heard Kerfuffle mutter.

The tear widened and grew and a golden swathe of light coloured the flagstones. 'It's time for you all to move on,' I told the spirits, and from the corner of my eye saw my guards begin to close in on Amaliel.

The little spirit, Clement, floated down to stand before me. He gave a small bow, and when he looked up he was smiling. 'Thank you,' he said and, taking hold of the hands of two other spirits, drifted towards the light. 'Don't be afraid,' he called to the others, 'the Soulseer has seen the curse lifted and granted us entry to beyond.' Then he stepped into the light, taking the two other spirits with him, and they were transformed from grey shadows into vibrant, glowing beings that easily could be mistaken for angels, but maybe that was what they now were.

'Goodbye Soulseer, until we meet again,' he said, looking back before he stepped through the tear and was gone.

The others began to follow. First one by one, then in pairs as the tear grew bigger and bigger until all but a few stragglers were gone. I noticed Kayla keeping well away from the light, although her expression was wistful. I remembered the warm glow and sound of tinkling laughter that had tempted me, but strangely enough my feet no longer felt the compulsion to take me into the beyond. Been there, done that I suppose.

My guards tightened the circle around Amaliel, edging him closer to the golden light, which began to change. Instead of pure golden rays promising happy endings, it darkened to orange, then to fiery red, until Amaliel realised what was coming and lost his nerve. With a shriek he thrust Angela towards the blackening hole, grabbed Philip by the arm and ran. Shenanigans and Kubeck threw themselves towards him – but too late. Amaliel was through and slamming the door behind him, and I heard the metallic rasp of bolts being shoved home.

The entrance to the other world wavered for a moment and then snapped shut and was gone.

'Shite,' Jinx said, running towards the door, 'I thought we were almost rid of him.'

Shenanigans lumbered over to Angela and picked her up from the floor. 'Are you all right?' I heard him ask.

'Hurry, he's getting away,' Kayla said.

'Pyrites, bash down the door,' I heard Jinx say.

'Take Angela now,' I said to Shenanigans and Kerfuffle and bent down to whisper in the little daemon's ear, 'I don't think she needs to see any of this.'

Kerfuffle got the picture. 'Come on,' he said, tugging on Shenanigans' sleeve, 'let's go.'

'Mistress, are you sure?' Shenanigans asked.

'You go ahead, we'll meet you there later. Kubeck – keep an eye on Henri.'

There was an almighty crash and Pyrites gave a roar as the door to the back room collapsed in a pile along with part of the wall.

I ran after Pyrites and my two men, the smashed leaded window on the other side of the room giving us a clue as to where Amaliel had gone. I got there last and peered outside to see Jamie's back disappearing through an archway across the gardens. I dragged a chair to beneath the window and hopped up onto it and, trying to avoid pieces of broken glass, climbed up into the frame and jumped down the other side. As soon as I hit the ground I was off and running along the path to the archway.

My legs pumped, my arms swung and never before had I felt so powerful, so strong, so alive. I bounded through the archway and slowed to a stop.

Jamie and Jinx were standing up to their thighs in a square ornamental pond in the centre of a walled garden. Their backs were to me, but from the agitated *swish*ing of Jinx's tail and the way Jamie's wings were pulled right back told me they were very unhappy. Kayla was sitting with her feet on the wall surrounding the pond and looked as dejected as my men. She had wrapped her arms around her legs with her cheek resting on her knees.

'Shite, shite, shite, shite, shite,' Jinx swore.

'What happened?' I asked, running up the path to join them.

Both men's shoulders sagged as they turned to greet me. 'We lost him,' Jamie said.

'He could be anywhere,' Jinx said.

'What?'

'Remember how Lord Argon used the pond at the golf club to travel between our worlds?' Jamie said.

'Wait a minute. Are you saying Amaliel has gone into the Overlands?'

'Only as a means of getting away from us,' Jinx said, 'he'll come straight back but somewhere else.'

'You know that, do you?'

'Why wouldn't he?'

'In case you weren't listening, he threatened my world.'

'In case you hadn't noticed,' Jinx said, looking me up and down, 'the Overlands isn't your world any longer.'

I looked down at my rose pink shimmering hands.

'I'm so glad you've regained your sense of humour. Doesn't it worry you Amaliel could be in the Overlands?' Then something occurred to me. 'I didn't think it was possible for a daemon to travel to the Overlands without being called upon. He told me he had no jurisdiction in my world.'

'He has possibly found his own gateway,' Jamie said, wading to the edge of the pond and climbing up onto the small wall surrounding it, 'but you needn't worry; he has no real power in your world. He can make a bit of mischief, maybe get a few stupid or greedy men like Philip to do a few things for him and make trouble, but he can't do anything major. That's what he needed you, or us, for: dominion over life and death would have made him powerful wherever he was.'

Jinx jumped down beside us with a squish of sodden boots. 'I'm more concerned about your safety than what Amaliel might get up to in the Overlands,' Jinx said. 'Anyway, if Baltheza hasn't already put out a warrant for his arrest he will do soon, and then there won't be anywhere he'll be safe ever again.'

With Amaliel gone, and Philip with him, there was only one thing we could do – go back to the palace and tell Baltheza.

'Baltheza won't be happy that we've lost him,' Jamie said.

'Baltheza is never happy unless he's torturing someone,' I said.

Jinx slung his arm around my shoulders and Jamie took my hand. 'Don't worry, we won't let anything happen to you.'

'I think brother, maybe we should take that holiday we were talking about,' but I saw the forced smile he gave Jamie. Jinx might have been playing it down, but I knew he was still worried that Amaliel was out there somewhere.

'What about Henri?' I asked.

'We'll drop him off in the cells pending our chat with Baltheza. He can make the decision of what's to be done with him.'

I let them take me back inside. Jamie flew me through the broken window and Pyrites helped Jinx through, while Kayla drifted ahead into the great hall. 'Oh my,' I heard her say and then she began to laugh. I must admit, when I walked into the chamber I had to stifle a giggle of my own.

'He been giving you trouble?' Jinx asked Kubeck, who had released Henri's collar and was now sitting on his chest.

Kubeck lifted up one of his meaty hands to show us the palm. A long gash ran from the base of his forefinger to his wrist. 'Knife up his sleeve,' the daemon said.

'I'm surprised you didn't kill him,' Jinx said.

Kubeck grinned. 'I think time down in the cells at Lord Baltheza's pleasure is a far worse fate.'

'I think he's having trouble breathing,' Kayla said.

'He is going a rather strange colour,' I agreed.

Kubeck climbed to his feet and dragged Henri up by the belt of his trousers, dangling him about two feet off the ground. 'Take him down to the cells,' Jinx said. 'Then we go to Baltheza.'

★

I didn't go back down to the chambers below the palace. Instead I waited with Kayla in the entrance hall; I didn't ever want to be in that godforsaken place again.

I was still worried about Amaliel's disappearance. Even as we stood there waiting for my two men and Kubeck to come back from the Chambers of Rectification, I worried that he could be hiding out somewhere in the human world while he plotted and planned. We had enough evil people of our own doing wicked things without him inciting them to do more.

Kayla didn't share my concerns. 'The Deathbringer's right. With a warrant out for his arrest he won't be safe anywhere.'

'He will, if he's in my world.'

'Not if Daddy sanctions a court assassin to go after him. Anyway,' Kayla flapped a hand at me, 'he won't last five minutes in the Overlands: too much technology, too many people. He will be a nobody there; an odd-looking nobody at that.'

'But daemons can make themselves look a whole lot different in my world – you being a case in point,' I reminded her, but she dismissed it with another flap of her hand.

'You worry too much.'

She may have brushed aside my fears, but I had this hard, cold feeling in my solar plexus telling me I had good reason to be afraid. I didn't push it though; there was no point. If Jamie or Jinx knew where Amaliel was they would have gone after him. He was too evil to be allowed to live.

When Jamie, Jinx and Kubeck returned, we went to find Baltheza and Kayla chose to come with us. Apart from Amaliel being free, I had other things on my mind, like: would I be spending the night down in the Chambers of Rectification myself? I doubted my men would let it happen, but who's to say? The news we had to give Baltheza was not good.

We reached Baltheza's chamber all too soon, and one of the guards banged on the door to Baltheza's chamber three times. 'Come,' we heard from behind the door.

'I hate that, don't you?' Kayla said. ' "Come!" it sounds like he's calling a dog.'

The soldier opened the door and we all filed in. I was beginning to find these constant meetings tedious; I could do without all the threats and innuendos of violence – and the smiling white-haired girl. She was beginning to wind me up big time, though that was probably because she scared me.

'Well, what news do you have for me apart from having turned my palace into a battlefield?' Baltheza said, not even bothering with any niceties. The girl at his feet hid her mouth behind her hand and her eyes glittered with laughter. This time, the boys didn't bother with any preamble.

'We found Amaliel hiding in the tunnels beneath the palace,' Jamie said, 'but unfortunately he escaped. His accomplice, Henri le Dent, however, resides in the Chambers of Rectification, at your leisure.'

'But Amaliel and the human do not.'

'You wanted the human?' Jinx asked.

Baltheza wrinkled his nose. 'Not particularly, but if he is of an interest to Amaliel I think he should be of an interest to me.'

'It *is* most odd that he gave up Henri rather than Philip Conrad,' Jamie said.

'You saved the child?' Baltheza asked.

'Yes, My Lord.'

'It is strange a father should be prepared to give up his daughter,' Baltheza said, reaching to pick up his goblet from the small table at his elbow.

'Not that strange,' Kayla muttered.

Baltheza regarded us over the rim of his drink. 'What do you think Amaliel was offering this Philip in return for his services?'

'We have no idea,' Jinx said. 'Though we know Amaliel has designs on both our world, and the Overlands.'

'Insanity.'

'Quite.'

Baltheza's blazing orange eyes turned on me. 'You are strangely quiet, daughter mine.'

'I have nothing to add to what you've been told by the Guardian and Deathbringer.'

'You have failed me once again.'

'I'd hoped not to.'

He gestured to his slave to pour him another drink. He didn't offer me one. 'I would speak with the Princess Lucinda alone,' he said.

'I don't think so,' Jinx said.

The slave handed Baltheza back his goblet and he tapped his long pointed claws against the metal, staring at Jinx as he did so. 'I will speak to her alone, but I'll promise you this: I mean her no harm at this time. We have matters to discuss which I will not speak of in front of an audience.'

'And what of her?' Jinx said, gesturing at the slave.

Baltheza gave a puzzled frown. 'She's nothing more than a poppet.'

'Really?' Jinx said, and I'm pretty sure the tension in the room ramped up a notch. Jamie and Jinx had certainly gone into guard mode.

Baltheza looked down upon the girl, wrenched the loop of the leash from around his wrist and threw it down at Jinx's feet. 'Take her if you must, but I will have a few moments alone with Lucinda.'

Jinx stooped down and scooped up the end of the lead. 'Thank you,' he said, and smiled at the girl, but it certainly wasn't a friendly aren't-you-a-pretty-little-thing smile, then he gave the leash a tug.

The girl uncurled her legs from beneath her and got to her feet, her own smile gone. She glanced at Baltheza, but he waved a hand for her to leave. 'We'll be right outside,' Jinx said and gave Kayla a pointed look.

Her expression was one of bemusement – she was obviously as bewildered as I felt. Added to my growing confusion was an underlying fear of being left alone with the daemon I now knew could not possibly be my father.

'I'll let you know if Lucky is in any danger,' she said, and it was only when the door had closed behind them that I realised Kayla may be just as unhappy as her father to hear the truth. I pushed the thought aside. He hadn't questioned the legitimacy of my being his daughter before; he was the one who had announced it, so why should he now?

'Sit down,' Baltheza said, patting the sofa.

I did as he said, but sat as far away from him as I could without appearing rude. If he noticed he didn't say, though I doubted his blazing orange eyes missed much.

'Time for some plain speaking,' he said, and took a swallow of his drink. He stared at me for a very long time, and I found it hard not to fidget under his watchful gaze. 'You look so very much like your mother, it could be she sitting where you are now.'

'I understand she was Kayla's aunt.'

He smiled and took another sip of his drink. 'She was really the sister I should have married, but I didn't realise until it was too late. Still, we had our moments together; Kayla being the product of one of them.'

'What?' Kayla said. I stared at him dumbstruck.

'Of course, it couldn't be seen that my mistress could bear me offspring whereas my wife could not, so the two went away for a visit to their parents and when they came back my wife was holding a baby girl in her arms.'

Kayla sank down onto the couch between us. 'I do not believe this.'

'Of course, it made things difficult between my wife and her sister, and Marla wouldn't have her in the palace, which meant I didn't see Veronica as much as I'd have liked.'

'That's hardly surprising,' Kayla said. 'I'm amazed I didn't suffer a nasty accident as a child.'

It was as if he'd heard her. 'Fortunately, Marla quickly gained affection for the child – and who wouldn't have? She was a beautiful little thing.' His voice wavered for a moment and he took another sip from the goblet. 'And now she is lost to me.'

'And me,' I told him – I could hardly tell him she was sitting in between us glaring daggers at his profile.

'When Veronica disappeared for a while, I wasn't surprised; I thought she was keeping her distance from Marla. It had been over three-thousand years, but family grudges run deep. Then there was a disturbance in the human world. A child was born; a daemon child – a special child.' His eyes met mine and it was then that I realised he knew. He knew I was the Soulseer.

'In retrospect, it was clear that Amaliel was already plotting, planning and scheming, but to my complete and utter surprise it was Kayla who somehow wheedled her way into the human world to be by your side.' He stood to pour himself another drink, and as an afterthought offered me one. I refused it – my head was spinning as it was.

'At first I thought she would see you dead and then return, but just as Marla became enamoured with Kayla, so Kayla became enamoured with you.

'Veronica had already returned, leaving you in the care of the human who you called your father and, after Kayla left, I had her arrested.' He let out a sigh. 'I now know this was due to Amaliel causing mischief, whispering words of discord in my ear.'

'So that's how he knew all about you,' Kayla said, 'from Veronica.'

Baltheza continued, oblivious. 'It's now clear Amaliel didn't tell me everything he'd learned, only what he wanted me to know. He told me she'd had a human lover. He told me you were the product of that liaison and not my daughter at all. He told me Veronica had betrayed me.' His lips twisted into a grimace.

'He's getting worked up,' Kayla said. 'Say something. Say something to calm him.'

I opened my mouth and shut it again, I couldn't think of a word to say that wouldn't make it worse.

Fortunately, Baltheza took a deep breath and then exhaled,

calming himself. 'He manipulated me into doing something I've regretted ever since and it was then that any semblance of friendship ended between us.'

So he knew I wasn't his daughter and always had – but why introduce me to the court as his, and continue the pretence for this long? I was truly confused.

'Years passed, and although I missed Kayla, I knew she would return at some point. Then Daltas started making noises about getting her back. I thought it was to do with him wanting to court her, therefore bringing himself nearer to my throne. I did not know that Amaliel was playing his evil games yet again. If I had, I would've resisted bringing you here. Why would I want the child of another and the woman I loved flaunted before me?'

'Why indeed?' Kayla said.

'But Amaliel used my fondness for Kayla to get me to agree to bring you here, and I fell for it, hoping that Kayla would come back.'

'I never knew he cared so much,' Kayla said, reaching out to touch her father's cheek. 'I always knew he had a soft spot for me, but—' she pressed her lips together into a tight line.

'So,' Baltheza said, 'now I've lost my true daughter and I have you – someone else's.'

'I'm sorry,' I said, which was totally inadequate, but the best I could do.

He smiled and this time it was a true smile. 'I like you,' he said. 'You're so very much like your mother and your sister. If nothing else is true, that at least is: you are Kayla's sister and she loved you, therefore, even if it weren't for you having two such dangerous allies, I wouldn't see any harm come to you.'

'Thank you.'

'Of course, the fact that you are the Soulseer does put a rather different perspective upon the matter.'

Kayla's hand jerked back from his cheek as though burned. 'What does being the Soulseer have to do with anything?' she said.

I stared at him and he stared right back, his fleeting, gentle, kind smile gone to be replaced by his usual cruel arrogance.

'Why should you care?' I asked.

'The dead can tell you secrets.'

'All the dead want to do is find peace, which was hard to do with your old friend Amaliel around. Did you realise he and the Sicarii were stopping them from passing over? If anyone, he was the one who wanted your secrets. Not me.' I leaned back in the seat and folded my arms. He wasn't going to have everything his own way and I wasn't going to act like a scared child; I'd had enough of his threats.

'Amaliel said—'

'Amaliel *said*,' I sneered. 'You've just spent the past fifteen minutes or so telling me why you shouldn't believe one word that manipulative shit has ever said, and now you're back to quoting him? Do you never learn?'

'Lucky,' Kayla said, laying her hand on my wrist, 'shut up before you really piss him off.'

'I will not,' I said, scowling at her. 'I'm fed up with him playing with my head and threatening me the whole time.'

Baltheza jumped to his feet and backed away from me. 'It's true?'

'What do you think?' I said, also getting to my feet. 'Here's the deal: I'll stay out of your way and you'll stay out of mine. That way we'll both live long and happy lives. If not, it will end badly for one of us, and as I have the Guardian and Deathbringer on my side, I wouldn't bet on it being me.'

Baltheza's eyes blazed and his mouth curled into a snarl as he glared at me. Then his lips began to twitch and he started to laugh. Kayla stood between us looking to him, then to me, and back again.

'That was close,' Kayla said, 'but don't think you're out of trouble yet.'

'So much like your mother; so much like your sister.'

'Have we a deal?'

'No,' he said, 'but we have a truce.'

'Fair enough.'

'I quite like having you around Lucky de Salle, so if it is your intention to leave this day, don't wait too long before you return to see me.' His laughter died away to be replaced by a deeper emotion. 'Is she here? Is Kayla here in this room?' I nodded. 'Is she well?'

'I'm dead Papa, how in all of the Underlands could I possibly be considered well?'

'She's mighty fed up she's dead, but otherwise she's the same old Kayla.'

'I want Amaliel's head,' Baltheza said, sitting down and slumping back on the couch as he reached for his goblet.

'No more than I,' I told him. 'We'll find him or, more than likely, he'll find us. We haven't heard the last of him I'm quite sure.'

'No,' Baltheza said, 'on that I think you're right. Before you leave I'll give you one piece of advice.' He beckoned me to move closer and whispered as though he thought Amaliel could still be listening. 'Do not underestimate Amaliel. It has become clear to me that he has been plotting and planning for a considerable amount of time. Don't for one moment think this is over. He wanted you here for a reason and, as you aren't dead, I'm not convinced he's done with you. Be very, very careful.'

With that happy thought in mind, and counting myself lucky that Vaybian had not been mentioned, I left him. My men were waiting outside with Baltheza's 'poppet', and from the glowering glare she gave me when I stepped into the hall, I gathered her smile had at least temporarily deserted her.

'Remember what I said,' Jinx said, dropping her lead into her palm.

She opened her mouth to speak, thought better of it, and flounced back into Baltheza's chambers.

'What was that all about?' I asked.

'She's one of Amaliel's spies.'

'Really?' I said, looking over my shoulder at the closed door.

'I have put it to her that it would probably be best for her health if Baltheza was never made aware of her previous loyalties.'

'Shouldn't we tell him?'

Jinx smiled one of his dangerous smiles. 'No, she's had a change of allegiance. She's now *our* spy.'

'She didn't look very happy about it,' I said as we started down the corridor.

'No,' Jinx said, 'she didn't, did she?'

I didn't ask for any more details. It was just another one of those occasions when it was probably better I didn't know.

'I could do with a drink,' I said instead.

'Now that sounds like a very good idea,' Jinx said.

Seventeen

We didn't reach the Drakon's Rest a moment too soon. Vaybian was fighting drunk and Kerfuffle had imbibed enough that he was willing to take him on. They were glaring at each other across our favourite table in the corner and it was only Shenanigans' tight grip on his friend's arm that stopped Kerfuffle from launching himself at Kayla's green captain.

'Oh dear,' Kayla said when she saw him trying to stand and put up his fists, while Kerfuffle grumbled at Shenanigans to let go of his sleeve. She wafted over to where her lover was still struggling to stand. 'Sit down before you fall down. I don't know why you do it; you know you can't take your drink.'

'She does realise he can't hear her?' Jinx said to me.

'As you said, she's always been bossy.'

Jinx plonked himself down on the other side of Kerfuffle and Jamie sat next to Vaybian, leaving me room to sit between him and Jinx. Kubeck sank down next to Shenanigans and Pyrites flopped down under the table next to my feet.

Leila appeared through the crowd of other patrons without being called and plonked three tankards and a goblet on the table, together with a carafe of wine for me and two more jugs of ale for the boys. 'Can I get you anything to eat?' she asked, which was really a very stupid question. Daemons on the whole were always hungry; at least my guard were. Usually we hadn't long finished breakfast before they were thinking about a snack, and then lunch, followed by afternoon tea, then of course supper, which was their biggest meal of the day. All meals, except – thankfully – breakfast, were consumed with vast quantities of ale. Even so, I had rarely seen a daemon drunk – tipsy, maybe, but nothing like poor Vaybian.

He lost the urge to fight sometime between my drinking my

first goblet of wine and the arrival of the food. On the whole, I think I preferred it when he was riling up Kerfuffle as he became maudlin once the aggression left him.

'All gone,' he said with a belch. 'All my friends. All gone.' He tried spearing a piece of something resembling a potato and it flew across the table and landed in Kerfuffle's ale, which didn't improve the little daemon's mood any. 'Even my lovely Kayla.'

Kayla rolled her eyes. 'Oh, for the love of the handmaidens of Osiris. Will he not shut up?'

'You should be pleased he's so bereft at your passing,' I told her.

'I wouldn't mind, but he added me on as an afterthought when he had finished mourning my six other guards.'

'Give the lad a break,' Jinx said. 'This is the first time he's even mentioned them since you died.'

'Don't you find it a bit weird – them talking to a dead person, I mean?' Kubeck asked Shenanigans.

'Them two are weird anyway, talking to dead people is only the half of it,' Kerfuffle said.

'Shush,' Shenanigans said, giving me and Jinx an embarrassed smile. 'He doesn't mean it.'

'Like hell I do,' Kerfuffle said.

Vaybian tried to spear another potato and this one flew off across the room. 'Little buggers,' he murmured. 'Can't catch 'em.'

'Try using a spoon,' Jamie suggested.

Vaybian peered at Jamie. 'Oh, it's you Guardian, where's the Deathbringer?'

'Across the table,' Jamie said, pointing at Jinx.

'You know something,' he said, in what I think he thought was a whisper, then gestured for Jamie to come closer. Jamie leaned a little closer, wrinkling his nose as he caught a whiff of the alcoholic fumes coming off Vaybian's breath. 'He's not half bad when you get to know him.'

'Hell's bells,' Jinx said, pushing his chair back from the table and stalking around to Vaybian.

'Don't you dare hurt him,' Kayla said.

He gave her a 'yeah, right' look and placed his hand on Vaybian's forehead. 'Sleep,' he said. The daemon's eyes drooped shut, and as soon as Jinx removed his hand Vaybian flopped forward onto his plate.

'I suppose we'd better get him back to the palace,' Jamie said.

'Let's finish our supper first brother. I, for one, have a fine thirst on me.'

'Hmm, so did he and look where it got him,' Shenanigans said.

We went back to the castle – there being no other place to stay – dumped Vaybian on the couch in our chamber and covered him up with a blanket. Kayla sank down beside him. My guards all flopped on or in the huge bed, while I used the bathroom and then went into the dressing room to change into something more comfortable.

The mirror told me I was still my daemon self, and I supposed that at least Baltheza would be pleased if he saw me again before I left. To tell the truth, I was getting used to this different me. Though, seeing myself in the mirror did bring back to mind my still uncertain parentage. I guessed it was something I should speak to Kayla about, no matter how scared of her response I might be.

I changed into a beige satin nightgown, and stopped in the doorway on the way out to take one last look at my reflection before blowing out the lamps. My reflection smiled at me.

'Who am I?' I asked her. 'Who were our parents?' If she knew any better than I, she wasn't telling.

In the morning, with Vaybian still looking a rather strange colour, we packed up to leave. I had made a promise to the souls at Dark Mountain, and I intended to keep it. But before we could go anywhere, there was Kayla's funeral to get through. It was to be a big affair, and although Baltheza hadn't ordered me there, it was made apparent that I was expected to go by the delivery of several packages containing appropriate funeral garb to my chamber.

In the Underlands it was customary for royal mourners to wear purple. The dress was not something I would wear by choice, but it was certainly beautiful and not at all flouncy. Apparently Baltheza had taken some notice of my tastes.

And then, when I thought he couldn't surprise me any more than he had already, he did so again.

Beneath the packages containing the dress, the underwear, the shoes and all the rest of my funeral clothing, there was a small, red leather box together with an envelope sealed with red candle wax. I opened the envelope first.

Lucinda, it read, *I know we haven't always seen eye to eye, but you are your mother's daughter, so how could I not care for you in some small part? The item in the box was once Veronica's and I thought you might like it as a keepsake.* It was signed with a flourish – *Baltheza*.

I opened the box with some trepidation. I wouldn't have been at all surprised if it contained something awful like a small withered body part. Fortunately, I was more than a little wrong. Inside the case was a beautiful gold ring lying on a navy velvet cushion. The stone was a translucent, deep green and polished smooth. It was oval in shape, but nestled in a heart-shaped setting. The rest of the band was plain gold – that was until you looked at it closely. On the outside it was engraved with intricate symbols that, to my inexperienced eye, could have been Celtic. On the inside there were two names – Kayla and Lucinda. She may have been absent, but those two words meant so much; they proved that she cared. They proved that she loved us.

I slipped it onto my right ring finger and it fitted like it had been made for me. I raised my hand, splaying my fingers, to study how it looked, and for an instant I thought I saw a flash of red and gold fire from deep within the stone, but then it was gone, leaving me unsure if the glimmer of flames had been a figment of my imagination. It had, however, fired my curiosity – when I had the opportunity, I wanted to find out more about the enigmatic woman who had been my mother.

★

I attended the funeral with my full guard, including Vaybian. Baltheza's eyes narrowed when he saw him, but he passed no comment, and acknowledged Jamie and Jinx instead. I did notice that he glanced down at my hand, and upon seeing the ring gave a small smile, though again he didn't remark upon it.

I stood by Baltheza's side throughout the ceremony and walked beside him as we followed Kayla's casket to its final resting place in the family mausoleum, acting every bit the royal daughter. The fact that Kayla was wafting around me making sarcastic and amusing comments about some of the mourners was not helpful, and on several occasions I had to raise a hand to my face as if to hide my grief, when actually I was trying to stifle slightly hysterical giggles.

We got ready to leave almost immediately after the funeral. There was little point staying around; Kayla may have been dead but she certainly hadn't gone anywhere, so my grieving process was on hold for the time being. Sadly I knew in my heart it was only temporary. I had seen the wistful expression on her face when the other spirits had passed over.

'Everyone ready?' Jamie asked.

'Where are we going?' Vaybian asked.

'First stop: Dark Mountain,' I told him.

Kerfuffle gave a theatrical shudder. 'If I never see that place again it would be too soon.'

'I know, but I promised I would release the souls of the Sicarii's victims and I intend to honour that promise.'

'You needn't come with us, if you and Shenanigans want to have some time with your ladies?' Jamie told him.

'I promised to serve Mistress Lucky,' Shenanigans said.

'You're allowed a few days off, Shenanigans,' I said.

'It's not like it'll be dangerous,' Jamie said. 'The Sicarii have all gone.'

'Well, if you're sure?' Shenanigans conceded, but I could see he was torn.

'I'll be fine. You two go and enjoy yourselves for a few days.'

And so it was decided. Shenanigans and Kerfuffle were going to stay at the Drakon's Rest and Kubeck was going to return to his family to let them know he was all right.

I did draw Shenanigans and Kerfuffle aside to ask them if Kubeck had a wife I was keeping him from, but the largest of my daemon guards gave me a toothy smile.

'No, he's going to see his brothers and cousins. They run a smithy together.'

'A smithy? As in a blacksmiths?' They both looked at me, puzzled. 'You know, where they make horseshoes, and I suppose swords and the like.'

'Oh no mistress,' Kerfuffle told me. 'They work in gold and silver.'

'I've heard Kubeck and his family make some of the finest jewellery that's highly sought after by the gentry,' Shenanigans confided. 'I looked into it because I thought I might get something for Leila.'

As for Vaybian, he stayed behind, though he didn't tell anyone what he was going to do, and no one asked.

'I'm coming with you,' Kayla told me. 'Vaybian can't see or hear me, and if he's going to spend the next few days getting drunk I'd rather I wasn't here to see it.'

So we set off; me and Jinx riding on Pyrites with Kayla at the back and Jamie under his own wing-power. I rode up front, enjoying the sensation of having Jinx's arms around my waist and his chest pressed up against my back. Jamie didn't say anything, but he kept close beside us, and I did catch the occasional sideways frown, especially when Jinx whispered something silly in my ear that made me laugh. I tried to restrain myself as I didn't want Jamie getting jealous; well – not much.

We camped in the forest opposite the mountain for the night, rather than venture inside when it was dark. It was silly really, as without lamps it would be pretty damn dark anyway, but I didn't want to find myself walking on dead people again.

★

The next morning was a different story and I wished we hadn't waited. Seeing the piles of bones and rotting corpses surrounding the mountain was far worse than I could have possibly imagined; worse even than the huge, foul pit full of the dead at the other temple. In the caverns beneath the monoliths there had been rats; here there were swarms of carrion crows and other scavenger birds, and seagulls hopping about the bodies. Their continual pecking and tearing at the remains of the dead made me want to retch.

At first we tried scaring the birds away, but they just flew up in a flapping, raucous cloud and returned almost immediately after the first few shouts, ignoring us completely.

'We should let Pyrites roast them,' Jamie said, wrinkling his nose in distaste.

So we skirted around the base, and the piles of feather-coated bodies, until we found the entrance again. Here there was a pathway through the dead where corpses had been heaped in careless piles, forming an obscene corridor of bones and mouldering flesh. The smell was almost indescribable; something between rotting flesh and bird guano. I didn't remembering it smelling so bad before, but then it had been a chilly night rather than a warm sunny day.

Inside the mountain the temperature was frigid. Jinx went in first, carrying the lamp; Jamie and I followed behind, my hand gripped in his. Pyrites was to circle the mountain acting as a look-out. We doubted anyone would come, but decided we'd rather be safe than sorry.

'I'll go with him. The last thing I want is to be inside another chamber full of restless spirits,' Kayla said with a grimace of distaste.

I was shivering, but I didn't think it had anything to do with the cold. The place reeked of evil, and the ruby rock passageway glowing in the lamplight could have been the entrance into hell.

The main cavern was as we had left it and the three grey-robed Sicarii still hung from the crosses, their now desiccated entrails hanging in withered loops down to their knees.

The echo of our footsteps as we crossed to the chamber gave me the creeps. It was as though we weren't alone.

'Let's get this over and done with,' I said.

Jinx stopped a yard or so before we reached the altar. 'Something's wrong,' he said, holding the lamp up high and turning full circle.

'What is it?' Jamie asked.

Jinx frowned. 'I'm not sure. I just have a feeling all is not right.'

'Can you see any spirits?' Jamie asked me.

I looked around. 'No,' I said. 'No I can't.' I closed my eyes and listened. 'I can't hear them either.'

Then there was a voice: a quiet whisper in the air. 'Scared.'

'Why are you scared? I'm here to help you.'

'Scared for you,' this time several voices said.

'There's nothing to be frightened of now,' I told them, 'the Sicarii are all gone.'

'There will be others. He will make others.'

Jinx turned another full circle, this time very slowly, stopping when we were in front of him. 'I—' he started to say, and then his brow bunched into a knot and he spun around to face the altar. 'There are three Sicarii,' he said as he started towards the three grey figures. 'There should be only two.'

He was right: the two who had come to the villa and whom Jinx had cursed to die. Jamie and I followed after him as he drew closer to the Sicarii. This was bad. Every single one of my senses screamed at me to turn and run, but my feet weren't listening to my brain; they continued to walk on.

Jinx jumped up onto the dais and stalked around the altar to where the third Sicarii hung. Now I was paying attention I could see the third body was fresher. The entrails were still shiny and plump, and even thinking that had me feeling a little lightheaded. The robe had been ripped open from throat to hem, and even though the head wasn't flopped forward like the other two, the victim's face remained hidden by a grey baggy cowl. Jamie's hand gripped mine all the tighter, and when I risked a glimpse in his direction his expression was one of grim anticipation.

Jinx stood below the third figure looking up. He glanced over his shoulder at us, then turned his attention to the body and stepped towards it, tilting his head so he could see up into the cowl.

He turned back to us. 'I think I may need your help, brother,' he said to Jamie.

Jamie and I moved closer. 'Stay here,' he said when we reached the dais, then gave my hand a squeeze and left me.

I wrapped my arms around myself. I was cold and I was scared; of what I wasn't sure. The dead couldn't hurt me.

Jamie linked his hands together to give Jinx a leg up so he could reach the Sicarii's cowl. Jinx hesitated a moment, then gripped the material of the hood between forefinger and thumb and pulled it back.

'Oh bugger,' he said.

'What?' Jamie said, unable to see as he was bent over, his hands entwined together holding Jinx up.

Jinx was in my direct eye line so I couldn't see either. I moved forward as Jinx hopped down and Jamie straightened to look up.

'Shit,' he said.

'Oh no,' I murmured and I had to turn away, though it was really too late for that. There are some images you never forget. This was going to be one of them.

It was a set piece: Amaliel had known we'd come. He knew I'd have promised to release the souls of the dead and this is why he had taken time positioning the body so the head was held upright; so we – no, I – would get the full, face-on impact of what he had done.

Philip Conrad's sightless eyes stared ahead, his lips drawn back in a rigour grimace. The robe had been positioned so that when the hood was pulled back, the material would gape open to show the extent of his terrible injuries, and they were truly terrible. He had died badly.

He had been alive when Amaliel had nailed him to the cross, and he must have had help to do so, so we knew he still had supporters. Philip had also been alive when Amaliel had sliced open his stomach, allowing his entrails to burst out of his body and slither down his legs. And he had been alive when Amaliel had cut open his breast, cracked open his ribcage and torn out his still beating heart. Only then had Philip sunk into the velvet darkness of death.

Jamie wrapped an arm around my shoulders and kissed the top of my head. 'I am so very sorry.'

Jinx wasn't so diplomatic. 'He was a little shite, but no one deserves to die like that.'

'So, now we know why he saved Philip over Henri: he knew there was one more way to hurt you,' Jamie said.

'Even though Philip betrayed you time and time again,' Jinx lifted my chin to look at my face. 'Sometimes you are too good for your own wellbeing.'

'I can't help it, it's the way I am.'

He caressed my cheek with his thumb. 'I know,' he said, his eyes twinkling, 'and I wouldn't want you any other way. Now, let's get on with what we came here for and do some good on this sorry day.'

We walked into the centre of the cavern and on the count of three Jamie and Jinx began to chant and I closed my eyes and called for the entrance to the hereafter to appear.

I opened my eyes when I heard the first voices of the spirits. They came from the roof, they came from beneath our feet, and they came from the tunnels leading into the cavern. Soon we were surrounded by hundreds of ghostly grey wraiths. This time, their cries of despair were silenced as they realised what was happening. My body began to tingle, and a nice feeling like I was floating upright in a warm, soapy bath flowed over and through me. I began to search the cavern for the dot of light I knew must be coming, and then there it was: a small, bright speck of gold dust within the red gloom. Within moments it was growing into a slit in the fabric that separated this world from the next.

The tall daemon, Dreyphus, floated over to stand before me. He smiled a happy smile that, had I been in human form, would probably have had my eyes misting up. 'Thank you,' he said. 'Thank you from the bottom of our hearts, you have set us free.' Then he turned and drifted towards the light. Unlike the spirits at the other temple or the great hall, these didn't hesitate. They began to crowd towards the golden glow spilling across the cavern, not even pausing to bathe in its radiance before crossing over.

This made me smile, and chased away the sadness in my heart for a few moments. Then I heard a voice; one that wasn't joyous or happy to be given the opportunity to move on. In amongst the grey figures crowding towards the light, I could see one fighting against the tide, and any happiness I was feeling evaporated.

'By Beelzebub's balls, why did I not see this coming?' Jinx said.

'What?' Jamie asked, and Jinx pointed towards the lone figure fighting to get away from the blinding light. 'Why doesn't he cross over?'

'Because he can't,' Jinx said, his tone bleak. 'He's like the Sicarii. He has done too much wrong to be welcome where they are going. He has been caressed by the fingers of evil and accepted its touch.'

'Lucky, help me,' Philip cried. 'Please, help me.' He broke free of the diminishing stream of spirits and ran across the hall towards me. 'Lucky, please!'

'Philip, I—'

'She can do nothing for you,' Jamie said, his voice harsh. 'You have brought this upon yourself, Conrad.'

'Is there nothing I can do?' I asked them.

'This is a matter over which we have no influence,' Jinx said. 'Each person is judged upon what's in their heart. Sadly, your friend has been found wanting and he knows it, otherwise he wouldn't have run from the light.'

Philip fell to his knees and tried to grab me around the legs. 'Please.'

The last of the Sicarii's victims passed through into the land beyond and the slit began to close. Philip turned his head, and upon seeing the entrance disappearing staggered to his feet. He began to smile and any sympathy I'd had for him vanished. He wasn't sorry for a single thing he'd done; he just didn't want to pay the price.

He turned to look at me. 'Seems I'm not so bad after all.'

'Scum of the earth is what you are,' Jamie said.

Philip grinned at him. 'Apparently not.'

Jinx smiled his dangerous smile. 'Well, I hope you enjoy it here for all eternity.'

Philip's own smile faltered. 'What do you mean?'

It seemed being 'bitchy' wasn't a purely female thing. Jinx gestured around the cavern. 'This is your home for all eternity: you died here, you stay here.'

'No,' Philip said.

'Oh yes,' Jamie said, his smile equally mean.

Philip glared at me. 'Put it right. Put it fucking right.'

I couldn't quite believe this. 'You what?'

'Your pet ghost travels around with you, so why shouldn't I?'

'Pet ghost?'

'Kayla, your friend Kayla, your pet ghost. I know all about her: your spirit guide.'

'I cannot believe him,' Jamie said.

'I think he's in denial,' Jinx said.

Jamie gave Jinx a sideways look. 'Really?'

'Nooo, just a f—' Jinx glanced at me, 'just a bloody idiot.'

'Philip, you either move on or you stay here,' I said.

'But. Kayla—'

'In our world Kayla was never a spirit, just a daemon in disguise. In this world her dying wish was never to leave me and this is what keeps her by my side. What did you wish for when you died? What was your last promise?'

'I just wanted the pain to stop.' His expression twisted into a snarl. 'Help me or I'll make you sorry.'

Jinx laughed. 'And how exactly are you going to do that, you pathetic little man?'

He glanced to where the entrance to the other side had been. 'I'll find a way. It may take me a very long time, but I'll find a way, and when I do you'll wish you'd helped me.'

'The only thing I can do for you is to help you pass over,' I said. 'Why can't you understand that?'

'He doesn't want to,' Jamie said. 'He's been a greedy, conniving little shit who betrayed his wife, his daughter and you, but to him it's everyone's fault but his own. Don't waste another moment's thought on him.'

Philip launched himself at Jamie, fists flailing, but it was an empty gesture. He fell straight through my angel and ended up in a heap on the ground. And that's where we left him, screaming abuse at us as we walked across the cavern, along the ruby red passageway and out into the sunshine, his vitriol still ringing in our ears.

'Can he hurt us?' I asked. 'Can a spirit full of so much hate and vengeance somehow find a way?'

'Do you want me to go back and make sure he's gone forever?' Jinx said.

'You can do that?'

'Never had to before, but in his case I'm willing to give it a damn good try.'

'We could all go back, and Lucky could open the door to make him pass on.'

I shivered. I couldn't do it. I would be condemning him to being whisked away to some terrible place by those black shadowy things. 'No, I couldn't, I wouldn't wish that upon anyone.'

So we trudged back past the piles of bodies and squawking birds and away from Dark Mountain and all its horrors until we were breathing fresh air and our bones began to lose the chill that had sunk into their marrow. And it was during this walk I felt myself change back into a human, almost as though my misery had driven her away.

Amaliel was out there somewhere and Philip's murder was a message – he would be coming for me; maybe not tomorrow, maybe not next week or next month, but hell, he had waited twenty-five years, so he was patient if nothing else. My men might try and tell me otherwise, but I knew it to be true.

Eighteen

Jinx and Jamie decided between them that we would take that little holiday Jinx had been talking about. At first my heart wasn't in it; I was too anxious. But gradually, between the two of them, they wore me down.

'A small cottage, on a beach next to the ocean where we can swim, fish and lie in the sun,' Jinx said.

Having seen the size of some of the creatures that lived in the seas of the Underlands, the idea didn't exactly fill me with enthusiasm.

'Come on Lucky, it'll be fun.' Even Jamie was up for it.

'Just the three of us. We'll do nothing but eat, drink and make merry all day.'

'How about me?' Kayla said.

'You can't eat and drink,' Jinx pointed out, rather unkindly I thought, 'and you certainly can't make merry.'

She frowned at him for a moment then glanced at me and began to smile. 'I'll promise to keep out of your way,' she said, her eyes sparkling.

'Then it's a deal,' he said.

'What's a deal?' Jamie said.

Jinx reached across and tousled his hair. 'Don't you worry your pretty little head.'

Jamie shrugged him off. 'Maybe this isn't such a good idea.'

'It will be brother, believe me, it will be,' and he gave Jamie a wink when he thought I wasn't looking.

And it had to be said, the spot they had found was idyllic: a small villa surrounded by lush, rust-coloured palms on the edge of an amethyst lake, Jinx eventually conceding to my reluctance to dabble my toes, or any other part of my anatomy for that matter, in the ocean.

There was a small village within walking distance where we could buy most of our provisions, and if we needed to travel further afield Pyrites was very obliging.

I had tentatively asked whether we should invite Vaybian along for Kayla's sake, but even she wasn't keen on that idea. 'Three's company, four's a crowd,' she said. 'Though you can't count me as I'm a ghost and Pyrites is more of a guard dog.' It was then that I got it.

So, 'making merry' was what they called it, and it was what finally sold the idea of the holiday to me; if Amaliel were to come calling I didn't want to die a virgin. Jamie had promised me that special moment together, and Jinx with all of his innuendos, some subtle, some not so much, had made his intentions quite clear.

If I said I hadn't thought about me and Jamie, and me and Jinx together – alone – I'd be lying. Some nights I lay awake thinking of nothing else, but the three of us – how was that going to work? Daemons didn't apparently have the same hang-ups as humans about a lot of things. I had found that out very soon after arriving at the villa.

It was hot, very hot and definitely too hot for leather trousers and boots. I'd collected some clothes from my wardrobe at the palace before we left – with the boys' help – though when I opened my bag when we reached the villa there were several, shall we say, rather skimpy items I didn't remember packing. I had included several long shift dresses and some loose fitting skirts and blouses, which were perfect, I'd thought, for this holiday.

I had wondered at Jinx and Jamie's rather limited amount of luggage, though it wasn't until I walked out onto the veranda to join my men for a celebratory holiday drink that the reason for them travelling so light became apparent. Fortunately, they were looking out over the lake with their backs to me.

'I think you may find you're a little overdressed,' Kayla whispered in my ear with a giggle.

'What do I do?'

'I would say "close your eyes and think of England", but that really would be a shame; they both have incredibly good bodies. I should've had a taste of the Deathbringer when I had the chance.'

'He said you had history.'

'History? A line on a page; a sentence worth if that.'

I don't know why, but Kayla confirming it made me a lot happier. 'I think I'd better . . .' I was about to turn and go back inside when Jamie glanced over his shoulder.

'Come on, your drink will get warm,' he said.

Jinx turned to face me and I swear my heart stopped for a second. I was certainly finding it hard to breathe. He grinned at me and he did that thing with his tail where it crept around his thigh and waggled at me.

I forced myself to take a breath, lifted my chin up and walked over to join them, hoping my cheeks weren't glowing as red as the burning sensation prickling my skin suggested.

'Jamie said you'd be embarrassed,' Jinx said, handing me a goblet of wine. 'You're not embarrassed are you?'

'Humans do have quite a few hang-ups about their bodies,' Jamie said.

'She's not a human.'

'She's been brought up in their world.'

I took a sip of my wine and looked out across the lake as it was probably safest. 'Actually, a lot of humans go to nudist beaches and holiday resorts,' I said.

'I bet you haven't,' Jamie said and couldn't quite stop himself from smirking.

'I've never really been on holiday except when I was a little girl with my dad, and he would've hardly taken me to a nudist beach.'

So we drank, they swam – I still wasn't particularly keen to find out what might be living in their waters – and we drank some more, and ate, and by the time the sun went down I'd grown comfortable with their nudity – well, maybe comfortable isn't quite the word; accustomed is probably a better term.

It was a temperate, balmy, perfect evening. The moons were rising in the sky, the stars were beginning to twinkle and the gentle breeze was as warm as an angel's breath. Although I'd relaxed by then over the wine, food and companionable conversation, it suddenly dawned on me that when it came to bedtime I would be crawling under the covers with not one, but two naked men, both of whom had promised their bodies to me. They had also professed to love me, albeit that Jamie hadn't actually used the word and neither had either of them actually said 'Lucky, I love you'.

They weren't in a hurry to go to bed, so by the time came I'd worked myself into a state of nervous anxiety, which I knew would totally blow any chance of this being a good experience for any of us.

While they took turns using the bathroom down the hall, I locked myself in the one in our bedroom and after stringing out everything I had to do for as long as I could, flopped down on the side of the bath and tried to fight down the growing tide of panic, which was in danger of engulfing me. Despite copious amounts of wine I was now stone cold sober, when I could have done with feeling a little drunk.

'What's the matter?' Kayla asked, floating through the door and across the room to sit beside me.

I sat staring at my hands. 'I'm scared,' I said eventually, and glanced up from under lowered lashes, waiting for the hoots of laughter. She surprised me.

'Do you love them?'

I nodded, feeling downright miserable. 'Too much, I think.'

'You can never love someone too much if they love you back.'

'Yeah, but do they?'

'You're kidding – right?'

I looked up at her with a frown. 'What do you mean?'

'They marked you. They *both* marked you, and neither one of them is willing to let you go. Do you know how unusual that is?'

'I don't even really know what it means other than Jinx telling me I was their "slave" or maybe even "sex toy".'

'That was before he realised how he felt about you. I think Jamie has always cared for you very deeply, and Jinx marking you brought out the green-eyed monster in him like you wouldn't believe.'

'You think?'

'Yep – and the Deathbringer actually used the "L" word, and I can tell you one thing: for all his laughing, joking, drinking and womanising, love is not a word he uses lightly.'

'What do I do?' I said. 'I've never done this with one man let alone two.'

'You lay back and let them look after you. They care for you, and in time you'll learn how to care for them and make them feel good.'

'I won't be a disappointment to them?'

'Don't be silly. They will love taking care of you. Trust me, by tomorrow morning you'll be wondering why you were so scared.'

'Wish me luck,' I said, getting up from the bath.

Ghostly lips brushed my cheek. 'You, my darling, won't need it.'

I had put on my favourite dusky pink, long, satin nightgown. It looked better on my daemon self as it suited her colouring, but it didn't look at all bad on me either. I wasn't brave enough to go to them naked. It would have been too brazen and I was too shy.

They had been busy while I'd been away. There was no orange lamplight for the occasion, instead the room was alight with a dozen or more flickering white candles and to my consternation they had both put on their trousers. Maybe I'd read the situation all wrong? Instead of being relieved, I was more disappointed than I could have possibly imagined.

It didn't go unnoticed. Jinx burst into gales of laughter and Jamie's eyes twinkled, though he did try to suppress his humour. Now I was dead grumpy. I stomped across the room, threw back the covers and slid into bed, which made Jinx laugh harder and Jamie, unable to restrain himself any longer, joined him.

I glared at both of them. 'I hope for your sakes there's a spare bedroom,' I said.

Jinx danced across the room and jumped up onto the bed and knelt down beside me. 'We are your guard and would therefore not be doing our duty if we didn't protect you, even if it is from yourself.' Then he took hold of my hand and raised it to his lips and kissed the back of my knuckles.

Jamie climbed up onto the other side of the bed, getting up close so he could put a hand on each of my shoulders, his fingers massaging my tight muscles. Despite myself I began to relax. 'There's no need to be scared,' he said. 'We'll take care of you.'

Jinx moved in close, his lips brushing my neck. 'We will be so very gentle with you – this time.'

And he didn't lie.

Jamie was laying on his front, his right wing covering me from my right shoulder down to my left hip. Jinx was pressed up against my left side and I could feel the weight of his arm resting across my waist. I shuffled around a bit and Jinx rolled onto his back and Jamie's wings closed behind him.

I wriggled up the bed and climbed out from between them, stepping over Jamie and hopping down to the floor. I glanced back over my shoulder, worried I had woken them, but no: Jinx rolled onto his other side and Jamie began to snore. I found my discarded nightgown on the floor and, slipping it on, wandered out into the quadrangle in the middle of the villa to sit on the edge of the ornamental pond.

It really wasn't a surprise to me when I looked down to see I was a shimmering rose pink, and my hair, blowing in the gentle breeze, was a glossy aubergine. You could say they had brought out the daemon in me. It was almost as though I had been freed from my frail human body. I felt stronger and more powerful than I'd ever felt before, even in my daemon persona. More importantly, I felt loved and cherished, and had I been human I think I may just have cried, the feeling was so bittersweet. Kayla had been right – now I couldn't imagine why I had been so afraid.

I wasn't even sure it was my daemon self that made me feel so strong and liberated. I think maybe it was my daemon lovers. Lovers – the word made me shiver, but not in a bad way.

I sat on the edge of the pond and trailed my fingers through the cool water and wondered whether this was me now. I did feel there was something permanent about it, like I was now wearing my own skin and everything before had been a disguise. It was strange, I had been afraid to be this other person, but now I didn't want to be any other.

As I lifted my hand from the pool, the green stone in my ring must have caught a glimmer of light from one of the two moons, as once again it appeared to burn with some inner fire, but when I raised it up to see, there was nothing there but sparkling green.

A splash from somewhere across the pond distracted me, my eyes jerking up to squint across the water's surface. Fear blossomed in my chest – Amaliel had used a pond to travel, and there I was alone, in the dark, sitting right next to his chosen means of transport. There was another splash that had my heart heading straight for my mouth – then a frog called out to its mate and I let out a shaky sigh. My men would never have brought me here if it wasn't safe. Never.

'Lucky,' I heard a voice call, and when I looked up Jamie was standing in the doorway. 'Come back to bed.'

Jinx's face appeared from around Jamie's left wing. 'We're getting lonely,' he said with an exaggerated wink.

I smiled and got up to go to them. As I walked through the door Jamie put an arm around my shoulder and Jinx slipped his arm around my waist. There was another splash from the pond and I glanced back over my shoulder.

'What's the matter?' Jamie asked.

'Are you cold? You're shivering,' Jinx said.

'I'm fine,' I told them, pushing my fear aside. I was spooked that was all. Amaliel would never find us here.

'I think Kerfuffle and Shenanigans are going to have to get used to sleeping in another room,' Jamie said, bringing me back to the now.

'What about Pyrites?' I asked, determined not to spoil our first night together with my paranoia.

'We'll have to find him a lady drakon,' Jinx said. 'He's old enough now.'

'Do they mate for life?' I asked.

'Yes,' Jamie said. 'When they find that one special mate they are bound together for all eternity.'

'Really?'

'Yes, really,' Jinx said. 'And, my lucky, lucky lady, you'd better get used to us, because the lad and I are the same, and we're going to be around for a very long time.' And with that he picked me up, swung me around and around then dropped me down on the bed, flinging himself down beside me. 'A very, very, very long time.'

At last the shadowy spectre of Amaliel slipped away into the dark recesses of my mind, even if only temporarily, as Jamie sunk down on the bed to join us and I became entwined in two pairs of strong arms.

My breath caught as their fingers and lips began to work their magic and it occurred to me that if, in the future, this was how every day ended and began, it wouldn't be such a hardship. Then Jamie pressed his lips against mine and my last vestiges of worry evaporated into mist – no, it wouldn't be any hardship at all.

Acknowledgements

I would like to thank Tony and Frances and Sarah and Paul for all their hard work. I would also like to thank Stephen Jones for his sage advice and encouragement. And lastly I would like to thank the lovely Jo Fletcher and my wonderful and supportive editor Nicola who have both taught me so much.

Sue Tingey spent 28 years with a major British bank before leaving the corporate life to work as Practice Manager for an Arboricultural Consultancy. She lives with her husband (and Koi carp) in East Grinstead, West Sussex. *Marked*, Book One of the Soulseer Chronicles, was her first novel. You can contact her on Twitter at @SueTingey and visit her at www.suetingey.co.uk.